THE
MACEDONIAN

FORGE BOOKS BY NICHOLAS GUILD

Blood Ties

The Ironsmith

The Spartan Dagger

The Macedonian

THE
MACEDONIAN

Nicholas Guild

A TOM DOHERTY ASSOCIATES BOOK
New York

THE MACEDONIAN

Copyright © 2017 by Nicholas Guild

A Forge Book
Published by Tom Doherty Associates
175 Fifth Avenue
New York, NY 10010

www.tor-forge.com

Forge® is a registered trademark of Macmillan Publishing Group, LLC.

The Library of Congress Cataloging-in-Publication Data is available upon request.

ISBN 978-0-7653-7846-0 (hardcover)
ISBN 978-1-4668-6161-9 (ebook)

Our books may be purchased in bulk for promotional, educational, or business use. Please contact your local bookseller or the Macmillan Corporate and Premium Sales Department at 1-800-221-7945, extension 5442, or by email at MacmillanSpecialMarkets@macmillan.com.

First Edition: December 2017

Printed in the United States of America

0 9 8 7 6 5 4 3 2 1

To my friends,
Gil and Barbara Feldman

THE
MACEDONIAN

1

The first storm of winter began just after dark. It had been unseasonably warm all day, as if summer had changed its mind and decided to linger in Macedon forever, but then, when the last smoldering red light of sunset guttered out and died, the wind blowing in from the sea grew suddenly cold. Soon damp clumps of snow were falling with noiseless, erratic fury into the dirt streets of Pella. People stood in their doorways and watched in awe. Yet no one spoke of omens. The gods were capricious this far north, and such things had been known to happen before.

Within an hour the courtyard of King Amyntas's palace was buried to a depth of nearly three fingers. By midnight the world was hushed and white and still. The busy life of men seemed to have perished with the sun.

Yet this was an illusion, for the palace itself was far from quiet. In the women's quarters Eurydike, the king's principal wife, choked on her screams as she labored to give life to a fourth child, and in the great hall the king and his companions drank unmixed wine and shook the air with their ferocious mirth.

Perhaps a hundred of the land's great nobles, the outlines of their hard faces sharpened by the dancing torchlight, laughed and shouted and beat their hands against the trestle tables that appeared arranged in no particular pattern and yet reflected a strict order of precedence. In battle these men surrounded the king's person, guarding his life with their own, and indeed their revels seemed a kind of battle, the sound of which hammered at the very walls.

A man appeared among the banqueters—not a grand figure like the others, yet not a servant. He looked about him as one might viewing the scene of some catastrophe. His tunic and even his short white beard were flecked with blood. He was Nikomachos, the king's physician and close friend.

As he approached Amyntas's couch and leaned down to speak to him, the hall fell into an uneasy silence.

"My Lord . . ."

The king, the flesh around his eyes seamed and cracked like an ancient leather mask, blinked uncomprehendingly and then threw an arm over the physician's shoulder to draw him closer. It was a gesture full of easy, wine-soaked familiarity.

"What is it, Nikomachos? Come to tell me that old men should know when to find their beds?"

He started to laugh, but stopped to draw the flat of his hand over the physician's beard and stare at the blood smeared across his palm.

"So—it was bad, was it? Is she dead?"

"She lives, My Lord, as does the child. Yet I cannot say if either will be alive tomorrow."

Amyntas, who was perhaps not so drunk as he seemed, studied his friend's face for a moment. They had known each other a long time, ever since the king's period of exile, when the Illyrians had briefly driven him from his own land and forced him to live among strangers. Nikomachos was a man to be trusted, a man who chose his words carefully.

"Is the child a male?"

"Yes, My Lord. It is a son."

"Then I had best come."

He stood up and, striding over the table in front of him as if it had been a log, sent his wine cup and a plate of roasted meat clattering to the stone floor with an impatient kick.

"Do not be alarmed, my comrades and brothers!" he shouted, smiling broadly. "Go on with your feasting, for soon I shall be among you again. It is a slight matter that calls me away, merely one of the inconveniences of domestic life."

In the laughter that followed, he motioned to two men lying on couches near his own. His voice, when he spoke again, was low and commanding.

"Ptolemy, cousin—and you, Lukios. You will accompany us. The birth of a prince is a public occasion, and I will not deny my son the attendance of his subjects, even if he may be dead by morning."

Ptolemy was the first to his feet. He was handsome and tall, with a glossy black beard that did not hide a faint smile that hid everything. He had the air of a favorite, and the king, who seemed uncertain in his gait, allowed himself to be steadied like a child just learning to walk. Lukios, an agreeable nobody with a face as polished and pink as a new apple—the indisputable sign of ancient lineage—followed along a step or two behind.

The corridor leading to the women's quarters was as black and airless as a burial vault. Amyntas took a torch from its wall sconce to light his way, yet the flame only seemed to gather into itself. He held the torch straight out in front of him, as if trying to force back the darkness, but his steps were guided more by habit than by sight.

"What happened?" he asked, his chin almost touching his shoulder as he murmured into Nikomachos's ear. "What went wrong? She is a strong woman . . ."

Nikomachos shook his head without disagreeing.

"Her age, perhaps, and this child following so closely on the last. And there were complications—it was a hard labor, and the boy came out clutching the birth cord. He seems to have crushed it, so that I have no idea how long he was without his mother's sustenance."

"He crushed it? Such a thing is possible?"

"Anything that happens is possible, My Lord." The physician offered a tense smile. "Your son did not seem very eager to be born."

"With five royal brothers ahead of him for the throne, I cannot blame him."

Amyntas allowed himself one quick syllable of laughter, as if the joke had only just occurred to him, and then turned suddenly grave.

"Yet it is strange that he should have crushed the cord. Never in a long life have I heard of such a thing."

"Perhaps it is an omen," Lukios said, speaking a little too eagerly. "Perhaps My Lord should send to Delphi."

"Yes, perhaps the House of the Argeadai has whelped another Herakles."

Ptolemy laughed, making a display of his contempt for the idea.

"It is never wise to neglect the gods," Lukios answered in a voice that suggested he would be just as pleased if no one heard him.

Amyntas, with an impatient gesture, willed him to silence.

"Yet the oracle would not loosen her tongue without an offering amounting to some few talents of gold," he said. "And then she would make only a riddling answer good for nothing except to tie a man's brains into knots. Besides, even if her prophecies were as easy to see through as her piss, the destiny of a sixth royal prince is certain to be obscure enough that I will not impoverish myself to find it out.

"Still, if he should be a Herakles after all, and will strangle serpents in his cradle, he could not have done better than to begin with one plucked from his own mother's bowels."

Only Nikomachos did not join the king in his laughter. His face was solemn as he appeared to study the flecks of dried blood still visible on his hands.

The birthing chamber was a small room, with only a single oil lamp to bathe the walls in its fitful light. The air stank of blood and exhaustion, so much that to breathe it seemed a labor at once unpleasant and useless. The Lady Eurydike lay in her bed, her breast so motionless beneath her thin tunic that for a moment it was impossible to tell if life still stirred within. Even her reddish-golden hair appeared faded to the color of dead leaves. Her beauty, which had once made the king's lust course through his veins like poison, seemed no more than a shadow.

They had washed the sweat from her brow and limbs, which looked as lifeless and yellowed as old wax. Only the eyes were alive, and like a dog's they immediately sought her master's face. They appeared to study him with the intimacy of an enduring hatred.

Amyntas did not even glance at her.

"Phew!" He shook his head in disgust. "Clearly it is no insignificant blessing not to have been born a woman. It is like a battlefield in here—before they have carried off the corpses. My kennels smell better."

With a wave he dismissed the Lady Eurydike's women, who bowed quickly and scurried away like field mice. The king looked about him, without seeming to notice the cradle in one corner of the room, and only when he had apparently found nothing else to interest him did he lower his gaze to the figure on the bed.

"You have seen hard service, wife," he said coldly. "Will you live, or no?"

She did not answer—one sensed she had not the strength—but she continued to watch him with the alert hostility of an animal.

Nikomachos was bending over her, the ends of his fingers resting on her throat.

"That is in the gods' hands, My Lord. But at least her pulse is stronger, so perhaps the bleeding has stopped."

"And what of my son?"

A look of anguished revulsion crossed the Lady Eurydike's face, like a twinge of pain, and for the first time her eyes dropped from the king's face to the dark corner where the cradle rested.

Amyntas, following her gaze, walked over to the cradle.

"The child is dead," he announced, without apparent emotion. "No, I was mistaken. He is merely asleep. There—he stirs again."

He crouched down and scooped up his son in both hands. Ptolemy and then Lukios approached for a closer look. The child began to cry in a thin, piercing voice.

"What say you, physician? Will my boy live?"

In silence, Nikomachos took him from his father's arms and brought him over to where the oil lamp rested. In the uncertain, yellowish light he gave the child the tip of his little finger to suckle on, which stilled his crying.

"I would not have said so an hour ago," he answered at last, "but, yes, I think he will do well enough."

"Then, My Lord, you must choose a name for him."

Ptolemy was looking down at the Lady Eurydike, as if he had spoken to her rather than to the king. He smiled, the way a man does when he has made a discovery that is pleasing to him.

"Yes, a name," Lukios repeated.

"Have you a suggestion, cousin?"

At the sound of the king's voice, Ptolemy turned his gaze back to him. He was still smiling.

"'Philip,' My Lord. If a name has any power, he may make you a tolerable commander of horse."

Amyntas laughed and nodded in agreement.

"Yes," he said. "Besides, it will serve to remind him how remote a title he has to my throne, for there has been no king of that name in nearly three hundred years. I agree—let him be called 'Philip.'"

"He needs a wet nurse more than he does a name."

Nikomachos, still holding the child in his arms, approached the bed. He stopped when, with an expression of something like horror, the Lady Eurydike turned her face away.

"Alcmene, the wife of My Lord's steward, was two days ago delivered of a dead child. Her dugs are heavy with milk."

He took his finger from between the child's lips, for the new prince of Macedon had fallen asleep again.

"I believe the Lady Eurydike is too weak . . ."

"Let it be as you think best," Amyntas replied, glancing at his son with a dismissing shrug. "Let Glaukon's woman have him. His mother, the bright gods know, will be of little enough use to him—now or later."

The king and his companions returned to the great hall. The Lady Eurydike's women crept back. Nikomachos watched with them for another hour, until he was sure his services would not be required again, and then took the king's new son away with him.

"We must have a word with the royal steward, My Prince," he murmured to the sleeping child. "There is nothing so very wrong with you that it won't soon be put right by a pair of milk-swollen breasts. You will do well enough for now."

For now, yes, he thought. *But even a few years hence, who could answer for anything?*

The physician clutched his young charge to him, feeling as if he had just uttered a curse.

Though still a young man, Glaukon had been steward to the royal household for three years. It was a post he had inherited from his father, whose ancestors had served the kings of Macedon since the time of the first Alexandros, more than a hundred years before. He could not have imagined any other destiny, since loyalty to the House of the Argeadai and obedience to the king's will seemed to him as natural as eating his dinner. He was trusted absolutely and he knew it. It was the pride of his life that he was so trusted, that no member of the king's court, not even the great nobles who were the Lord Amyntas's companions and whom he called "cousin" and "friend," stood higher in his confidence than humble Glaukon, who tallied the wine jars and managed the palace slaves and went down to the bazaar twice a week to sit under an awning and haggle with the traders and the farming folk, the king's purse resting on his knees.

Thus, where another man might have been prey to a thousand anxious reflections about being summoned out of bed in the middle of the night, wondering if some small, secret crime had at last been discovered, if his last hour might not be upon him, Glaukon simply wiped the sleep from his eyes and dressed himself. He hardly even considered what might be amiss at such an hour. Whatever it was it would wait upon his own good time and he would deal with it then. He was an honest man and fitted to his station. He had no misgivings.

Besides, his mind was too clouded with a private grief to allow place for dread.

The messenger, one of the king's pages, a boy of about ten who looked as if he had been dragged from his bed as well, had simply told him that he was expected in the kitchens. Probably there was some trouble with one of the servingwomen—there was always trouble with the servingwomen—but what it could be, and why it could not have waited until the morning, he did not consider.

He had forgotten about the Lady Eurydike's travail. Or perhaps he had dismissed it from his mind. Just then the ordeal of childbirth was not a subject that held much delight for him.

His own little son, who had not lived long enough even to cry, whose corpse had been taken away in the deepest black of night like something unholy . . . The ashes of his funeral pyre were hardly even cold, and his mother—sweet Alcmene, so full of blighted love for the child she would never hold to her breast—his mother could not stop weeping. Sometimes life was more bitter than death.

Glaukon lived just outside the palace compound, in a quarter of the city that was all the king's property and built when Archelaos, in his tomb almost twenty years, had moved the capital from Aigai to Pella. To be allowed to live in one of these houses, more spacious and private than anything a servant could hope for in the palace itself, was a great mark of favor, yet the honor seemed diminished almost to nothing on such a night, when a winter storm left the streets choked with snow. The royal steward cursed the weather and might have cursed the old Archelaos himself, had such a thing been seemly and had not the bright gods saved him the trouble, leaving the king to fall by the hand of an assassin before he had a son grown to manhood so that all the days since had been filled with chaos and treachery—this not even the Lord Amyntas's reign, now in its tenth year, had been able utterly to quench. Perhaps it had been an impiety to abandon Aigai, for all that the kings, even Archelaos, were still buried there. Glaukon, sullenly kicking his way through the drifted snow, his feet shod only in sandals, would not have taken much convincing that he lived in an evil and sacrilegious age.

The kitchen fire had long since gone cold and gray, but the room was still quite warm. Someone had kept a brazier going and Nikomachos, the king's physician, sat facing it, resting his head on one hand as he appeared to study the tiny wisps of flame that fluttered here and there among the coals.

On the other side of the brazier, on a bench that also held a cup of wine, was an old woman with a bundle in her arms, her lips moving almost soundlessly in some private meditation. She was Iocasta, born in a remote mountain village but a servant in the royal household since long before anyone could remember. She did not even raise her eyes when Glaukon entered but went on muttering to herself. It would not have been any different if Lord Amyntas himself had come in, for Iocasta was too full of years to defer to anyone.

It was a considerable moment before Glaukon realized that the bundle in her arms held a child, a baby no more than a few hours old. His heart seemed to die within his breast.

"The Lady Eurydike is delivered of a son," Nikomachos announced quietly. "Yet she cannot nurse the child—his coming into the world was a terrible business, for him and for her."

He stood up, as if he had been waiting half his life to say so little.

"Take him to your own wife, Glaukon, and let them comfort one another."

The two men exchanged a glance, and then Nikomachos turned and started down the corridor that led to the great hall, disappearing almost at once into the shadows. Glaukon crouched beside Iocasta's bench, reaching across to pull the sheepskin away from the child's face.

The king's new son slept on, a few wisps of dark hair clinging to his scalp, his round face with its puffy eyelids giving him an appearance of intense concentration.

Let them comfort one another. It occurred to Glaukon that the physician was both compassionate and wise.

"What is his name?"

Iocasta glanced up and scowled, as if she resented the intrusion.

"Philip," she said at last. "'Lover of Horses'—perhaps the Lord Amyntas intends him for a stableboy. It would be better so."

She drew the sleeping child closer to her bosom and stared at the flames of the brazier, which moved with liquid slowness. What she saw there did not seem to please her, for the creases in her withered old face settled into an expression of something between pity and dread.

"He began life by trying to break the cord that held him to his mother. Did you know that?"

Glaukon only shook his head. Old women sometimes spoke with the voice of prophecy, but he was not sure it was always wise to listen. Certainly it was not wise to question.

"I think he did very well," she went on, "for mother and son will live their lives as enemies—until one is the undoing of the other. See what a beginning they have made: he almost killed her being born, and the Lady Eurydike, had she had but the strength to speak, would have damned him even as he slipped from her womb. Her belly could not be more full of venom if it held vipers in place of guts. She is a Lynkestian, a mountain woman, and she knows how to hate."

"You are from there yourself, are you not, Iocasta?"

Without raising her eyes from the child, she nodded slowly, allowing herself a tight smile, as if to acknowledge an unintended compliment.

"I am. And that is why I understand her. And that is why I know there is no more terrible destiny than a mother's curse, even if she has not breath to utter it."

For a long moment she said nothing, and then she held the child away from her and put him into Glaukon's arms. The youngest of King Amyntas's sons stirred a little, opening his eyes briefly before returning to a profound sleep.

"Take him away," she said. "The sight of him oppresses my heart, for his life's blood will be spilled through treachery."

The king's steward walked home through the cold and deserted night, carrying his royal burden against his chest. The snowstorm had stopped abruptly so that the ground was a featureless white in the moonlight. The very air had taken on an unearthly clarity so that everything stood revealed, almost as if in daylight.

Glaukon thought of what he would see in his wife's face when he woke her from her tortured, restless sleep and put this child, still wrapped in its sheepskin, into her arms.

I return our son to your breast, he thought, knowing these to be words he could never speak. *Our son . . .*

He stopped for a moment—because he had to, because he was almost blinded by his own tears—and raised his eyes to the dark heavens to thank the gods for their mercy.

Above him, in the western sky, glittered the Constellation of the Toiling Man.

"Herakles . . ." The word escaped before he realized he had spoken it.

"And this too is prophecy," he murmured. "So perhaps, my little prince— my son—perhaps your destiny will not after all be so obscure."

2

The stallion was eighteen hands high and wild as a demon. The muscles beneath its smooth black coat bunched and rippled as it trotted back and forth within the stout wooden railings of the enclosure, tearing up the earth with its hooves, searching for a means of escape. By now it knew there was no escape, but its fury would not allow it to be still.

"This one is fine, is he not," said Alexandros, first prince of Macedon, looking on as he leaned against the gate. He was tall and fair and almost inhumanly beautiful, and his whole carriage suggested the easy animal grace of the born warrior. He watched the stallion through pale blue, predatory eyes that reflected an odd mixture of admiration and envy, as if the beast were both a possession and a rival.

"We found him out on the eastern plains, with a whole herd of mares all to himself. Before we could drive him in here he broke a horse's shoulder with one kick and almost killed its rider."

The prince turned around toward the men who were with him, and his gaze fell on his two young brothers. Perdikkas, the elder by a year and already with a few tufts of copper-colored beard on his chin, dropped his eyes almost at once, causing Alexandros to smile with what might have been affection but was more probably contempt.

"What would you say, Perdikkas, if I were to offer you this splendid animal? Would he not be worth a little danger? I will make you a present of him if you can stay on his back to the count of ten."

But Perdikkas, who, despite his new beard, was still only a boy, shook his head, not even daring to look his brother in the face.

"Do you plan to live forever then?"

All the strong, brave young men who were Alexandros's friends laughed at his jest, making the boy blush with shame.

"Our brother Perdikkas is well enough as a horseman," spoke up the youngest of King Amyntas's sons, his voice still piping almost as high as a girl's. "But he is not the rider to attempt an untamed stallion—at least, not that one—and he is also not a fool to get his neck broken simply because you dare him to. However, if you really don't want the horse for yourself, offer him to me on the same terms."

Philip looked up at his eldest brother as a man might look into the sun. He even shaded his eyes, his grin showing white, even teeth in a face more remarkable for strength and intelligence than for beauty. Alexandros was his hero, but he was not in the least intimidated by him.

This was so obvious that Alexandros was forced to laugh.

"Little brother Philip, 'Lover of Horses,'" he said, putting his hands on his knees and crouching slightly, as if he were talking to a very young child. "For all that I put you on your first mount before you were old enough to walk, that black demon will trample you into paste."

They both turned to watch the stallion, which lowered its head for an instant and then reared up, slashing at the air with its hooves, seeming to issue a challenge of its own.

"Don't be mad," Perdikkas murmured—his voice was hushed with dread, giving the impression he was afraid the stallion might overhear him. "Philip, that horse is a man-killer."

He turned to his elder brother with something like real anger.

"Alexandros, put a stop to this folly. If you encourage him in his own rashness, Philip's blood will be on your hands, just as surely as if you had murdered him."

Everyone laughed, even Alexandros, although his laughter betrayed a certain uneasiness. No one laughed harder than Philip.

"He is right, Philip. Even I would hesitate . . ."

"But I would not." The face of Amyntas's youngest son was set and serious. He was not to be resisted. "I mean to have the stallion, brother. Will you retract your challenge? Then I will know you think me as great a coward as yourself."

There was a sudden, dangerous silence. Alexandros seemed too shocked even to be angry. He actually looked as if someone had struck him.

And then one of his companions, a youth named Praxis, rested his hand on the prince's shoulder.

"Come, Alexandros. Be reasonable," he said in the soft, consoling voice with which one speaks to a grief-stricken woman. "You cannot allow yourself to be goaded into this piece of folly because a child calls you a name. Spank him for his impudence if you must, but let that end it."

Alexandros struck the hand away.

"No. Rope the stallion and let little brother Philip have his wish. 'Lover of Horses'—we shall see. If he wishes to kill himself, then let him!"

He raised his arm and, out of sheer impatience, threw it down again.

"Have I to do the thing myself?" he shouted, scrambling over the enclosure rails as if he really meant to. "Throw a rope across the brute's neck that Philip the Demigod may climb on his back—do it at once!"

It required almost a quarter of an hour to rope the stallion, and then a second rope was required before it could be brought to a halt and kept from rearing up and lashing out with its great hooves at the men who struggled to restrain it. In another horse so much violence might have been nothing more than simple panic, but this one seemed to seethe with fury, with the desire for revenge.

"Well, Lover of Horses, he is yours for the taking. I wish you joy in him."

Alexandros grinned savagely at his youngest brother, who in that moment felt a kind of grief, as if he had lost something forever. This the first prince of Macedon saw in his face, but misunderstood.

"If you are afraid, you need only say so. No one will think you a coward."

The word stung like a nettle, but Philip only shook his head.

"I am not afraid," he said and jumped down from the enclosure fence.

Two grooms, working with the quick, deft movements of men who feel themselves at risk and wish to be away, were already slipping a bridle over the stallion's head. Philip made his slow approach from the front and left, and the beast watched him through a huge, wild eye as if it knew that this was the only adversary who mattered. It whinnied slightly as Philip put his hand on its neck.

"That's done, then," he murmured, running his palm along the smooth coat, so black it seemed to cast back the sunlight like a polished gemstone. "You mustn't be frightened. You and I will get along very well together."

The stallion tried to strike out with its head but only succeeded in brushing against Philip's shoulder with its nose—the touch felt almost like a caress.

Philip took up the reins and, with deliberate suddenness, before the stallion had time to react, grabbed a handful of mane and jumped up onto its back.

"Slip the ropes!" he shouted, the stallion already bucking wildly beneath him. "Slip them—and stand clear!"

It was not advice anyone needed to hear more than once. Philip saw the ropes slide away, saw the grooms running for the fence, and almost simultaneously felt himself surging straight up. Then, in the next instant, he seemed to be hanging suspended in empty space—the stallion had simply dropped from beneath him.

He came down again with a sickening jolt that felt as if it had shattered his insides, yet somehow he managed to clamp his legs around the stallion's back and keep from tumbling off. He yanked back on the reins, trying to assert some kind of control, but the beast had a mouth of iron so that the bit seemed useless.

The stallion reared, snatching at the air, and then kicked back so that its whole body made a sharp twist to the left. Philip was hanging on to its mane by then, with no thought except somehow to avoid falling beneath those terrible hooves. Twice, three times he kept himself erect, knowing that if he lost his balance, he would probably be dead almost as soon as he hit the ground. And then . . .

He hardly knew what happened, except that he was going down—it was like diving into a pool. The stallion lashed out, and a terrible pain, like a flash of hot, white light, seemed to explode inside his head. He threw his arms out to break his fall, and then rolled, trying to get away before the stallion caught him again.

And all at once it was over. Philip pulled himself over onto his back and looked up at the sun. His face hurt and he could taste blood, but he was alive.

He seemed quite alone. Philip turned his head and saw the stallion perhaps fifteen or twenty paces away, calmly standing there, ignoring him. It was almost insulting.

Alexandros came running to help him up, but Philip shook him off. He scrambled to his feet unaided, and after a few seconds he was sure he would not fall down again.

"I'm all right," he said, and then he brought his left hand up to his cheek. He was bleeding just below the eye, but he wouldn't die of it. "I'm fine—get a rope and I'll try again. This time I'll beat him."

"We will have old Nikomachos see to you." Alexandros bent down to look at the wound on his little brother's face. "The bone may be broken . . ."

"Alexandros, rope the horse!" Philip shouted—suddenly he was in a fine rage so that he actually stamped his foot.

"Philip, the horse is yours if you want him so much!" Alexandros shouted back. "He is a demon, as black inside as out, and you are lucky to be alive. Be content—you have proved to me that you are a man."

"But I have not proved it to *him*!"

Tears were already coursing down his face. Philip held out his arm, pointing in the stallion's direction, the fist clenched and trembling. And then, from one instant to the next, his anger broke.

"Rope the horse," he said softly. "Have it done, brother, or I will do it myself. He may be a demon, but he will not defeat me. I know his tricks now. I will ride him."

"'I will alone,' little brother?" Alexandros smiled, but with a kind of repressed impatience, as if it were being squeezed out of him, as he alluded to the story old Glaukon always told of Philip's first attempts to walk—barely a year old, he furiously pushed away all attempts at help, shouting in his lisping baby's voice, "I will alone, I will alone!" "You only fell on your bottom then—you may break your neck this time."

"Have it done, brother."

The smile faded. He had only to look in Philip's eyes to know that argument was useless. Alexandros raised a hand, in a gesture that was like a shrug, and gave the order.

Philip sat down on the grass, nursing his head and his pride, watching while the grooms went about their work. The stallion's front legs had become entangled in the reins, so this time it was not so difficult to capture and subdue—besides, it no longer seemed afraid of the confrontation with mere men, as if it sensed it could win against any rider.

"The gods punish pride," Philip whispered to himself, his eyes narrowing slightly as they measured the hard, black shape of his adversary. "Whether yours or mine, my friend, we have still to determine."

He got up and walked stiffly to where the grooms and their captive were waiting for him. As soon as he gave the signal, and the ropes slipped from around the its neck, he tightened his legs against the stallion's flanks and dropped down so that his chest was almost touching its neck.

Snorting wildly, the stallion reared up and then jumped with all the power of his hindquarters, but, as Philip had expected, came down rather lightly on its forelegs. He anticipated the stallion's leftward twist by throwing his weight in that direction, and it was as if his mount came to catch him before he fell.

The stallion reared again, neighing with what sounded like incredulous rage. Again and again, with mounting fury, it tried to shake itself free of its unwanted burden, but each time Philip was able to keep his seat. Finally it seemed to give up on that tactic, stood perfectly still for a moment, and then began galloping back and forth within the enclosure.

"Open the gate!" Philip shouted, hardly able to make himself heard. "Throw open the gate!"

Rider and horse, looking as if they had fused together into a single being, tore over the hard-packed earth of the enclosure, out through the gate and onto the windswept grasslands beyond. The pounding of the stallion's hooves was no more than a blur of sound—the horse burned over the open ground as if it wished to burst its heart. Never, never had Philip ridden an animal that could run like this one.

But no living thing could go on like that forever. Gradually the stallion began to slow and, as it slowed, it began to answer to the reins. Soon, when they were down to little more than a canter, Philip was able to turn its head back the way they had come. The wooden rails of the enclosure were hardly visible.

"Enough for one day," Philip murmured now, letting his hand slide down to stroke the stallion's black, sweat-lathered neck. "Time to go home."

He pulled in with the reins, bringing the horse to a stop, and then touched its flanks with his heels. It started forward at a walk, as if long accustomed to its master's will.

Alexandros and Perdikkas, surrounded by Alexandros's friends, met them at the enclosure gate. Philip jumped down, took a step forward, and offered the first prince his hand.

"I beg your forgiveness, brother," he said, his eyes on Alexandros's face. "I spoke in anger, with nothing to guide my tongue but injured vanity. I forgot the justice I owe to one of proven courage."

For a moment Alexandros did not seem to know what to do, and then he frowned, the way one does when reproving a child.

"If you had been killed, the king our father would have blamed me."

"If I had been killed, the king our father would not even have noticed."

In a burst of startled laughter, Alexandros threw his arms around his youngest brother's shoulders. The stallion stepped back a pace and whinnied, as if at the sight of blood.

"Groom—you there!" Alexandros shouted. "Take the Lord Philip's horse to the stables and see that he is well rubbed down. My brother is hard with his animals."

The laughter was now general—only Perdikkas kept apart from it.

It was not until after nightfall, when her daughter's husband had already crept into her bed, that the Lady Eurydike heard of Philip's triumph. She had turned her face to the wall so that her naked back was pressed against Ptolemy's chest, and he whispered the story to her as he gathered in the soft weight of her breasts. He knew it would elicit in her that sullen anger, like the contemplation of an old injustice, which somehow always shaded into desire. Even as he entered her he had no way to be sure which passion caused her breath to catch, or if she would have recognized there could be a difference.

Afterward, and for a long time, she did not speak.

"Nothing more has happened than a boy mastering a horse," he said at last. "It was only chance that he did not break his neck."

"It was not chance."

"Of course it was chance."

Eurydike laughed. It was a gloomy sound in the darkness.

"Had it been Alexandros, or anyone else, I might agree, but Philip will never die until someone kills him."

Ptolemy made no answer. The Lady Eurydike had once more turned away from him so that her hair, which was like tarnished honey, cascaded heavily across her white back.

He did not love her. She was merely useful, he told himself. She was the key with which he would one day open the door to power. He told himself it was enough that Eurydike loved him—loved him with the blind, devoted passion that the gods visit upon those whom they mean to destroy. Yet their intrigue had exposed a vein of sensuality in him that he had not even suspected of existing, for it was deeply stirring to have excited such desire in a woman, and all the more so because it knew no rival. Beside him, neither her husband nor the children of her own body meant anything to her.

Moreover, for all that she had borne many children and was almost forty, she was still beautiful.

Yet the very wildness of her passion, exciting enough in an embrace, was at other times unnerving. It was dangerous, precisely because it knew no limits.

The king was old—dying, so everyone said. They were safe from his wrath, but what did Eurydike care for safety? She had beckoned Ptolemy into her arms long ago, when the slightest whisper would have meant their deaths, yet such had been her lust that the risks had meant nothing to her.

In an instant, in one of those sudden swings of mood that seemed to transform her utterly, she turned back to him, a smile on her lips.

"When you rise from here, will you go to my daughter's bed?" she asked as if she already knew the answer—as if she only wanted the self-torturing pleasure of hearing him speak it. "Does your bride know how you wear away your strength laboring over her mother's body?"

Like a restless and unwelcome spirit, the thought of his wife stole into Ptolemy's mind. Likewise called Eurydike, and as unlike her mother as it was possible to imagine, she was a pretty, quiet, pious girl who made daily offerings at the shrine of Hera, patroness of domestic life, that she might grow quick with a son and thus find a way into her husband's love. A son, as if that would make any difference . . .

"Yes, of course she knows. By now, everyone knows."

"Except the king, who is beyond caring, even if he did know."

With a fit of savage laughter, she lunged at him, baring her teeth to bite him on the chest. Ptolemy grabbed her shoulders and thus just prevented her. She would have done it, had done it before. He had scars to witness for him.

"You are mad." His hands slipped up to her throat. He thought how easy it would be to kill her. Perhaps it would be the best thing, he thought. It would be the sort of death she might relish. "You are as savage as an animal."

"Yes."

"Yes."

But he did not kill her. Instead, he found himself once more full of desire. Her flesh seemed to burn under his touch. He took her breasts in his hands, digging his fingers into them as if he would tear them from her body. And still she laughed—pain meant nothing to her.

She moved closer to him, dragging herself beneath his weight.

When it was over, and she had burned his lust to ashes so that he almost hated her, she reached beneath the bed and took out a pair of cups and a small jar of wine. Yes, he was thirsty. His throat felt as if the inside had been coated with pitch, but he resented that she should find him so predictable.

"He may yet break his neck," he said with a certain malicious satisfaction, although he knew the remark had no power to wound her. It was a few seconds before she even remembered who he could have meant.

"Philip? No." The Lady Eurydike shook her head, almost grimly, as if acknowledging a defeat. "Yet it would be safer for you if he did."

"He is only a boy—I am not afraid of him."

"You should be."

She smiled at him, and even in the dim light from a single oil lamp he could read the contempt in her smile—he was her lover and she hated this her youngest child, yet Philip was still her son and thus enough like her to be a match for all the Ptolemies who had ever lived. This she believed in the very core of her soul, and it made her hatred more like love than love itself.

"He will kill you," she said matter-of-factly, the smile dying on her lips. "Alexandros has courage, but he is vain. You can outwit Alexandros. And I can control Perdikkas. But Philip . . . As you plan your treason, Philip should never be far from your thoughts."

"The king is old and infirm and cannot last through the next winter. When he is gone, there will be only Alexandros, who trusts me as his friend. Perdikkas and Philip are boys."

"You say that as if boys never grew into men."

"Some of them do not."

"Do you mean to kill my sons?" she asked as if she expected to find the answer amusing. "Will you be king in their place? The Assembly of the Macedonians elects the king. What will they think if they find you with your hands reddened by the blood of three royal princes?"

She shrugged her naked shoulders and brought the wine cup to her lips, seemingly indifferent.

"Since it is power you wish, you shall have it. I will see to it that you are great in the next reign. But if you wish to live to enjoy such power, keep your ambition within bounds—for your own sake if not for mine, since I know how little I mean to you. And do not speak again as if you would harm my sons."

His wine cup was empty, so she refilled it. Then she kissed his lips with the most abject tenderness.

"Yet be careful of Philip. Do not make the mistake of thinking that because he is only a boy he is not the most dangerous of enemies."

Ptolemy knew she was right. He could feel the truth of it in the cold fear that held his bowels clenched like a fist.

"He may yet break his neck," he said at last. "It still might happen. Some horses are never truly broken—they wait upon the time, and then they kill."

Philip himself entertained no such doubts. He had a fine new horse and he was on the threshold of manhood. Neither of these held any terrors for him, and life had not yet taught him there could be anything more to hope for. The king and his mother were distant figures, and his cousin the Lord Ptolemy he hardly knew. His family, as defined by his affections, consisted of Glaukon and Alcmene, who occupied the place of parents, Alexandros and Perdikkas, and his half brother, Arrhidaios, his closest friend.

Thus, a few days later, it was to Arrhidaios that he revealed the most recent of his triumphs. He had trained his new possession, now bearing the name "Alastor," to answer to the pressure of his knees instead of to the bit alone.

"You see?" Philip almost shouted with exultation as the great black stallion began pacing slowly to the left. "Soon he will learn to do the same at a gallop, and then I will be able to keep my hands free at all times, even in a cavalry charge."

Arrhidaios laughed. "It is a good thing you will never be king," he said. "You are so in love with war that your reign would be a scene of continuous bloodshed."

But Philip did not seem to hear him. He slid down from the horse, his bare feet striking the ground as if he intended to anchor himself to that spot.

"Want to try him?"

Arrhidaios merely shook his head, letting his long arms cross over the neck of his dappled gelding. He was two years older than Philip and by nature more cautious, as befitted the second son of a king's second wife.

"He understands that he has found his match in you, but everyone says he is a demon. Who knows if, with another rider, he might not decide to take his revenge?" He shrugged, bringing his wide, bony shoulders up into little points. "'Alastor'—trust you to name your horse after the cruelest and most wicked of the gods. Would you frighten us all out of our lives?"

Philip placed his hand on the stallion's neck, as if to demonstrate its placidity.

"Don't be such a coward," he said. "Try him. See? He's as peaceful as a plow ox."

"I'm quite content where I am, thank you. I've no inclination to find my death beneath that black brute's hooves."

Then they could both laugh, and Philip grabbed handfuls of the stallion's mane and scrambled up again onto its back.

"Let's race to the river and back!" Philip shouted, his mount already skittering nervously.

"It would hardly be a contest. This nag breathes like a bellows if forced above a trot."

"Then let's go hunting."

But there was little game this near to Pella, and what there was had long since grown wary of men on horseback. Thus the two royal princes quickly abandoned even the pretense that they expected to use their iron-tipped javelins for anything more than target practice. They rode at will over the broad plains north of the city, sometimes chasing furiously after a wild pig that would appear suddenly just out of range and then just as suddenly disappear into a ravine, sometimes engaging in mock battles against an invisible foe, enjoying themselves after the aimless fashion of boys who have nothing to do but to grow triumphantly into men.

At last, when their shadows began to lengthen over the yellow grass, they turned their faces back to where the buildings of the king's capital made a broken line against the horizon. It was almost dark by the time they had left their horses with the grooms of the royal stable.

"I'm hungry," Philip announced as if the discovery came to him as a surprise. "We'll have to hope Alcmene saved us some dinner."

But of course Alcmene, who was not a woman to leave such things to chance, had saved them some dinner. They sat at a wooden table in her kitchen while she filled their bowls with a meat stew rich enough almost to sate their hunger if they but held their faces over it and breathed in the steam that rose from its surface.

And all the time they ate, Alcmene scolded Philip—for being late, for risking his life on "that dreadful animal," for having forgotten to take a lunch bag with him, for his general heedlessness—all the while calling him "Prince" and "My Lord." She was perhaps thirty years old, a plump and motherly creature with the pale blue, despairing eyes of one who has long since resigned herself to barrenness, and Philip was the idol of her life, upon whom she lavished the love she could not give her own unborn children.

Philip, for his part, did not answer, did not even really listen. Alcmene's complaints against him had been in his ears ever since he could remember. They were like another woman's caresses. He merely ate and made jokes with Arrhidaios.

"Where is Glaukon?" he asked suddenly.

"Like a good servant, about his master's business," she replied as if meeting an accusation. She loved Philip above any living thing, but her husband was her standard of all the manly virtues—if a prince could not model himself upon the king's chief steward, then so much the worse for the prince.

"A page came for him not an hour ago. Doubtless he will tell you about it when he returns."

"Doubtless."

Philip smiled at Arrhidaios, tore a piece of bread in half, and shrugged. Almost everything he knew of life in his father's court he had learned from listening to Glaukon. It was not a topic about which he was very curious, for to a boy of his age war was the only item of statecraft of any real interest—or, at least, of interest to the boy who was Prince Philip of Macedon—and during the last several years of this reign the nation had been at peace.

Nevertheless, almost against his will, he had absorbed it all, all the kitchen gossip, all the intrigues and the rivalries, everything that Glaukon thought fit to tell him—and there were few secrets that did not reach the ears of the king's chief steward. The result was that Philip saw the men and women who surrounded the king not as they saw themselves but as they appeared to the eyes of an intelligent servant. He was not cynical, for cynicism implies an expectation of something better, and Philip expected nothing. It was just that these rulers of the earth did not seem to him so very grand.

A moment later the door opened. It was Glaukon. As soon as his gaze came to rest on Philip he frowned, just the way he had frowned once when he had caught the youngest prince of Macedon stealing apples from Alcmene's larder, with a kind of pitying regret.

"You are sent for," he said in a flat voice. "You as well, My Lord Arrhidaios. The king your father is dying."

Philip experienced the words almost as a physical shock: *The king your father is dying.* But the shock was merely surprise, for he did not feel himself at all involved in the fact. All good Macedonians loved their king, and Philip was a good Macedonian. But that this king was his father meant nothing. What, after all, was a father? Someone hopelessly remote—like a king.

"Then we must go."

Philip was a little taken aback by the sound of his own voice. It seemed to belong to someone else.

On the walk to the palace compound, Glaukon told them what had happened. "The Lord Amyntas was visited with a stroke. It came without warning— he simply collapsed. He is paralyzed along the whole left side of his body. His speech is hardly more than a whisper, but his mind is clear. Nikomachos does not believe he will live more than a few hours more. He called for his son."

"Then he meant Alexandros," Philip announced with the tone of someone stating the obvious. "He wishes to see his heir."

"He did not mean Alexandros."

For some reason, Glaukon looked embarrassed. Although it was a warm night, he drew his cloak around him as they walked, and his pace quickened. It was obvious he did not intend to elaborate.

When they reached the long antechamber to the king's private apartments, the chief steward paused before a great oak door.

"Go inside," he said. "Both of you, go inside. I will wait here. A king is a man like other men, and his death is properly the concern of his family. This room no longer holds any place for servants."

Philip and Arrhidaios exchanged glances. It seemed a strange business, and neither of them had ever been inside the king's bedchamber.

The door opened soundlessly, and the two boys entered. The room was surprisingly small and seemed all the smaller for the number of people it held. No one spoke, or even looked up to see who had come in—their whole attention belonged to the figure on the bed.

At first Philip thought that the king must already have died, he was so still. He looked incalculably old, which is the way one always imagines the dead to look. A blanket covered him to the waist, and his hands, lying at his sides, were as pale as wax. His eyes were shut and he did not appear to be breathing.

Then he opened his eyes.

He glanced about him, searching the faces gathered around his bed, seemingly bewildered, as if their presence was only one more frightening proof that he was dying, as if he could not quite remember who they were: his sons, chief among them Alexandros, his beautiful countenance creased with anger, as though he imagined himself somehow cheated; the king's two wives, with expressions like birds of prey; cousin Ptolemy, his face suitably grave; even cousin Pausanias, a king's son himself and the last of his line, giving the impression he was more frightened of death even than was the dying man. The House of the Argeadai was there complete. The only stranger was Nikomachos, the royal physician.

When the king's eyes fell on his youngest son, they rested there. Now Philip was frightened. He did not dare look away, for his father's gaze held him, as if they were alone.

At last Amyntas, king of Macedon, opened his mouth to speak, although the sound of his voice was lost even in that stillness. The strain seemed to tire him beyond bearing. Nikomachos brought a cup of wine to his lips, but he shook his head. Then he made a tiny movement with the fingers of his right hand—a gesture of summons. He had never taken his eyes from Philip's face.

Philip approached the bed and knelt beside his father, covering the king's withered hand with his own. The dying man seemed to gather the last of his strength.

"Sometimes," he said, speaking so softly the boy could hardly hear, "sometimes, before they stop a man's breath, the gods reveal their will to him, perhaps only that he may know what folly his life has been."

He closed his eyes for a moment, giving the impression the effort of these few words was unendurable. Then he opened them again, and his hand stirred beneath Philip's, as if he would grasp the boy's fingers.

"Philip, my son, the king's burden . . ."

But it was too late. The sentence was lost in his last breath. All at once his face changed in some indefinable way.

Nikomachos reached down and touched the side of the king's neck.

"He is gone," the physician murmured, although it seemed the loudest sound in the world. "What did he say, Prince?"

Philip looked up, his eyes glistening with unspent tears.

"Nothing."

3

Philip walked back through the silent darkness of a city that had lost its king. He had knelt by the bed, still holding his father's hand, as the physician Nikomachos closed the third Amyntas's eyes. Then there was a murmur of voices as, one after the other, the Argeadai began to adjust themselves to the awesome reality of death.

All at once Philip felt the weight of a hand on his shoulder.

"Let go," Alexandros said, giving him a rough shake. "Let go of his hand before the fingers lock shut around yours. Time for you to go home."

He looked at his youngest brother as if their father's corpse were his personal property.

"Save your tears for the funeral."

By now the household slaves were washing the dead king's limbs, preparing him for the purifying fire. Amyntas, lord of the Macedonians, already belonged to the past.

There was an unnatural quiet. Philip saw not a living face as he made his way back to Glaukon's house. The precincts around the palace were dark and still, as if everyone were in hiding—as if the numb feeling in his own breast had spread out through the whole royal quarter.

He no longer understood himself. The king had lived a stranger to him yet, almost with his last breath, had called him "my son," making his heart tremble like a bell struck once after years of silence. Was a son's love so accessible that this man could reach inside him and take it in handfuls, now, when it was too late for both of them? Was this grief, this sense of having been plundered? If this was grief, then Philip felt contempt for it. What else he felt he did not know.

Alcmene was still awake. She sat on a stool beside the hearth, her hands in her lap. There was still fire enough to keep the cooking pot warm.

"Are you hungry?" she asked, looking up at him with her imploring blue eyes—she had given him dinner out of the same pot not four hours ago, but Alcmene believed in food as the sovereign remedy for all afflictions, of the body and the soul both.

Philip shook his head. He did not know why, but at that moment he could not have trusted himself to speak.

"Then take some wine, My Lord."

Instead, he knelt beside her, placing his head on her lap. Without knowing why, he was suddenly overwhelmed by sorrow. His eyes filled with tears, and a great sob convulsed him. Alcmene put an arm over his shoulders and stroked his hair.

"I know, I know," she murmured, the sound of her voice like a caress. "I know, my little prince—it is bitter to learn this truth so young."

By sunrise everyone in Pella knew of Amyntas's death, and at noon every man under arms was gathered in the amphitheater, which stood at the summit of a small hill near the city's outskirts, with the purpose of choosing a successor. Even Glaukon, although he had never known battle, wore a breastplate into assembly and carried a sword, for these things were the emblems of citizenship. Whether he served or not, every Macedonian was a soldier, and the army elected the king.

Philip, Perdikkas, and Arrhidaios were still too young to take part, so they remained at the base of the hill, waiting with the crowds of women, children, and foreigners. They waited without suspense since, like everyone else, they knew what the decision must be. Tradition held that the nation would survive and prosper only so long as it was ruled by a descendant of Herakles, and thus only the House of the Argeadai could provide a king. Alexandros was the eldest son and labored under no disability that rendered him either incapable or offensive to the gods. Had he been a minor like his brothers, a regent might have been appointed or he might even have been set aside, but he was of age, a proven warrior, and popular with the army. He had also been his father's choice. His election was assured.

Perdikkas's attention seemed focused on the plane trees that lined the outside wall of the amphitheater. Their upper branches stirred slightly in a breeze that was not detectible from the ground, and Perdikkas watched with sulky concentration, as if he took even this as a personal affront.

"They have been about it a long time," he said finally. "Perhaps they do not mean to make Alexandros king after all."

It was impossible to tell from his expression whether the idea pleased him or not. The way that he plucked at his few tufts of beard suggested that he could not decide himself.

Philip glanced down at the dust on his sandals, as if embarrassed.

"They must first make sacrifice and offer prayers that the gods will favor their decision. Be patient."

As if in answer, a great shout rose from the amphitheater, followed by a mounting wave of sound, harsh and insistent, like stones breaking against one another—it was a clang of swords upon breastplates as the Macedonians under arms affirmed their loyalty to a new king.

"You see?" Philip grinned broadly as if at some personal triumph. "They have made their choice."

"Yes, they have made their choice." It was the first time Arrhidaios had broken his silence.

"You mustn't be dismayed." Perdikkas regarded him with a sly smile. "It only means that you and your brothers now belong to a collateral branch. Or did you cherish an ambition to be king?"

"It is to be hoped that none of us cherish such an ambition," Philip answered—before Arrhidaios had a chance. "We must pray that Alexandros has a long reign and fathers many sons. The Macedonians will then be free to make war on their enemies, instead of on each other."

Perdikkas and Arrhidaios both looked at him as if he had spoken like a fool, and Philip himself experienced an instant of doubt whether perhaps he had.

Yet that doubt vanished as quickly as it had come when a man in full battle dress appeared at the entrance to the amphitheater and walked a few paces down toward the waiting crowd before coming to a halt. He carried an ax in his right hand, and he led a dog by the coil of rope he held in the other. The crowd fell silent.

Perhaps it was the sudden hush, but in that moment the dog seemed to become aware of danger. It began to bark, the sound gradually rising into a panicky squeal, and for the first time fought against the rope that held it. It was an old dog, stiff in its movements, and there were gray hairs mixed in with the patchy brown on its muzzle. There was something pathetic about its terror.

The soldier was very efficient. He simply hauled the dog in until he held it by its rope collar, then knelt down and, in a single, deft movement, struck it across the top of its skull with the flat side of the ax head. The dog was only stunned, but it offered no further resistance. It did not even cry out when the soldier laid it across a flat stone by the side of the path leading down from the amphitheater, placed his sandaled foot across the dog's neck, and once more raised the ax.

The next blow was certainly fatal, for it caught the animal just at the edge of its rib cage and severed its spine.

It took the soldier only a few more seconds to cut the carcass in half. When that was done, he wiped his ax clean on a patch of grass and stood up, holding the dog's hind quarters in his left hand. These he threw to the other side of the path—they left a thin trail of blood in the air—before he disappeared back inside the amphitheater. By this grisly ritual, as old as the foundations of the state, was the election of a new king of Macedon announced.

A moment later Alexandros came into view. He wore a breastplate and there was a sword in his belt, but his handsome head was bare. The sight of him brought a cheer from the waiting crowds, but he did not acknowledge it. He merely glanced about him, with his cold blue eyes, as if waiting for the tumult to end.

At first he stood alone in the columned entranceway, but gradually the space behind him filled with men. Unlike their king, they all wore helmets and many of them carried spears.

The crowd grew silent and began to fall back along either side of the path, clearing a way for the king and his soldiers, who would now march to the center of the city, to the temple of Herakles, in a ceremony of purification.

It was then, at the last moment before the army of Macedon began its solemn procession, that Philip happened to turn his head and noticed Pausanias, standing a little way down on the other side of the path, among a group of Athenian merchants.

Himself the son and grandson of kings, his rightful place was with the other great nobles, the companions who now ranged themselves behind Alexandros and would henceforth be at his side in war and in council. It was strange to see him there, among foreigners, as if he were one of them and not a member of the royal house itself.

But Pausanias did not now look like an Argead. He shifted his weight nervously from one foot to the other, and his eyes were never still. He seemed almost ready to flee.

"What is he doing out here?" Perdikkas asked in a tone that suggested he felt himself insulted.

"Perhaps he was afraid of what might have happened to him inside," Arrhidaios replied. "Perhaps he was afraid that Alexandros's first action as king might be to condemn him to death."

Philip said nothing, for Pausanias was discovering that he had been noticed and he appeared to be trying to recall where he had seen these boys before. When his gaze settled on Philip he actually seemed to take fright—his face darkened and he scowled, as if caught in the midst of some shameful act. After a moment he began to edge his way back through the crowd, which soon engulfed him.

Perdikkas, however, had already lost interest.

"Here they come!" he cried, just as the new king, with his army behind him, came out of the shadow of the entranceway. "Glory to the king of Macedon! Glory to the House of the Argeadai!" He waved his arms as he shouted, in a perfect ecstasy of excitement.

Alexandros, as he walked past, only glanced at his younger brother, but that glance was full of withering contempt.

King Amyntas's body had been consigned to the fire, and his bones had been washed and wrapped in a gold-and-purple cloth for burial among his ancestors in Aigai. The next day was set aside for his funeral games.

The Lady Eurydike watched them from her seat beneath an awning on a patch of slightly rising ground just at the eastern edge of the playing field. It was a place of honor to which no one disputed her right, for she was the new king's mother and the line of direct descent now ran through her sons.

She was almost the only woman present, for the games were not a public event, and the dead king's family and court made up both the participants and the audience. All the great nobles were there, eager to display their prowess at wrestling or horse racing or with the discus—Alexandros himself would compete in the footraces. And the Lady Eurydike, as Amyntas's widow and the mother of his successor, was expected to acknowledge the winners with gifts and tokens of victory.

At the moment about a dozen of the companions were testing one another in the javelin throw. Ptolemy was one of these. What pleasure it would give her to set the laurel wreath upon his brow! What a moment that would be: *Here is my lover, the strongest among the strong!*

But she knew this would be denied her, for the honors of the day, which should have been his, would inevitably go to younger men—boys, really, striplings for whom time cast no shadow and whom, for that alone, she almost found it possible to hate.

Her eyes might have filled with tears of resentment had she not turned them away and pretended to discover the contestants less interesting than her fellow members of the audience.

Alexandros was on the sidelines, surrounded a small circle of youths who had been his friends since childhood, and each of whom expected to stand high in the reign that was just beginning. Alexandros was handsome, gifted, and brave, but experience had yet to find anything to teach him and such was his fierce pride in himself that he believed it never would. The sight of him bruised Eurydike's heart, for she could not bring herself to believe that the gods would suffer him to live a long life.

And a little distance away, with Glaukon the steward, the physician Nikomachos, and Nikomachos's son young Aristotle, whom everyone spoke of as a lad of great intellect, was Philip—it was so like Philip to put himself among low-born men, little better than servants. He seemed to disdain the company of his equals, valuing only such as were clever or talented or blessed with some particular virtue. It was hard to remember that the blood of kings flowed through his veins.

Yet of all her sons it seemed to her that, in a strange way, Philip was the most like Amyntas.

Eurydike hated her youngest child, hated him precisely because, even as he quickened in her womb, she had learned to hate his father.

The House of the Bakchiadai had ruled Lynkos as kings in their own right for as long as anyone could remember. The Argeadai claimed sovereignty over the whole of Macedon, but it had not been so since the days of the first Alexandros, for the Lynkestai made war and entered into treaties, sometimes with the enemies of the Argeadai, just as they saw fit. So it was that King Arrhabaios sought among the women of the royal house of Illyria a bride for his son and heir Sirrhas, who had recently lost his wife, the mother of his son. This Illyrian woman gave birth to two stillborn sons and then died herself after the birth of a daughter—named Eurydike.

And Arrhabaios, beholding the weakness of the Argeadai, had forced Amyntas to take his granddaughter as a wife, that the rulers of Macedon might one day have his blood in their veins. Eurydike, at fifteen, found herself a bride in a strange court, surrounded by people she had been raised to see as enemies and oppressors.

But she had been dutiful. She had borne Amyntas a son, then a daughter, then another son, and the king her lord had treated her with the kindness of indifference. Theirs had been much like any other royal marriage, an obligation of rank, understood as such on both sides and therefore tolerable.

And then her father, Sirrhas, who had long since come to the throne and dreamed of throwing off the tyranny of the Argeadai, had sided with his father-in-law, Bardylis, king of the Illyrians. There was war, and Amyntas was forced to yield territory and to countenance, if not accept, the independence of the Lynkestai.

So he took his revenge upon his wife.

Such was his rage that he might have killed her had he dared, but he did not dare. Instead, he became inflamed with senile lust, using her like a tavern whore, though she was still weak from the birth of her second son—perhaps he had meant to kill her in that way, that thus no blame could attach to his name.

How she had learned to loathe the weight of him on her belly. And how he had delighted in degrading her, in indulging the most unspeakable appetites! The things he had done to her, and made her do . . . Even after all these years, she still remembered that time with a thrill of horror.

At last it became obvious that she was once more with child. Amyntas never touched her again.

And for of all this, Philip carried the burden. She had nearly died when he was born, and they had taken him away to be cared for by another—to become another woman's son and almost a stranger to the mother who had given him life. Perhaps, if it had not been so, if she had been allowed to nurse him at her own breasts . . . But her milk had dried up, and with it, the last chance to find the love for her son that was untainted by the curse of a wife's loathing for the husband who had wounded her soul.

Perhaps, in the end, Philip would serve her even worse.

"I should be among the competitors," Perdikkas announced sullenly, without looking at her. "I would be, had you not discouraged me."

The Lady Eurydike turned her eyes to her middle son, who was seated at her right hand. She smiled, for she loved Perdikkas, with a mother's love for the weakest of her children. Perdikkas was an intelligent boy and yet still a fool, after the manner of one who can believe something which he knows to be false.

"In what would you have competed?" she asked. "As an athlete you are not gifted."

"I am as good as anyone else."

He frowned, still keeping his gaze on the javelin hurlers. He frowned because he knew himself to be physically awkward and did not care to admit it, perhaps even in the privacy of his own heart.

"You are young, and prowess on the field is also a matter of experience."

In fact, as they both knew, she had discouraged him lest he make an exhibition of himself. This was not the time to excite the laughter of Alexandros and his friends.

"These are your father's funeral games," she added. "Sometimes it is best to maintain a dignified composure."

He started to say something, and then thought better of it. To save his feelings, she allowed her attention to return to the field.

Each competitor had already taken three of his five throws, and it was already clear that the contest was between only two men. Ptolemy was not one of these, although his three javelins had buried their points in the earth respectably close to the others.

He was sitting on the ground, waiting his turn for the fourth throw, with his javelin balanced across his knees. One of the other men turned to him and said something that made him throw back his head and laugh, and his beard seemed to gleam in the sunlight like polished iron. There were already a few patches of gray in its shimmering blackness—the thought of it touching her skin made Eurydike's breath catch—but otherwise he still had the look and bearing of a youth.

Though she labored to keep all expression out of her face, Eurydike could feel her bowels melting like hot wax. She was always surprised and perhaps a little frightened that the mere sight of this man should exercise such power over her. It must be so that the gods only visited love such as this on those whom they meant to destroy. Surely at last she would die, or pray for death, over some folly into which her passion had betrayed her, for love had not rendered her blind. She knew the sort of man she loved, dangerous and without scruple, greedy beyond reason for the power that must finally elude him—a man fated to a bad end. And she knew he did not return her love but was only using it as the tool of his ambition. She knew all this, but she was helpless. That was the full measure of the gods' enmity that they allowed her to see so clearly the destruction to which she hurried.

Yet what was that against the sight of him, against the press of his arms and the smell of his warm flesh? Even at the end, and no matter what terrors and suffering that end held in waiting for her, she knew she would not be able to regret anything.

Ptolemy's last two attempts did nothing to change the outcome of the contest, which was won by Craterus, eldest son of Antipatros, Lord of the Edonoi. Knowing how these things were to be managed, Ptolemy embraced Craterus and congratulated the father on the prowess of his heir—Ptolemy was a man who made friends wherever he could. He then walked over to sit on the ground at the Lady Eurydike's feet, thus demonstrating to anyone who cared to look what favor he found and how high he stood among the House of the Argeadai.

"It is a sport for boys," he said as if to no one in particular. "In my youth I was unsurpassed, but one's strength fades. At my age I should be content to sit on the sidelines and applaud the triumphs of a son."

"And you will when your son is of an age to compete—and there is yet hope you may have others."

The Lady Eurydike smiled. No, she was not taunting him. She knew he was not greatly grieved that his second wife seemed to be barren.

"Yes, I am not yet so decrepit that I cannot father children," he answered.

Perdikkas coughed uncomfortably. Perhaps he merely disliked being ignored, but he seemed embarrassed. That his mother and his sister's husband were lovers constituted a fact that was at once obvious and impossible to acknowledge, even to himself. Therefore he was even more than usually eager to attract Ptolemy's attention.

Ptolemy responded by letting his gaze settle upon the playing field, where the footraces were shortly to begin. Alexandros, stripped, his perfect body glistening with sweat and oil, was crouched on the ground with his head almost directly between his knees in some odd ritual of preparation. He would win this race, and he gave the impression that he knew it, and knew as well that his victory would be no fawning tribute to rank but his own, an entirely personal triumph, for he could run with a speed and unresisting grace that made it seem as if his feet hardly touched the earth.

The contrast between Macedon's new king and his ungainly, apprehensive brother could not have been more striking.

"Now that he is king, Alexandros should show you more favor," Ptolemy said. He turned his head and, without warning, broke into one of his blinding, unfathomable smiles. "He does not accord you the dignity he might—it is both wrong and foolish of him."

The footrace began. Alexandros quickly surged into the lead. The crowd roared its approval, but the three of them seemed isolated in their own silence. They might not even have been in the same place but somewhere of their own making, conscious of no one but each other. Ptolemy was still bathing Perdikkas in the entangling warmth of his notice, while the boy, almost blushing with pleasure, tried to think of some appropriate answer. It all seemed so playful and harmless they might have been lovers.

Eurydike felt a stab of cold go through her heart as she looked at them, her favorite son and this man who was more to her than the breath beneath her ribs, and tried to discover the snare in that baffling, irresistible smile.

Philip would not be denied. He was still too young to compete in his father's funeral games, so he decided to stage his own. He would hold a horse race, with himself, Arrhidaios, and the reluctant Aristotle as the competitors. Then there would be wrestling, then archery, then a poetry recitation, since Aristotle, who seemed to have the whole of Homer committed to memory, must be allowed to win something.

But the horse race was the real soul of the scheme. Philip would of course win—on his new stallion, how could he possibly fail to win?—but victory was almost unimportant against the pleasure of the ride itself: galloping over the vast, empty plains beyond the capital, the wind flowing like water over one's naked body, in one's ears the hypnotic beat of the horses' hooves against the earth. He could forget everything that had happened over the last several days, during which life had seemed as coiled as a serpent. He could forget all that and become once more simply a boy riding a fast and dangerous horse. Surely the race alone was prize enough.

There was a grove of oak trees about half an hour's walk north of the city gates. It would serve as a goal and they could hold the other contests there, safe from the observation of Alexandros and his friends—Philip had conceived a certain horror of his brother's mockery. Then they would come home, where Alcmene would give them a victory dinner. Perhaps she would even leave the wine sufficiently unwatered to allow them to grow drunk.

For the soldiers at the north gate it was a little respite from the boredom of guard duty. They laughed and offered to place bets on the outcome, and one of them agreed to give the starting signal. He stood about twenty paces in front of the three young riders, holding his sword aloft. When he brought the point down, Philip touched his heels to the stallion's black flanks and jolted instantly ahead.

In those first few moments he always had the sensation that the air was being sucked out of his lungs—there was nothing that could prepare one for the speed of this animal. The landscape blurred before his eyes; the only sounds he could hear were Alastor's fierce hoofbeats. Philip let the reins go loose and bent forward until his face was almost touching the stallion's neck, and he experienced once more the odd sense that horse and rider had somehow merged into a single being, as if he could feel with its body and it were thinking with his mind. He was filled with a wild, chaotic joy.

After the first surge, the stallion's gallop settled into a rhythm that left him free to return to himself. He knew that his companions were far behind—Arrhidaios's dappled gelding was no match and Aristotle, who was not even a Macedonian, hardly knew what a horse was—so he pulled in a little on the reins.

"Alastor, you will kill us both someday," he murmured, and at once the stallion dropped its head and slowed to a gentler pace.

Philip could already see ahead to the little grove of oak trees that marked the end of the race.

By the time he reached them, the stallion was lathered with sweat. Philip galloped a short way into the grove, where the sun filtered through to make hand-sized patches of light on the ground, and then he pulled the stallion to a halt and walked it around in a tight little circle until they were facing back the way they had come. He had been careful not to push his mount too hard over such a distance, but he was gratified to see that he had left Arrhidaios some two hundred paces back and Aristotle another hundred paces behind that. They were both still at a gallop and closing fast.

In a sudden burst of high spirits, he raised his arm and shouted a war chant, goading Alastor forward to a canter.

It happened just as he left the grove behind him and broke once more into the sunlight, and it happened with an awful suddenness. Philip glanced up, and in the same instant a terrible, feral cry shattered the air. His heart seemed to turn to ice as he saw swooping down at him a huge owl.

He saw its terrible eyes, full of death. He saw its claws, its talons long and tapered. It was coming straight for him, dropping through the empty sky like a stone. Philip had never felt so helpless. He could not even raise his arms to defend himself. He was transfixed with dread.

And then, at what must have been the last possible moment, the owl spread its great wings so that they seemed to blot out the whole of existence.

Philip felt it brush against his face, felt a sudden twinge of pain, and then . . . nothing.

He did not even remember falling. All at once he was simply lying on the ground, staring up at the sky, watching the owl rise on its great wings. It wheeled about in one vast turn and then disappeared.

4

"One only has to look to see the meaning of this," Glaukon said after he had heard the story. "There is the surface of things, which sometimes conceals the truth, and then there is the truth itself. In this case, the one is merely a version of the other."

Philip and his friends had ridden straight back to Pella. After so bizarre an event none of them had any heart left for games. Besides, the wounds left on Philip's face by the owl's talons were deep enough to require the services of a physician.

Yet it was not these that made Glaukon look so grave while Nikomachos painted over with a yellow salve that stung worse than nettles the two long parallel cuts on Philip's jaw.

"The owl, as everyone knows, is sacred to Athena, and now the goddess has marked you for her own—whether for good or ill she will reveal in her own time. She is full of wisdom and cunning and, for all she is a virgin, loves men of valor. She was the patroness of Herakles himself."

"And of Odysseus," Philip announced. "'The goddess, gray-eyed Athena, smiled on him, and stroked him with her hand.'"

"'And said to him, "He must be sharp and full of cunning who will surpass you in guile, you who are so devious and full of tricks."'"

Aristotle grinned—he and Philip had been playing his game of capping each other's quotations almost since they had first learned to read. His father merely grunted and went on with dressing Philip's wounds.

"Perhaps she means to be your patroness as well," Glaukon continued as if no one had spoken. "Or perhaps this was a warning that you have somehow incurred her displeasure. Go to the temple, My Lord, and make sacrifice to the goddess. Offer prayers that you may know her will."

"This is good advice." Nikomachos frowned at his son as if to keep the boy from making an objection. "Caution is a great virtue where the gods are concerned. And remember to reapply the salve every twelve hours—birds are filthy creatures, whether they come from the gods or not."

"Nothing is lost by offering prayers—even if it was only a frightened owl startled awake by your noise and blinded by the sunlight. The natural and obvious explanation is usually best; nevertheless, prayers do no harm."

Apparently feeling that he had taken sufficient revenge, Aristotle lapsed into an innocent silence, glancing about his father's surgery as if he had never seen it before.

But in matters of religion Philip was not encumbered with his friend's skepticism, so that afternoon, before he returned to Alcmene's hearthside to face her anxious and loving inquisition, he walked to the temple district.

Athena was not an important goddess to the Macedonians, so the shrine devoted to her worship was a humble business, little more than an altar with a few columns to mark out the precinct and a wooden roof to keep the rain off. Except that she did not like her offerings burned, Philip did not even know the rituals of her cult, so he left her an oat cake and a few cuttings from his hair and hoped that these would not give offense—like everyone else, the gods were full of singular preferences. He then sat down on a little stone bench just inside the entrance and tried to compose a suitable prayer.

His face itched where the owl had torn him, and he felt awkward, as if he were trespassing. Suddenly he was conscious of being very young and very unimportant. He could think of nothing he had done that might be displeasing to the gods, and the idea that he should have been singled out for divine favor struck him as preposterous. Who was he, after all, but a minor prince who would grow up to fight as a soldier for the king his brother? Why should any god, even Athena, imagine that he might be worth the trouble? What could she possibly want of him?

He looked at the statue of the goddess that stood in a niche behind the altar. It was a small but exquisitely made statue of a woman who was handsome rather than beautiful, with a silver breastplate over her long blue tunic, from beneath which one sandaled foot emerged. She was holding a spear.

"What would you have to me, Lady?" he murmured, a little surprised by the sound of his own voice. "What may I do to find your blessing?"

There was no answer, of course. He would have to wait for some sign of favor—if, indeed, he was to be favored—and then hope that when the time came he would know the goddess's will.

Beginning to feel a trifle foolish, he went outside again.

There was a procession of maidens coming out of the temple of Hera, and he waited for them to pass. One turned her head to look at him as she walked by. She smiled, and Philip realized that he knew her: she was some sort of cousin, just the same age as himself, and her name was Arsinoe. It struck him all at once that she was the most perfect creature he had ever seen.

He had not even presence of mind enough to smile back, and she turned her eyes away as if at a rebuke.

"You are an idiot, Philip," he said to himself. "Is that really her?"

Yes, it was. He could remember playing with her when she still wore a short tunic and had dirty knees. Had that been so long ago? She hadn't seemed very remarkable then.

He wondered what her knees were like now.

"Did the goddess reveal herself to you in there?" It was Aristotle—Philip hadn't even noticed his approach. "You have the look of one who has been privileged to glimpse the divine."

Philip turned to him and smiled, putting both more and less into the smile than he felt.

"I have, but the Lady Athena was not involved."

Alexandros had grown up believing that the king of Macedon must be the happiest and most fortunate of men, but his father had not been dead many days before he began to realize the proportions of his mistake. As prince and heir, he had understood with perfect clarity what would be expected of him once he ascended the throne, and he had never doubted that he would be a good king and do his duty, which was, after all, a perfectly simple business. The king should dispense justice to his subjects, favor to his friends, and death to his enemies. The king lived under the blessing of the gods, who made him virtuous in peace and terrible in war. The king was the darling of fortune. It had all seemed so straightforward and obvious. Now he felt as if nothing would ever be obvious again.

He had not understood how weak a nation he was to rule and how completely it was hedged about by enemies. The northern provinces of Lynkos and Orestis were in a more-or-less open state of rebellion. Athens was allied to the Chalcidian League, which threatened Macedon's access to the Thermaic Gulf. And now the Illyrians were demanding assurances that the new king would honor the treaties agreed to by his father.

The ultimate solution lay with the army, which Amyntas had neglected. Alexandros knew how to be a soldier, knew precisely what needed to be done. In the end Macedonian valor would overcome every difficulty.

And Macedonian valor could be restored, he felt certain, if only his nobles would stop intriguing and leave him in peace to reform the army. All he needed was time, just a little breathing space, but this, it seemed, he was not to be allowed.

No one else seemed concerned about the army. All anyone talked about was the succession.

This, Alexandros realized, was to some degree his own fault. He did not really care for women and had put off choosing a bride. His father should have insisted—it was really Amyntas's fault—but for the last several years his father had been too busy preparing for death to think about anything else. Thus there was no son to follow him, and both of his brothers were still in their minority, which would mean a regency if he died within the next few years. Nevertheless, either Perdikkas or Philip would have to be designated as the heir.

The choice should have been obvious, since Perdikkas was the elder. But Perdikkas was a weakling and unpopular. Philip would be a more approved choice, especially since . . .

No, he could not bring himself to name Philip the heir. In truth, he was beginning to grow a little afraid of Philip.

To be king, Alexandros had discovered, was to be constantly trapped in seemingly insoluble difficulties. He must either wage a war with Athens that he knew he could not win or accept a peace that would gradually strangle the nation. If he defied the Illyrians, they were likely to begin raiding the northern frontiers, but if he acknowledged the existing treaties, King Bardylis, the old bandit, would take it as a sign of weakness and press him all the harder. He must choose either Perdikkas or Philip, and neither was safe. Life had become a snare in which he found himself ever more entangled.

The only escape was in revelry, and even that was beginning to fail. More and more, at the nightly banquets with which he celebrated the beginning of his reign, Alexandros found himself morosely drunk, watching his barons pelting each other with wine cups and greasy, half-gnawed beef bones, wondering how he could stand the company of such filthy brutes. A month before he had been one of them and happy, yet to be a king, it seemed, was to forfeit every illusion. The gods must truly have laid a curse upon the House of the Argeadai, for to be lord over the Macedonians was to be a swineherd.

"My Lord finds no pleasure in this?"

Like a man startled awake by a loud noise, Alexandros did not immediately recognize the voice—in fact, for just an instant, he wondered if it could have been his own. Then he turned his head and saw Ptolemy, who had sat down at his right hand, on the bench where by custom no one ever sat except at the king's express invitation.

Ptolemy was his near relation and his friend. Ptolemy was like an elder brother, except cut off from the direct line of succession and therefore no threat. He wanted nothing for himself. Indeed, since he had been a great favorite of the late king's and stood well with his successor, what could he want that he did not already have? He was a man Alexandros found it impossible not to trust and his presence made him feel better—willing, even, to overlook the presumption.

"They are little better than cattle," Alexandros murmured, making a guarded gesture that nonetheless took in the whole room.

"And it is just as well, for cattle are very easily led."

Ptolemy smiled and although Alexandros found the smile unaccountably disturbing he found the idea comfortable enough. Yet he frowned anyway, since that seemed safer.

"Not these. Every one of them imagines himself the cowherd—or at least the principal bull."

Alexandros threw back his head and laughed. And then he stopped, suddenly realizing that he was more drunk than he had thought.

He glanced at Ptolemy, wondering if he had made a fool of himself, and saw the same unreadable smile on his lips, as if it had been carved into his flesh.

"I try to lead them, these cattle who are my subjects," the king of the Macedonians said, almost as if to himself, "but at every crossing they lower their heads and scratch at the earth with their hooves, wanting one path while I direct them to another. It is not even disobedience—not yet—only perversity."

"It is the art of kingship never to seem to direct to one path or another, but to create the illusion that there is only one path. Most men are only confused by choices. They are always happier for not realizing any exist."

Ptolemy allowed the smile to die away, and his voice dropped to that of a lover whispering a confidence.

"Do we speak of the same thing, My Lord?" he asked. "Do we speak of the succession—and of your brother Philip?"

Alexandros was too taken aback, by both the boldness of the question and the eerie sense that Ptolemy had somehow read his very thoughts, to do more than nod.

"It is as I suspected." Ptolemy looked grave now, like a physician discovering the first symptoms of illness. "A new king always sits uneasily upon his throne, particularly when he has no son. He fears his subjects as if they were a giddy woman who may sweep him aside if some new man takes her fancy. Philip is still a boy, but the signs of greatness cluster around him—it is even whispered that the old king understood the gods' will in his last moments, that had he lived another hour he would have displaced you as his heir and named your brother."

He held up his hand to forestall the inevitable question.

"It is enough to know that it is said, My Lord. It will do you no good to know by whom. But if Perdikkas is named the heir, as is only right, since he is the next in age, then all such voices will be stilled."

"And now there is this business of the owl," Alexandros murmured through clenched teeth. He had heard of it, for everyone spoke of Prince Philip's strange encounter—an owl, and in broad day. How could it not have been the Lady Athena? He had heard the story, and he had tried to dismiss it. He did not want to believe there was anything of the gods in it, yet he did.

"Yes. It is all over the city. Send Philip away," Ptolemy went on. "Wait awhile, and then name Perdikkas heir. By the time you call Philip back, everyone will have forgotten you even have another brother."

"How can I send him away? People will imagine I am afraid of him."

"If you are wise, you *are* afraid of him."

The two men exchanged a look that was almost like hatred but was not.

"Yet he is loyal to me and everyone knows it. If I seem to punish him against justice, it will be taken for a sign of weakness."

The smile returned to Ptolemy's lips, only now Alexandros imagined himself to understand its meaning.

"The Illyrians seek assurances of your goodwill," he said. "Why not arrange an exchange of diplomatic hostages? It will satisfy the Illyrians without creating the impression that you are afraid of them, and it will get Philip out of the way."

"Yes, precisely." And now Alexandros smiled, as if at his own cunning. "It would do him good to see a bit more of the world than old Glaukon's hearthstone. Philip will probably even bless me for it, since his has never been a quiet spirit."

"No one will think badly of you, only that you mean to keep your father's treaties since you pledge your brother's life to them."

"And my brother will come to no harm." Alexandros turned to his kinsman with something almost ferocious in his expression, for Philip was still his brother. "We will have him out of the way for half a year or so, and then he will come home, no worse for having been gone. I will not have him murdered by savages."

Ptolemy continued to smile, but his eyes were dead and lightless.

"As everyone knows, My Lord, the Illyrians are famous for their hospitality."

For several days Philip's face itched where the owl had left the marks of its claws. That was a normal part of healing, Nikomachos had said. There was no evidence that the wounds were turning putrid. Nevertheless, he had warned, with his customary gravity of manner, one should resist the temptation to scratch.

But no one can be virtuous all the time, and one morning, while Philip still rolled about on his sleeping cot, hardly even venturing to open his eyes, a hand automatically found its way to his jaw.

Sleep fled at once. He sat bolt upright, wondering if he could possibly be mistaken.

No, he could feel them. Between the two angry red welts he could feel a coarse stubble. His beard was coming in.

He ran his fingers over his throat and jaw, but the rest of his face seemed to be perfectly smooth. Hair was growing around the two cuts left by the owl's claws, and nowhere else.

If he had needed confirmation of the goddess's omen, then this was it. "You are mine," she was telling him. "I have marked you and I have made you. You belong to me."

There was no longer any space in his mind for doubt, for in token of her favor the Lady Athena had given him his manhood.

Within a matter of days his face was covered with a reddish-gold down so that the change was obvious to everyone—so that when he was summoned into the king's presence the two brothers met for the first time as men.

Alexandros was supervising cavalry drill on the vast unplowed flatlands north of Pella, and Philip had to ride straight through the afternoon to reach him.

That day's exercises were at an end, and perhaps as many as three hundred horses were tethered in groups of eight or ten, their heads pointing in to the center of a circle, their graceful necks stretched down to the earth as they companionably ate knee-high, yellowing grass, which the lowering sun shadowed to the color of old leather. The smoke from scores of cooking fires tainted the air, and as Philip passed, weary men glanced up from their suppers and then immediately lost interest. Some few who knew him smiled or raised a hand in greeting, but most looked at Alastor first, making sure they were out of the way of his great hooves, and did not even notice the rider.

Philip found his eldest brother squatting on the ground with five or six of the other men, eating flatbread rolled around pieces of roasted meat from a little iron cooking pot. The king wore a dirty linen tunic that only reached to his knees. His handsome face was stained with dust and dried sweat, and he ate with a bronze knife that could have belonged to a cobbler's son. Here he was merely a soldier among soldiers.

Alexandros raised his eyes as the shadow of Philip's horse fell across him, and then he grinned and threw out his arms in comic surprise.

"Little brother, can it be? Is that a beard on your chin, or is your face just dirty?"

Everyone laughed with the king, even Philip.

"Come down from that black demon and wash the dust from your throat with some of this frog piss." Alexandros held up a wineskin. "Groom! Take the Lord Philip's horse."

The messenger sent to Pella to fetch him had told Philip nothing except that it was the king's pleasure he should come at once, yet Alexandros seemed in no hurry to explain his summons, and Philip decided that explanations could wait. He was astonishingly hungry. He upended the wineskin so that a thin stream trickled over his tongue, and then he tore off a strip of bread and used it to scoop out a few chunks of meat from the pot, devouring them greedily although they were still hot enough to burn the roof of his mouth. For perhaps half an hour, everyone was content to eat in silence.

When he was finished, Alexandros wiped his fingers on his tunic and lay back on the grass with his hand behind his head, closing his eyes. Almost at once he began snoring gently, for he had the soldier's knack of falling asleep as if by an act of will. No one paid any attention.

"I have to inspect the defenses—do you want to go for a walk?"

It was just sundown. Alexandros hadn't opened his eyes yet, but he sounded wide awake.

"Yes, fine. I was beginning to think you were dead."

Alexandros did not laugh. For an instant he looked as if Philip had slapped him. Then he stood up.

"Let's go," he said. "Soldiers have to see that the king cares how they perform their duty."

As they made their tour of inspection, Philip studied the way his brother conducted himself, and he began to understand why Alexandros was so popular with his soldiers. He seemed to know everyone's name, and he had time for everyone. He inquired after their wives and children and the condition of their horses. He spoke with men about their performance on the drill field, praising and sometimes criticizing but always giving the impression that every detail of the day's exercises was held in his memory. Thus did he tighten the bonds of loyalty, for an army must believe that its commander understands his business and is not too grand to care about the humblest among them. It seemed a lesson worth remembering.

"What do you know about the Illyrians?"

It was the blackest part of the night, and they had only just finished checking on the last man at the last guard station. The only light was from the sentry fires. Philip glanced at his brother's face and noticed that it was creased by an expression he had never before seen there, as if Alexandros had been made uncomfortable by some inner doubt.

"Little enough," he answered. "I know that they are a nation of thieves, that they oppress their subject peoples and cause trouble for their neighbors. I know that their king is named Bardylis and that he is old and considered cunning. What else is there to know?"

Alexandros threw back his head and laughed. The laughter went on too long, and there was something hollow about the sound.

"Whatever there is," he said finally, "you will know it before any of us. Bardylis is frightened by the warlike reputation of Macedon's new king and wants some assurance of our continued goodwill. Thus there will be an exchange of hostages—he sends me one of his numberless descendants, and I send him you. Remember, when you are among them, to keep your eyes open.

"It will not be for long, and you will be treated as an honored guest. I almost envy you, little brother."

Somehow Philip could not shake off the sense that he was listening to someone else's voice.

5

The Illyrians had always held a prominent place in Philip's imagination. In the endless games of war that had occupied his childhood, the Illyrians were heavily favored for the role of opponent. For some perverse reason, Arrhidaios, when it was someone else's turn to be king of Macedon, invariably wanted to be an Athenian general, but in the opinion of Philip and his other friends the Illyrians made the best enemies. They were cruel and cunning, and their horsemen were almost a match for the Macedonian cavalry. Besides, they enjoyed that aura of fascinating villainy that belongs only to half-savage races.

So Philip's first reaction when told that he was about to be turned over to King Bardylis was a shudder of dread, for he had heard enough stories of how the Illyrians treated prisoners that the prospect of falling into their hands made his flesh crawl. Then he decided that this was cowardly of him, that a diplomatic exchange of hostages would be quite another matter, and that the whole thing was likely to be a marvelous adventure. He even began to look forward to it—always provided that he was able to forget the expression on Alexandros's face as he told him.

But as the summer wore on, it seemed to Philip that his sojourn among the Illyrians was fated never to happen. The only horsemen who threaded their way across the bleak mountains that formed the frontier between the two kingdoms were dispatch riders, for the negotiations made no progress, as if Bardylis were using them toward some hidden purpose of his own.

The delay played on Alexandros's nerves.

"What is the old bandit planning?" he raged. "Does he imagine we will be content to wait forever?"

"I could go myself."

The Lord Ptolemy shrugged, as if unconvinced that his personal intervention would serve in such a case, but he was a shrewd judge of his new king's temper—Alexandros accepted at once.

"Yes, by all means. Go as soon as you can."

Ptolemy left the next morning. Twenty days later he returned, with an agreement. There was to be a straight exchange of hostages, fifteen days hence, at the Vatokhori Pass. If there were any additional understandings, only Ptolemy, and perhaps the king, knew of them.

And Philip did not care. He only cared that in ten days' time he would be on his way north. He would be away from the smothering haven of his family, surrounded by strangers, living a man's life. It would probably even be dangerous—he hoped it would be dangerous. He did not know how he was to endure the few remaining hours he would be forced to abide in Pella.

But he kept his impatience hidden, for Alcmene's sake.

Poor Alcmene, whom he loved with a son's love, how her haunted eyes followed his every movement! He remembered how, through all of his childhood illnesses, it had been just the same, as if she half expected him to fade from sight forever.

And on the morning of his departure there was the formal leave-taking, with the king there to embrace him. A small crowd had gathered, among whom he saw his mother and—it made his heart swell within him—his cousin Arsinoe. As he climbed on his horse he caught Arsinoe's eye and smiled. There was just a hint of a return before she dropped her gaze. His mother hardly even glanced at him.

"Take this, Lord," Alcmene murmured. She had approached as silent as a shadow and stood holding up to him a stout leather bag, even as her hand came to rest stealthily upon his knee. Alcmene was afraid of horses, and particularly of Philip's, so only the courage of desperation could have allowed her to venture so close. "It is a long way to that place, and you will be hungry."

Philip laughed that even now she could not bring herself to call the Illyrians by their name, or even to admit their existence. He went not to them but to "that place."

He took the bag, which was still warm and smelled of cooked lamb—doubtless its contents would feed him for a month—and leaned down to kiss her lips.

"You worry too much, Alcmene," he said, still laughing. "Old Bardylis may, in the end, cut my throat, but he is unlikely to starve me."

Pulling back hard on the reins, he turned and galloped out of the palace courtyard so that his escort were hard-pressed to catch up with him.

Even in late summer the mountain winds that poured down through the Vatokhori Pass felt laden with snow. Philip shivered inside his fleece cape. He could not help himself. He had the impression he would never be warm again. A stream flowed across the trail, its water so cold that it seemed to tinkle like shards of broken ice as it lapped over the stones.

On the other side of the stream, mounted on horses with coats already ragged from their winter growth, were an Illyrian warrior and a soft, spindly limbed boy of perhaps eight or nine years, who clutched at his horse's mane as if afraid of falling off. The boy was presumably of the Illyrian royal house, although he hardly looked the part—his nose was dripping, and the only thing that gave animation to his face was the dissatisfied expression that was concentrated around his otherwise rather lifeless eyes. He showed no hint of interest in the party of strangers he had journeyed so far to meet in this desolate place.

The warrior, on the other hand, studied Philip with an intense and hostile gaze. His huge left hand held the reins with an almost feminine gentleness, but the rest of his strong, agile-looking body seemed taut with rage.

"Perhaps they plan to cut my throat after all," Philip whispered to himself, even while he touched his heels to Alastor's withers—for all that fear writhed in his bowels like a serpent, it would not do to appear afraid. As his horse walked forward to meet the Illyrians, he could hear the splash of its hooves in the shallow stream like the cries of terror-stricken women.

"I am Philip, son of Amyntas and prince of Macedon," he said in a voice that surprised him with his steadiness. "I am he for whom you have come."

The warrior said nothing. He only reached over to slap the other horse on the rump so that it too stepped into the icy water. As they passed, Philip glanced at the boy, who looked at nothing, whose eyes were glazed with indifference, as if he neither understood or cared what was happening around him. Deep in his soul, Philip felt a quaver of horror.

He turned back to his companions, men with whom he had traveled for four days and nights, and raised his hand in farewell, forcing himself to smile. One of them rode forward a few paces, seemingly about to speak, and then merely caught at the bridle of the Illyrian boy's horse, leading it back with him.

"There is nothing to keep us, then." Philip looked at his new guide, assuming the voice of command he had learned from listening to Alexandros. "Take me to King Bardylis."

The Illyrian appeared not to have heard him. For perhaps a quarter of an hour the two of them remained there in silence, watching the backs of the retreating Macedonians until they disappeared from sight. Then the Illyrian swung his horse around and returned the way he had come, leaving Philip to follow if he would.

By the time they made camp that night they were high into the mountains, and the wind tugged at their meager fire so that one hardly felt its heat. Philip huddled inside his fleece cape, utterly miserable. Sleep was impossible, not only because he was in danger of freezing but because the Illyrian, who was sitting well away from the fire with his back against a rock, seemingly oblivious to the cold, had not spoken to him all day. The obvious explanation was that the man probably knew no Greek, but Philip still was not quite sure that he dare fall asleep.

He judged he was safe enough, however, since the Illyrian had already had more than seven hours in which to act and did not give the impression he was the type who would need to wait for sleep to render his victim defenseless. He was an immense, savage-looking brute with a black beard that seemed to begin immediately below his eyes—eyes that never seemed to close, the restless eyes of a predator. A fur jacket covered his chest but left his arms bare, and the right one bore a wide, ragged scar that ran from shoulder to elbow. No, this was not a man who would hesitate to kill, and, after all, there was nothing to stop him. Philip was a hostage and carried no weapon.

Thus, he concluded, since he was alive now he would probably live at least long enough to reach King Bardylis. It made no immediate difference, however. He still couldn't find his sleep.

They traveled for three days through a series of mountain valleys that Philip was reasonably sure did not belong to the Illyrians' native territory but was instead part of their small empire of conquered tribes. In the midst of grasslands that would have fed great herds of sheep and cattle, the villages were poor and desolate looking, full of dirty, potbellied children with hopeless eyes. And their parents seemed frightened, giving Philip and his guide a wide berth when they encountered them on the trails, never speaking or even glancing up from the snow-crusted earth upon which they stood. None of the men carried weapons, and they gave the impression they would have run away if only they had dared, as if generations of the most brutal subjection had taught them the futility of pride. Philip had never seen anyone behave with such frightened servility, for among the Macedonians the king himself was only a man like other men, before whom even the humblest peasant would have scorned thus to abase himself.

It was strange to see misery and shame in a setting of such grandeur, for the northern mountains were so majestic a landscape that Philip could hardly believe the gods would ever have allowed mere mortals to dwell in them. Yet it was also a cruel place. Winter had already begun here, for all that the clear sunlight was still strong enough to hurt one's eyes, and everywhere the living water that oozed down the sheer rock faces of the mountains was frozen to marble, as if suspended in the act of falling. Overhead, in the pale sky that seemed as wide as creation, hawks swung about in great effortless circles, like silent prophecies of death.

On the early afternoon of the fourth day after their rendezvous at the

Vatokhori Pass, Philip and the Illyrian, whose voice he had yet to hear, rounded an outcropping of rock that turned out to be one face of a narrow passageway between two mountains. As they rode down this corridor of stone, a natural fortification that twenty men could easily have held against five hundred, Philip had only to glance about him to see the evidences of human contrivance—a narrow rampart carved out of the granite wall some fifteen cubits above his head, a pile of boulders arranged so that the touch of a man's hand would have been enough to send them sliding down on an intruder, a pair of sentry posts hidden in shadow. Philip could see no one, yet he could sense that he and his guide were being watched. It was clear they had reached the entrance to some stronghold.

The passageway opened onto a meadow about a two-hour journey across at its widest point and surrounded on all sides by steeply slanting rock walls. Built into the eastern wall, and at this distance almost invisible against it, was a city of stone buildings, humble enough if one compared it to Pella but a city for all that. To the inhabitants of these mountains, it must have seemed the center of the world.

Philip and the Illyrian exchanged a glance—it was almost as if the man felt he had been tricked into even this, for he looked away at once—and then rode into the snow-covered valley. Not a quarter of an hour passed before Philip heard the low rumbling of horses' hooves and, a few minutes later, saw perhaps as many as a hundred riders bearing down on him at a full gallop.

When they were about fifty paces away, the horsemen slowed to a trot, and then to a walk, forming up into a line some twenty riders across, and then, when the distance separating them was no more than eight or ten paces, they stopped.

His guide caught at Philip's bridle and reined in his own horse. They had come, it seemed, to the end of their journey.

Someone shouted something in a language Philip had never heard before, and the Illyrian shouted back—so, his tongue was not dead in his mouth after all. Philip understood not a word of the exchange, but he could recognize that the one in the center of the line of horsemen, who had been the first to speak, was Bardylis. After all, he was too elderly to be anyone except a king.

"Well, then, Zolfi," the frail-looking old man called out, this time—and presumably for Philip's benefit—in thickly accented Greek, "so you have at last brought me my great-grandson."

"Your grandmother was my second daughter, the child of my third wife," Bardylis explained when he could spare the time from eating. He was so thin he looked like a desiccated corpse, yet in the course of the banquet given to honor his hostage he had clawed through plates of goat flesh and millet,

washed down by numberless cups of wine, with all the rapacity of a true conqueror. "At least that is my recollection, yet at this reach of time it is possible
I could be mistaken. I was in my twenties when she was born and had more to
do than to pester myself about girl babies. I cannot even remember her name.

"I gave her to old Arrhabaios of Lynkos as a bride for that son of his. She
died in childbirth, full forty years ago. Nevertheless, through her my blood
runs in your veins. I am your ancestor, boy—ah, hah, hah!"

Everyone in the tiny room laughed, even Philip. He had discovered he
rather liked his old skeleton of a great-grandsire, although there was a certain
offhand quality in the king's manner toward him that he distrusted by instinct.

Even Bardylis's retainers laughed, for all that most of them probably
understood very little Greek. Even Pleuratos laughed.

Bardylis had outlived all of his sons, and thus Pleuratos, whose father had
been the king's firstborn, was generally looked upon as his heir. He was just
on the threshold of middle age, a strong, heavily built man, very serious in his
manner but with eyes which were a trifle too small for his face, giving it an
expression of baffled perplexity. Up to that point in the dinner, no sound had
issued from his lips.

Among the lessons Philip had learned from listening to old Glaukon's descriptions of court life at Pella was that much can be inferred from watching
men's faces at a banquet, where everyone is obliged to seem as if he is enjoying
himself and, in fact, no one finds it possible to relax, even for a moment. "A
man must be a fool to find banquets entertaining," Glaukon used to say, "for
they are simply the business of intrigue carried out under another form. One
has but to look about one to understand this. Follow men's eyes and you will
see clearly enough where the lines of power are drawn. The only people who
are at their ease on such occasions are the servants."

Philip had never attended a royal banquet at Pella, but he saw clearly
enough that Glaukon's observation had the force of truth. Men ate and made
jokes and smiled, but their eyes never lost their anxious expression as they
threw darting glances about the room, always measuring the strength of one
against the weakness of another—and trying to judge their own position
between the two.

And it was clear to him that Pleuratos was not only Bardylis's heir but
his rival as well. Bardylis was king now, but the future belonged to his grandson, and, since men must live in both, his nobles were forced to divide their
allegiance. Philip wondered how much support Pleuratos could already command. Probably it didn't matter, since time must inevitably favor him.

A girl, perhaps eight or nine years old, appeared in the doorway from what
was presumably the kitchen. She carried a jug of wine, placing it on the table
before Bardylis, who put his thin arm around her neck in an embrace to which
she seemed perfectly accustomed.

"My great-granddaughter, Audata," he said, displaying her to Philip as if she were a prize of war. "It is only at the last that one learns to appreciate female children. I love this one extravagantly."

Then, motioning toward Philip, he said something to the girl, who followed his gesture with large, speculative eyes. Then she walked around the table to where Philip was sitting and pulled on the sleeve of his tunic. When he turned his head to hear what she was saying, she kissed him—not on the cheek, as he might have expected, but full on the mouth. Then she turned and walked out of the room, without glancing back.

Philip discovered that he was blushing. Pleuratos looked annoyed, but said nothing. Bardylis laughed.

"My grandson is eaten up with jealousy!" he shouted. "For it would seem that his little Audata has learned to find the woman within herself—see? Already the chick begins sharpening her beak! Ah, hah, hah!"

And then, suddenly, the king ceased to laugh. His face clouded, as if with some long-forgotten grief.

"I remember her name now. Dakrua—her name was Dakrua. You could be her son, young Philip of Macedon, for she had your eyes."

And then he seemed to dismiss the matter from his thoughts.

"I knew nothing of the relationship," Philip said quietly, keeping his voice deliberately neutral.

The remark overtook Bardylis in the midst of another huge mouthful of food and seemed to come as an unwelcome surprise. He swallowed hard.

"I suppose, by now, everyone's forgotten. That is the great diplomatic advantage of surviving into one's old age. I remember what everyone else has forgotten."

His eyes, which were the same blue gray as Eurydike's, even as Philip's own, narrowed slightly, as if the king meant something more than he was disposed to say.

6

As she leaned forward to refill her son Alexandros's wine cup, the Lady Eurydike discovered she had to fight back a rising sensation of panic. It had come to her more and more of late, this feeling of utter helplessness before some terrible but unspecific danger that haunted a future she could imagine only as more fearful than death, from which death might at last be a merciful escape. A cry of warning rose to her lips—against what? She could not have found the words to answer, even to herself. So she strangled it behind a thin, unconvincing smile.

What had they been talking about? Did it matter? She couldn't seem to remember.

Alexandros looked bored. He had hardly touched his food, and he was drinking too much wine, which inclined him to sullenness. He longed to be away, that was obvious, back with his soldiers, back to the familiar and easy companionship of other men. The company of women, even of his own mother, made him restless.

Which was precisely the difficulty.

"You have been wearing yourself out," Eurydike said, picking up the thread. Her voice reflected just the right balance between sympathy and reproach. "You need looking after."

"The army is what needs looking after, Mother. These ten years and more it has been allowed to sink into decay. One can scarcely believe . . ."

"The army is nothing without its king, and you take better care of your horses than you do of yourself. Besides, a king's duty does not lie with the army alone. You need a wife."

She smiled again, ignoring the irritation that flickered across Alexandros's handsome face.

"And doubtless you have thought of someone—just to save me the inconvenience of looking?"

Eurydike shrugged her shoulders and smiled as if to say, *Of course.*

"My brother Menelaos has a daughter of marriageable age," she answered instead, although she had only to look at the notch that was forming between her son's eyebrows to know that she was speaking in vain, that Alexandros would not marry her niece Philinna, that he would probably never marry at all. "There would be political advantages, since the ties with Lynkos . . ."

"Lynkos is in rebellion." For an instant Alexandros seemed on the verge of rising from his seat, but he did not. "Menelaos conspires with the Illyrians against me. If the fact that he is my uncle cannot purchase his loyalty, I fail to see how I will benefit from making him my father-in-law."

"She could give you a son—"

"The succession is secure," he answered, cutting her off—his voice was rising as if he thought he might need to shout her down. "I nominated Perdikkas as my heir a month ago. There is no necessity to speak of wives."

That he knew how the haste of anger had betrayed him into a mistake was apparent from the way he dropped his eyes.

But Eurydike, with a mother's wisdom, decided, for the moment, to ignore it.

"Is the thought of a woman then so distasteful to you, my son?" She reached across the table and placed her hand gently on his. He did not shrink from her touch. "It is a little thing, over in a moment, and then a king's duty is done. You must remember your own safety as well, for how many of the kings of Macedon have fallen not in battle but at the hands of wicked subjects? An assassin will think before he strikes if there is a son to avenge the father's death."

"My brothers would avenge me."

He knew it was not true, so that the words seemed to die even on his lips. Eurydike had to choke back the temptation to laugh—laughter that would quickly have shaded into hysterical weeping.

"Perdikkas would avenge you?" she asked, not even trying to keep the disdain out of her voice. "Perdikkas? Oh, I think that any man possessed of the audacity to slay you could trust himself with Perdikkas. And Perdikkas, after all, would be king."

She waited, to see if he could bring himself to pronounce Philip's name, but he remained silent. It suited them both to forget for the moment that he even existed.

"I will consider it," he said in a way that implied he had already rejected the idea.

"Do consider it, my son. Consider all that you might purchase with those few hours spent in a woman's arms . . ."

Alexandros smiled, showing his teeth so that the smile seemed to become a kind of threat.

"And what, Mother, has cousin Ptolemy purchased for himself in your arms?"

Praxis was an effeminate, vicious, mean-spirited youth, with nothing to recommend him except a distinguished ancestry and a well-formed backside. None but the coarsest tastes could be long satisfied with such a one, and therefore it was not surprising that, after a brief infatuation, Alexandros had cast him off, nor that, characteristically, he had failed to appreciate the danger posed by discarded lovers. Praxis was not even discouraged from remaining at court, where he sulked like a woman and treasured up his sense of injury—and where the Lord Ptolemy, recognizing a useful instrument when he saw one, wasted little time in seducing the boy.

The trial of a single night was enough to convince the Lord Ptolemy that he had chosen well, since Praxis would submit to anything, would endure any indignity—seemed, in fact, to relish brutal and contemptuous treatment—provided only that he was allowed to believe that he excited the most passionate desire. The gods had jested in giving him a man's body, for he was born to play the whore's part and would spread his buttocks with cringing gratitude for any use one thought to make of him.

"Praxis, my beloved, with your slave's heart, full of resentment and cringing jealousy, what a revolting little creature you are," mused Ptolemy as, in the middle of the night, thinking to cleanse his throat with a swallow or two of wine, he sat up in bed and chanced to glance down at the form asleep beside him. "And how admirably you will suit my purposes."

And, as he drank his wine in the still darkness, he felt a thrill of something compounded of about equal parts fear and exhilaration, for he knew he had the bowels for anything that served the limitless ambition that glowed like an ember in the core of his soul, consuming all else that it might burn the brighter, and his own daring both appalled and fascinated him.

It was perhaps only at moments like this, when he was utterly alone with himself, that he understood the enormity of the risks he was prepared to take, had in fact already taken, to gain that which he desired the way no man had ever desired a lover. What was mere flesh—or even life itself—compared to the attraction of power? The longing for power could transform everything, making even his own dread, as he contemplated the death he courted, into an almost sensual pleasure.

Certainly it had transformed him, for Ptolemy had lived at court from the first hour of his life. Archelaos, his grandfather, had ruled then, a vain, swaggering man—the second son of his second son, Ptolemy remembered him quite distinctly, how his laughter seemed to make the walls shake, even the smell of his beard. He had been the sort of man who seemed to beckon disaster to him. Finally it came. One of his nobles, a man named Crataeas, had murdered him for breaking his betrothal to the younger of the king's daughters.

There had followed eight years of chaos, the years during which Ptolemy grew to manhood. Archelaos's son Orestes followed him to the throne and shared his fate, struck down by an uncle, Aeropos, the old king's brother, who took his place, ruled a few years, and died. Then two more kings were proclaimed and murdered between one winter and the next, first Archelaos's second son, Amyntas the Little, Ptolemy's own father, then Aeropos's son Pausanias.

And then, when the Macedonians had assembled under arms to elect a new king, Ptolemy, with that ruthless clarity of vision that is the sign of those born to rule, saw at once that he stood no chance of succeeding his father—after all, he was hardly more than a boy, and the Macedonians wanted a strong king to put an end to the bloodshed and the weakness—that to put himself forward would only mark him out as an ambitious and dangerous youth, the sort of young men new kings fear the most, and most quickly find some pretext for condemning. Therefore, he made sure to be among the very first to declare himself for Amyntas, son of Arrhidaios.

Pausanias had left a son of his name, a child not yet fit to leave his mother, and some had thought to elect him, putting the power of the state in a regent's hands. But a boy as king invites murder and chaos, so when Ptolemy rose to his feet, striking his sword against his breastplate to command attention, many among the Macedonians were prepared to listen.

"How much more must we endure before the nation falls to pieces and is consumed by our enemies?" he shouted. "Let us not invite destruction, and let us—for once—have a king to rule us whose lineage is not smeared with the blood of treason. There is yet among us one descended of the Argeadai, ripe in his manhood, whose abilities have been tested and are known . . ."

In the end, of course, there had been no other choice. Ptolemy's wisdom had consisted of seeing this a little sooner than the others.

And he had gone on to prove that his loyalty extended beyond a timely word in council. When the Illyrians drove the new king into exile, Ptolemy went with him, negotiated with the Thessalians for military support, and served as a captain of horse in the yearlong campaign to regain Pella and Amyntas's throne.

There had been rewards, for the lord of Macedon was generous in his gratitude—lands, honors, important commands, and at last the king's only daughter for a wife. But never enough.

For Ptolemy, the son and grandson of kings, could not but ask himself why any other man should be raised to glory over him. His claim by blood was as good or better, since Amyntas's grandfather, after all, had been the last born of old King Alexandros's sons. Yet Ptolemy was the servant, and Amyntas was the master.

So Ptolemy set about taking his revenge. First he had seduced the king's principal wife, the mother of his heir, laboring hard between her legs that she might grow so besotted with love that she would be blind to all else. And then, with Amyntas dead, he had prepared the destruction of the royal sons.

It had been a masterstroke, this business with Philip: the boy dies while a hostage of the Illyrians, and Alexandros, his brain clouded with rage and remorse, declares war against Bardylis, only to be defeated and to fall himself in battle. Alexandros was headstrong, and brave to the point of folly, so why should he not be killed? What could be more easily arranged?

And then, of course, it would be necessary to buy peace with the Illyrians—Ptolemy had already settled on the terms with Pleuratos, Bardylis's ambitious grandson and a man with whom one could do business. Macedon would forfeit the northern provinces and would be obliged to pay a heavy yearly tribute, but better a diminished realm provided only that it was one's own.

For Perdikkas, the last of Amyntas's sons, would still be too young to rule in his own right and would require a regent—and who more fit than his brother-in-law, the Lord Ptolemy?

And in time, when Perdikkas had been taken from this world by some misfortune—for they were an unlucky family, the sons of Amyntas—then who would the Macedonians elect to succeed him but his brother-in-law, the Lord Ptolemy?

It would all be so simple, provided only that Pleuratos fulfilled his end of the bargain and made sure of that brat Philip . . .

The first time Bardylis heard Philip refer to his captors as "Illyrians," he corrected him at once. "We are Dardanians. To a Macedonian the distinction may not seem important, but it does to us. The Illyrians consist of many nations, but we are their leaders—a Theban would not think it a compliment if you called him a Boeotian. It is the same with us."

And the Dardanians, Philip quickly discovered, were obsessed with war. They had no thought of war as an instrument of statecraft, nor were they a race of soldiers like the Spartans, for they cared nothing about the moral discipline of war that the Spartans carried into their daily lives and had thus made into something almost noble. Indeed, it seemed unlikely the Dardanians could even have conceived of such a thing. Ideas like glory, service, and discipline meant nothing to them, for theirs was the philosophy of bandits. They had no scruples about anything. The only virtue they recognized was courage, which they had in abundance, but, beyond that, they saw war as a child might see it, as a kind of game—a game brought to the final extremity, where wounds and death were the hazards and the rewards were rape and plunder.

And this, merely this, was to the Dardanians the very pinnacle of life.

Yet the wisest and best of men do not always make the most amiable companions, particularly when one is just coming into manhood, and Philip found life among this brigand nation decidedly to his taste.

Most of the Dardanian nobles spoke at least a little Greek, and Philip quickly learned a hundred or so words of their original language, enough to allow him to mix freely even with common people, who made no scruple about adopting almost as one of their own this foreign prince who was descended from their king, could ride as well as any of them, and seemed afraid of nothing. Philip enjoyed himself immensely—he enjoyed their society and, most particularly, he enjoyed the barbaric excitement of their cavalry exercises.

Soldiers drilled, and every soldier hates drill. But the Dardanians were not real soldiers and therefore their practice for war was both less disciplined and more amusing—a game, really, which they pursued with the obsessive enthusiasm of children.

In the early days of winter, while the plain that stretched before their city was still only two or three spans deep with the season's first real snowfall, they held mock battles, using lances with their tips wrapped in cloth and charging each other in long, ecstatically shouting lines of cavalry. As they galloped through the powdery snow, their sure-footed horses threw up soft clouds that almost hid them from sight, and men who were careless or unlucky enough to be knocked from their mounts would usually pick themselves up laughing, perhaps spitting out blood and broken teeth as they brushed the ice from their beards.

It was war without the numbing threat of death—and what, after all, did Philip know of death? The game filled him with a strange exultation that canceled all fear and weariness, that made him feel like an immortal. He would ride all day, never stopping, until Alastor's sides were lathered with sweat.

The first time or two they admitted Philip to their sport, while they still regarded him as a stranger, the Dardanians treated him with that condescending deference that is usually reserved for children. Yet they saw quickly enough that "the Macedonian boy" could be thrown to the snowy ground many times and would always come back. He was neither cowardly nor weak, and he took their laughter with good grace. He was also relentless. After the third day they stopped calling him a boy, and soon, very soon, when he had acquired the knack of this sort of warfare, the sight of "Philip the Macedonian" mounted on his great black stallion, bearing down on them at a heedless gallop, his lance tip swinging around to take aim at their hearts, was enough to stir a thrill of terror in men who had been raiding his father's border villages before he was born.

All afternoon would be consumed with this wonderful game, and then everyone would ride home to the baths, to sweat the stiffness out of their aching bodies and drink strong wine and display their injuries, boasting to one another about how they had received them. In this too Philip took vast pleasure and pride, for in the midst of the Dardanians he now truly felt himself accepted as a man among other men. He had put aside his boyhood forever.

Yet, though the Dardanians treated him as one of them, he was still a prisoner, for old Bardylis's watchdog, the man he had called Zolfi, was never far away. Even as Philip rode back toward the gates, he had only to glance down at the ground to see the shadow of his warder's horse. So he had no trouble remembering Alexandros's charge: "Remember, when you are among them, to keep your eyes open." And his eyes, as he studied the catwalks and towers of the city wall, were those of an enemy.

They build fortifications, but without conviction, he thought. *They cannot credit they will ever need them—they cannot conceive that anyone would ever dare to bring war to their own gates. I could conquer this city in half a day.*

And in imagination, almost between one breath and another, he did conquer it. The walls lay in rubble and a haze of smoke hung over the sacked and ruined buildings. Old Bardylis, come as a penitent to beg for his people's lives, how his eyes would widen when he saw his great-grandson grinning at him from beneath the commander's bronze war helmet!

And then, of course, Philip remembered the narrow, rock-walled pass leading into this valley, and how easily a handful of men could defend it against an army. What would numbers matter there, except as more dead bodies to choke off the entrance?

Philip promised himself he would find some pretext to scout the position. Perhaps there was a weakness he hadn't noticed.

He goaded Alastor forward, resisting the temptation to turn his head. Zolfi could not read his thoughts, but it was possible for a man to betray himself with a glance.

Inside the gates Philip was surprised to find little Audata, calmly sitting on the broad stone rim of an empty cistern, her arms wrapped around her knees as if to fend off the evening wind that was already beginning to stir. It was the first time he had seen her since the night of his arrival.

Without actually looking at him, she raised her face in a way that suggested she meant to be noticed. And Philip did notice her, for hers was less a child's face than a woman's. Indeed, it occurred to him, she was quite beautiful, with bronze-colored hair and high cheekbones that gave her a delicately feline appearance—perhaps it was this that created the impression of unawakened sensuality, but

Philip couldn't help remembering the way she had kissed him. He smiled at the recollection, feeling suddenly rather awkward.

"Aren't you cold?" he asked, leaning down so that he almost seemed to be lying across his horse's neck. It was a second before she turned her blue-gray eyes to him, and then she seemed not to have heard.

"Will you ever be a king?"

He must have looked startled, because she repeated the question.

"Will you be a king, Philip? Great-Grandfather has said I am to be the bride of a great king someday."

"It will be a black hour for the Macedonians when they are obliged to choose me, for I have two elder brothers." He laughed, although suddenly his distance from the kingship, which had never troubled him before, seemed almost a grief.

"Yet stranger things have happened," she answered. "Perhaps you will be a king after all."

From almost directly behind him, Philip heard a string of curses— although he understood not one word of them, they could not have been anything else—and, with a kind of start, as if awakened into a cold and unforgiving present, Audata slid down from the edge of the cistern and scurried out of sight. A horse drew up beside Philip's. Its rider was Pleuratos. For a moment Pleuratos glared at him, seeming to hate him in a silence that was itself a curse, and then he turned his face away and rode on.

7

Bardylis in his eighties could still ride almost as well and as tirelessly as in the days of his youth, but in the summer of his seventy-second year, during a punitive raid against the Taulantii, his horse had been killed from beneath him and he had mangled his left leg in the fall. The bones had never healed properly, and as a result he was obliged to walk using a stick.

He was not a man to suffer his infirmities patiently—or even to admit he had any—so the stick was a permanent grievance. When he walked about with Philip he preferred to leave it behind and to lean instead on the young man's shoulder, which was just at the right height. Perhaps this was what created the intimacy between them, or perhaps something about Philip stirred into tenderness some long-forgotten memory. Or perhaps Bardylis simply liked being able to leave his stick behind. In any case, it soon became apparent that the king of the Dardanians had developed a particular fondness for the company of his great-grandson.

"I wish you would stay with us," Bardylis said one morning as the two of them were strolling down to the city gate and back, which was the farthest limit the old man would venture on foot. "I wish you would forget all about being a Macedonian. Then I would set Pleuratos aside and make you my heir. My grandson is a lout, you know. He is good for nothing except plundering villages—he has no subtlety of mind. You would make a much better king."

"It is the general opinion that plundering villages is all any Dardanian is good for," Philip answered. They laughed at this together, for Bardylis was not a man to cherish any illusions. "Besides, if I defected, what would Alexandros do to the hostage he is holding?"

"Cut his throat." Bardylis's voice was perfectly level, as if noting a fact of no importance. "He is also a great-grandson. You have seen him—having his throat cut would leave him vastly improved. Why? Did you imagine I would be fool enough to send someone whose life I valued?"

He turned to Philip and smiled. It was a pleasant enough smile, but it sent a chill through one's heart.

"Remember, Philip, should you ever chance to become a king, that the tree of royalty remains sturdy only so long as one remembers to prune away the weaker branches.

"Now I have shocked you," he went on, sounding rather as though he had achieved the effect he desired. "And now you will not wish to become my heir. But there was never any chance of that, was there, for you will never forget that you are a Macedonian, and you plan to take possession of all this not by inheritance but by conquest."

He made a sweeping gesture that seemed to take in the whole world, and then let his arm drop back to his side, as if the strength had suddenly left it.

"You see, Philip, I have noticed the way you look about you, coveting the very walls of my city. I do not resent this, since it is natural enough, particularly in a young man who feels the lust for glory surging within him. I remember my own youth, and the dreams of future triumphs that haunted my every thought. And thus I know it is only a kind of game you play inside your head. Take care, however, for others doubtless have also noticed. And they might put a less tolerant construction on it."

"Against which are you warning me, Great-Grandfather—against attacking your city or against Pleuratos?"

The old man's laughter was high-pitched and brittle, a sound somehow reminiscent of splintering ice.

"Not much escapes you, does it, boy?" His voice was wheezy, as if the effort of his own hilarity had exhausted him. "Philip, you will surely be a great man someday, provided you live, yet I think the Dardanians are safe enough, even from you, for no Macedonian would ever dare to lead an army into this place."

"Then it is Pleuratos."

"I have said nothing," Bardylis answered, tightening his grip on Philip's shoulder. "It is not a matter in which I choose to interfere."

"Nevertheless, I will learn to be careful of my back."

"That is always wise."

In the end, Bardylis offered no objection when Philip proposed to take a riding tour of the surrounding mountains. "Go," he said. "Satisfy yourself, for I would have you free yourself of any illusions. All that you will discover is what experience has taught many others, and at terrible cost—that this valley is impregnable. The cliffs are high, and covered with ice this time of year—be careful of your footing."

The old king favored him with another of his wintry smiles, as if to suggest a warning within the warning.

And so it was that one bitterly cold morning, about two months after he had first come among the Dardanians, Philip set out to survey the valley's rocky perimeter. He carried provisions enough to last four days, and, as always, riding behind him like a reminder of mortality, was the man Zolfi. Philip had grown so accustomed to his silent presence that he seemed hardly to notice it anymore.

He found that the cold no longer troubled him. He had adopted Dardanian dress and wore a fur jacket that left his arms exposed, but he felt perfectly comfortable—perhaps, he thought, the southern races treated themselves too kindly. Perhaps one suffered from the cold only as much as one expected to. At any rate, he felt himself to have grown harder among these northern savages, less fastidious and altogether more of a match for the world's cruelty. He remembered the boy he had been those first few days away from Alcmene's hearthside, shivering inside his fleece-lined cloak, and a smile of something like contempt pulled at the corners of his mouth.

He would need to be hard, he thought, even as the shadow of the city gates passed over him, for before he returned this way he would be required to defend his life.

For days Philip had sensed that Zolfi was only waiting upon his chance. The man meant to kill him. It was a deed that could not be owned, since otherwise he would already be dead, but Zolfi was like a fox sniffing at the rabbit's burrow.

It would be made to seem an innocent death. There would be no sword cuts, not even any marks of a struggle on Philip's body when it would be turned over to the Macedonians for burial, nothing that would oblige Alexandros to seek vengeance. A riding accident, perhaps, a fall under his own horse's hooves that would break open his skull like a melon and leave his brains to leak into the snow. "He was dead even before we reached him," the Dardanians would explain. "He was an impetuous boy, and that black beast of his . . . We put it to death." And the Macedonians would nod, grim-faced and perhaps a little suspicious, but willing at last to accept that such a thing could happen easily enough. It would be something like that.

Philip did not know why, or by whom, but he was sure the order had been given for his murder. He could sense the change: Zolfi no longer boiled with barely suppressed hatred but seemed almost happy. The hunting dog had at last been let out of its cage and could scent a kill. He only wondered if old Bardylis knew—knew, rather than guessed, for surely he had guessed—and had perhaps even consented. Somehow he could not quite bring himself to believe it.

Thus the surveying expedition served a double purpose, for Zolfi must be given his opportunity before he decided to make one for himself. Philip knew that his only possible defense lay in choosing the time and the place.

The snow on the valley floor was deep enough that a man on foot might have worn himself out struggling through a distance of five or six hundred paces, yet the horses had little enough trouble, their thin, knobby legs thrusting into the unblemished whiteness with a playful, seemingly effortless delicacy. So muted was their contact with the frozen earth that it was almost as if the snow buoyed them up, as if it were some vast, foaming sea through which they swam like dolphins. Philip had never felt so alive, and his whole soul filled with fear-annihilating joy. For long stretches he lost all sense of time and place, of his own mortal existence. And then he would remember, but only as one remembers the fading terrors of a dream.

They spent that night in a stone hut perhaps an hour below the summit of the western mountains, sharing a charcoal brazier with six of the men who guarded the valley's narrow approach. In their midst Philip knew himself to be safe, just as he knew that the sunrise would mean an end to safety, perhaps even to life. Tomorrow would have to be left to itself, and even when it came he knew he could only hold himself in readiness and wait upon Zolfi's pleasure.

It was impossible to plan anything because it was impossible to anticipate how death might come, yet his mind kept endlessly turning on this one theme. Still, that was better than yielding to the black, shapeless terror that seemed to wait for him, just beyond reach.

The next morning, while the dawn was still only a pale pink sliver against the darkness of the eastern sky, they all shared out a soldiers' breakfast to which Philip contributed two loaves of bread that were only a day old, along with a jar of rough red wine that still had fragments of grape husk floating in it. The guards had all been there for half a month. They were due for relief soon, and they talked about home as if it were on a different continent instead of just across the valley—perhaps that only made it worse for them.

"If I were a great prince, I would never stray farther than the closest wineshop," one of them said. "You wouldn't catch me crawling over these mountains in winter."

There was a general murmur of agreement.

"Yes, the man is wise who knows to stay home."

"Drunk on a whore's belly."

Everyone laughed except Zolfi, who appeared not even to have heard.

"What makes a prince want to come here, Philip?" the first man asked, making the question sound like a reproach.

Philip smiled, even as fear turned his bowels to water.

"I am still too young for whores," he said.

This made everyone laugh all over again.

As soon as there was light enough to see by, Philip set off on the steep trail that led up to the spine of the mountain range. Zolfi followed silently, keeping fifteen or twenty paces behind. They had left their horses at the hut, for the path was narrow and the frost had loosened a treacherous amount of rock. The climb was arduous but without particular difficulty or danger, and they were both well rested and strong. They made such good time that when they reached the summit the sun was still only directly across the horizon.

Philip had but to look about him to know that old Bardylis was probably right. Not five paces from where he stood the mountain broke off into a sheer drop. There were trails in the rock face, but they were slippery with ice at this time of year, and if the man climbing them put a foot wrong there would be nothing to break his fall. No one but a fool would try to bring an army up that side, so the only way in was through the pass, which was impregnable if defended by even a handful of men. Thus the Dardanians were safe inside their valley.

He could feel the faint winter sun on his back. There was no wind, and a terrible stillness seemed to have descended on the world. In the distance the snow-laden peaks of mountains glittered in bright daylight while the valleys below were still buried under the shadow of night. It was like being at the very edge of existence. Only a little way in front of him the land simply fell away into an emptiness seemingly as vast as death itself.

Yes, death was close. He could almost smell it. He felt it beckoning to him.

He let himself be drawn a step or two closer to the edge—slowly, like a man in a trance. It was almost true. He felt his mind emptying, as if he were about to shed existence like a garment the weight of which had begun to oppress him. He seemed to stare directly ahead, captured by the obliterating grandeur. Yet something nagged at him. His eyes kept flitting down to the snow-covered ground.

Then, between one heartbeat and the next, he was quick with life again. This moment, this instant, was all that mattered. There was no time to think—there was only now.

Before he knew what he was about, Philip found he had thrown himself down. He had simply taken a dive at the ground, and was actually astonished to find himself with his face in the snow.

Then he knew everything. With a sharp twist of his body, he rolled away from the precipice and almost immediately slammed into a pair of legs—he heard a little grunt of surprise as the man stumbled against him, and for some reason the sound filled him with a cold, pitiless fury.

He pulled his left arm free and struck out with it so that his elbow caught Zolfi almost precisely behind the knees and made him start to topple over helplessly.

But it wasn't quite enough. Philip knew, without giving the thought a chance to form in his mind, that it wasn't quite enough.

He pitched over onto his back, twisted around, and kicked straight out with both feet, striking Zolfi just at the base of the spine.

Zolfi made a sharp little cry and threw out his arms to try to catch himself, clawing at the snow like an animal, but he was too close to the edge. He just slid forward, helpless, and then plunged headfirst into oblivion.

There was a high-pitched scream of terror that seemed to echo for a few seconds through that vast emptiness, even after it had stopped abruptly.

Philip was glad he had not had to see the man's face.

At first, while the dread of it still gripped him, like claws that pierced his flesh, he could not bring himself to move. In his whole life he had never known such fear. He lay there, his legs wide apart and his arms thrown out to the sides, appearing to cling to the earth as if afraid that he too would tumble off into the void. The sky seemed to be spinning wildly over his head.

At last, little by little, the fear began to drain away. Finally he was able to sit up and then, on his hands and knees, he crawled toward the edge. He had to lie down again on his belly before he could bring himself to look over.

The corpse lay just above the floor of the pass. Philip thought he could see a smear of blood on a bare stone shelf two hundred or so cubits above that, about halfway down—Zolfi must have struck there first, and was probably dead long before his body came to rest.

It was his shadow that had killed him. It had stretched before him on the snowy ground as he came rushing toward Philip to push him over the edge, and the sight of it was what Philip had been waiting for, without even realizing. On such a little thing did a man's life turn, on forgetting all that it meant to have the light at one's back.

The sun was just at its zenith when he returned to the stone hut. One of the guards was sitting outside the doorway, preoccupied with the contents of an iron cooking pot that hung from a tripod over a small fire—when the smell reached Philip's nostrils it made his guts clench with nausea.

Finally the guard looked up and, seeing Philip, frowned with perplexity.

"You're alone," he said as if he thought that Philip might not have noticed. "Where is Zolfi?"

"He had an accident."

"Is he dead, then?"

"Yes."

The guard, who had a narrow, worried face and was thin enough that his legs gave the impression of being unnaturally long, considered this for a moment, then held up a bony finger to make a gesture describing the arc of a falling object.

"Yes."

He nodded gravely, as if Philip had confessed to murder, and then let his hands fall to his thighs with a slap and stood up, having apparently lost interest in his meal.

"Then we had better fetch his body before the wolves find it. I hope you know where he came down."

The impact had caved in Zolfi's whole face so that nothing was left except a ragged, blood-soaked wound. The scars on his right arm were distinctive, but otherwise the broken, torn corpse they found wedged into an outcropping of rock could have been anyone. They wrapped him in a blanket the guard had brought along for the purpose, but the smell of blood made the horses skittish, and Philip had to blindfold the dead man's mount before they could tie the body onto its back. This was no longer anything human, just a load of carrion.

"I wouldn't care to die like that," the guard said as they cleaned their hands in the snow—carrying what was left of Zolfi down from the rocks had been a gruesome piece of work. "I don't know what you two were thinking of, climbing around up there. Those mountain trails are treacherous if you weren't born to them. I leave all that to the goat herders, and welcome. As for civilized men, anywhere you can't go with a horse, you're better off not going."

Philip was wiping his hands dry on his tunic. Only the scrupulous care he brought to the task betrayed his excitement.

"I would think even a goatherd might prefer keeping to the flatlands."

"Around here the flatlands are for us. We chased the local people out generations ago, and they have to find their pasture where they can. But don't waste sympathy on the likes of them. They almost never fall. They're like animals, with all their sense in their legs. Hah, hah, hah!"

The guard was too pleased with his own joke to notice that Philip wasn't laughing. It was like the Dardanians, he thought—they held the peasants of these mountains in such subjection that they had at last forgotten even to be afraid of them. In his mind Philip saw twenty or thirty men silently working their way up these trails . . .

One had only to put swords in their hands—and teach them not to be afraid to use them.

"You will have to spend another night with us," the guard went on as he mounted his horse. "There's too much of the day gone to make it back before sunset, and it's bad luck to bring a corpse under the city gate at night. It's too bad about Zolfi."

"Did he have a wife?" Philip asked, experiencing a sudden twinge of guilt.

"No, no wife. But the Lord Pleuratos will be as displeased as any widow. Zolfi was his good right hand."

The men on watch along the walls must have seen him coming: a rider alone, leading a horse with what was obviously a corpse tied across its back. Either that, or the officer in command at the pass had sent someone on ahead the night before, because Bardylis and half his court were waiting at the city gates as Philip approached.

While the others stayed behind, Bardylis rode forward to meet him, just out of hearing.

"What happened?" He frowned, and his gaze settled on Zolfi's hand, which was sticking out of the blanket.

"He slipped on the ice. Apparently he was the one you should have warned." The king's frown deepened, and then he nodded curtly.

"That will do to tell the others—now what really happened?"

"He tried to kill me."

"And you killed him instead." Bardylis seemed genuinely impressed. "You have done well for yourself, Philip of Macedon, for Zolfi was no barnyard cock."

"I have done better than you can possibly imagine."

Bardylis started to laugh—a breathless, surprised little laugh—and then seemed to think better of it. For a moment it was almost possible to believe he had understood.

"I make no inquiries," he said, "for sometimes it is better not to see into the hearts of young men, but when you look like that, Philip, you make me glad that I am old and near death."

Without another word he turned his horse, and the two men rode back through the city gates together.

That night, Philip was tormented by dreams. He had slept peacefully enough in the garrison hut, where the air was heavy with the murmur of other men's snoring, but now, covered in blood, his face nothing but a rim of glittering, splintered bone, Zolfi appeared at the foot of his bed, demanding to know how Philip had the effrontery to be alive.

He awoke—or, rather, he opened his eyes, for the dream seemed still to be with him. In the doorway, surrounded by a flickering nimbus of light, hovered the dark outline of a human form.

"Philip! Philip, are you asleep?"

Relief flooded through him as he realized the voice was that of a child.

Audata's hand had been shading the lamp she carried. She raised it and revealed her face.

"Great-Grandfather says you are not safe here tonight," she said, once she was satisfied of having his attention. "Come with me."

She knelt beside his bed, as if he were the child whose fears she must comfort away. Her face was grave and oddly beautiful.

"If there is danger, I am surprised the king involves you in it," he answered, seeming to choose the least of the many things he might have said to her in that moment.

Audata reached out and touched his hair.

"I have nothing to fear from anyone who dwells in this house, Philip of Macedon." She stood up abruptly. "Come—now."

He let her take his hand and lead him out into the corridor, where the only sound came from their naked feet against the stones.

Philip could not overcome the sensation of having made some decision at the very core of his being, a decision about which he understood nothing except that it was not concerned with Bardylis's fears for his safety. Indeed, if there were assassins waiting somewhere in the silent darkness, he hardly thought of them. He seemed aware of nothing except the strength of those delicate fingers as they curled around his.

They had not very far to go. She guided him around a corner and then stopped in front of a door that was standing slightly open. She gestured that he should follow her inside, but Philip's attention was on a slit of light along the floor some ten or twelve paces farther on.

"That is Great-Grandfather's room," Audata murmured. "He does not sleep well and keeps a lamp burning by his bed all night. I think it is because he is so old."

Philip supposed it more likely to be because Bardylis was a king and knew better than to trust the darkness, but he said nothing.

"Come."

It was a small room but perhaps not too small for a child—and she seemed to have it all to herself, which was unusual enough even for the great-granddaughter of a king. The light from her lamp was guttering out, but Philip thought he saw a doll lying on a shelf. Unaccountably he found the sight of it disturbing, as if he had forgotten to think of Audata as a child and found the reminder something of an embarrassment.

She had a bearskin robe on her bed. They slipped beneath it, and within a few minutes he knew from her breathing that she was asleep. Once she turned and nestled her head against his arm. He stayed awake a long time, filled with a strange contentment from which he did not want to be parted.

It was perhaps an hour before dawn when the door opened soundlessly and Bardylis stepped in.

"You are awake?" he whispered. "Good. Come away, and we will have a little stroll before breakfast. Try not to wake her—it is well to leave young children to their rest."

He handed Philip a fur-lined cloak, although his own was of cloth and showed years of wear.

"Put it on, for the morning is sharp."

Philip glanced back at the still figure of Audata, her face nearly covered by the bearskin. It caused him a twinge of regret to think she would wake up to find him gone.

"Come, Prince of Macedon." Bardylis had his hand on Philip's elbow, as if ready to drag him from the room. There was a curious urgency in his voice.

The old man closed the bedroom door behind them with something almost like stealth. Philip noticed that he carried his stick with him.

As they began their accustomed walk to the city gate and back, Bardylis looked about him at the gray stones of his capital. There was a faint smile on his lips that suggested a mingling of pride and regret.

"I became king of the Dardanians when I was seventeen," he said as if that fact explained much. "Sixty years and more—there is hardly a soul living who can remember any king but me.

"Men will grow bored with a king, as with a woman. It does not matter whether he is a good king or a villain, if he reigns too long, his subjects will look to his successor as if the change from one to another could remake the world. Thus, even as I live, Pleuratos accumulates followers, men whose loyalty is of a kind to make him king already in their hearts. I do not resent this—I even understand it, for I am old enough to be sometimes weary of power. For such reasons have I given Pleuratos more latitude than is perhaps wise."

"Why do you tell me this?" Philip asked. The question surprised him, for he had not meant to ask it, yet he really wanted to know.

Bardylis looked up into his face, and the smile tightened a little. He did not seem surprised.

"Perhaps because you have already guessed it. Or perhaps to prevent you from making the same mistake someday. A king should remain a king, and his successor's reign should not begin before the gods ordain it. Do not try to cheat the future, Philip, but mind the years of your own life."

"I will never be a king, Great-Grandfather."

"No? Then little Audata will be vastly disappointed."

He laughed at this, as if at a children's game.

When they reached the city gate Philip saw his horse, bridled and waiting.

"It is time for you to go back from whence you came," Bardylis said in the manner of a host announcing dinner. "I cannot answer for your safety here, my boy, and your life has become strangely precious to me. A rider was sent ahead not an hour ago, so your way through the pass will be clear. The satchel on your horse contains food and a little purse of Athenian drachmas, enough to see you to the end of your journey. I can give you no more than half a day's grace and then surely men will be sent after you, so do not idle on your way.

"And remember, when you are home and begin to feel yourself safe, that you have not outrun your dangers, that the beast who hungers after your life may stretch its reach as far as Dardania, but its den is in Macedon."

For a moment his old eyes seemed about to cloud with tears. He stood with his hands on his great-grandson's shoulders, ready to embrace him, and then he caught sight of the first traces of the morning sun, pouring over the eastern mountains like blood. Suddenly he grinned.

"I was thinking of Pleuratos—he will be so furious when he finds out."

8

The mere thought of death will drive a man until his heart bursts, but a horse, which fears nothing in imagination, must be fed and watered and rested, or it will not go on. Thus Philip had traveled no more than three hundred some odd *stadioi* before darkness obliged him to stop.

Even assuming that Bardylis had indeed managed to purchase him half a day's start, he doubted that Pleuratos's men were more than a few hours behind him. They would be able to ride their horses without mercy, and to change them for fresh mounts at any of the three or four Illyrian villages through which they would have passed, asking after the young foreigner who traveled alone on a black stallion. The border with Lynkos, where King Menelaos might be unwilling to watch his nephew murdered by strangers—even if they were Illyrians—was at least three days away. Tomorrow, perhaps, or certainly the following morning, his pursuers would catch up with him.

Half an hour before sundown, Philip left the mountain trail he had been following and managed to find a cleft in the rock that offered some conceal- ment. He would be safe enough there until morning. He tethered Alastor, wrapped himself in a blanket, and waited for night.

By the time stars began to appear over the western horizon the cold was really quite terrible, but under the circumstances it would have been madness to build a fire. Philip remembered hearing once that as long as a man stays awake he can't freeze to death, so he found himself a particularly rocky and uncomfortable patch of ground on which to keep his vigil. He entertained himself by trying to define the scope of the conspiracy against him.

Because of course Pleuratos had no motive of his own which could have justified the risks—someone had bribed him to have Philip murdered. And the bribe would have had to be considerable.

What could it have been? Money? Power? No. A man who is almost ruler of the Dardanians does not commit such an act for something as trifling as money, and the only person capable of increasing Pleuratos's power was Bardylis. No matter how many times Philip turned the matter over in his mind, he could not arrive at a motive for Bardylis to set this plot in motion and then betray it. That left only territory.

Who would offer the Dardanians territory to effect the death of an obscure prince? Only someone among the Macedonians. And among the Macedonians, who was in a position to make such an offer? Only Alexandros and his agent in the negotiations, Ptolemy. That Ptolemy was involved, Philip never even troubled to doubt. But Alexandros? His own brother?

Well, it wasn't as if such things had never happened before.

If Alexandros wanted him killed, then Philip's only chance of survival was to go into exile and never come back. It was a bitter thought.

But was such a thing possible? Alexandros? He loved Alexandros. He would gladly have laid down his life for him. And Alexandros knew it.

No, he could not bring himself to believe that Alexandros would have been guilty of anything so pointlessly base.

Then was it possible that Ptolemy, for some reason known only to himself, had acted alone?

It occurred to Philip that he hardly knew the Lord Ptolemy, that his cousin and brother-in-law, with whom he had been acquainted all his life, was the sort who remains an unreadable mystery, even to those closest to them in blood and feeling. He liked Ptolemy—Ptolemy was charming and easy to talk to—but he could not make the slightest claim to understanding him. Some men had no intimates. Some minds are as impenetrable as stone.

Yes. It was possible. All at once, and with the force of revelation, Philip saw that anything was possible.

Sitting there in the freezing darkness, he suddenly felt giddy with dread. And at the same time he was conscious that all fear—at least that purely individual terror that paralyzes the soul—had left him. The dangers facing him, his family, his king, and his nation were of a magnitude to render his own personal survival a matter of little importance, even to himself. Perhaps no one else in the whole world suspected the truth.

He had never known what it was to be so alone.

And then, somewhere in the distance, he heard the hoot of an owl, reminding him that he was not utterly deserted.

"Mother of Battles," he whispered, "Virgin Goddess, Lady of the Gray Eyes, hear my prayer."

At first, he was not even sure for what he should pray. Perhaps it did not matter, since if She heard She would understand.

"Lady Athena, Wise Goddess, protect me now as you did once my ancestor, the divine Herakles. Lend me something of your strength and your cunning."

Merely to speak the words made him feel better. He allowed his heart to be comforted.

In the first gray light of morning, he was surprised and a little frightened to discover that he had fallen asleep. At least the cold hadn't killed him—or had it?

He couldn't seem to feel his feet at all. And then, as he began wriggling his toes, the sharp stabs of something that was not quite pain convinced him that he was still alive.

He had to get away from this place, he thought, or the blessings of life might be somewhat temporary.

Alastor snorted indignantly as Philip untethered him and slipped on his bridle. They picked their way carefully over the short, rock-littered path that led back to the main trail, since it was still perhaps a quarter of an hour before dawn.

Would his pursuers sleep a little longer? Would they make themselves breakfast before they set out again? Would they trouble to build a fire? Philip knew that his life might hang on such trifles.

Two hours after setting out, he realized that he no longer knew precisely where he was. Yesterday the way had been unmistakable, but today the countryside did not look the same as it had three months ago. And the trail kept branching off, so that it was like trying to negotiate a spider's web.

Perhaps that was for the best. Philip knew that so long as he kept to a generally southeastern direction he could not go far out of his course, and the men behind him would be slowed by the difficulty of tracking him. The wind had blown the snow into drifts, leaving long stretches of his path bare, so that his horse's hoofprints would be difficult to find on the frost-hardened ground.

He looked over his shoulder, beginning for the first time to feel safe, and his eyes immediately settled on a pile of steaming horse droppings about thirty paces back on the trail.

"Alastor," he muttered, "exercise a little discretion." And then, suddenly, he had an idea.

He dismounted and, using a broken-off section of bush, managed to sweep the horse droppings into his sleeping blanket, folding them up into a tidy package. A few minutes more and Philip was able to obliterate all trace of his passage.

"May one hope that you will remain continent for yet a little longer?"

It would be easy enough to lay a false trail. He would not be able to use that trick more than once, but it might purchase him an extra hour—besides, if these men were really going to kill him, which seemed likely, there was no reason to deny himself the satisfaction of tormenting them a little.

And, as for spending the next night in a blanket smeared with horseshit, if he lived to suffer the inconvenience, he would imagine himself blessed among men.

At the next fork, he dismounted and left Alastor with his reins trailing on the ground, measured off about fifty paces down the righthand trail, dumped out his bundle and went back to continue on to the left.

By late afternoon Philip had reached a small valley, perhaps two hours from side to side, that was choked with forest. There was plenty of shade, and the evergreens broke up the wind, so the snow lay more heavily on the ground. There was no chance of disguising his passage over such terrain, so he did not try. He simply rode on, hoping to get through before the light failed.

When he made the rim, and the ground was once again hard under his horse's hooves, he looked back and noticed that the valley was open from several directions. He knew that by now his pursuers could not be more than an hour or two behind him, and if they were worth anything as trackers, they would know it too. They would not push on any farther tonight—why should they, when time was so obviously on their side? And, besides, they would want to overtake him in daylight. They would camp tonight in this valley, in the comforting shelter of its forest.

Philip decided he was weary of this game. He would go over to the offensive. An idea was beginning to take shape in his mind.

He made sure that his trail was obscured and then dismounted and led his horse over the stony ground until he discovered another path into the valley.

Just before dark he found a small clearing in the forest where a few yellowing shoots of grass were visible in the patchy snow. He tethered Alastor and took the bit out of his mouth.

"I will return for you," he murmured, stroking the horse's glossy black neck. "A few hours, and I will be back. Perhaps, after all, there is a way out of this trap."

The Dardanians were not hard to find—why should they try to conceal themselves when they were the hunters? Philip merely followed the main trail, and then the smell of woodsmoke, and then the light from their campfire. He crouched in the underbrush, staying downwind and out of sight, and watched them cook dinner.

There were four of them, lumpy shadows huddled around the fire. He was close enough to hear them complaining about the wretchedness of their lot, so far from the comforts of home, their voices floating through the darkness like phantoms.

"I spent half of my share from last summer's plunder on a slave woman, and after but five days in which to pleasure myself with her the Lord Pleuratos sends us on this chase."

"Never fear—she will doubtless find someone to keep her amused during your absence."

A few syllables of laughter, followed by a dangerous silence, followed by the sound of someone clearing his throat.

"I saw that woman the day before she was sold—you paid a hundred and twenty drachmas for her? She has a mole on her belly as big as my thumb, and in three years her breasts will hang like empty wineskins. You are a fool, Bakelas. That slave dealer has robbed you."

"You have not lain with her," Bakelas answered, sounding injured. "I gave the fellow two drachmas on account and told him I must know what I was getting before I would agree to his price. She squeezes the seed from a man as if her thighs were a date press—I am hard as iron this very minute, just from thinking of her. And any man who worries what a slave woman's breasts will look like in three years' time is a bigger fool than I ever was. By then the Lord Pleuratos will probably be king, and we will each have enough to buy ten new whores every winter."

"Well, you will never get home to Wartbelly if we do not catch this boy, may the gods curse him. The Lord Pleuratos will have our heads if he cannot have Philip's—"

"We will catch him, probably tomorrow. Those tracks in the snow couldn't have been more than two hours old. He does not know the terrain, and he is only a boy. Tomorrow we will catch him, cut off his head, and go home."

They talked for a while longer and then, one after the other, they stretched out to find their rest. They did not even trouble to post a guard. It was almost insulting.

Philip was disappointed they had seemed to bring no wine with them. He had a half-formed idea he might wait until they were all wine-fogged and snoring and then sneak into their camp, steal a knife, and cut their throats, one at a time, while they slept. He had no scruples about such a deed—they meant to kill him, did they not? Life had very suddenly ceased to be a game.

Nothing of the sort would be practical now, however, for he would be a dead man if one of them woke up. And one of them was sure to wake up. There was nothing to do except to wait an hour or so, until he could be certain none of them would be on the watch, and then sneak away into the darkness.

Still, it was worth something to have seen his enemies. They were men now, finite in number, and he had learned to hate them.

So the next morning, standing in a dense clump of trees, stroking Alastor's nose that he might not betray them with a whinny if he smelled their horses, Philip watched his pursuers head out of the valley. He would give them a start and then he would begin to track them—it might take them the rest of the day to figure out that they had lost all trace of him, and longer than that before it occurred to them to double back. He might have thought of something by then, and at least it would be one more day of life.

The countryside quickly flattened out, becoming more open and offering fewer places of concealment—yet, if they caught sight of him, the chances of escape were slightly better than they would have been on a narrow mountain trail. Philip was careful, however, and followed his pursuers' progress with the greatest caution.

Every few hours he would allow himself a glimpse of them. Once he watched as they fanned out over a little network of trails, trying to find some sign of him. They regrouped after a bit and went on. They never gave any sign of retracing their own steps, as if it hadn't occurred to them that he would do anything besides run before them like a startled rabbit. After all, it was only a boy they were chasing.

Toward nightfall they reached a meager jumble of twenty or thirty stone huts, a farming community that looked poor and precarious but might have stood on that same spot for four hundred years, and stopped to question the inhabitants.

Philip had passed two or three such little settlements in the past few days and had always avoided them, knowing that the people who lived there would have no choice but to betray him—why should they do anything else when they were defenseless and accustomed to fear the Dardanians?

He dismounted and watched from the protecting shadow of a cliff face as Pleuratos's men interrogated a peasant with a gray beard, who was probably the village elder. The other villagers formed a wide and submissive circle around them. Philip couldn't hear anything, even though the men seemed to be shouting, but he saw enough to have a sense of how Bardylis and his warriors kept their vassal peoples properly cringing and docile.

They bullied the old man, pushing him and even slapping at him with the flats of their swords, as if they would cut him to pieces if they did not care for his answers. Clearly he had reason to fear for his life.

Finally, when they seemed satisfied that there was nothing he could tell them, they let him go and sat down around a cooking fire over which a pot hung from an iron tripod. They began to eat, occasionally shouting what must have been demands for something to drink because the villagers brought them out eight or ten jars—probably every drop so poor a place contained.

They will stay here for the night, Philip thought. *Why should they not, since in an hour the light will be gone? They will welcome the chance to be at their ease. One can hope the local people know how to brew strong beer.*

Night began to fall and Philip, when he was sure it would cover him, began to work his stealthy way in toward the little cluster of buildings. Passing soundlessly from one place of concealment to another, he could hear others moving around him in the darkness as, singly or a few at a time, the villagers began sneaking away, to hide themselves until the morning, when these intruders would once more leave them in peace.

Some were not so lucky.

A couple of the village women, not very pretty, perhaps, but young and full of terror, were huddled beside the cooking fire. They served Pleuratos's men and waited, not daring to run away. One of them was quietly sobbing to herself, her face hidden in her hands. Philip was close enough by then to hear her quite distinctly.

The Dardanians appeared to find her distress amusing—one of them kept picking up the hem of her tunic with his sword point, laughing when each time she flinched and tried to snatch it away.

"You can see what her legs look like soon enough, Bakelas. Have a little patience and finish your dinner."

All four of them laughed at this.

By then Philip was crouched behind a pile of wood that had been stacked beside one of the village dwellings. He had found the broken handle of an ax, a slender shaft of wood not as long as his arm, but probably the best weapon he could hope for in such a place. All he lacked was the opportunity to use it.

Everything depended on surprise. His opponents were armed with swords, and there were four of them—men who would afford him not an instant of mercy. It was well to remember that.

Kill them, he thought. *Kill them, quickly and quietly and with no shrinking. Wait in patience until you can catch one of them alone.*

He did not have to wait long.

"Don't be shy, girl. Let us see if your backside is fit for anything except sitting on."

He sounded drunk. Good. One could hope that his companions were not more temperate.

Philip heard laughter and then whimpered pleading, and watched a shadow passing high up on the stone wall of the hut opposite—a man half dragging a woman by the wrist.

"Come along, girl. Which one of these hovels is yours? I don't fancy having you on the cold ground."

The woman's voice, just a high, hysterical murmur, reached him in snatches. "Please not . . . Please not." She couldn't fight, or even resist. She could only beg.

Philip waited until they had passed by, and then followed.

The hut did not even have a door, just an old blanket fastened to the lintel to keep the wind out. The Dardanian dragged his captive inside, in his haste yanking the blanket loose from one of its nails.

"Now let's have a look . . ."

There was the sound of tearing cloth, followed by a short, sobbing scream and then, for a few seconds, only silence.

It was hard, but Philip decided to give this pig a moment or two to rut in the mud—leave him alone until this business had his full attention.

He couldn't hear the woman anymore but, after a while, he heard the urgent, satisfied grunts of a man taking his pleasure.

Enough—more than enough. He pushed the blanket aside and stepped over the threshold, letting a slash of pale moonlight fall across the floor. He almost stepped on the Dardanian, who was crouched on all fours, his tunic hitched up and tucked into his belt, so intent on quenching his lust that he seemed to hear or see nothing.

All Philip could see of the girl were the soles of her feet.

"Bakelas . . ."

The Dardanian's head jerked up, and he began to twist about to discover who had spoken. The heavy end of Philip's ax handle caught him directly on the temple, and from the sound it must have broken his skull. He pitched over with a groan so that he fell on his back, naked from the waist down, his eyes open. From the expression on his face, one might have thought he was merely embarrassed. Philip knew at once that he had killed him.

The woman was lying on her back, her breasts and belly shining in the moonlight, her legs still wide apart, as if she expected Philip to throw himself down in Bakelas's place. She was surprisingly young, hardly out of her girlhood—hardly older than Philip himself. She was also terrified. Too terrified, fortunately, even to cry out.

Philip raised a finger to his lips, commanding silence, and then reached down to pick up the woman's tunic, which was torn almost to pieces. He held it out and she grabbed it to her, covering herself as best she could.

Then, quietly, she began to sob. It was no good trying to stop her, so Philip left her alone.

The Dardanian's sword was lying beside him, and Philip picked it up. There were still three men left, and a sword was better than a piece of wood.

"My husband will hate me," the woman said, with a kind of astonished quietness. She had stopped sobbing, as if her grief had stunned her into calm. "He will never look at me again."

"Unless he is a fool, he will be glad enough that you are simply alive and will keep his peace."

"Do you really think so?" She looked up at Philip with touchingly obvious gratitude.

"Yes."

Again, Philip signed for quiet. He heard someone approaching.

"Bakelas—Bakelas, come along. You have had her to yourself long enough. It is time to share."

The blanket over the door was swept aside and a man stepped into the hut. For an instant he just stood there, his arm still raised to hold the blanket. Perhaps at first he didn't even see that anything was wrong.

Philip had waited beside the doorframe. He took a step forward and, with savage force, drove his sword up so that its point caught the man just under the rib cage, burying itself almost to the hilt. The man opened his mouth, as if he meant to cry out, but all that came from his lips was a thin spray of blood. He was dead even before his knees struck the earthen floor.

"That's two," Philip murmured. He yanked the sword loose and wiped the blade clean on the Dardanian's tunic. Suddenly the air in the hut was rank with the smell of death. He turned to the woman.

"You will wait here," he said. His voice and his heart both seemed to have turned to ice. "You will make no sound. I must attend to the two who remain— if I do not kill them they shall surely kill me, and then they will remember you. If you wish to live, you will not leave these walls."

He did not wait for her to answer, since at that moment she hardly even existed for him. He simply left her there.

Outside, Philip drew a deep breath of the cold night air and, for just a moment, thought he was about to faint. He had just killed two men in the space of a few minutes. He had never killed anyone before—somehow Zolfi didn't seem to count. And now . . .

He forced himself to stop thinking about it. He was not at liberty to indulge such weakness.

There were still two more left.

They were sitting before the fire, one on either side. They were drinking beer from a pair of small jars, talking in low, sullen voices. They heard nothing, they saw nothing. They did not even glance up. It was almost too easy.

Philip stepped up behind one of them, raised his sword, and brought it slashing down upon the man's neck. There was a grunt and a thick, sudden welling of blood, and then the man collapsed over on his side. He lay on the ground, his legs twitching violently, but he was dead. It seemed possible he did not even live to feel the stroke that killed him.

The second Dardanian, seeing what had happened, scrambled backward, in his haste to get away almost pitching over on his back. His eyes were wide with terror. Philip experienced a spasm of disgust, as if at the first scent of a decaying corpse.

"Stand up," he commanded. "Stand up. Take your sword in your hand and defend yourself. I have grown weary of slaughtering Dardanians as if they were sheep."

The man never took his eyes from the point of Philip's weapon. At first he seemed too stunned to move, and then suddenly he pushed himself up. He didn't appear to know what to do next.

"Draw your sword—or would you prefer that I simply killed you?"

The words had the desired effect, for the man flinched, just as if he had been struck in the face, and then he showed his teeth in something halfway between a grin and a snarl.

At last, and without hurry, he drew the sword from his belt.

"You arrogant little boy," the Dardanian said, in a coarse whisper that was full of contempt. "Do you imagine I am afraid of a Macedonian baby, simply because he finds he is not afraid to kill from behind?"

"I won't kill you from behind."

"No." He laughed as if he were only just seeing the joke. "No, you won't."

The man was perhaps a span taller, and perhaps ten years older. His bare arms were knotted with muscle. His hair and beard were a tarnished yellow, which somehow only increased the general impression of self-sufficient cruelty. How many had he killed, face-to-face, in single combat? He had the look of one who lives only to fight.

All at once he made a lunge, not a serious attack so much as a probe. Philip caught the point of his sword with his blade and parried the thrust aside. The man retreated a step or two.

"Very well—then someone has at least taught you the elements." The Dardanian grinned all over again. "The dogs will still have made a meal of you before you are a quarter of an hour older."

They circled one another, the light from the fire glinting off their weapons. It was almost as formal as the courtship dance of a pair of birds.

And then Philip lunged. A sudden rush, the sound of iron against iron, and then retreat. The Dardanian pressed the attack, and Philip could hardly get away in time.

And then again. And again.

"I will kill you, little boy," the Dardanian taunted, his voice lilting with mockery. "I will put your head in a leather bag and take it home to Lord Pleuratos."

Philip stepped back, letting the point of his sword drop a little. He was afraid, yes, and he hoped he looked it.

The Dardanian took the bait. A quick shuffle, and he rushed in for the kill. He was slashing with his weapon now—each time the blade coming a little closer. Philip seemed about to be overpowered.

And then, even as he turned the Dardanian's blade away so that he could almost feel the cold iron against his face, he dodged a little to one side, twisted out of the way, and let the other man step into the space he made.

It was a trap—only at the very last did the Dardanian realize that he had allowed himself to come too close. Suddenly Philip crouched and threw his weight against him, striking him just under the ribs with his shoulder.

As the Dardanian toppled backward, Philip swung his weapon in a low, narrow arc. The point buried itself in the man's arm, just above the elbow, and a heavy black line of blood appeared at once.

It was over. The Dardanian's sword dropped from his hand. Philip swung again, and the flat of his sword caught the man on the face. The blow could have done no real harm, but the Dardanian fell to his knees with a scream of surprise and pain.

"I will not kill you from behind."

Philip stepped forward, ready to finish him . . .

"Stop!"

Astonished at the sound, he looked about him. Slowly, out of the darkness, came perhaps as many as thirty or forty men—in the flickering light from the cooking fire, their faces looked grim, almost demonic. One of them he recognized as the village elder.

Philip waited, his sword still raised to take the Dardanian's life. The elder bowed to him.

"Stay your hand, Lord. Leave him to us."

9

Death from the sword of an enemy would have been a blessing. But that a man, any man, should die thus . . .

When the Dardanian saw what was to happen, he began to scream—and that scream, before they choked it off, was like no human sound. Philip could only crouch on the ground and watch, too frightened to move, too awed even to look away.

The villagers tore him apart. With sharpened stones, with their bare hands, they simply ripped him to pieces, the way starving men might attack a joint of roasted meat, their frenzy not subsiding until there was nothing left except a few cracked and ragged bones.

And when it was over, and the smell of blood hung in the air like a pall, someone held a cup of beer to Philip's lips and made him drink.

"Do not judge us, Lord," the village elder said. "Until you yourself have lived under the yoke of the Dardanians, do not judge what we have done. Now come to my hut and sleep."

In the morning he found Alastor tethered outside. There was no trace of the Dardanians.

"We cut the throats of their horses and buried them all, men and animals, in a place no one will ever look for them. You have never been here, Lord—those men have never been here. The Dardanians would crucify us, down to the sucking babes, if ever they guessed what has happened here."

"They will never hear of it from my lips. I will never speak of it, or of this place, to any living man."

"We know this, Lord." And the look in his eyes said, *Were it not so, you would now be buried with them.*

Philip tried to control a shiver of dread he felt as he took the elder's hand in his own.

"Go in peace, Lord, for you have brought us the blessing of revenge."

Philip mounted his horse and rode south. He did not even turn to look back.

Early in the afternoon of the next day, Philip reached the Vatokhori Pass and entered the Kingdom of Lynkos.

Menelaos, king of the Lynkestians, tended to ignore the king in Pella, but at least he was a Macedonian. Philip no longer felt himself at the mercy of strangers.

He camped on the flatlands and, for the first time since parting from Bardylis, dared to indulge in the luxury of a fire. He knew he was no safer for having crossed a border, but in two days there had been no signs of pursuit. He seemed to have this mountain wilderness to himself.

Nevertheless, he slept with his sword drawn.

The next day found him on a wooded plateau within an hour's ride of King Menelaos's stronghold at Pisoderi. The trail would cross some pleasant little meadow, bathed in light, and the next moment the trees closed around one like a cloak. An hour past midday Philip heard the distant whine of hunting horns.

Alastor first sensed the presence of danger. With a low, nervous whinny, the stallion halted in the middle of a narrow clearing. Philip leaned forward to stroke its neck.

"What is in your nostrils, you black demon?" he whispered. "What would you tell me if you had a man's voice?"

But in that tense, watchful moment there was nothing, only the silence of something waiting to happen.

And then, in almost the next instant, he heard it. He knew what it was even as the forest hid it, even as it thrashed through the undergrowth in its panicked flight. He drew his sword, swung a leg over Alastor's back, and dropped to the ground.

When at last it broke through into the clearing, he was astonished at its size—a great boar, perhaps two cubits at the shoulder, as big as any two men. Its tusks were gleaming white, and its cruel little eyes glittered with rage. When it saw Philip in its path it stopped short, tearing at the earth with its hoof as it lowered its black head for the attack.

Philip held his sword with the point angled down, knowing he would have only one chance. Face-to-face with this murderous beast, he felt a strange joy.

"Come to me, my pretty," he murmured in that singsong voice one uses with young children. "Come to me, that we may know which of us will be alive a minute hence."

As if answering a dare, the boar snorted angrily and charged him. Philip stood his ground, trying not to think, keeping his arm straight and his sword point lined up with a spot between the boar's shoulder blades, as if only that spot were hurrying toward him and not five or six talents of muscle and bone, with tusks as long as daggers. It was the hardest few seconds of his life.

The impact was tremendous. Philip felt all the air go out of his body as he was lifted up, like a mote of dust someone has swept from his garment. He had no idea whether or not his thrust had gone home—he had no idea of anything. He did not even remember striking the ground.

He must have been knocked unconscious, at least for a few moments. He opened his eyes, a little surprised even to be alive. The boar was dead, almost at his feet, with Philip's sword buried up to the hilt, precisely between its shoulder blades.

That made him feel better—at least he had not lost his nerve in the last instant. It nearly made up for the tear in his thigh, as long as his middle finger and about as deep, where the filthy brute had managed to gore him.

Almost as soon as he became conscious of the wound, a stab of pain shot up from his knee all the way into his groin. At first he could not even breathe, but then the pain subsided into mere burning ache. There was blood, but not too much. Philip decided he would probably survive.

Then he moved his leg and the pain came back, this time so bad that it made him feel giddy. His horse was standing some twelve or fourteen paces away, grazing on the thin grass—it seemed an uncrossable gulf.

"Alastor, come!"

The stallion raised its head and looked at him as if to say, *Now what do you want?* Nevertheless, it came and stood beside its master.

Philip raised himself to a crouch, keeping the weight off his bad leg. Then he reached up and just managed to grab a handful of Alastor's mane. With much effort, and enough pain to make his hair damp with sweat, he at last was able to stand up.

But climbing up on the stallion's back, as he came to realize, was simply beyond him. He was considering what to do next when three mounted men galloped into the clearing, reining in their horses at the sight of him. Their lances were already drawn and ready.

"It is an offense to hunt the king's boar," one of them said in the slightly choppy dialect of the mountain peoples. "It is an offense punishable by death."

"The boar seemed under the impression it was hunting me," Philip answered, grinning at his own joke.

For a long moment no one spoke, as if they had reached some sort of impasse.

"Why did you dismount?"

It was a different man who at last broke the silence. Philip merely stared at him. At first he had no idea what the fellow was taking about.

"Why did you get off your horse? A man is safer if he keeps to his horse."

"Yes, but the horse isn't," Philip answered, when he understood. "Besides, I didn't have a lance—only a sword."

They all looked down at the body of the dead boar.

"That looks like an Illyrian sword. I can tell by the hilt work."

"It is an Illyrian sword." Philip let his eyes narrow, as if he fancied himself insulted. "But I am a Macedonian."

"You made a good kill," the man said after a moment, seeming to ignore Philip's claim. "Still, boy, you were a fool to have tried it. And all for the sake of a horse."

"He is my horse, and I put a high value on him."

Philip held his gaze, until at last the other man was forced to look away—wondering, perhaps, why this raw youth appeared determined to make an enemy of him.

The silence now was hostile and oppressive. Philip still stood beside his horse, clutching a handful of mane. His leg throbbed with pain until he was beginning to feel quite sick, yet he was determined at all costs to keep his feet. He was only afraid he might faint, which would have struck him as a shameful weakness.

After an interval that seemed to go on forever but was probably only a few minutes, two more men rode into the clearing, one slightly ahead of the other. Philip's captors raised their lance points in salute, but even without this he would have known the man with the curly brown beard that did not quite cover a purplish birthmark on his left cheek. He had seen Menelaos seven years ago, in Pella, during one of the infrequent periods of peace between Macedon and her nominal vassal.

"We caught this one poaching, My Lord King!" shouted the man who had tried to identify Philip's sword as Illyrian. "He claims he was merely defending himself, that the boar attacked him, but—"

"Does anyone go hunting boar with nothing but a sword?" Menelaos broke in impatiently. He was only a year or two short of forty and had been king for a long time. One had the impression he understood how it was to be managed. "You really are a fool, Lysander."

And then he seemed to dismiss the man from existence and turned his attention to Philip.

"Who are you, boy? That is no scratch you have there on your thigh—perhaps you should sit down and take the weight off it."

"I am a Macedonian, My Lord," Philip answered, still standing, although his legs felt as if they were turning to mush. "I am also your kinsman, your sister's son."

The Lord Menelaos peered at him for a moment, as if he doubted his sanity, and then his eyes widened with surprised recognition.

"Philip? Can it possibly be you?"

When Philip nodded, the king of Lynkos broke into a loud laugh. "That beard is an excellent disguise," he said, clapping his hand to his chest in sheer exuberance. "The last time we met you weren't more than seven or eight—just a little boy. You were still playing with toy soldiers!"

He laughed all over again at the recollection and then suddenly stopped, looking down at the sword hilt sticking out from between the shoulder blades of the dead boar.

"Well, nephew, you are not a boy now. And tonight, when we dine, you will sit at the head of the table with the companions, even though it is certain you have yet to kill your first man. For to have killed a beast such as this one, and with nothing but a sword, carries with it full as much honor."

King Menelaos was doubtless more than a little astonished when his sister's son all at once broke into a fit of almost hysterical laughter.

"Your brother is off chasing shadows in Thessaly," Menelaos said, absently scratching at his beard as if the birthmark itched. "Jason of Pherae was assassinated, and the Aleuadae chose the occasion to shake off the control of his successor. They appealed to Alexandros, naturally, and he was fool enough to answer their summons. I hear that things have not gone well for him down there."

He grinned, showing strong, uneven teeth. Alexandros was his kinsman and had once been a great favorite, but the king of Lynkos would never love the king of Macedon. It was like a principle of logic.

"Is the Lord Ptolemy with him?" Philip asked innocently. He took a sip from his wine cup to cover the apprehension rising in his chest like panic. But Menelaos only shrugged.

"One supposes he must be—the flea is never found very far from the dog."

The laughter at this witticism was general and immoderate, for the Lynkestians understood what was due to their king. Philip, as the dog's brother, was allowed to scrape by with a polite smile.

"Alexandros should watch that one," the king said, lowering his voice and leaning confidentially toward Philip, who sat at his right hand. "The Lord Ptolemy is the sort of friend a man of prudence keeps close to him—and never trusts. How is my sister, by the way?"

Menelaos kept his face studiously neutral, but Philip knew perfectly well what he meant. So. Even in Lynkos they knew that the Lord Ptolemy neglected his wife's bed in favor of her mother's.

Philip, however, merely nodded as if acknowledging the most ordinary of courtesies. "Very well, so far as I know. I have been away and have heard no news of Pella since the beginning of winter."

There was no reason why Menelaos should have looked surprised, for how could he have failed to know of the recent exchange of diplomatic prisoners, which had taken place practically at his doorstep? He merely smiled—the cold, dangerous smile one only sees on the lips of men who know the power of life and death.

"How did you find the Illyrians?" he asked as if this too were known to him already. "Are they the savages you imagined?"

For just an instant, as a thing that registered itself in the tiniest movement of his eyes, the king of Lynkos betrayed that the answer he received was not, for once, what he anticipated.

"Yes. They were everything I had imagined."

Philip was eager to be on his way—and, indeed, Uncle Menelaos was not very pressing in offers of hospitality—but it was full ten days before his leg was healed enough to allow him to sit a horse. Still, as soon as he was able he was once more on the road south.

By late afternoon the mountains were behind him and he had entered the vast plains of Macedon. Pella was still a day and a half away, but already, riding through the waist-high grass, he felt himself to be home.

He spent that first night with shepherds who, in exchange for one of his small silver coins, were willing enough to share their dinner and to offer him a place in their stone hut to spread his sleeping rug but who were too proud of being Macedonians to treat him as anything except an equal. To them he was simply a youth with a fine horse and a full purse—valuable things in themselves but conferring no special dignity. They did not inquire as to his parentage, or even his name, and neither did he volunteer them. Philip half suspected it would have made no difference if he had. His own people, he thought with a certain pleasure, were no one's slaves.

Still, because hospitality was a duty to the gods and because everyone welcomes a compatriot, they were amiable enough. He asked after the news from Pella.

"You know Pella?"

The question suggested a certain wariness, but no more than might be considered usual before a stranger—*Pella*, after all, could only mean one thing—and the man who put it, even if his rock-hard countryman's face never changed expression, managed to imply that he wondered by what right his young guest concerned himself with the doings of the king.

"I have family there," Philip answered, rather pleased with himself for having avoided an actual lie. Then he smiled and shrugged his shoulders as if admitting to some kind of fault.

The shepherd, who was in the middle of life and looked somehow as if he might once have been a soldier, appeared satisfied with this. He cleared his throat and spat into the fire, frowning as he listened to it hiss.

"Seen your family lately?" he asked. When Philip shook his head, the shepherd nodded, giving the impression he had expected no more. "Well, they will tell you that we have a new king. Old Amyntas died this summer—in his bed, may the gods be thanked. The son, so I hear, is already off in the south, making war."

His disapproval, though unstated, was perfectly plain, yet when someone laughed he looked nettled and turned on the man with real anger.

"If you think the king does ill, Duskleas, then go and tell him so to his face. That is your right, if you have the bowels for it, but I will not sit here and listen to you snickering about the Lord Alexandros behind his back."

"Yes, Kaltios, we all know that . . ."

But whatever Duskleas might have said died on his lips when he saw the scowl on the face of the man called Kaltios.

"I know how much respect is due the king of the Macedonians, that is all. That is all a man needs to know if he would not shame himself before the deathless gods."

There was no answer to this, and for a long time the men around the shepherds' campfire abided in a comfortless silence.

At last, feeling that the obligation lay with him, Philip hunted around for something to say.

"The king's war does not prosper, then?" he asked.

For a moment Kaltios looked at him as if wondering whether he too might be offering an impertinence, but at last he turned his face away and stared sullenly at the fire.

"How long has it been, I wonder, since Macedonian arms have prospered? And how long before they do again?"

It was nightfall when Philip reached the walls of Pella. The bonfires were alight beside the city gate, and the captain of the watch had to raise his torch to see his face.

"Then it's really you, my young Lord? So the Illyrians haven't killed you after all—but then perhaps they thought that black demon of a horse would save them the trouble."

Philip felt his bowels turning to ice, but he laughed along with everyone else.

"Is the king still in Thessaly?" he asked.

"You have heard of that, then?" The captain shook his head as if embarrassed. "Yes, he is still there. The Thebans have taken the field, and one hears rumors that they are demanding stiff terms before they will accept a peace."

"Is it Pelopidas who commands them?"

"The very same."

Philip made no reply, but urged his horse through the opening gate. Pelopidas the Invincible, the Champion of Thebes, considered by many the greatest general in the world—it was almost a relief. To be defeated by Pelopidas carried no disgrace.

And defeated Alexandros certainly would be if he was fool enough to let the Thebans tempt him into battle.

Even after dark the city was a busy place. Winter was nearly over, but the weather was still dry and that most sociable of people, the citizens of Pella, filled the streets to buy and sell, to argue, haggle, and gossip. There were stalls with cloth awnings where anyone with a few coins in his purse could find wine, roast meat, figs, live ducks, green melons from Lesbos, swords, and body armor from Phrygia, Thracian horses, manuscripts from Athens and Ionia. The whores were out and enjoying a decent trade. A fair number of the men were already a little drunk, and there was much laughter.

This was the city in which Philip was a prince of the Royal House of the Argeadai, yet his homecoming was perfectly ordinary. Here and there someone who knew him might shout his name and wave, and a few people stared, as if he were a curiosity, but for the most part he was unregarded. As he rode through the crowded, narrow streets, his presence among this busy multitude struck no one, least of all himself, as in any way remarkable.

People were too preoccupied with their own lives to give much heed to princes—the king was far away, ruining himself in foreign wars, yet this too might go unheeded.

It was only when he entered the royal quarter, where the streets were cobbled, that Philip noticed the heavy, foreboding silence of defeat. Yes, here the news from Thessaly had made itself felt.

He left Alastor with the grooms at the royal stable.

"Is the king's steward anywhere within?" he asked in the kitchen—from long habit he had entered the palace of his fathers through the servants' wing.

"At home, I expect," replied one of the cook's helpers, a woman who had treated Philip to bits of apple when he had been barely able to walk. He noticed now the way she glanced at her fellows, as if they were all privy to some secret, but he said nothing.

"Then I shall look for him there, Kinissa. I thank you," he answered this woman, whom he had known all his life.

As soon as he turned the corner and entered the street where he had played as a child, he knew what that glance had meant. When he looked up at the roofline of Glaukon's house he was seized with an odd kind of panic, as if all at once he no longer recognized the place.

There was no smoke coming from the chimney. The hearth fire, which

Alcmene had kept alive since the day she had entered this house as a bride, had been allowed to flicker out.

Philip opened the door soundlessly, with almost a robber's stealth, and stepped inside. The first thing he saw was Glaukon, sitting on a stool beside the hearth, his arms resting dejectedly on his knees. He looked as if he had not slept in days.

When at last he noticed Philip's presence, he looked up.

"Your mo—" He stopped himself and then swallowed hard, as if to cleanse his mouth of some bitter taste. "Alcmene is dead."

10

The king of Macedon seemed to encompass in his own person all the weaknesses and follies of youth—he chose the wrong favorites, he would not listen to advice, and he grotesquely overestimated both his strength and his talents. Long before he had time to outgrow them, these faults, combined with a disposition for war, would result in the destruction of his country. The recent disaster in Thessaly had left Ptolemy convinced that, his personal ambitions aside, he would have to find the means of displacing Alexandros. It was virtually a duty to arrange his assassination.

Opportunities were not meant to be squandered, and in Thessaly Alexandros had been very close to achieving a significant hedge against the threats of the southern powers. Jason of Pherae had marched on Larissa and expelled the Aleuadae, who, as everyone knew, were as vicious and untrustworthy a family of brigands as had ever set themselves up to plunder their neighbors—the Larissans doubtless had been delighted to see them go. But then Jason had been assassinated and his successor poisoned, and the Aleuadae had called upon Alexandros to restore them to power.

Alexandros had been right to agree: Pherae was in chaos and, once the ruling family there stopped murdering each other and settled on a new tyrant, it would have put a useful check on her power to have the Aleuadae back in Larissa as Macedonian clients. And there was no denying that Alexandros's capture of Larissa had been a soldierly piece of work. The difficulty was that the young fool did not have the least conception of when to stop.

He should, upon achieving his little victory, have simply withdrawn. But no, that didn't square with his notions of what was due to a great conqueror, so he had started establishing garrisons all along the line of the River Peneos—didn't the idiot realize that he had no forces to spare, that the northern borders, which were where the real danger lay, had already been stripped bare for this little adventure, that there was neither any necessity nor even the required soldiers to fortify the south? Hadn't Ptolemy, his kinsman and friend, who had killed his first man ten years before Alexandros was even born, pointed this out to him? Yes, of course—endlessly. But the king had ears only for those who told him that he was Achilleos reborn and was destined to stride the whole of Greece like a colossus.

Well, the garrisons had achieved nothing except to unite all of Thessaly against the "northern invaders" and to give Thebes an excuse to intervene with a force headed by no less a figure than the great Pelopidas. Within two months of marching south, Alexandros found himself back across the border, only this time with a hostile Boeotian army operating on Macedonian soil.

But at least Alexandros had finally grasped the full scope of his folly. After two days of sulking in his tent, too depressed in spirit even to come out and face his own soldiers, he had sent Ptolemy off to Pelopidas's camp to inquire concerning his terms for a withdrawal.

The Thebans had the advantage of numbers, but they knew enough to be cautious in hostile territory and so their mounted patrols intercepted Ptolemy a good hour's ride from their outer perimeter. They seemed surprised to find a man alone, but he had decided against an escort—it did not strike the right chord of humble supplication, and, besides, he preferred that no version of this meeting except his own should find its way back to Alexandros.

He brought his horse to a halt and allowed the Theban cavalrymen to surround him.

"I am an emissary from the king of Macedon," Ptolemy said, glancing around at them in that slightly annoyed manner that is the diplomat's natural defense against fear. "I come to treat with the Boeotarch."

No one answered him—they were only soldiers, and in their eyes he was merely another prisoner. One of them, whose manner more than his uniform distinguished him as the captain of the patrol, rode close enough to take the reins of Ptolemy's horse from his hands. The king's emissary submitted to this in silence and allowed himself to be led back to the Theban encampment.

Along the way there was plenty of time to consider the appalling humiliation involved in being brought in this manner before a man like Pelopidas—Pelopidas, who, with hardly any weapons except his own daring and the help of only a few like-minded friends, had come out of exile to deliver his city from the conqueror's yoke and had gone on to crush, apparently forever, the might of Spartan arms. What must such a man think of Alexandros, the boy-king of Macedon, who ruins himself and his country in a fit of adolescent vanity? With what contempt must he view this king's ambassador?

That he had forced Ptolemy into this mortifying position was yet one more grievance to be tallied against Alexandros. Yet there was some comfort in remembering that the account between them would be settled one day. And that day was not far off.

But in the meantime it was still necessary to decide how the present part might best be played. Whom would the Boeotarch be expecting? The northern rustic, faithful as one of his lord's hunting dogs? Or the intriguer, ready to strike an advantageous personal bargain behind his king's back? Or some combination of the two, since, as the bright gods knew well enough, the rest of the world tended to regard Macedonians as devious simpletons?

Or perhaps merely the gray-bearded statesman, the senior member of his dynasty, whose loyalties are to the state, the royal house, and the king, in that order. A man who feels the tug of hereditary allegiances but has not let them blind him to the painful truth. A patriot. Yes. All things being equal, Ptolemy thought he might find that role the most congenial.

Yet finally the choice would have to be left to Pelopidas himself. Let him see whatever he wished to see.

The Theban camp was a masterpiece of defense. The walls were of earthwork with wooden towers every forty or so paces, and these were surrounded by a double ring of ditches, the outer ring rather shallow but fortified with sharpened stakes and the inner ring astonishingly deep—if a man did not tear his belly open on the one, he was likely to find himself buried alive as he attempted to scramble up the steep, crumbling slopes of the other. Even if he had the necessary forces, Alexandros could easily wear out a couple of months trying to force a breach, by which time Pelopidas would have cut him to shreds. And this virtually impregnable fortress had been thrown together in perhaps three days.

But such was the character of the Theban army, which ranked as probably the best the world had yet seen. They fought with inhuman courage and efficiency, and they left nothing to chance.

The camp's sole entrance was a drawbridge leading to a timber gate. Inside there was a marshaling field and, beyond that, row after row of white linen tents. In the center of these, set apart but only slightly larger than the rest, was one guarded by a pair of spearmen and flying the pennant of the Boeotarch. Ptolemy and his escort came to a halt before it.

The tent flap came up, and a man walked out into the sunlight. He was about fifty and wore a plain homespun cloak that might once have been brown or black but had faded to no particular color at all. The man did not even carry a sword, yet he had the bearing of one long accustomed to command. At first he did not speak. His pale blue eyes, as pitiless as a hawk's, studied Ptolemy's face with something like amused curiosity.

"I am Pelopidas," he said at last. "And you, I should imagine, are the Lord Ptolemy. Come inside—I fear all I can offer you is some rather indifferent wine . . ."

"The king your master shows a becoming love of glory," Pelopidas said after he had refilled his guest's wine cup. "I think, however, that in this one instance a little caution would have been even more becoming. Certainly he realizes that he has overextended himself."

"If he does not, it is not for want of being told."

Ptolemy shrugged and avoided looking the other man straight in the face. It was a gesture he hoped would suggest the right quality of embarrassed diffidence, for it would not do to appear to criticize Alexandros directly.

The Boeotarch responded with a clipped syllable of laughter, as if to say, "Yes, we are both men who have seen something of life, are we not? And we know what boys are like when they grow too full of themselves."

What was there to do except to frown and to make some show of wounded dignity?

"The king has a generous and heroic nature," Ptolemy said in a tone that implied the rebuke was directed more to himself than to Pelopidas. "And the Aleuadae have long enjoyed the patronage of our royal house."

In the silence that followed, during which Pelopidas's cold, measuring eyes never left his face, Ptolemy entertained the uncomfortable suspicion that this man could look straight into his mind. *You are not what you would appear,* those eyes said. *You have no secrets I have not guessed.*

"The Aleuadae are a race of scoundrels," the Boeotarch replied at last, a faint smile playing across his lips. "And they impose upon your master's good nature. Yet they may keep Larissa—for the present. I am prepared to make this concession because I admire the king of Macedon and would be his friend."

"My king has need of friends." Ptolemy returned the smile, since he felt a returning sense of safety, as if once more he understood what the conversation was about. "And the goodwill of My Lord Pelopidas is not to be despised. Yet may one inquire what the Boeotarch, whose impulses are not those of a private man but who above all else cherishes the interests of his city, will expect as the price of such generosity?"

No, he had understood nothing. He could see as much in the way the light changed in the man's eyes. Some souls will remain a mystery, impenetrable, like the will of the gods.

"The interests of Thebes and Macedon are one," the Boeotarch answered smoothly, as if he were explaining something to a talented child. "Peace and serenity in the northern states. No adventures. No . . . disturbances. To that end we are prepared to offer King Alexandros an alliance . . ."

As he rode back across the empty grasslands toward the Macedonian camp, Ptolemy felt in his chest the flutterings of a vague, cold terror, as if Black Death had opened her wings to throw their shadow across his life.

He thought of Philip—dead by now probably, although he had heard nothing. He had been so clever to send that precociously dangerous boy off to have his throat cut, although what they would do now if it came to war with the Illyrians, he couldn't even begin to guess.

And in his ears he still heard the Boeotarch's words, like a muttered prophecy of doom. It was as if the gods had decided to destroy him with weapons of his own forging.

"We will expect to receive hostages, My Lord—guarantors of the peace we hope to preserve between us. They will live in Thebes, in the houses of our great men, and they will be treated as allies and honored guests. It will be an opportunity for them, an introduction to the world beyond your own kingdom such as, I daresay, few of your young Macedonian nobles could ever dream of. It would gratify me, My Lord, as a sign of your friendship and trust, if among them you might think to number your own son."

The morning after his return to Pella, while the sky was still a pale, silvery gray, Philip went with Glaukon to the burial ground outside the city walls. The grave was unmarked, and Alcmene had been dead for nearly a month, so the earth that covered her funeral urn was already beginning to look worn and windswept. In half a year, when the grass was high, this spot would seem to disappear.

The two men sat down beside it, and Philip rested his hand on the burial mound in a gesture that was almost a caress. He had not slept. His eyes were wet with tears.

"She had not been well since you left," Glaukon said. "One day she sat down beside the hearth and simply died. Not even Nikomachos can say what killed her, but I think it was grief."

"I was so glad to go—I feel as if I murdered her."

But Glaukon shook his head, frowning, as if disappointed that it should not be so.

"It was not your choice but the king's. And the fault lies with neither of you." He closed his eyes as an expression of pain crossed his face. "More and more I have come to believe that the gods meant to punish Alcmene for her arrogance."

Philip began to say something, but the words died on his lips. What, after all, could he have said? He felt, suddenly, that he was in the presence of some great secret that it would be a presumption of challenge.

Perhaps it was best, after all, to be silent and listen.

"Alcmene did not understand," Glaukon went on, almost as if he were explaining the thing to himself. "To her you were simply the child she had nursed at her breast—no more than that, a creature of flesh and blood, more precious to her than her own. She put you in place of the baby who had died, and she believed that somehow the love she bore you had made you hers. She was wrong to believe it."

"Was she?" Philip's voice was so choked with emotion that he could hardly speak. "For all that she was not my mother, I loved her as such. Who in all the dark world had a better claim on a son's love? The Lady Eurydike? You see how weak are the ties of blood."

Glaukon looked at him and smiled joylessly, for Philip always spoke thus of his mother—as someone remote and separate.

"I was not speaking of blood," he said. "You do not belong to your mother the queen, no more than you did to Alcmene—no more than you will ever belong to any living man or woman. You belong to Macedon and to the immortal gods, who hold your life in their keeping against some purpose of their own. They made plain their will on the very night of your birth, which was blessed by Herakles, and there have been signs and portents since—you know yourself that what I say is truth. Thus I knew they would bring you back alive from the land of the Illyrians."

With an almost imperceptible shrug Glaukon appeared to separate himself from his insight into the miraculous, implying that what was so plain to one such as he could not help but be the truth.

"Alcmene could not see that all was in the gods' hands," he went on as if confessing some private shame. "She could not see because her love for you blinded her to all else, and thus she was afraid, and thus her fear killed her. Her fear was both a weakness and a blasphemy, for she should have trusted in the will of heaven."

Philip did not know if he believed Glaukon's words, but they had the effect of clearing his mind. He remembered Ptolemy, and that made him ashamed of having surrendered to a private grief. Alexandros, his brother and king, had yet to be warned.

He went to find Perdikkas.

"I have been named the heir," Perdikkas said as almost his first words. "And quite properly, as I am next in age." He smiled, as if at some purely personal triumph. Almost as if he somehow expected Philip to be jealous.

"You may succeed faster than you expect."

They were in Perdikkas's bedroom, which adjoined their mother's private apartments, and Perdikkas was still at his breakfast. He sat, calmly chewing on a piece of bread dipped in wine, listening as Philip unfolded the odd story of his adventure in the north. He did not seem particularly impressed.

"You are like a woman," he said finally. "You see conspiracies everywhere. If someone wanted to kill you, it is far likelier to have been old Bardylis than the Lord Ptolemy, who is our kinsman and friend. The whole idea is preposterous."

"There is nothing preposterous about a king of Macedon being murdered by a kinsman. The Argeadai have murdered each other for generations—it has almost the sanction of custom."

But Perdikkas merely glared at him.

"Come with me," Philip said at last. "We can leave this morning and reach the king's camp in two days. We will seek out the Lord Ptolemy and confront him, in Alexandros's presence. Then we will all know the truth."

"You would confront him?" Perdikkas was so appalled that he pushed his breakfast away from him and stood up. "You would accuse him of attempting to murder you—and to his face? What if he should . . . ?"

"Should what? Deny it? Of course he will deny it."

"Then what is the point?" Perdikkas almost shouted.

But Philip seemed for the moment to have lost interest. As if he had suddenly remembered that he was hungry, he reached down to pick up the piece of flatbread his brother had been eating, tore off a large hunk, and stuffed it in his mouth. Then he poured himself a cup of wine and sat down.

"Finish your breakfast," he said, gesturing toward the chair his brother had abandoned. "We have a long ride ahead of us."

Perdikkas merely repeated his question.

"What is the point?" he asked, more calmly this time. "If he denies the accusation—and he can hardly do anything else—then you will have gained nothing."

Philip put down the wine cup, wiped his mouth, and sighed with animal contentment.

"Ptolemy imagines that I am dead by now." He glanced longingly at his brother's bed, thinking that the wine had been a mistake, for he was very tired. "If we catch him by surprise, before some idiot puts the news of my return into a dispatch bag, then I don't imagine his denial will be very convincing."

"And then what?"

"And then Alexandros will kill him," Philip answered. It was with some difficulty that he refrained from adding, "Or I will do it myself."

Perdikkas had not sat down, and when Philip glanced up at him he instantly averted his eyes.

"Alexandros will not believe him guilty. I do not believe him guilty. I do not care to associate myself with such an accusation."

"Why? Because you are afraid, should I be right, of how he might avenge himself against you?"

The silence that followed confirmed the truth of what Philip had said only half in earnest.

And perhaps, Philip thought, *perhaps Perdikkas is not wrong to refuse.* Perdikkas, after all, really was the heir—perhaps it was best if he did not become embroiled in this.

"What will you do?" Perdikkas asked at last. His eyes were almost pleading.

"Do?"

You belong to Macedon and to the immortal gods, who hold your life in their keeping against some purpose of their own. Philip could only smile at the recollection, for truly Glaukon was a credulous old fool to believe such a thing. Yet perhaps it was now necessary to behave as if it were so.

"Do? I shall find our brother, Alexandros. And I shall tell the king of Macedon that he walks about with a serpent coiled against his bosom."

The war in Thessaly had entered its diplomatic phase, but diplomacy, in the king of Macedon's opinion, was the occupation of cowards, nothing more than a method for losing battles without having to take the trouble to fight them. As much as possible, Alexandros tried to avoid the actual negotiations, and it did not occur to him to be offended that they seemed to go on just as well without him.

What he could not avoid was the nagging suspicion that he had somehow revealed a weakness in himself, that control was slipping away from him, that he and everything that mattered to him were gradually becoming irrelevant. This made him both angry and afraid, and both of these emotions he focused on Pelopidas of Thebes.

Nothing made any sense. Nothing was the way it was supposed to be, and no one else gave any indication that they noticed or cared. Pelopidas was supposed to be a great hero, yet the only things that appeared to interest him were proscription lists and the wheat yield. Alexandros was sensationally disappointed, while Pelopidas, for his part, seemed actually to like him, treating him with that mixture of interest and forbearance, which might have characterized the relations between a man and his half-grown nephew. It was maddening.

Every evening the Lord Ptolemy, who showed no distaste for the conference table, came to Alexandros's tent and explained how things were progressing. The king listened quietly, nodding now and then when some sign of agreement was required of him, wondering in silence, *Where is the glory in this?*

In silence, because he had come to depend upon Ptolemy and did not care to draw his scorn.

"There must be hostages, then?" he asked when the terms of their capitulation to Thebes were almost settled.

"Yes, My Lord." Ptolemy nodded gravely, for his own son was to be one of them. "That there must be both hostages and tribute money, this we knew from the beginning. The only question was how much would the Lord Pelopidas demand of each."

"But not Philip this time, eh? My conscience troubles me about Philip, and I would not have him go on his travels again once we get him back from the Illyrians."

"Nothing has been said of Philip. I think I can assure you that Philip will not be among those who take the road south."

There was a look in Ptolemy's eye as he said it—the look, almost, of a man who has taken his revenge. Yet how could that be? Alexandros might have forgotten it except . . .

As always when he was on campaign, the king took his dinner out of the same cooking pot and drank the same wine as the poorest man who carried a spear in his army. Around him might be the great nobles of his realm, but they too lived and ate as common soldiers. These days, perhaps, Alexandros drank a little more, and his companions were never far behind him, but by sunset they had had only enough to take some of the sting out of defeat and, perhaps, to make them a little incautious. There was no other way to explain what happened when Alexandros happened to raise his head and saw the shape of a horse and rider approaching.

I know that horse, he thought, and then, out loud, "I know that horse!"

He stood up. Yes, he was right.

"Little brother . . . by the bright gods, what are you doing here?"

But Philip just managed a glance and then looked past him. And that look might have gone straight through a man, like sunlight through water, burning itself into his soul.

"My Lord Ptolemy, see who's . . ."

Alexandros turned back just a little, but enough to see what his brother had seen—the Lord Ptolemy, his face stretched tight, his eyes glazed with something between fear and resentment, staring at Philip, as if he had just been shown the instrument of his own death.

11

Philip slept that night in his brother's tent, and when he awoke the next morning he put on a clean tunic and washed his face in water that still smelled of snow. He was to be presented that day to the great Pelopidas, an honor that was intended to console him for not being allowed to kill Lord Ptolemy.

Because Alexandros didn't believe him either—at least, he had said he didn't.

"You are afraid of him," Philip said at last, after their arguments had all been exhausted. "Why? He is only a man, after all. I never thought I would see you afraid of anyone."

"I am not afraid of him, and he is not a traitor. The Lord Ptolemy, who is, I might remind you, a kinsman, has served this family well since before either of us was born."

"Yes, he is a kinsman. He is married to our sister and was bedding with our mother even while our father was alive. I am overpowered by these proofs of his loyalty."

For a moment Alexandros said nothing—he was too angry. The subject of Ptolemy's relationship with the Lady Eurydike was not one he relished. Besides, he couldn't immediately think of an answer.

"You shouldn't have threatened him," he said at last.

"I shouldn't have had to!" Philip shouted, stamping his foot like an angry child. "He should already have been dead by then, and by your hand, not mine. Besides, it wasn't a threat when I said I wanted to see if it was blood or poison in his veins—a threat is something you don't mean to do, and I meant to kill him. You shouldn't have stopped me, brother. I can only hope Ptolemy allows you to live long enough to regret it."

A guard lifted the tent flap and peered in at them. It was impossible to say whether he was more alarmed or embarrassed.

"All is well, Kreon," Alexandros said quietly. "The Lord Philip is merely throwing a tantrum."

Philip shot the man a look that made him drop the tent flap as if it had suddenly caught fire.

"You should have let me kill him," he murmured through clenched teeth.

"You have changed, Philip." Alexandros looked at him speculatively, cocking his head a little to one side, precisely as if he were trying to judge the age of a horse. "We send you off to the barbarians for a winter, some common bandit tries to kill you—probably with no motive except to rob your purse—and you come back a different person."

"I have grown up, My Lord. I have put aside my innocence and joined the estate of men. I can recommend it to you."

For an instant Alexandros looked as if he couldn't decide whether to be offended or amused. Neither man moved. It could have come to anything. And then the king of Macedon threw back his head and began to laugh.

"Well said, little brother," he gasped when the fit had left him a little. He threw an arm over Philip's shoulder, giving the impression that the entire conversation had been forgotten. "I wonder if tomorrow you will have the cheek to be so forthright, when you meet the greatest soldier in the world . . ."

The Lord Ptolemy was one of those who witnessed Philip's presentation, which took place in the Theban camp, when the king and his honor guard arrived a few hours after dawn. As was his custom whenever the king of Macedon honored him with a visit, Pelopidas was waiting at the gate, quite alone, his hands clasped behind his back. He did not bow to Alexandros—no one would have expected such a show of respect from so great a man, whose absolute power was probably greater than any king's—but he did step forward and hold the bridle of Alexandros's horse while he dismounted. Then they embraced, like father and son, and Alexandros led him back through the ranks of his retainers to where Philip waited.

"It gives me pleasure to introduce to your notice the youngest of my father's sons," Alexandros said, throwing an arm across his shoulders. "My brother Philip, who has just returned from a sojourn among the Illyrians and, like the boy he still is, brings home many stories of his adventures."

Everyone laughed, everyone except Philip and Pelopidas. Philip could only blush hotly, but Pelopidas did not so much as smile.

"Whatever tales he tells, I would encourage you to listen with respect," Pelopidas said at last—he had the habit of dropping his voice in such a way as to enforce the strictest attention. "His eyes are full of cunning, yet they are the eyes not of a child but of a man. I do not think it would occur to him to brag."

His words produced a dangerous silence, for everyone there had been a witness to the scene of the night before, when Philip had accused the Lord Ptolemy to his face, calling him a traitor and actually drawing his sword. There would have been bloodshed had not the king grabbed his brother's arm and wrestled the sword away from him. Even at that moment, in the presence of so distinguished a foreigner, Philip's hard, pitiless eyes were fixed on Ptolemy, who felt a knot forming in his belly, as cold as iron.

No. They were not a child's eyes.

Pelopidas made a jest and everyone laughed, easing the tension—had he somehow guessed what was happening? Ptolemy could hardly hear the laughter, because inside his armor he was sweating with fear.

That boy knew, absolutely knew. He had come back from the very jaws of death, and he knew everything. He was more dangerous than a hundred Alexandroses. Everyone laughed at his suspicions, but in the end he would make himself believed and then it would be Ptolemy's turn to spill his life into the dust.

But when Alexandros was dead, Philip would be harmless.

During the course of the day, Ptolemy met with Pelopidas's lieutenants to settle the final details of the treaty between Macedon and Thebes. It was the work of the file, the smoothing out of the rough places that, in a year's time, one side or the other might find rubbing them raw. It was the sort of business with which Alexandros had no patience—which was one more reason he was a bad king.

In the evening there was a banquet. Pelopidas, as the host, sat at the head, with Alexandros at his right side. What was astonishing was that Philip sat at his left—and the Boeotarch of Thebes seemed to have full as much to say to the youngest brother as to the eldest.

Ptolemy was not close enough to hear their conversation, but he was well placed to watch and found a kind of morbid pleasure in comparing Pelopidas's modes of address as his attention moved from one to the other. With Alexandros he was all hearty cheer, full of jests and loud laughter; they spoke briefly, like men exchanging formal salutes, and then would each turn aside and seem to ignore one another. But with Philip the great general and statesman dropped his head and spoke in what looked like a familiar murmur, as if the two of them had been in each other's confidence for years. Their conversations went on sometimes for several minutes, and when Philip spoke—and he did speak, occasionally at length—the Boeotarch favored him with his complete attention, forgetting sometimes even to smile. It appeared to be a dialogue of equals.

And finally, after witnessing this for perhaps an hour, it occurred to Ptolemy, with something like genuine surprise, that he was jealous. Alexandros, predictably, was both too vain and too stupid even to notice, but Ptolemy did—and felt it as an almost physical anguish. He envied Philip the interest and respect of so great a man, for certainly Pelopidas had never taken him as seriously. And with envy was mixed fear—the fear that shadowed his every thought of Philip—for he was forced to wonder what quality there might be in this mere boy that could be so lacking in himself.

But whatever it was it would be swept into oblivion, almost as soon as they returned to Pella. Philip without his brother was merely a clever youth who could safely be ignored and, when once the sons of Amyntas were all together again at home, Ptolemy had something in the nature of a surprise prepared for Alexandros.

At last Philip gave up. He could not persuade his brother that the Lord Ptolemy was a dangerous traitor who should be destroyed the way one destroys a viper. He did not doubt his own conclusions, but the weight of Alexandros's disbelief, plus the prestige Ptolemy seemed to enjoy as a result of his negotiations with the Boeotarch, finally persuaded him to silence. He did not enjoy being made to feel like a fool.

Very well, he thought. *If Alexandros puts no value on his own safety I cannot force him into prudence. The king must choose for himself whom he believes.*

And thus, when the treaty with the Thebans was concluded and the king's nobles, celebrating defeat as if it were victory, had drained the last cup of wine with their conquerors, Alexandros, his brother, his trusted friend and cousin Ptolemy, and the whole host of the Macedonian army took the road back to Pella, precisely as if nothing had happened.

Five days later they reached the city gates, and everyone was still alive. Thus did Philip, in a disgust that was almost indistinguishable from shame, return to the private pursuits of his life.

But he was not alone. There was general relief that a war with Thebes had been averted, and a city is never so frivolous as when it is full of humiliated soldiers. There was much drunkenness when the army returned, and the whores earned a good living. And the revels of Alexandros and his nobles had never been merrier.

Philip, still smoldering with anger, at first concentrated on hunting. All alone he rode far across the plains, sometimes not returning for two or three days at a time, and conducted a great slaughter of deer and wild pigs.

Once, he killed a boar almost as big as the one in Lynkos. He burned the fat and the skin as a sacrifice to appease the envy of the gods, roasted a shoulder for his dinner, and left the rest to the crows. He did not bring the head back with him to Pella, although such a kill would have earned him a place at table among the King's companions. He did not mention the incident to anyone. He had not yet finished sulking.

When at last he abandoned the field it was not to be reconciled with his brother but because his cousin the Lady Arsinoe had once more entered his life.

And he had seen her, as before, outside the temple of Athena.

Though her shrine was obscure, the gray-eyed Athena was almost never without an offering of wheat cake and honey, and this because Philip, believing that he lived his life cradled in the goddess's hand, wished to show his gratitude. Almost every morning he went to the temple district to make sacrifice and to pray. It was only there, in the whole city of Pella, that he felt at peace, as if his life was lived to some purpose. It was only within the narrow walls of this smallest of shrines that he could believe existence was not what it appeared to be, some vast, pointless jest. He always came away restored in spirit.

Nor is it always chance when two young people meet where they have met before. A place that has been lucky once may be lucky again—this every hunter knows, and every lover. And who can say what promptings of her heart had brought Arsinoe here to make sacrifice to the lords of life, whether of piety or of something else?

The rest was easy. A nod, a smile, a word—a promise to meet again. Love grows quickly in the heated breast of youth. Soon Philip could hardly think of anything else. With men his words came readily enough, but in her presence he was almost mute. He had only to look at her to make his heart pound and his throat close off with a longing that was more like pain than pleasure.

"Could you . . . ?" he would begin. "Could I see you . . . ?"

"You see me now," she would answer, smiling in a way that both seemed to mock him and to thrill his soul.

"I cannot speak here. I would feed my eyes on you—I would . . ."

"Then perhaps it is best if we do not meet, if you really mean to devour me."

Yet she understood, and the hunger in her woman's heart was as great as his own.

"Perhaps someday," she would say. "But not now—not yet."

And she would smile again, turning his bowels to water.

He had seen her five, perhaps six times since they were both children, playing in the dust, fighting over a painted wooden ball. Where, then, had been her flashing eyes and her hair the color of fallen leaves? Perhaps he simply had not noticed. Now she consumed him. His mind was numb and he could not sleep. Love is a thing the gods send when they wish to torment us.

Or, just perhaps, to preserve our souls, against the times when all else lies broken in the dust.

·   ·   ·

Even since his return to Pella, Ptolemy had been driven to the point of near exhaustion by the demands of two greedy lovers. Each night the Lady Eurydike required him in her bed, and the hunger of her lust seemed never to be satisfied—seemed, in fact, to feed upon itself. In the blackest part of the night they would lie there, clinging to one another, slippery with warm sweat and panting for breath. She seemed intent on burning herself to ashes with the heat of her own desire.

And then there was Praxis, with his blond, curling hair and his doglike loyalty, who would wait doglike outside the door to Ptolemy's apartments, cringing in the shadows, sometimes until dawn. For the most part he would be content with a good thrashing, but from time to time his demands for love became more urgent.

During the day, Ptolemy would sit in council with the king, hardly able to sit at all for the throbbing pain in his groin. He had tried cold water, lemon juice, heated mud, everything. His member felt tender and bruised, and each night he had no idea how he would ever manage to fill a man's part, but somehow he did.

The king's mother and the groveling pederast. Soon they would each have their part to play in the little drama he was planning to stage: *The Death of Alexandros*—Eurypides could hardly have done better. And it would have to be very soon, or he himself would perish from weariness—either that or become impotent—before he ever had a chance to listen to the audience's applause.

His wife, he knew, cried herself to sleep at night, wondering how she had so sinned against the bright gods that they punished her with her husband's indifference. Well, let her weep. She would weep the harder when her brother was dead. And harder still afterward, when she realized how completely she had outlived her usefulness.

And at last the time had come to carry his plan beyond the bedroom, and to make Praxis ready, for the first and the last time in this life, to do his duty as a man.

"Do you understand what is required?"

"Yes," Praxis answered, touching his lover's hand as it held the sword. "I understand."

"One quick thrust—up under the ribs and to the heart. He will not be armed. He will not be expecting this. And you will kill him before he has a chance to react."

"Yes."

"You have practiced? You are ready?"

"Yes."

Ptolemy smiled, putting the sword into Praxis's hand and touching his hair. They were alone together in one of the sweating rooms in the garrison of the king's own guard, of which they were both members. Two men, naked and alone, two shadowy presences in a cloud of steam dense enough to muffle their voices.

"You hate Alexandros, don't you—yes, I know you do."

He let his fingers slide down the boy's smooth neck, thinking that no one would imagine this puppy capable of murder. Yet Praxis was as vicious as a bitch in heat, and as dangerous. And he was besotted, with love and with malice, which was nothing more than love gone putrid.

"Well, you will have your revenge. And when you have had it, I will protect you. I will have all the king's power when he is dead, and I will use it to shield you. I will raise you above all other men."

Ptolemy had only to glance down to see how the thought excited Praxis. He took the boy in his arms, stroking his back and shoulders.

"No one will ever dare to scorn you again," he whispered. "You will be feared and envied. You will be the man who killed the king."

Praxis kissed him with all the urgency of submissive lust, and the Lord Ptolemy let him, kissing him back. *Why should not this fool have his little moment of joy?* he thought.

This licking dog imagines he loves me, he thought. *Yet he is not mine. His heart is all Alexandros's, if he but knew it. And tomorrow I shall be rid of them both.*

12

Alexandros had declared that he would hold games to celebrate the treaty with Thebes, which he was rapidly convincing himself constituted some sort of personal triumph. Macedon would be great again because she now enjoyed the friendship of the Boeotian Confederacy and of its great leader, Pelopidas. Any mention of hostages was tactfully avoided.

The king still persisted in regarding his youngest brother as a child and did not allow him to compete, not even in the horse races, which, as everyone knew, he could easily have won. Perdikkas, on the other hand, was now almost a man and had besides been accepted as the heir. He was not given any choice—he finished last in the javelin throw and, later, was thrown by his horse in the second race and badly bruised. He went home to sweat out his humiliation in the baths, complaining that Alexandros showed him less respect than he did even Philip.

Ptolemy's son, the child of his first wife, competed for the first time and placed fourth in the javelin, which was his father's weapon. Everyone said he did very well, but Ptolemy was someone whose vanity everyone was eager to flatter.

Hardly anyone even noticed Praxis, although afterward it was mentioned that he had carried a sword all that day but had not competed with it in any event.

Alexandros was particularly splendid. He won both the footrace and the horse race—some said this was why he had excluded Philip, that he feared to come second behind his youngest brother—and he took third place in the wrestling. Someone later said that he had declared it the best day of his life.

On this occasion the king held to the old custom and allowed no women or foreigners among the spectators. In theory the games were open to any free man of Macedonian birth, but in fact no one competed except members of the court. Everyone felt himself among friends, and there was much drinking. Even the grooms were drunk. In the middle of the day, one of them fell from a horse he was taking back to the royal stables to be rubbed down and fed. He simply dropped to the ground and was dead, as if the shock had stopped his heart. But even in the presence of so bad an omen, the games went on.

If Philip could not compete, he could at least watch. He did not allow himself to be offended by Alexandros's decision, even though he knew it was unjust, but enjoyed himself immensely, cheering on his brothers and friends and growing as drunk as everyone else.

Perdikkas came back in time for supper, which was to be eaten out of doors, just as if they were on campaign. His knee was purplish black and he walked with a stick, as indeed he was probably in as much pain as he pretended. During the meal he sat beside Philip, who treated him with consideration and made sure he had plenty of wine to take the edge off his suffering.

"Games like these are a brutish relic," Perdikkas said when he was drunk enough. "That grown men should disport themselves like children . . ."

"Games keep the martial spirit alive—besides, brother, you only dislike them because you are not good at them. But I agree with you that *these* games are childish."

Philip had hardly touched his wine, but lately he felt no inclination to speak anything but the truth. It was, he had decided, one of the compensations for being the youngest of three brothers and thus so far removed from the succession.

"Why? Because Alexandros and his friends behave like green boys?"

But Philip, after appearing to consider the point for a moment, shook his head.

"No. They are childish because they celebrate a defeat by pretending it is a victory."

"Then you think the alliance with Thebes a bad thing?"

"No, because it is a necessary thing—and, in any case, it is hardly an alliance at all, but rather a capitulation. What I regret is the conduct of policy that made it necessary. In that the Lord Ptolemy is quite right. Alexandros did blunder in overextending himself in Thessaly."

"But Ptolemy never said . . ."

Philip only smiled, but his smile mirrored such withering contempt that Perdikkas did not dare even to finish his sentence.

"Perdikkas, since it seems possible you may be king one day, you would do well to listen more to what men do not say."

When he realized that he was merely tormenting his brother, Philip turned his head away and started pushing bits of meat around his plate with a torn piece of bread, although at that moment the sight of food disgusted him.

"I believe I shall grow very drunk tonight," he said. "I believe I shall drown myself in this Lemnian red until my piss is that precise same color, and then I shall puke violently all over one of Alexandros's favorites and be carried off to bed to snore until tomorrow nightfall. That would be, I fancy, the proper way for a loyal Macedonian to celebrate this most recent of our king's glorious triumphs."

"Shut up, Philip—it is dangerous to talk thus."

"Dangerous? Nonsense!" Philip threw his hand across his elder brother's neck and shook him good-naturedly. "What danger could anyone imagine there is in a loyal drunkard? Only look around you, Perdikkas."

With a gesture of his free hand he seemed to take in the whole of Alexandros's outdoor banquet, a jumble of tables and benches covering an area of perhaps fifteen paces square, illuminated now by a paling of torches set up on iron staffs. Indeed, the King's companions were making so much noise that his two younger brothers could have been shouting treason and no one would have noticed. Men who the month before had been commanding an army in Thessaly were now hurling wine cups and pieces of mutton at each other.

"I look forward to many such occasions in the new reign. I expect to grow into quite an accomplished table soldier, the very archetype of the modern courtier. That you even think there is anything of danger in such an innocent ambition is proof that you have not drunk enough wine."

Philip's gaze settled on the Lord Ptolemy, who was seated only a few tables distant from the king, and his eyes narrowed.

"Now there is danger, if you have but eyes to see it," he said, pulling Perdikkas toward him to murmur the warning into his ear. "Look at him, brother. I have been watching him this half hour, and he has yet to refill his wine cup. A man who stays sober in such a gathering as this is a man to be feared—the Lord Ptolemy is so drunk with ambition that he dares not relax. He is like a serpent, coiled to strike."

And indeed, Ptolemy's javelin was within easy reach, sticking point first into the ground beside him. At the sight of it Philip felt a twinge of something almost like an intuition, but, as always after a day of games, there were many weapons strewn carelessly about. So Philip dismissed his little flutter of dread, half-ashamed of it.

"I see that you are drunk enough," Perdikkas sneered.

"No, brother—were I drunk enough I might think our cousin Ptolemy the best man in the world. It is only when my head is clear that I mistrust him."

But Perdikkas appeared not to have heard, for he laughed suddenly and his eyes were on the king's table, where Aristomachos, the king's current favorite, had risen to entertain the company with an obscene song about a donkey and a tavern master's daughter. The comic effect was heightened by the fact that Aristomachos was so deep in wine that he tended to forget the crucial verses and would then grow red-faced and angry when his audience shouted them up to him. Finally he became so enraged that he let go of the edge of the table, to which he had been clinging for balance, and his legs promptly buckled underneath him. He never did finish the song, but no one cared because everyone knew it already—people went on singing snatches of it all during the banquet.

Kreon of Europos then climbed up on the shoulders of Parmenos, son of Archos of Tyrissa, and defied all comers. Several men took up the challenge and soon they were all pelting each other with pieces of bread dipped in wine. The conflict soon became general and, since each hit left a red stain on the face or breast, soon everyone looked as if he were bleeding from a dozen mortal wounds. Peace was only restored when the combatants ran out of bread, because by the time the grooms brought a fresh supply everyone had grown bored with the fight.

Philip, who had taken no part in these entertainments, had fallen peacefully asleep, his arms cradling his head as they rested on the table. He did not wake up again until the banquet was over and his bench was snatched from beneath him to be added to the bonfire with which the king's outdoor revels always came to an end. His head was sore and his tongue tasted like something that had crawled into his mouth to die as he watched the fire slowly lapping over the pile of rough wooden furniture.

And as soon as the flames had reached as high as a man's head, the war dance began.

The war dance was performed not to mark some great triumph of Macedonian arms but as a celebration of war itself. It was an act of worship, a ritual submission to the gods' love of courage and cruelty. And only those who had fought beside their king, and thus had shed their own mortal terror, could participate. So Philip, once more, found his place among the onlookers.

By tradition it was a wild, ecstatic ceremony, performed to the frantic music of drums and cymbals and to shrieks that seemed to tear the night air like a knife cutting through linen. If men were drunk enough, they sometimes jumped through the flames, coming out of the other side—if, indeed, they did come out, and sometimes they did not—smoke blackened and with their hair burning.

And it always began with the king's slow circling around the fire, his arms extended and his head thrown back as he searched for the delirious oblivion that kills the fear of death.

Alexandros, his naked body oiled and shining, his long honey-colored hair swinging around and then, for an instant, trembling in the air like a golden flame, Alexandros, lord of Macedon, was glorious in his godlike beauty as he danced alone to the ominous, throbbing music. He was like a being transported, breaking free from his mortal existence . . .

The bonfire threw ghastly shadows over the faces of men as, slowly, they began to join their king in his delirious, trancelike ecstasy.

Sitting on the ground beside his brother Perdikkas, the two of them clapping their hands in time to the mad rhythm of the dancers, who howled and shouted, throwing themselves about in their frenzied joy, Philip had forgotten all his dark imaginings. He was happy and at peace with himself, lost to everything except the moment. He hardly knew anything was wrong until he heard the drumbeat stop.

But the silence was like cold water, dashing him awake. All at once there was Alexandros lying on the ground, his hand to his side and dark blood running out between his fingers. Standing over him was Praxis, holding a gory sword, glancing triumphantly about at the faces of men too stunned to move.

At last, perhaps to dispel their uncomprehending horror, he raised the sword above his head.

"Death to the tyrant!" he shouted, making as if to strike again. "Glory to—"

Philip, suddenly mad with rage, bounded to his feet. He would kill the traitor, with his bare hands if need be. Yet he had hardly taken a step before Praxis's voice was cut off—drowned in the sound of a mortal groan as a javelin shattered his chest. He was dead even before his knees struck the bare earth.

Praxis was dead. He no longer mattered. Alexandros was dying, even as Philip knelt to cradle the king's head in his arms.

"I'm cold," he whispered through parched lips. "I'm cold, Philip."

Philip drew his cloak around his brother's shoulders.

"Is this what death is like? Is this . . . ?"

Suddenly his eyes rolled back in his head and he was gone.

For a moment Philip thought his heart had turned to ice—he seemed to feel nothing. And then, as he lifted his hand away from Alexandros's corpse and saw that his fingers were coated with blood, in that moment all the grief of this dark world seemed to concentrate within his breast and a cry of fierce, animal pain broke from his lips.

He staggered to his feet and looked around him. Not a step away, Praxis lay on his side, his hands still clenched around the javelin that had torn his life away. Philip reached down and picked up his sword, still wet with the king's blood.

"Who killed him?" he asked. Tears were streaming from his eyes. And then, when no one answered, Philip shouted out the words like a challenge. "*Who killed him?*"

"I killed him."

From the knot of onlookers, the Lord Ptolemy stepped forward. His eyes narrowed when he saw the expression on Philip's face.

"He seemed ready to strike again. I thought . . . Is the king dead, then?"

"Yes," Philip answered, weighing Praxis's sword in his hand. He discovered he had to fight against the temptation to step forward and run the man through. Was it only because the Lord Ptolemy happened to be standing closest? "They are both dead. They are both far out of reach."

13

The king's ashes were still warm in his funeral urn when the Macedonians met in solemn assembly and elected a successor. There was only one candidate, but it was deemed proper, in view of Perdikkas's youth and inexperience, to appoint a regent. Again, there was only one candidate. For at least the next few years, the substance of power would rest with the Lord Ptolemy.

After the assembly it was discovered that Arrhidaios and his brothers, King Amyntas's sons by his first wife, had disappeared from the city. They were doubtless wise to do so, because Ptolemy almost certainly would have regarded them as potential rivals and found some pretext for executing them, but their flight occasioned speculation that they might somehow have been involved in the king's murder.

No one raised the possibility that treason extended any further. Praxis was dead and his corpse had been publicly crucified and then left to the crows. Everyone knew he had nursed a sense of injury ever since Alexandros had thrown him off—and that seemed to end the matter.

Certainly no suspicion fell on the Lord Ptolemy. Had he not, in a vain attempt to save the king's life, by his own hand killed the traitor? Had not the Macedonian Assembly named him regent to the new king, and was he not now as great as if he wore the crown himself? Even after Ptolemy divorced his wife and married her mother, the Lord Amyntas's widow, no one thought to accuse him.

No one, except Philip.

Had he known, even in that first moment? It was impossible to determine the steps by which suspicion had hardened into belief and then into certainty. Still, he knew.

"The Lord Ptolemy displayed admirable presence of mind," he told his brother Perdikkas. "He had his weapon ready at hand and struck down the traitor so quickly one might almost imagine he had been expecting . . . I wonder who or what Praxis was about to hail when death overtook him."

Perdikkas, who had never loved Alexandros very much, and for whom the novelty of kingship was still fresh, did not relish this line of inquiry. He could not quite make out its direction, but he suspected enough to be uneasy.

"Praxis was a jealous lover. Thwarted passion can drive even women to murder." He looked at Philip and smiled sourly, as if he had settled everything.

"But he called Alexandros a tyrant, do you remember? He shouted, 'Death to the tyrant!' as if he were avenging some general grievance. Do you think he expected to die? I don't—I think he expected to be congratulated."

"Everyone knows that love addles the brains."

"Perhaps." Philip pursed his lips, appearing to consider the possibility. "But Praxis was notoriously stupid. The idea of calling our brother a tyrant did not find its way into his head by itself."

Perdikkas glanced nervously about. They were sitting together in the king's room warming their hands over a charcoal grate, for the nights had turned cool since Alexandros's death. They were alone—that the two royal brothers should be thus alone was perhaps a measure of how completely the Lord Ptolemy had made himself master of the state—yet Perdikkas could not control the shudder of anxiety that passed through him. He was the king, and still he was afraid.

"Your suggestion is almost treasonous, Philip."

"How is it treasonous? I am speaking to the king my brother about how the king our brother was murdered."

"But Ptolemy is the regent."

"Then, since you name him, it appears that you have followed my train of thought to the same conclusion. It was Ptolemy's will that guided the assassin's hand. And now, as you so correctly point out, he is the regent and holds power in your name."

Philip allowed himself a cruel smile.

"It is Ptolemy, and not Praxis, whose corpse should be crucified over the king's funeral mound. Come, Perdikkas—you are sometimes a wretched coward, but you have never been a fool. You know that I am right."

Yes, Perdikkas knew. Yet at the same time Philip understood that he would never own that he knew, perhaps not even to himself. He was too frightened for that.

"Ptolemy loved Alexandros. Ptolemy is loyal. Ptolemy would never have—"

"Yes, oh, yes, he would." Philip put his hand on his brother's knee. It was a gesture at once of affection and of pity. "He has. The Lord Ptolemy has found it within himself to murder a king. And if you do not pull yourself straight and act the man, he may imagine he is at liberty to murder another."

. . .

Perdikkas no longer knew what to make of Philip. Philip had changed, almost out of recognition. A few months in the mountains with the Illyrian barbarians and he had come back a different person. One could see it in his eyes.

When they were boys growing up together, Perdikkas had always felt himself the superior. He was the elder by a year, so why should his little brother not defer to him? And Philip, who was so strong-willed in everything else, had accepted his place as the last and least of the king's sons.

Yet after his return, even while Alexandros was alive, it was almost as if Philip had outgrown them. It was almost possible to envy him, for when he spoke it was with the self-command of a man—a man conscious of his powers, a man seasoned by the lifetime of experience that Philip had somehow compressed into the short span he had been away from them. A man one ignored at one's peril.

He was not the same.

At first, Perdikkas had been prone to take offense—was not Philip still a boy, his little brother? Now, however, with Alexandros dead, it was strangely comforting to listen to the measured authority of his voice. Even when the words themselves filled him with terror.

The Lord Ptolemy has found it within himself to murder a king. It was impossible to believe such a thing. And yet, when Philip looked straight into one's face and spoke the words, it was impossible not to believe. Thus, the season of Perdikkas's fear found its beginnings in that conversation with his brother.

And, as always when his soul was overburdened, he turned for comfort to his mother.

But Eurydike too had changed. The death of her eldest son had cast its shadow over her, and at the same time her marriage to the Lord Ptolemy had infused her with a desperate energy. She seemed less happy in that marriage than determined to be happy, and her nervous vivacity of mind was tainted with something almost like madness.

"This is what it is like," Perdikkas might have whispered to himself, "when the gods have sent us love as the chosen instrument of our destruction."

So as she listened to her son, Eurydike's long, agile fingers played with the beads of the gold necklace Ptolemy had given her as a wedding present. She did not even seem surprised to learn that Philip had accused her new husband of treason and murder. It was not even possible to tell if she did not half believe it. She merely listened, her face as expressionless as a death mask, with only the nervous movements of her fingers hinting at an inner tension.

"Philip had best be more careful," she said when the recital was over. "He should remember that, although a prince of the royal house and your heir, he is still no more than a subject."

"He says that he is *my* subject, Mother—not Ptolemy's." Perdikkas glanced down at his lap, as if his brother's fealty was a burden he was not sure he had the strength to bear. "He says that I have but to speak the word and he will kill Ptolemy. He says I have but to declare myself of age and he will end the regency with Ptolemy's life. He will challenge Ptolemy in the assembly and kill him there, for all to see. I believe he would do it."

"Yes, of course he would do it. Or at least he would try. Philip, whatever his other failings, was never lacking in stomach."

Eurydike actually smiled, as if the idea amused her, and for once her hands grew still.

"But he must be prevented from doing it because the Lord Ptolemy is your loyal servant, as he was your brother's."

His mother had a way of quietly gazing into his eyes the power of which Perdikkas had never found a way to combat. She seemed to hold his will prisoner when she looked at him thus, because it was impossible to quell within himself a surge of cringing love for her, or to quite believe that he could ever love her enough. She was his adored mother, and he was a scoundrel if he did not believe everything she told him. Ptolemy was his friend—had always been his friend. His mother loved Ptolemy, and therefore Perdikkas must love him. Ptolemy was a good man, and Philip's mind was maggoty with baseless suspicion. For that moment, at least, he believed it, even while his reason rebelled against the idea. And afterward, of course, he would be trapped.

"Yes, of course he is loyal, but—"

"And Philip is a fool to imagine anything else," Eurydike interrupted, still holding him with her gaze. "We can only believe that his mind had grown clouded with grief. We have all been made to suffer through Alexandros's sudden death. I, his mother . . ."

At last she turned her head away as she appeared to suppress a pang of sorrow.

"Yes, Mother."

When she looked at him again her eyes were shiny with unspent tears and her smiling lips trembled. Perdikkas felt his face burning with shame that he had even uttered Philip's name.

She put her hand over his.

"We will not speak of this again," she said.

Still, Eurydike was not so blinded by her passion for the Lord Ptolemy that she did not understand his nature. She had only to look to her own domestic arrangements to see the treachery of which he was capable.

In order to marry her he had first to divorce his wife, her own daughter, and a woman who has been cast off by her husband has nowhere to go except back to her family. Yet, since her brothers were not of an age to have their own establishments, she could only return to her mother, who was now Ptolemy's wife. Thus she remained part of her former husband's household.

And he continued to visit her bed, possibly more now than when she had been his wife. He made use of her as casually as he might have one of the servant women—not because he especially wanted her but simply because he knew it would be tolerated by both women in humiliated silence. It seemed to amuse him that, whereas before he had betrayed the daughter with the mother, now it was the other way about.

Eurydike had never been close to her daughter, who bore her name but had always been called "Meda" within the family. And they had not lived together since she was fourteen and King Amyntas had first given her to Ptolemy as a wife. Eurydike had always thought of Meda as a rather lifeless creature, so it surprised her, when they were once more under the same roof, to discover the intensity of the child's anguish.

It was from Meda's own lips that she first heard that Ptolemy had begun returning to her bed. And the words were spoken not in triumph, as one might have expected, or even rage, but with a remorse that took all the guilt for the deed upon herself. Meda was appealing for her mother's forgiveness, begging her to understand that the touch of this man's hand deprived her of will and reason. He did not force himself upon her because he did not need force—she was powerless to resist him.

And Eurydike had understood. She knew how it was possible to know the evil in a man, even to hate him for it, and yet to be the willing slave of his desire. She knew Ptolemy's power over the flesh. She and her daughter had sat together in a corner of her room, their arms around each other's shoulders, sobbing with grief. And their tears were for each other, for they knew that they were both tangled hopelessly in the web the gods had woven for them.

So why should Eurydike not believe that Ptolemy was behind her son's murder—except that to believe it would have been to run mad? Ptolemy was capable of anything, this she knew. Would it make any difference if he had killed Alexandros? Would she have been able to tear herself away from him? Perhaps, but only long enough to drive the sword into her own bosom. To believe such a thing was to die, and therefore she could not bring herself to believe it.

Yet the voice within her, whispering that it all might be true, could not be stilled.

Thus there was a sense in which she almost welcomed Philip's accusation, if only because, in the silence that enclosed so much of her life, it gave her suspicions words that, after all, were not her own.

"My son Philip believes that Praxis did not act alone," she said, murmuring into the darkness of their bedroom even as Ptolemy's hand slid over her breast.

"Did he tell you this?"

She could already feel his breath on her neck, and her heart began to beat wildly, like an animal throwing itself against the bars of its cage.

"Does it matter who told me?" She ran her hand over his chest until her fingers rested against the jagged scar just below his rib cage where, as a youth, he had taken an arrow in battle against the Illyrians. "He believes it—that is enough."

"Has he named an accomplice?" His beard just grazed her chin. As always, the stiff hairs seemed to cut at her like pieces of broken flint, and she grew almost faint with longing.

"Yes. He says it was you."

She crushed her mouth hungrily against the yielding softness of his lips, as if she would devour him. She felt starved for him, as if the appetite fed upon itself. With a leg thrown across his hips, she pressed herself against him, feeling every contour of his naked body on her own.

"You will not touch my son," she whispered, making it sound like a curse. "You will put this limit at least upon your ambition, that you will not raise your hand against my son."

"Why? Do you love him so much?"

"You will not touch my son."

"Why?"

"He is my son. That is enough."

When it was over, and they lay in each other's arms, bathed in sweat, Ptolemy turned his head to look up at the ceiling, shrouded in darkness.

"No one will credit such an accusation," he said at last. It seemed as close to a denial as he could bring himself.

"At least, no one will say they credit it."

He did not so much as glance at her, but his face seemed to harden, as if stung by a rebuke. Then he sat up at the edge of the bed and poured himself a cup of wine. He did not speak again until he had drunk nearly half of it.

"I am the regent," he said. His back was to her, so she could only judge by his voice. He seemed almost to be boasting. "I cannot have it whispered about that I have been involved in treason."

"Then you have nothing to fear, since Philip, when he makes an accusation, is not the type to whisper it."

"Do you mock me, woman?"

"No." Eurydike drew the blanket up over her breasts, for suddenly she was cold. "No, I do not mock you. I am only surprised."

"Surprised at what?"

"That the whole world should be so afraid of you, and you so afraid of Philip."

"You have always warned me against him."

"Yes." She nodded, although she knew he would not see the gesture. "You are right to be afraid."

Ptolemy did not reply, but finished his wine and then set the cup down by his foot. He seemed to be debating with himself whether he should rise from the bed.

At last he lay down again, but he held his arms close against his body and made no move to touch his wife.

"Philip must be sent away," he said, making it sound as if the idea had just come into his head.

"You would send him into exile?"

"No, not exile. He will join the hostages in Thebes, where he will be safe and out of the way. The change will help to rid him of these grotesque fancies. Philip will like Thebes. My own son is there."

"I do not think he will like it any better for that."

But Ptolemy had already closed his eyes. It was as if he had not even heard.

What thoughts visited Ptolemy in the long night? Was he haunted by the ghost of the king he had murdered, or was he beyond remorse? Philip tried to imagine what that could be like, but found he could not.

He could only mourn. Alexandros's bones had already made their journey to the royal tombs at Aigai. The earth was piled high over his burial chamber— he was as remote as the deathless gods. So Philip was left to console himself by pouring libations over the grave of his foster mother in hopes of quieting her restless spirit, and his own.

There was nothing he could do. He would gladly have killed Ptolemy, even at the cost of his own life—then the royal house of the Argeadai would at least be free of this mad fire of ambition which was burning in its vitals. Then Perdikkas might perhaps have some chance to grow into his kingship. Now Perdikkas was imprisoned by fear, and fear would die with Ptolemy, but fear was what kept him from sanctioning his own release. Philip could not bring himself to strike against the king's will, for he would not make himself a traitor. Perdikkas might be weak, but he was still the king, and his commands must mean something.

There seemed no way out.

He wished now that he could lay his head on Alcmene's lap, just as he had done when he was a child and had hurt himself in some rough boy's game. His soul felt bruised, as if the slightest touch would make it bleed. And now there was no tenderness left in the world.

"Do you come here often?"

He glanced up and was astonished to discover Arsinoe standing just a few paces from him. Before he could think of what to say she closed the distance and knelt beside him so that her trailing hair just brushed his shoulder.

"My father is buried not far from here," she said. "I saw you, and . . ."

"Has he been dead long?"

"My father? Yes, for over a year now."

"Do you still feel the pain of it?"

Instead of answering, Arsinoe placed her hand on his arm, just above the elbow.

"And who lies here?" she asked.

"My mo— The woman who raised me. Her name was Alcmene. She died while I was with the Illyrians."

Even while he spoke, it was with the greatest difficulty that Philip was able to maintain his composure. He loved Arsinoe—at least, he assumed that this strange feeling that tormented him whenever he saw her must be love. Yet now he only wished she would go away, because her presence only made everything else harder to bear. Yet at the same time he felt he would die if she left him, simply break in half like a stone split by the ice that had found its way into some tiny flaw. He felt the strongest temptation to throw himself into her arms and weep like a child, like Alcmene's child, and she would despise him for that. He would despise himself.

So he did nothing. He merely waited, unable even to look at her, until she decided his fate.

"Do you want to be with me?" she asked finally.

At first he did not understand what she meant. Was she asking him if he wished her to stay? How could he answer her when he did not know himself? Then he felt her hand as it slipped inside the neck of his tunic.

"Do you want to be with me?"

She kissed him on the lips, and he felt such a turmoil of pleasure that he could hardly breathe.

"You need not be alone, Philip, for I love you."

It was past twilight now, and the burial grounds were empty. They were quite alone in the covering darkness, safe from all eyes, but this hardly mattered to them. In that moment, only they two lived and had being. The world beyond their two bodies was not even a shadow.

She took his hands in hers and guided them to her breasts. Then, sliding her arms around his neck, she drew him to her.

As they made love in the cool grass her soul seemed to pour into him, like wine into water, so that he became someone else, a stranger to himself, lightened of all his burdens, his heart alive again within his breast, godlike, blessed with a happiness that would never die.

"I love you," he whispered, the words almost speaking themselves. "I want only to be like this forever. I will never leave you."

14

It was shortly after midday when Philip first beheld Thebes. It was still more than an hour's ride distant, so he could see little beyond the city walls, which caught the sun so that they gleamed like polished marble.

He and his escort had left the seaport town of Rhamnous at first light, after two days aboard a heaving ship. There had been no leave-taking at Pella—in what seemed like the middle of the night he was roused from his bed by a palace messenger and taken straight into Ptolemy's presence.

"Your travels begin again," the regent told him. "A ship bound for Boeotia will leave at dawn, and you will be on it. You will enjoy Thebes, Philip. The weather is pleasant, and a young man who wants to be a soldier can learn much there. It will do you good."

Philip thought of Arsinoe, the taste of whose kisses were still on his lips, and he felt as if a sliver of ice were being pushed through his heart.

"I do not wish to leave Pella. I am tired of being sent around like a diplomatic satchel. Send someone else."

"There is no one else. The Thebans are not interested in entertaining kitchen slaves."

"You have no right to do this, My Lord. In this matter I will appeal to the king."

"I speak in the king's name, Philip. The king will not see you—the king will still be asleep in his bed when you are out of sight of land."

He had only to look at the way the regent smiled at him to know that it was so, that he was not being given a choice.

"Then give me an hour or two to make my farewells."

"There is no time, Philip."

The two men regarded each other for a moment. There were no secrets between them. Without a word spoken, they understood each other perfectly.

Philip turned on his heel and left the room.

Guards met him outside the door and took him straight back to Glaukon's house, where he had less than a quarter of an hour to prepare for the journey. The king's steward, who knew better than to ask questions that could not be answered, watched in silence as Philip filled a wicker basket with a few clothes.

"If anyone should come asking for me, say I would have stayed if I could."

"Who might come, My Prince?"

Philip looked only at his hands as they folded the winter tunic Alcmene had made for him before he went among the Illyrians. And now, once more, he was bound for the polite captivity of a diplomatic hostage. At the end of this journey would he find yet another assassin?

"No one, Glaukon," he answered, shaking his head. He might love the slender, sweet-armed girl who had given herself to him in that field of sorrow. It was even possible she might love him in return, yet he had no right to involve anyone in his fate. "No one at all."

No one at all. The words echoed in his mind as he looked down from the mouth of the pass onto the wide plains of Boeotia. Even in the mountains the heat had been ferocious, and the grasslands that stretched before him were burned brown by the sun. This was a hostile place, and he felt himself alone in it.

The men around him were the lightly armed cavalry soldiers of the Theban army. They had been waiting on the wharf at Rhamnous and conducted themselves toward him as if they were a guard of honor rather than a prisoner's escort. Yet they were distant in their bearing, whether as a mark of respect or for some other reason he had no way of knowing. He had found himself eating his noon meal with only the officer for company, while the men, sitting a little way off, huddled round their lunch bags ignoring them. It had struck him as odd behavior in the soldiers of a democracy—in Macedonia the king himself was not so grand that he disdained the common cooking pot and the companionship of even his humblest subjects.

He kept thinking of Arsinoe. What must she think of him? She probably imagined that he had known he was about to be sent away and had taken her quite casually, to sneak off without a word or gesture. She probably hated him now.

And there, across the plain, glistening in the sun, was Thebes—his place of exile. The sight of it hurt his eyes.

"She is beautiful, is she not, Prince?" said the officer in charge of Philip's escort, a man named Ganelon, who, although barely twenty, had already served in four campaigns and had been to Macedon with Pelopidas. "She is the queen of cities, as cultured as Athens and as warlike as Sparta. You will find much to admire within those walls."

"I would have preferred to continue admiring her from a distance," Philip answered. This reply Ganelon affected to find vastly amusing, and his laughter covered what might otherwise have become an embarrassing silence.

In the mountains there had been a breath of wind to vitiate the heat, but as soon as the road they had been following dropped into the central plains the air itself seemed baked and exhausted. Harvest time was over, and the fields they passed were cut to stubble so that the bare earth showed through. Philip noticed, however, that the bottoms of the irrigation ditches were still black with mud, so water must have been plentiful. The farmhouses they passed appeared well kept, surrounded by vines and olive trees, and the animals that grazed here and there for whatever the scythe had left behind were fat and sleek. Obviously, the Boeotians prospered.

And it was clear they had taken measures to protect their prosperity. The road, which lay narrow and straight beneath the horses' hooves, was perfect for a peasant family fleeing to the protection of the city walls but could not but leave an invading army strung out and exposed to ambush. And the walls themselves, rising from the very edge of a high bluff, would be no easy matter to breach. All the advantages of terrain and construction would lay with the defenders, so that after a long siege the Thebans might be starved into submission but, so long as their army remained intact, their city was unlikely ever to be taken by storm.

The road grew so steep as they approached the city walls that Philip was tempted to climb down and walk to spare his animal. Yet his escort kept their mounts and their agile little horses, smaller than the horses of Macedon so that they almost might be colts, seemed accustomed to laboring up and down this harsh grade.

As they reached the main gate a man stepped out from beneath its shadow and approached them. He was in the middle of life and, except for the restless intelligence of his eyes, undistinguished in his appearance. He wore a simple brown soldier's cloak, which, after the fashion of the southern Greeks, exposed the right arm but covered the left all the way down to the wrist. It was his right hand that he extended to help Philip down from his horse.

"Welcome, young man," he said in the manner of a family friend. "You are to be my guest during your stay among us. I am Pammenes."

Of course Philip knew the name. His host was one of the triumvirate of leaders who in little more than a decade had created an army without equal in the world and had made of Thebes a power with no real rival except Athens.

Pelopidas, Epaminondas, and Pammenes—when still young men, after being driven into exile by the Spartan-backed oligarchy who ruled Thebes, had returned home in secret, and, disguised as women, had broken in on a dinner party at which the three polemarchs were celebrating the end of their year in office and assassinated them. That same night the other pro-Spartan oligarchs in the city were hunted down and killed.

There followed four years of war as the Spartans attempted to reassert their control of Boeotia, at the end of which the world was astonished to see them beaten and humiliated. The best professional fighting force in Greece went down to defeat before a small, hastily assembled citizen army. Commanders of vast experience and brilliant reputation found themselves overmastered by unknown men they would hardly even have considered soldiers. Thebes had emerged as a great power—and all this was the work of three men.

Pammenes was descended from the old Theban aristocracy, but his family had lost everything during the years of Spartan domination. He did not seem to regret his poverty, or even to notice it, as that first night he entertained his young houseguest over a plain dinner of goat flesh and boiled millet.

"Pelopidas mentioned you often in his letters," he said to Philip, refilling his cup with a vile, unmixed wine as thick as horse blood. "You made an impression on him. So did the Lord Ptolemy, although of a different sort. It is a great pity about your brother the king—to die so young, and at the hands of a friend, is indeed bitter."

His face, as he spoke, was as bland as milk, and his words seemed at once to imply everything and nothing. Pammenes, one suspected, was a man who hid behind his appearance of mediocrity, wearing it like a disguise.

"Bitter, yes. But not unexpected."

At first Pammenes affected to be surprised by this answer, but in the end he merely shrugged his shoulders and sighed as if at the last in a long series of anticipated disappointments.

"No, not unexpected," he said, carefully looking at nothing. "Pelopidas was perhaps wise to insist that the Lord Ptolemy's own son be among the hostages delivered over to us, since it is in everyone's interest that the new regent's ambitions be curbed."

He tasted his wine and made a face. The subject of the Lord Ptolemy's ambition appeared to have disappeared from his mind until he spoke again.

"If I may speak frankly, Prince, I am a little surprised to see you here in Thebes. The regent must be nodding—or perhaps he wishes to display the harmlessness of his intentions."

Philip must have looked puzzled, for his host smiled.

"You must know," Pammenes continued as if explaining the solution to a riddle, "that your presence here is the best possible guarantor of the new king's life. The Lord Ptolemy's tenderness toward his son may not be very great, but as long as we have you he will respect the peace and make no attempt to remove your brother Perdikkas."

Now it was Philip's turn to smile. He tore a corner from a flat piece of bread and used it to wipe up a bit of drippings from his plate.

"I think you miscalculate. Cut this throat, My Lord, and for the rest of his life the regent will count you dearer to him than a brother."

As if to underscore the point, he dropped the fragment of bread into his mouth and swallowed it without taking the trouble to chew.

Pammenes shook his head.

"Suppose, my young friend, that the regent decides he is not content with the substance of power. 'I would be king,' he says. What would he do then?"

"Have Perdikkas murdered," Philip answered. He frowned, apparently at a loss to discover the point of the question.

"The way Alexandros was murdered, so that no one lives to stand accused to it?"

"Yes, of course. The assembly will not condone treason."

"Yet even suppose that your brother the king dies in his sleep. Would Ptolemy feel himself secure of his crown?"

Philip's eyes narrowed. He was beginning to see the point.

"No, he would not," he said slowly. "Many would side against him, knowing there is one still closer in blood . . ."

"And you are he?"

"And I am he."

"And you are in Thebes, Philip." Pammenes lifted his wine cup, seeming to test the weight of it in his fingers. "And Thebes might decide it is to her advantage to support your claim to be king of Macedon. All this the regent knows, and thus your brother's life is safe. One can only speculate what there is about you that the Lord Ptolemy fears so much that it is stronger even than his ambition."

"Possibly nothing more than that I know my brother's blood is on his hands."

"Yet you are alive." After setting the wine cup down again, without tasting it, Pammenes smiled once more, this time with a bit less condescension. "How is that, Prince?"

Philip discovered that he was blushing hotly—less from shame than from some cause he could not have named, even to himself.

"The Lord Ptolemy is my mother's husband," he said finally. He had found that if he took a long, slow breath he could pronounce the words with a reasonable appearance of calm. "I am informed she keeps the bed tolerably warm for him, but perhaps she is not so utterly blinded by love that she would fail to notice the murder of yet another son. Perhaps the regent, when he falls asleep at night, prefers to hope that the next morning he will wake up in this world instead of another."

For a moment Pammenes regarded him in silence, and when he spoke at last there was no longer any trace of a smile on his lips.

"I understand now, Prince, why Pelopidas was so taken with you," he said.

"For it is clear you have the makings of a great man. Never in my life have I seen one so young with so cold a mind."

In the morning Philip was given breakfast and told to go out and explore the city. "You are not a prisoner in Thebes," Pammenes told him. "How can you be a prisoner when we have no interest in menacing your safety and all your enemies are in Pella? You are my guest. You are free to come and go as you like and no one will keep watch over your movements."

And it was true. This time there was no Zolfi to dog his steps, and not even the watch soldiers at the gates paid any attention to him. Indeed, they did not even seem to know who he was—for the first time in his life, Philip discovered the pleasure of moving through crowd-filled streets as a stranger, anonymous and unrecognized.

The marketplace was disappointingly small. Still, upon inspection it turned out to have much to offer a young man who still carried Bardylis's Athenian drachmas in a pouch tied to his belt. He had not lived a life that much accustomed him to handling money, but he felt himself to be luxuriously rich.

Naturally, the first thing he purchased was a sword. It was a foot soldier's weapon, with the blade less than a cubit in length. It was flexible and well balanced—when he held it by its leather-wrapped hilt it felt right in his hand.

Philip had spent his boyhood following Glaukon about the marketplace at Pella, so he knew how to haggle. When the trader finally had his one silver coin he rubbed it carefully between his fingers as if worried that his customer might at last have somehow contrived to cheat him.

There were manuscripts for sale, but it was cheaper to listen to the professional reciters who gathered their audiences outside the wineshops and for a few coppers would entertain with scenes from Aeschylos, taking all the parts, or Hesiod's genealogies of the gods or passages from Homer. Standing in the sunshine as he listened to the death of Hektor, Philip thought of his friend Aristotle, who was in Athens now, studying philosophy—Aristotle seemed to know Homer complete, even the catalog of ships' names that put everyone else to sleep. The recollection made him feel homesick.

He remembered Arsinoe and the taste of her mouth, and he imagined it just possible, as he looked down at the cobblestones of a Theban street, that he would die of longing for Pella.

"Beg me not!" The reciter's voice rose until it almost cracked as he spoke the words of Achilleos. "You cur, to beg in my old father's name. I would have the gods bless me with such wrath that I might hack the flesh from your bones and eat it!"

In his mind's eye, Philip saw his brother die again on Praxis's sword, and all softness died in his breast.

Perhaps, Philip thought, when he killed the Lord Ptolemy he would drag his body nine times around the city walls, until there was hardly enough left of him to burn.

But that must wait. Alexandros's ghost must wait for his revenge. For now, Macedon belonged to the regent.

"It is only poetry, Philip. You look as if you were about to kill Hektor yourself."

He turned his head, at first not recognizing the voice. It belonged to a reedy youth who was just tall enough to make him adjust his gaze up about four fingers—Philoxenos, his cousin and the Lord Ptolemy's only son.

Philoxenos was almost precisely a year older than Philip and, while he might have outgrown the awkwardness of childhood, he had never acquired the charms of manner and person that were so marked in his father. He also lacked the regent's capacity for deception, for when he smiled, as he did now, he betrayed everything he felt.

The two young men had detested each other all their lives.

"I came looking for you," he said. "Thebes must seem strange after Pella—I thought you might take comfort in a familiar face."

It might even have been true.

Eventually, however, after he became quite convinced that Philip wasn't going to answer him, Philoxenos allowed his smile to flicker out.

"My father wrote and said—"

"And you write him," Philip broke in. "The regent, it seems, has his spies everywhere."

"He said you were making wild and treasonous accusations."

"Oh, hardly that, cousin. I merely suggested that he was behind the king's murder."

A look of wild fear came into Philoxenos's face and he actually appeared to shrink back, as if he had seen a snake in his path. At last, and with a visible effort, he brought himself to smile again.

"Who would believe such a thing?" he asked in a tone that suggested the question contained its own answer. "I think your wits have been turned by grief, Philip."

And in that moment Philip knew that the son knew nothing of the father's villainy. If Ptolemy should ever be brought to trial before the assembly, Philoxenos would be condemned with him, for that was the law. But he was entirely innocent. He did not even suspect.

Why should he? Philoxenos was one of those who would always believe the common report, and the regent would never reveal himself to this booby.

The realization tasted almost like shame. Philip suddenly discovered in himself the strong desire to make amends.

"Doubtless you are right," he said, offering his own smile—he was pleased to observe that Philoxenos seemed relieved. "And, yes, it is agreeable to see a familiar face." He put his hand across his cousin's shoulder. "Come, let us buy a wineskin and find a bit of shade, and we will drink together to the pleasures of exile."

15

As regent to a boy king who by now was almost afraid to look at him, the Lord Ptolemy enjoyed all the authority of a sovereign. He was chief priest and officiated over the daily rites of sacrifice that guaranteed the nation's safety. He was commander of the army in time of war. In treason trials before the assembly he alone had the power to accuse, and in all lesser matters he was the sole judge of law. His enemies, however, had committed no offenses that could fall within even the most elastic definition of treason, Macedon was at peace, and religious ritual bored him. He had stolen Amyntas's wife and murdered his son. He had all but stolen his crown. He had satisfied the ambition of thirty years, only to discover that the achievement was hollow and that revenge over the dead smells of their corruption. Had it not been for Philip, he might simply have lost interest.

Philip was all that he had left to fear, and fear alone could remind him of the sweetness of life. But Philip was far away.

Philip at the ear of Pelopidas. The thought of it clawed at Ptolemy's entrails like a fox digging its burrow. Yet nothing that Philip could say in Thebes could be half so dangerous as what he had already said in Pella—the regent had only to catch Perdikkas's eye for an instant, and have him glance away as if sick with shame, to know that the king, in his heart, knew that Philip had spoken the truth. It had been the wisest thing to send him to Thebes. Six more months in Macedon, and Ptolemy would certainly have felt compelled to have him killed. Philip was simply too dangerous to be left at home.

Still, it was odd how much Ptolemy felt his absence. When the boy had turned on his heel and begun his journey into exile, Ptolemy had experienced it almost as a defeat. It was humiliating to feel such fear of a mere boy, and somehow worse to experience that fear as an almost sensual pleasure.

Thus it was perhaps not entirely by chance that one evening, about a week after Philip's departure, Ptolemy returned from a day of hunting and, as he left the royal stables, found himself tarrying to listen to the hoofbeats of a great black stallion as it tried to kick down the gate to its stall.

"That would be Prince Philip's horse, My Lord," the chief groom told him. "He's as restless as a demon. He feels the want of exercise since the prince went on his travels again."

"Then why don't you send one of the stableboys out with him?"

The chief groom laughed. He was a tall, gangling man and there was a notch-like scar on his left cheekbone he had carried since he was fourteen, when King Amyntas's warhorse had tried to scatter his brains.

"No one is fool enough to trust his life to that one, Lord." He shook his head and laughed again. "He will let no one near him. With the prince he was as gentle as a kitten—I have seen him eat slices of apple from Lord Philip's hand. Yet he knows but one master. It would be another man's death to try riding him."

"What is the beast's name?"

"Alastor, My Lord."

The late-afternoon sun filtered in through the stable doors, and the air was heavy with the scent of fresh hay and horse sweat. The Lord Ptolemy had had a good day hunting, and his arms were stained with the stag's blood. He felt tired, but it was the like the weariness of his youth, suggesting reserves of strength.

Alastor. It was like Philip to name his stallion after an avenging demon. It was like an open dare.

"We will take him with us in the morning," Ptolemy answered, a little surprised to hear himself speak. "It is a waste of a good mount to leave him here—I will ride him tomorrow when my own horse tires."

"My Lord, I—"

"I will ride him, Geron. You will see that he is made ready."

"Yes, My Lord."

As he bowed, the chief groom's face was dark with trouble, as if he were being compelled to commit an impiety.

In the cold light of the first hour after dawn, watching as the great stallion was brought out into the courtyard by mounted grooms—they had him double roped and were walking him out between a pair of geldings to keep him calm—the Lord Ptolemy knew a moment of doubt. "This horse is a man-killer," he whispered to himself. But like the shadow of a flying bird that passes swiftly over the ground, the thought flickered through his soul and then, in an instant, was gone. Only its memory lingered, and with it the brassy taste of fear.

No, he would not wait, since fear was a burden that fattened upon itself.

"Geron, as soon as we are beyond the city gates, where he cannot scour me off against a wall, you will take my horse and I will ride the Lord Philip's."

The chief groom said nothing, but he frowned in disapproval.

As soon as the Lord Ptolemy had dismounted, the grooms jumped down from their geldings and began to peg their leads to the ground, keeping the ropes short so that the stallion could not pull his head back. At last Geron came forward with the bit—it was a training bit, used only with the unruliest animals, a cruel piece of worked iron that would cut to shreds the mouth of any horse that fought against it—and slipped it over Alastor's head. Then he walked back to where the regent was waiting.

"He is a brute and will use every weakness against you, My Lord. Do not be shy with him, but teach him quickly that you mean to be the master."

"That is always good advice."

The Lord Ptolemy managed a tight little smile that only hinted how much he might have taken offense, but the chief groom read its meaning in full and bowed.

"My father put me on my first horse before I could walk, Geron. I commanded the king's right wing in battle when I was not yet seventeen. This is but another stallion with too much fire in its blood—I will manage."

"I meant no offense, My Lord."

"And I have taken none." He allowed the smile to die away. "When I have my legs over him your men may resume their mounts, but let them keep their ropes tight. I think it best to let him grow accustomed to my weight, and to let the bit teach him to behave himself."

"It shall be as you command, My Lord."

He understood well enough what the knave was thinking: Philip had ridden his Alastor for the first time with nothing but a rope halter—it was said he could command the stallion with just a whispered word and the pressure of his knees—but Ptolemy was not a reckless boy to hazard his life needlessly. If he could break the horse to his will, that was victory enough.

At first with the bit in his mouth the stallion was restless and skittish, even striking out at the two geldings with his hooves. Gradually, however, he began to settle down, and at last the regent made his approach.

The Lord Ptolemy had indeed lived his whole life around horses, and he knew the astonishing range of emotions they were capable of expressing. Thus he understood that the low whinny that seemed to come from deep within the stallion's chest registered less fear than something very like a smoldering outrage.

Could a horse resent an insult? It would seem so—Philip's Alastor seemed to take it as an offense that any other man should presume to curb his will. The Lord Ptolemy found he was almost glad.

"I know not what Philip used to break your will," he murmured as his hand came down lightly on the stallion's neck, "but I fancy that this time simple force will answer well enough. I am no boy to suffer your little whims."

Alastor rolled his great black eyes and pulled his head away, but had grown strangely quiet.

The Lord Ptolemy grabbed two great handfuls of mane and threw himself over the stallion's back. When he was well mounted he picked up the reins and gave them a sharp upward pull. Instantly the stallion bellowed with pain.

"Do we understand each other now?"

With a nod to the grooms mounted on either side of him, Ptolemy dug his heels into Alastor's shining black flanks and the stallion jolted forward.

Alastor was not easily curbed. He fought the bit and the rider, rearing up so that his front hooves clawed at the air, but in the end, when his mouth was streaming with blood and the slightest tug on the reins dug into raw flesh, he seemed to give up.

Within half an hour Ptolemy decided to let the grooms slip their ropes that he might ride alone. After a few minutes he urged the stallion into a canter and then into a slow gallop, and for the first time he sensed the beast's enormous power.

At last, when he felt some confidence in his control, he let the stallion have his head and they tore over the empty ground together so fast that the world became a blur before his eyes.

Yet, in the end, Alastor answered to the bit and slowed to a docile trot.

The Lord Ptolemy turned back toward his hunting party.

"Take him back to the stables," he said, sliding down to the ground and handing the reins to Geron. Alastor was lathered with sweat and the muscles in his great flanks quivered under the skin. "Let him ponder today's lesson—I will ride him again before he has had a chance to forget it, but at present his mouth is too tender for the day's hunting."

He climbed back on his own horse and rode away to amuse himself.

When he returned from hunting, the Lord Ptolemy always liked to take a cup of wine and a little fruit and then nap for half an hour. He always woke up in a cheerful mood, but he had discovered over the years that the crude fellowship of other men had a tendency to blunt his gaiety. Thus he preferred to pass the hours before the nightly revels of the King's companions either alone or in the company of women. Eurydike, when it suited her, could be a very agreeable companion, and she was too proud to prevail upon his good humor to ask for favors. Thus the early evening had become a time he usually spent with his wife.

On this particular evening, after his encounter with the black stallion that had belonged to her son, he was strangely reluctant to be in her presence. He could not have explained why, not even to himself, but he was not particularly pleased when, after a longer-than-usual sleep, he opened his eyes and beheld her, smiling one of her unreadable smiles that always seemed to mirror back some doubt he had smothered into unconsciousness in his own breast.

He knew, the instant he saw her face, that she had heard something. Well, that was to be expected. There were no secrets from the regent's wife.

"What hour is it?" he asked, making a show of wiping the sleep from his eyes—he wondered why he troubled himself with these petty deceptions and felt suddenly ashamed.

"It is just twilight."

The Lady Eurydike handed him a cup of wine and, although he did not really want it, he took a swallow before setting it down on the floor beside his bed.

She rose from where she had been sitting beside him and lit a lamp. The light from it threw a yellow aura about her arm, like the mantle of a goddess.

"You must have been tired," she went on, not looking at him. "Was the sport good today?"

There was an edge in her voice that made him wary. He waited a long time before answering.

"Only fair."

"Then perhaps you are tired from riding."

"Someone told you about the horse."

"Does that surprise you?"

"Nothing about you surprises me anymore," he said, conscious of lying and of being a trifle offended that the insult seemed to have so little effect. The Lady Eurydike hardly even appeared to have heard.

"I would warn you to beware of how you trifle with Philip's horse," was all she said.

"Philip is far away," he answered before he could stop himself—why did he sound, even to himself, as if he was afraid? "He will be in Thebes for a very long time, and thus it cannot matter to him what I do with his horse."

"Everything about you matters to him, and distance is not safety. Yet I was not thinking of Philip. Please do not suppose my aim is to defend the rights of my son."

She was standing in almost the precise center of the tiny bedroom, turned slightly away from him so that he could see only a little of her face. Who could say what she felt about her son, whom she said she hated and yet was her flesh, an intimacy that can sometimes be more important than love.

"Then what am I to suppose?"

She moved her head, as if to look back at him over her shoulder, and he thought it likely he would never forget her expression. She was afraid, but not in the usual way. It was as though she could see into the future as clearly as if time were no more than a window. There was a kind of awe mixed in with her fear that made it terrible to behold.

"Suppose nothing," she said at last. "Believe only that I wish selfishly to preserve your life. Stay clear of Philip's horse. As you would fear to put yourself in his hands, fear his horse. Understand, husband, that there are limits to what you may safely dare—trifle with Philip and he will destroy you."

"It was my impression we were speaking about a horse."

Ptolemy picked up the wine cup from the floor and drank off what was left. His throat was oddly constricted. He preferred to think it was merely because he was annoyed.

"Are you so blind that you cannot recognize that they are both part of the same thing? The gods have shown you the instrument they have chosen to destroy you—can you not see it?"

When she spoke again, a weariness had come into the Lady Eurydike's voice. "I am a wicked woman, and the gods will punish me for it," she said. "They punish me already, through every hour of my life. And still I have not yet known the worst."

At the banquet that night the regent decided he needed the consolation of old friends about him, so he invited Lukios to sit at his table. As a general rule, the Lord Ptolemy found more than a few minutes of his company irritating. Lukios's conversation was generally about nothing except his horses and his food, and since the death of his wife the previous year even these topics tended to disappear into the vast, wine-soaked silences to which he was increasingly prone. Yet at least it could be said for him that Lukios was a man empty of both talent and ambition and was therefore perfectly safe. Besides, they had known each other since boyhood.

By the midpoint of the evening Ptolemy began to suspect that he might be drinking too much, for at one point he discovered himself actually bragging to Lukios about his exploits with Philip's stallion.

"We give horses too much credit," he found himself saying. "Everyone talks a lot of rubbish about their spirit so that we almost imagine them breathing fire through their nostrils, but I tell you I have known women who have more spirit than any horse that ever lived. This black demon of my stepson's is a fine enough animal, but I broke him to my will in a single afternoon. I think I may use him as a hunter—I do not think he really has the stomach to make a proper warhorse."

"What you say about women is both wise and true," Lukios answered, nodding in heavy agreement. "Some women are very fine."

"I was speaking of horses, you dolt."

"Yes, of course you were."

"Perhaps you should marry again," the regent said with a pang of contrition—Lukios, after all, was very far gone in wine so that it was a miracle he was even listening.

"Perhaps I should."

"What sort of wife would you like?"

"A young one—beyond that I am not particular."

"Very well. I shall ask Eurydike to look about for you."

"You were always a true friend, Ptolemy," Lukios said with considerable emotion. His eyes brimmed with tears and then, suddenly, he appeared to forget all about it. He seemed on the verge of falling asleep.

"There are some who think I am unwise to hazard myself with the horse," the regent continued, not quite sure what kept drawing him back to the subject of Philip's stallion. "What do you think?"

Lukios belched, which one gathered had the effect of clearing his brain.

"I think if a child can ride him, you can. It is easier to mount a horse than a woman."

He laughed immoderately at this, until Ptolemy fetched him a clout on the side of the head, and then he was silent.

"Your seed is going rancid and curdling your wits," Ptolemy announced, with the air of one administering a reproof. "Have you no servant girls upon whom you can relieve yourself?"

"My wife was of a jealous disposition and filled the house with old women."

"Oh. That is a great misfortune."

"Yes. Especially as now she is dead."

"Have you seen Philip's stallion?"

"No." Lukios turned his head to look at Ptolemy and then blinked as if startled by a light. "Why do you keep going on about Philip's stallion? You sound like my wife when her mind was full of maggots because I had looked at some other woman. Can you be jealous of the boy?"

In wine there is truth, Ptolemy thought. *This drunken clod has seen into my soul.*

He considered making some sharp answer but decided against it. A quarter of an hour later, Lukios was quietly asleep, his head lying across his folded arms.

When the banquet was over, before finding his own bed Ptolemy strolled over to the royal stables. For some reason he thought he would sleep easier if he saw the stallion one more time, perhaps if only to remind himself that a horse is, after all, only that.

What he found there was not peace of mind but a blanket spread out over the floor, covering what was obviously a human form. What he found was the stunned silence that always accompanies death.

"Alastor killed one of the stable lads," Geron told him. "The horse was restless, and the boy went to see if anything ailed him."

"He went in the stall with him?"

"Yes, he was a new boy, just in from the countryside. He was probably accustomed to dealing with plow oxen. It is a great pity. The Lord Philip will be very upset when he learns we have had to destroy his stallion."

Ptolemy looked down at the corpse beneath the blanket. From the quantity of blood that had soaked through, the horse must have kicked the boy's head into pulp.

"I forbid you to destroy him," he said before he knew he had intended to say anything. "It was the boy's fault, not the stallion's. We will not sacrifice a good animal only because a stable hand was careless."

Walking through the darkened courtyard toward his own quarters, the Lord Ptolemy felt a terrible pain clutching at his bowels. When he discovered that he could not go on, he dropped to the ground and retched violently.

In the moment, on his knees in the darkness, trembling and sweating with the weakness that overcomes a man when he has emptied his stomach after a night of drinking, he felt horribly afraid.

"Why did I not have the stallion destroyed?" he asked himself. "Why, except that I did not dare?"

He got to his feet as quickly as he could, lest someone discover him in that posture, and hurried away to find the oblivion of sleep.

16

Philip very quickly discovered that his friendship with Philoxenos was destined to be short-lived. The bulk of the Macedonians in Thebes had been drawn from among the families of the Lord Ptolemy's supporters—after all, the time spent as a diplomatic hostage was considered to be an important episode in a young man's life—and none of them were ignorant of Philip's hostility toward the regent. Besides, no one could be sure that this regency was not simply the prelude to another royal murder and Ptolemy's direct assumption of the kingship. For both of these reasons it was considered wise to adopt an attitude of subtle hostility toward the king's younger brother. For Philoxenos, who had never been noted for originality, it was no more than a matter of falling in with the prevailing atmosphere, which he alone might have had the prestige to dispel. Thus very quickly Philip found it more agreeable to pass his time among Thebans than among his own countrymen.

This did not distress him very much since, although he was a prince of the royal house, Philip had never felt particularly at ease among the Macedonian aristocracy. He preferred the company of soldiers and stable hands, of artisans and merchants and scholars—of men who, as he had once put it to his brother Perdikkas, "knew something besides how to pick their teeth." His mother always claimed that his taste for lowborn friends resulted from his having been raised by the king's steward, and it was even possible she may have been correct, but Philip's was a restless, probing intelligence, not easily satisfied with the smug contemplation of his ancestry. He wanted to understand the world and all its arts, and he took his lessons where he could. In Macedon he had learned about politics and commerce from listening to his foster father, Glaukon. Old Nikomachos had taught him the rudiments of medicine. From the stonemasons, carpenters, and other craftsmen who worked on royal building sites he had gleaned a knowledge of mechanics. And he had absorbed all the poetry that came his way. In Thebes he set himself to learn the secrets of war.

The campaigning season was then at its zenith, but Thebes suffered from the inconvenience of being temporarily at peace. So her armies vented their ferocious energy by staging elaborate drills on the plains of Boeotia, drills that were distinguishable from war itself only by the absence of the slain.

These Philip watched from the city walls. No one prevented him—Pammenes was amused by his interest. Philip became so familiar to the soldiers of the watch that they often shared their midday meal with him, and he would sit at their feet and listen to their stories of battles long since fought.

But it was the drills that chiefly fascinated him. At first he found them perplexing, for they were infantry drills and the Macedonians were a nation of horsemen—their own foot soldiers were little more than a rabble. Yet the Thebans had won great wars through the valor of their hoplites, who were considered the finest fighting men in the world, better even than the Spartans. Philip was hard pressed to understand how foot soldiers could be used with such effect.

One day he discovered he was not alone at his favorite observation post above the city gates. He had not heard anyone approaching on the narrow stone stairway that led up to the arch—he simply turned and discovered that there was standing behind him a tall man with a scar running down his left temple and into his beard, which was beginning to show a few threads of gray among the black. His mouth was creased and frowning, and his eyes, which were unfathomably dark, seemed to glitter with anger, but Philip quickly grasped that the expression was habitual and not directed at him. Indeed, his gaze was fixed on the plain below, where the army that had forced Alexandros to sue for peace was disposed in three long columns of men, like three fingers from the same gigantic hand.

"I had heard the Macedonians had sent a spy among us," he said, without even troubling to glace at Philip. "It is a climb up to this vantage point—I thought I would come and see what you find so worth the trouble of looking at."

"The logic of the thing is more apparent from up here. The battle order appears as it must in the commander's own mind." But by then Philip already knew to whom he was speaking, and he was determined not to let his embarrassment show. "Why has Epaminondas strengthened his left wing to a depth of fifty men?"

"Because the Spartans always put their best troops on the right. Then they wheel in to the center like a gate opening and roll over the opposing army. I wish them to be crushed against a wall, so I fortify my left side."

Something like amusement showed in the face of the man who three years earlier had conquered Kleombrotos at Leuctra.

"Pammenes warned me that you would be full of intelligent questions. What else do you want to know?"

"Those in the front and center of the left wing—their uniforms are different. Who are they?" Philip asked.

"Those are the Sacred Band," the Boeotarch replied, his eyes narrowing slightly as if to pick out the faces of individual men. "You do well to remark them, for they are the backbone of our forces. When they perish, Thebes will be lost."

"Sacred—why are they called that?"

"Because they have taken an oath to conquer or perish. New recruits join in twos and are chosen from among pairs of lovers. They fight shoulder to shoulder so their courage in battle is the tenacity of men who are protecting that which is most dear to them."

"And they do not retreat?"

"They never have."

"Such courage could well become an expensive luxury for a commander."

Epaminondas seemed for a moment as if he were about to become displeased. Then he seemed to change his mind. Then he laughed.

"I can predict you will be an interesting acquaintance, young Philip of Macedon. You have a rare gift for seeing beyond the obvious." He put his hand on the young man's shoulder. "You are quite right, of course. When the struggle goes against one, it is an advantage to be able to break off and live to fight another day. Yet it is an advantage of which we Greeks have tended to avail ourselves rather too freely. That is why I called the Sacred Band our 'backbone'— they stand firm and shame us into following their example. Many a battle has been lost because of too great an eagerness to snatch defeat from the jaws of victory."

His eyes once more returned to his army, with a look as soft as a caress. For a long time he did not speak.

"Would you like to come down from this lofty vantage and see how the army of Thebes looks at close range?" he asked finally. "The first thing a spy should learn is that there are no secrets—except the secret of the men themselves."

By the time they climbed down from the city gate the drill had already been broken off and troops of the Theban infantry were sitting about on the ground. A few of that vast number propped their shields up with their lances to make a little shade in which to take a nap, and many busied themselves with repairing their sandal straps or sharpening their short, broad-pointed swords or performing any one of the hundreds of little tasks with which soldiers busy their hands. As Epaminondas led Philip among them, some watched their commander with expressions of weary curiosity but most ignored him. They had seen him before.

"It is not the same in Macedon, I would guess."

With his right arm Epaminondas made a gesture that took in the whole field. There was the merest trace of a smile on his lips as he spoke, as if he were displaying some costly possession which he expected to be coveted.

"No, it is not. The Macedonians are horsemen."

"Ah, yes, I see your point," he answered. It seemed to amuse him that he had nettled Philip. "But cavalry is useless against disciplined troops, and the soil of Greece is so full of stones that horses are forever going lame."

"Discipline is not perfect even in Greek armies, and I have heard it said that Pelopidas uses cavalry to great effect. Besides, Macedonian horses are bigger."

Epaminondas seemed to consider the matter for a few seconds, and then he reached down and picked up one of the huge hoplite shields that littered the ground and handed it to Philip.

"Here—take this as well," he said, giving Philip a spear that was half again as tall as he was. "Now, if you were a horseman, would you charge a wall of men thus armed? That shield is four layers of oxhide, strapped with bronze. It would turn aside an arrow like a straw in the wind, and there is hardly a javelin thrower alive whose arm is strong enough to pierce it. How would you attack it from the back of a horse? How would you keep from being impaled?"

Feeling a fool, Philip put his left forearm through the loops on the back of the shield and tested its weight. Out of his wounded pride he had answered back one of the greatest soldiers in the world, and now Epaminondas must think him a callow boy without the brains of a peacock.

Truly, the man who could carry such a shield throughout the long course of battle was no weakling.

"I see your point," he said, clearing his throat to hide his embarrassment. "A phalanx of such men must be as impregnable as a turtle."

At first he could not understand why Epaminondas was laughing.

"Young Philip of Macedon, I believe there is in you the makings of a commander, for you have seen in an instant what the Spartans have been unable to grasp in three hundred years. As impregnable as a turtle, yes, and every bit as ponderous."

Epaminondas was quite explicit about the limitations of hoplite infantry: "They are so heavily armed that, really, they cannot fight at all except on level ground, so for as long as anyone can remember, battles between Greek armies have been little more than shoving matches in which one side tries to overpower their opponents, shatter their discipline, and force them to flee. Possession of the battlefield itself was all the victory a commander could hope for because pursuit is difficult for men weighted down with body shields and full armor. And that meant your enemy could always hope to regroup and fight another day. Nothing was ever permanently settled, and therefore no one was ever genuinely safe. Victory and defeat were alike in their unreality. The whole business, as you can easily imagine, took on the character of a child's game. It has been the business of my life to make of warfare something decisive.

"An army is not genuinely defeated until it is destroyed as a fighting force—until it has been hunted down with sufficient slaughter that it will never again pose a threat to anyone. This is where the lighter-armed peltast infantry prove their worth, for they are capable of pursuit. They can maintain formation at a run and roll over a panicked enemy like a millstone crushing grain."

"And would not cavalry serve even better?" Philip asked. They were at dinner in Pammenes' house, and he had drunk enough of his host's wine to have found his courage again.

Epaminondas frowned, and Pammenes, who had been silent during most of the discussion, suddenly burst into laughter.

"Philip, my young friend, you must wait until Pelopidas returns from the north before you will hear anything of cavalry," he said finally. "For Epaminondas can hardly bring himself to admit that a horse makes even a decent pack animal."

"That is not the case." Epaminondas picked up his wine cup and then put it back down without bringing it to his lips. It was obvious that he was struggling hard not to appear offended, and just as obvious that he was. "Pelopidas has demonstrated time and again the role that cavalry can play in determining the outcome of battle. I, who fought beside him against the Spartans, would be the last to belittle his accomplishment."

"I beg your pardon, my old comrade," said Pammenes, placing a hand upon his friend's arm. "It was never my intention to suggest—"

"I know it was not."

The two men, who between them shared supreme authority both within Thebes itself and over the great league of states it dominated, joined hands across the table in a gesture of reconciliation that demonstrated more eloquently than any words their perfect confidence in one another. The moment was brief, but it stirred Philip of Macedon, who was its only witness, to the depths of his being, for it showed what was possible when ambition was replaced by generosity of spirit.

In Pella, they would have been at one another's throats.

"Yet I think," Epaminondas went on as if nothing had happened, "that even Pelopidas, were he among us, would concede pride of place to infantry. Cavalry can swell the tide of victory, but it labors under too many disadvantages ever to be more than an auxiliary force."

He picked up his wine cup again and this time drank. It was still in his hand when a shadow of suppressed anger returned to his hand.

"But it is evident you doubt me, Prince."

Philip was momentarily saved the ordeal of a reply by a renewal of Pammenes' intemperate laughter.

"My friend Epaminondas assumes that because he has triumphed over some of the best armies in the world no one has the right to question his judgment as a soldier."

"Such an assumption would strike me or anyone else as entirely justified." Philip addressed his remark to Pammenes, but out of the corner of his eye he noted the ghost of a smile on Epaminondas's lips. "And I am neither so callow nor so stupid as to dispute strategy with one of the world's greatest commanders. I am merely surprised, since the traditions of my own country favor cavalry to the neglect of infantry. I wish only to learn . . ."

Then it was Epaminondas's turn to laugh.

"Clearly our young hostage's services to Macedon are destined to be as much diplomatic as military." He reached across the table and cuffed Philip good-naturedly on the side of the head. "I have been on this earth long enough, my boy, to know when I am being flattered, but you too are wise to tread lightly around the vanity of those whom the world calls great."

With his own hand the hero of Leuctra freshened the wine in Philip's cup. When he spoke again it was in the confidential manner of an old friend.

"I may be brewing up a disaster for Thebes ten or twenty years hence, and yet I think I do no more than explain what a few more months among us would reveal to you in any case. So I will enlighten you as to the proper relationship between infantry and cavalry . . ."

The summer heat was fierce over the Boeotian plains, making the air dance. One felt the sun's scorching weight pressing down on one's back, and merely to glance up into its light was like being struck with a hammer. Soldiers rose early to finish their drill while it was still morning, and by the middle of the afternoon everyone in Thebes was hiding under whatever shade they could find. The city seemed half-asleep.

Philip liked to spend the time in a wineshop called the Yellow Fig, just inside the main gate. He liked it because the wine was not watered beyond decency and because the woman who owned it, a widow not far past her twentieth year, seemed to enjoy flirting with him, and because it was much frequented by mercenaries.

Greece was full of men who had no profession except that of arms and who would fight for anyone who paid them. They had no country, no prejudices, and no loyalty except to their own commanders. Because their lives took them everywhere—some of them had fought for the king of Persia, even against their own cities—they bore no ill will toward foreigners.

Philip was something of a favorite among them. He was an aristocrat, but he did not hold himself aloof. Indeed, he seemed to admire these rough infantrymen with the dust of a thousand roads on their sandals, as if the warrior's virtues were the only ones that mattered. And, besides, he liked to listen to their stories. A soldier always enjoys having an audience for his stories.

"Now Jason—there was a man to work for," remarked Theseus, a heavy-limbed Aetolian with a face like leather, who had "followed the spear," as the saying was, since he was fifteen. He was expanding on his favorite themes: the merits and failings of the various commanders under whom he had had the pleasure of serving. "He always paid us on time. And in silver. The Pheraeans could starve, but his soldiers never missed a payday. Tyrants make the best employers. When I heard Jason had been assassinated, I made sacrifice of wine for the repose of his ghost. By the gods, I loved the man!"

"I was there. You were drunk on that awful Thasian that tastes like piss, and you knocked over a jar on your way outside to throw up. We all agreed, it was a touching gesture."

Everyone laughed at this, even Gobryas, who told it, who was Theseus's closest friend—even Theseus himself.

"Theseus is narrow-minded," Gobryas went on to explain. "He recognizes no other virtue in a general beyond possession of a full treasury."

"There is no other virtue." For emphasis, Theseus hit the table with the flat of his hand, hard enough to make the wine cups jump.

"What about indecisiveness?"

Gobryas smiled as Theseus nodded reluctant agreement. Unlike his friend he was thin and bony, with eyes that seemed lost in the immense depth of their sockets.

"Yes," Theseus conceded with the air of one having been reminded of the obvious, "there is much to be said in favor of indecisiveness. A commander who knows his own mind will most often win or lose pretty quickly, and either way a fellow is out of work. I like a protracted war with plenty of truces so you have a chance to spend your wages. By Aphrodite's backside, what if I were killed in battle with my pay pouch still full of drachmas—wouldn't that be a bloody waste!"

"Athenian politicians make the best generals. They'd rather talk than fight any day, and they usually don't know what they're doing."

"Except a man has to be a fool to work for the Athenians. Two times out of three that belching club they call their assembly will cut off funds for the war, and then you can whistle for your money. Democracy! Phugh!"

There was a general murmur of assent from around the tiny room, which was almost as hot as it was out on the street and certainly a good deal closer.

Philip, who was still tolerably sober, studied the faces of the men around him with the cold and ruthless calm with which his friend Aristotle used to cut open frogs to measure the length of their entrails. He felt he was learning a valuable lesson about the necessity of considering a subordinate's motives. Perhaps if Alexandros had learned it, he might still be alive. Or perhaps not, since a mercenary's motives had at least the merit of simplicity.

"What is the Athenian army like?" he asked when the issue appeared settled and everyone seemed in danger of falling into a comfortable stupor.

"Like?" Gobryas stared at him fiercely, as if the question constituted some manner of insult. "It isn't like anything. Most particularly it is not like an army."

"What it is like," interjected Theseus, "is an elderly maiden's defense of her virginity—half-hearted and unnecessary."

This jest had such merit that Theseus himself laughed at it, longer than anyone else. When he was finished he had to wipe the tears from his eyes.

"Then how has Athens survived, since she seems to be constantly at war with someone? Why have not the other states long since overwhelmed her?"

The two old soldiers regarded each other for a moment and then, in the same instant, turned their gaze on Philip, who was beginning to wonder if he had not touched on some sore point between them.

"Athens hardly needs an army," Theseus announced at last in a tone that bordered on indignation. "She has her ships and one of the best ports in the world, so she cannot be starved out. Her wealth is derived from trade, so she will not suffer greatly for having her countryside ravaged. And her walls are not easily breached so long as the citizens have the heart to defend them. The Athenians can afford to be poor soldiers."

"Have you ever served under Athenian commanders?"

"Philip, why do you ask so many questions?" Gobryas's deep-set eyes, which before had registered indignation, now narrowed with suspicion. "You live in the house of Pammenes, and we see you constantly in company with Epaminondas—did they send you to spy on us?"

Philip found he was not able to suppress a smile.

"They accuse me of spying for the Macedonians."

"Which, of course, being a Macedonian yourself, you do."

"Of course." Philip shrugged his shoulders as if to acknowledge, what could be more obvious?

"Then why do you spend so much time with common louts like us?"

Gobryas, to his credit, was no longer suspicious, merely curious.

"Because I would learn the military arts," Philip answered. "And because, while wars may be fought in the minds of commanders, battles are fought on the bare ground. There is much that happens there of which men like Pammenes and Epaminondas, for all their genius, know nothing. Or perhaps have merely forgotten. Forgive me if I offend against your natural humility, but I suspect that 'common louts' have full as much to teach of war as the greatest general—even if he be a Theban."

Theseus leaned across the table to take him by the ears.

"Philip, I love you, for you are a clever lad," he said and then administered a rough kiss to the top of Philip's head before releasing him. "It is much to be regretted that you were born a prince, since you have the makings of a fine mercenary."

And then he looked about him, as if he had just that instant noticed where he was.

"Madzos, you whore! Where are you hiding our wine?"

The mistress of the house, who was pretty and still quite young, came out from the back room, carrying a large urn that still glistened with drops of water from the well bottom where it had been left all that day to cool. Great patches of her tunic were also wet so that it clung to her breasts and belly in a manner that could not help but make a man's mouth go dry. She smiled at Philip and, as she set the jar down in the center of the table, her hip just happened to brush against his shoulder.

They all watched spellbound as she retreated back into her sanctum.

"What a pair of breasts!" Gobryas murmured with something like awe. "Her little nipples are as hard and sharp as spear points. A man would have to be careful he did not impale himself."

"I would volunteer to risk it."

Theseus sighed heavily and then turned his attention back to Philip.

"She likes you," he said with the air of having discovered something. "What I would not give to be in your place—if I had been lucky enough to take her fancy I would give up soldiering. I would settle down here in Thebes and divide my prowess between the wine jug and that pretty brown backside."

"The two are not perfectly compatible," Gobryas pointed out. "It is no easy business keeping your dagger stiff with a skin full of drink. Better leave her to Philip."

"Yes, but he is a prince and will find better ways to spend his life than in the arms of a tavern wench."

"What better ways? There is no better way."

Everyone laughed at this except Philip, whose cheeks burned as if he still felt the pressure of Madzos's flesh against his own.

And then he remembered the softness of another's caress, and his own words, whispered into the darkness—*I want only to be like this forever. I will never leave you.*

17

"So—your mother informs me that you could not wait for her to find you a husband. How far along are you, girl?"

Arsinoe blushed crimson as much with smothered rage as with shame. It infuriated her to see the Lady Eurydike's tight little smile as she sat there, her hands folded in her lap, waiting for an answer. For this reason, as much as any other, she would not meet her gaze but kept her eyes on the floor.

This was not what she had expected when she had gone to her mother, not knowing what else to do, not knowing what to expect. Tears, perhaps. Or curses shouted after her as she was hounded out of her home. Certainly not the stern, set face, the frozen silence in which the very sound of her daughter's voice seemed to wither and die. And, in the end, the voice that carried no hint of pity, or even regret. "You must speak to the Lady Eurydike—since Amyntas was your grandsire's cousin, and since you claim her son for the father. She must dispose of the matter as she sees fit."

Since you claim her son for the father. How those words had stung her heart!

But at least the interview was being conducted in the privacy of the mother of kings' reception room—at least she had been spared the smiles and mocking jests of the whole court. At least, for now.

"A little more than two months, My Lady."

"You can be so precise? You surprise me."

"I have missed my time twice now, My Lady. And the Lord Philip has been gone eight days beyond the moon's second turning. I saw him last the night before he left."

"His departure was conveniently timed, since it prevents him from disputing the intimacy—my son is very young, Arsinoe. And you have had no lover since?"

"No, My Lady."

"But there have been others before him."

It was not even a question. Arsinoe risked a glance and saw at once that she had no secrets left. The Lady Eurydike knew everything. Her own mother might have suspected, but the Lady Eurydike knew. The expression of those eyes did not admit of a doubt.

"One other, My Lady, but he is not the father."

"How long ago, my child?"

The mother of kings' smile broadened just a shade, and with a little start of surprise Arsinoe realized that she had been tricked. Yes, of course—what hope had a mere girl against the cunning of age?

Still, there was no point in lying now.

"Six, seven months ago. And only once. I am no harlot, My Lady."

She looked at this woman with the purest hatred. Everyone knew that the Lady Eurydike had, for years before his death, wronged the old king's bed. Many said she and the Lord Ptolemy had murdered him—what were Arsinoe's little transgressions compared to these?

And yet it was the Lady Eurydike who sat in judgment, as if she spoke with the voice of Hera.

"Of course not, my child. If you say you are not a harlot, then you are not. I may be forgiven, however, if I do not perfectly trust that the weight in your belly is my son's work.

"Yet you are a kinswoman . . ."

Arsinoe waited through the silence that followed, unable to conquer the feeling that it hardly mattered what became of her. It was all gone now—she had thought she might be Philip's wife, but she had lost that gamble. Philip's wife . . .

The Lady Eurydike's eyes flashed with malicious triumph. Why did this business please her so much? Whose happiness did she believe herself to be destroying?

Yes. How she must hate her son.

"Yet you are a kinswoman, and I cannot let you ruin yourself utterly." Her lover's mother straightened her back, like a cat stretching itself in the sunlight. "We must arrange a marriage for you, lest your child come into the daylight a bastard. You shall have a husband, although not one such as you would wish. Not one so pleasing to your vanity as my son might have been."

As king, Perdikkas was expected to host his cousin's wedding, but fortunately all that was required of him was his presence on the day. That was enough. There was nothing of pleasure in these family duties, and before he heard she was to marry the Lord Lukios, he had hardly even noticed Arsinoe's existence.

Lukios, for all that he was an ox and a fool, was a great friend of the Lord Ptolemy's—all the more so now that the regent had found him a bride less than half his age. The man's gratitude was almost as embarrassing to witness as his lust, and it was appalling enough to witness the way he pawed the girl during the wedding banquet, running his hands over her bare shoulders as if, now that the actual ceremony was concluded, he could hardly restrain himself mounting her on the spot. She bore it with a calm that was almost like insensibility. It was almost possible to pity her.

"Look at him," the Lord Ptolemy murmured, leaning toward Perdikkas, who was sitting beside him, as he refilled his wine cup. "The more drunk he becomes, the more amorous—and he is very amorous. Their wedding night would make an amusing spectacle. I will be sorry to miss it."

As each day of his reign succeeded the last, Perdikkas grew more and more afraid of his stepfather. And never more than when the Lord Ptolemy seemed most intimate and confidential. It was like watching a serpent writhe to display its pretty skin.

"You may not miss it," Perdikkas said, his voice as flat as he could make it. "Behold—My Lord Lukios seems determined to consummate the marriage under our very eyes."

This made Ptolemy laugh. He threw back his head and roared with mirth. By the time he was finished he was wiping tears from his eyes.

Then he threw his arm across Perdikkas's shoulder and drew him toward himself.

"He does not know it yet, but this union has already proved fruitful. The lady is even now quick with child."

The regent laughed again and then, when his laughter ceased, they both watched as, across the banqueting hall, the bridegroom cupped a hand over his new wife's breast and drew his wet, bearded lips across her throat.

"Your brother, it appears, has sown this field ahead of him."

"What! Alexandros?" Perdikkas was genuinely shocked. "I never thought—"

"Don't be such a blockhead, my son. Alexandros has been dead for four months. The honor goes to Philip."

"Philip?"

Ptolemy nodded gravely, a smile twitching at the corner of his mouth.

"Philip. The girl admitted as much to your lady mother."

"Philip?" In his momentary confusion of emotions, Perdikkas could not be certain whether he was more surprised, angry, or envious. Philip, after all, was a year his junior—why was it always given to Philip to . . . ? "What will Lukios do when he finds out?"

"Perhaps, since Lukios is such a fool, she will succeed in convincing him that the child is simply ahead of its time, but if not, what can he do?" The regent pushed his stepson away and then slapped him good-naturedly on the back. "Perhaps he will beat her, if he feels so inclined, but he will not disown either her or her brat. Even Lukios is not that stupid. After all, I arranged this marriage for him, and he will never know who is the real father. He must never know. He will be quiet. But for the moment Lukios feels himself very heavily in my debt." He laughed again. "It is a rare jest, my son, is it not?"

All at once Perdikkas could feel a spasm of dread coiling in his bowels like a serpent. *This man betrays for the pleasure of betrayal*, he thought. *If he betrays his friend, would he not betray his wife's son? Would he not betray his king?*

My son. What weight could a man like the Lord Ptolemy give to the claims of kinship or of sovereignty?

And in that moment he saw with blinding clarity what he had known all along but had kept hidden from himself, that Philip was right, that somehow or other Ptolemy had contrived Alexandros's murder. Praxis had never been more than his instrument—which was why he had to die without being given the chance to utter his accomplice's name.

And before I come of an age to deprive him of his regency, he will murder me.

Life, his own life, was slipping away through Perdikkas's fingers like grains of sand.

I am a dead man, he thought.

Arsinoe's wedding night was, at least in some respects, less terrible than she had imagined. By the time they were conducted up to their chamber, the groom was far too gone in drink to claim due possession of his bride—in fact, he had to be helped into bed and soon fell asleep, clutching her right breast in his soft, thick hand and breathing wine fumes into her face. In spite of this failure, he awoke the next morning very well pleased with himself and boasted to his friends, who attended them at breakfast, that he was a little afraid that her screams of ecstasy might have disturbed them during the night. He seemed actually to believe it himself.

The next night and the next he did not touch her, offering no explanation for his lack of interest, but on the fourth night he managed sufficient show of manly fortitude to actually penetrate, and then promptly fell asleep. As it turned out, the Lord Lukios's performances of his matrimonial duty usually had this effect so that once he began to snore even before he had heaved himself off her belly.

Arsinoe quickly learned to regard her husband with indifference. Experience, it is said, breeds tolerance, and his lovemaking, which at least had the virtue of brevity, became after a time only mildly distasteful to her. Besides, he was too old and loved wine too much to be very ardent. She found she was not inconvenienced more than once or twice a month. For the rest she hardly saw him.

Yet she lived a life of misery. Bitterness consumed her so that it poisoned every hour of her existence. Philip had deserted her, and his family had concocted this ludicrous marriage partly to keep peace with her mother and partly, she was sure, as some sort of grotesque jest. She hated them, but most of all Philip. She wished sometimes that the Lord Lukios was not quite such a jelly so that she could have told him the truth and been certain of his taking his revenge. Even if he had killed her, it would have been worth something to die knowing that Philip was next. But she was married to a supple fool who was no doubt a coward in the bargain, so, when a month had passed and she found it necessary to inform him that she was with child, she did not discourage him from believing that the accomplishment was entirely his own.

"I am very pleased," he said. "If it lives and is a son, we shall name him for the lord regent, who is the true author of our happiness."

He could not understand it when Arsinoe suddenly turned pale and left the room.

It was the beginning of winter and on the plains north of Pella the tall grass, long since withered brown, was already covered by snow about a handspan deep. Game had been plentiful all year, and the hunting was excellent. The regent and his followers had been out almost every day.

Usually they did not return until nearly dusk, when they would ride into the central courtyard of the king's palace, blood-smeared and shouting, and the Lord Ptolemy would summon the chief steward to him to discuss the preparations for that evening's banquet and, incidentally, to show off some prize stag he had killed. The Lord Ptolemy, who was as much the master there as if he had been king himself, was usually in a fine temper when he came back from a day's sport.

But not this day. It was no more than an hour past midday when the regent, accompanied by only a handful of men, came back through the city gates. Although the winter sun was bright, he rode with his cloak wrapped tight around him.

Glaukon, as the king's principal servant, made a point of being on hand when the royal hunting parties returned, but today, when the regent returned so unexpectedly early, he was almost too late to pay his respects. It hardly mattered, though—the Lord Ptolemy brushed past him in the courtyard, apparently without noticing his existence.

"What is the matter? Is he ill?"

There were none of the companions about, only a few stableboys who were attending to the horses, and Geron, the chief groom, so Glaukon addressed his question to him.

Geron shook his head. "Not ill," he said, "merely frightened—for which no man should blame him. He has had a strange experience."

"What happened?"

As Geron told it, it was strange indeed. It seemed that an enormous owl had come dropping down out of the sun, coming close enough to shadow the regent's face with its wings before it pulled away.

"It circled three times above the Lord Ptolemy's head, uttered a dreadful cry, like the curse of a demon, and then flew off. It was a terrible omen."

"Perhaps not." Glaukon frowned, giving the lie to his own words. "The Lord Philip had a similar experience little more than a year ago. The owl even cut his cheek with its claws, and he has passed through many dangers since. Perhaps this time too it is a blessing from the gods."

"I think not this time."

Geron held out his left hand and opened the fingers. Lying across his palm was a fragment of polished bronze, broken across the broad end and then sharply tapered to a point.

"It was clutching this in its talons. The owl dropped it before flying off. It fell almost under the hooves of the Lord Ptolemy's horse."

"What is it?"

"It is the tip of a hunting spear." Geron looked about him, as if to make sure he could not be overheard. "I would not say this to another living soul, Glaukon, but you and I have been servants together in this house since we were boys. I believe the Lord Ptolemy has received a warning that death is near. I believe he understands it to be such."

For a moment Glaukon looked as if he hadn't heard. He appeared to be thinking about something else.

"What horse was he riding today?" he asked finally.

"Why, the Lord Philip's," Geron replied—it was not clear whether he was more astonished by the question itself or its possible implications. "The great black stallion."

"Alastor."

"Yes. Alastor. The same horse Philip was riding when . . ."

"Yes, exactly."

"And how did he behave? Did the owl frighten him as well?"

"Anyone would have thought so, but no. The horse was merely still and watchful, as if he understood everything."

"Exactly so," Glaukon said as if to himself.

He turned and began walking back through the gates leading out beyond the palace compound. The chief groom shouted something after him, but he appeared not to hear.

When he reached his own house, Glaukon sat down beside his hearth on the stool that had been Alcmene's—since her death he always sat there when he was troubled in his mind. For perhaps a quarter of an hour he hardly moved.

"What do the gods intend?" he whispered at last. The sound of his own voice seemed to shock him awake. He stood up and went into Philip's old bedroom.

When the prince had been once more hustled off into exile, he had hardly been given a chance even to stop for a few clothes. The rest were all still in his room, in a chest at the foot of his bed. Glaukon lifted the lid and took out the heavy cloak Philip had been wearing when he returned from among the Illyrians.

Glaukon gathered it up in his arms and carried it away.

At that hour the stables were almost deserted. There weren't more than six or seven horses in their stalls and not a groom in sight. In any case, no one would have challenged the chief steward's presence there.

He heard the stallion before he saw him, a low, nervous whinny, less a challenge than a warning. Alastor was in the last stall, behind a gate that looked as if it had been recently reinforced—this, clearly, was an animal his handlers treated with respectful caution.

His eyes rolled when he saw Glaukon, and his nostrils flared with menace. The blow of a hoof against the heavy wooden gate made it tremble as if it were made of straw.

As a member of the king's household, Glaukon had lived his entire life around horses. As a boy he had served as a groom and had played his childish games in these very stables, running between the legs of the royal war steeds as if they were as insensible and harmless as so many tables. Horses were familiar, unintimidating creatures, and none of them caused him the slightest apprehension. None, except for Philip's great black stallion.

The horse was neighing—a deep, throaty sound, full of menace—and Glaukon watched the huge muscles twitch beneath its sleek black coat and felt on his tongue the brassy taste of fear. There was no particular peril, since the stall was barred with oak timbers as thick as a man's wrist, but he was afraid anyway. Some creatures, like some men, simply carry with them an atmosphere of danger.

The cloak Glaukon had taken from Philip's chest was over his arm. He laid it across the top of the gate and stepped back.

The effect was immediate. Alastor grew quiet. He took a step forward and touched the cloak with his nose.

"So you remember," Glaukon murmured. "You remember your true master. You have not forgotten him."

He took an apple from the pocket of his tunic and cut out a piece with his knife. The stallion ate it from his hand. He did not resist when Glaukon stroked his muzzle.

"He will come back to us one day. And then we will see how the gods' will is done."

18

"I leave for Athens in the morning. There is a treaty that must be renewed, and I am obliged to make the journey. The Athenians never trust their delegates with any real authority, so one either goes to them or suffers through a thousand delays. Would you care to accompany me?"

Thus casually was the invitation issued, halfway through dinner as Pammenes was wiping up the gravy at the bottom of his bowl with a fragment of bread. His face, dominated by his long upper lips and his slightly bulbous nose, was furrowed in concentration, for he was a man who took eating seriously.

"Yes, of course. Thank you. I would like that very much."

Pammenes looked up and smiled, not without a certain amount of mischief. "Good. Perhaps, when you have seen her, you will decide that Athens is the greater prize and will leave poor Thebes in peace. A day's travel by land and two days by ship, since it is a rough journey over the mountains. Besides, everyone's first impression of Athens should be as she appears from the sea."

He picked up the wine pitcher and was about to refill Philip's cup, but then seemed to think better of it.

"We will be leaving the city well before dawn that we may avoid as much of the midday heat as we can, and it is disagreeable to awaken in the dark with one's head buzzing like a hornet's nest—perhaps we have both drunk enough for one night."

An hour later Philip was in his bed, his head buzzing not with wine but with thoughts of the journey and of Athens. She arose in his imagination all white, a perfect city, pure, crowned with light. Her columns gleamed under sunshine that was like the benediction of heaven. Her streets were populated with philosophers, poets, and statesmen, her temples and courts echoing to the sound of their wisdom. Athens seemed as distant from the life that he knew as Olympos itself, for it too was inhabited by gods.

It was a distance the beginnings of which stretched out over hours and hours of dusty, rock-strewn roads, until at last they looked up and saw a tern gliding overhead, its wings spread wide and set.

"We will be in Rhamnous soon," someone announced. "We will dine on octopus and mussels tonight—I can almost smell the water."

Only a few moments later they made the summit of a hill and saw the Euboean Gulf glittering in the late-afternoon sunlight.

The journey by boat took them first to Carystos, where they tied up for the night, and then, in a long sweep around the Attic peninsula, to Athens itself.

They arrived in the hour just before sunset, with the red light of dusk streaming over the great fortress of the Akropolis so that her marble buildings, which were in fact a pale, yellowish gray, looked as if they had been stained with blood.

"What is that?" Philip asked, shading his eyes as he pointed out a squat box of columns at the very summit.

For some reason Pammenes seemed to find the question amusing.

"That, Prince, is the temple of Athena Parthenos, patroness of the city. It is worth the climb to see, for it is perhaps the most beautifully decorated building in all Greece and the statue of the goddess is one of the wonders of the world."

"Then I will go there tomorrow, and I will offer sacrifice to the Lady of the Gray Eyes."

"Have you chosen her for your patroness as well, Philip? Would you have her love you as she did Herakles? Are you ambitious even in your devotions?"

But if Pammenes had intended to be teasing, he did not achieve his object. Philip merely turned to him with an expression the Boeotarch, for all his long experience of men, found impossible to read.

"I chose nothing," he said at last, measuring the words out so that each seemed to carry the same weight. "Instead, I was chosen."

It was apparent that the Athenians did not believe in making elaborate provision for the comfort of visiting diplomats, since the Theban party were obliged to find accommodation for themselves at an inn near the waterfront, where no one seemed to have the least idea that Pammenes and his young companion were anyone except a pair of ordinary travelers. They had dinner that night in company with the master of a trading vessel out of Syracuse and a Lydian slave merchant who was on a buying trip for a string of brothels in Egypt; their conversation was not only entertaining but a genuine education.

"Life itself is a brothel," the Lydian observed in his liquid, strangely accented Greek. "One pays at the door, makes a choice based entirely upon appearances, and then goes out again feeling that the experience fell short of the expectation. This is the constantly repeated pattern of every man's existence— we are always disappointed and always surprised at being so. We are all fools, but the Athenians are the biggest fools of all for they believe in the possibility of wisdom. Have you listened to their philosophers? I am glad to be an honest man who trades merely in whores."

"Athens is not so bad," replied the master, who was sixty and apparently from some remote part of the Italian peninsula. He picked up his wine cup with the tips of his fingers, holding it around the rim as if to test its weight, and then set it down again. "But I would rather be a clod-scraping farmer with dung between my toes than live in any city. When I am in a city for longer than it takes to dispose of my cargo, I always end in the law courts. I think half the men in any city between Carthage and Antioch live solely by bringing suit against foreigners. Cities fester with corruption. By the way, if you have filled your holding pens within a day or two, I can give you a cheap rate for transport to Naukratis, as I have a shipment of papyrus waiting for me there."

The Lydian's eyes narrowed as he reassumed his identity as a canny man of affairs.

"What would you charge?"

This seemed to be a question calling for the nicest philosophical discernment. The master stared into space for a moment, as if consulting some inner voice, and at last said, "Half a drachma a head."

"I am sure you are getting nothing close to that for your present consignment." The Lydian smiled. He was not a man to be imposed upon. "What did you say it was? Wine?"

"Yes, that is true. But wine, when it is off-loaded, leaves the hold clean and sweet. Women, on the other hand, are a dirty cargo—a ship carries slaves for a year and you will never get the smell out. After three years there is no choice but to haul it up on the beach and burn it."

"My girls are young and healthy. Half of them have not even begun to bleed yet."

"The young ones are the worst. Two days in the hold and they stink like ferrets."

"I will offer you a drachma for every three, simply to spare myself the trouble of further inquiries."

For just an instant the master frowned. One might almost have supposed he was about to take offense. Then his face went smooth again, and one realized that its momentary change of expression had had its origins in something else. "Two drachmas for every five."

"Done."

Having struck their bargain, the two men lapsed into silence, as if they could no longer trust each other with the most harmless conversation. Pammenes, who had remained silent all through the meal, caught Philip's eye and smiled.

"I am always amused when men speak of the ruthlessness of politics," he said later, when they had gone down to the docks in hopes of escaping the heat—the sun had long since set, but the very walls of the houses were still warm to the touch, making the prospect of a sea breeze very welcome. "Yet what are politics except the relations of everyday life played out on a somewhat larger scale? I have made this tedious journey to treat with the Athenians on questions of commerce and military policy, and I am obliged to have no thought except for the profit of Thebes. Substitute my own interests for those of Thebes and I am a merchant from Lydia, trading in the flesh of young girls. Or a teacher of rhetoric, instructing his students in the best means of perverting the conclusions of a jury. By contrast, the statesman is all openness and generosity, since he confines his treachery to foreigners."

"Then the Lydian was right—life is a brothel."

"Say rather that it is a war and that the condition of happiness is not having to fight it for oneself alone."

The next morning, after Pammenes had gone off in search of someone with whom to negotiate his treaty, Philip found himself quite at liberty. He had been away from home for several months by then and the idea of exploring yet another foreign city alone oppressed him. He longed to see a familiar face. To the best of his knowledge Athens contained only one, that of his childhood friend Aristotle. Thus, when he reached the central marketplace, he asked directions to the school of the philosopher Plato.

"Oh, yes, it is about a quarter of an hour's walk beyond the gates. Just follow the road until you come to the Grove of Akademus—you will know the place when you see it. Do you plan to enroll then, youngster? Will you go home in a year or two and overthrow your city's government?"

The old stonecutter to whom he had addressed his inquiry seemed vastly amused by this suggestion. He laid his tools down on the marble section of column upon which he had been working that he might be at liberty to laugh all the harder at his own joke.

"One goes there to study politics?" Philip asked when the laughter had subsided enough that he thought there was some chance of being heard. "Such was not my impression."

"It is a school for treason and blasphemy, or that is what people say," the stonecutter answered, after first wiping his eyes. The description was offered without any apparent malice. "I myself have doubts. I knew Sokrates, whose disciple Plato claims to be—his booth was just here, next to my own, when I was apprenticed to my father—and there was no particular harm in him, although he was lazy and a poor workman. If he carved a capital, it would always come out a little crooked. Yet that does not make a man a criminal. It was after the war with Sparta and tempers were short that they made him drink his hemlock. In such times a fool who loves the sound of his own voice is not safe."

Philip thanked the man for assisting him and started in the direction that would take him to the main gate. He was not sure which impressed him more, that in Athens they executed their philosophers or that they cared enough about such matters to take the trouble. It was certainly not in every city that any workman could point one's way to the doorstep of the local sage. No wonder that Aristotle had been eager to come here.

The road leading into the countryside was straight and heavily traveled so that the dust that quickly covered one's feet had long since been ground fine under the wheels of a million oxcarts. Already, by midmorning, the sun made the back of Philip's neck burn. He wondered if Aristotle might have a pitcher of wine about him, or if philosophers were above noticing the heat.

The Grove of Akademus was a pleasant place. Flies buzzed in the shade of plane trees that someone had once planted in neat rows but which had long since grown tall enough that their branches laced together to make an unbroken canopy. Men gathered in little clusters of two or three, and sometimes as many as ten or fifteen sat at the feet of some wise teacher, scratching away at their wax tablets as he spoke. Everywhere there was the murmur of voices.

Philip found Aristotle by himself, sitting with his back against a tree trunk, reading a scroll. Aristotle glanced up at the sound of his name. He did not even seem surprised.

"My father wrote to me that you had been sent to Thebes as a hostage," he said as he stood up. The scroll dangled from his hand so that one end almost touched the ground. "I take it, from your presence here, that the terms of your captivity are not too harsh."

"No, it is not harsh. It is not even captivity. I could return to Macedon tomorrow and the Thebans would merely shake their heads at my rashness and wish me a safe journey. They have all been very kind. Pammenes is here on diplomatic business and brought me with him as a treat."

"Pammenes?" Aristotle allowed himself to look impressed. "I should like to meet him if it can be managed conveniently. All the Theban oligarchs are well thought of here. Plato holds them up as models of the enlightened and selfless ruler—he only wishes they would pay more attention to philosophy."

"Does a ruler need philosophy?"

"Plato thinks so. Let me introduce you to him. He has a weakness for royalty. Since you are a prince, he may even invite us to lunch. You will find him amusing . . ."

And he was amusing. Plato turned out to be a man in his early sixties, white-haired, effeminate, and voluptuously fat. The servant who stood beside him at the table and kept his wine cup filled was perhaps twelve years old, and from time to time, while he talked about Sokrates or the Ideal of the Good or the indignities he had suffered at the hands of his disciples, the great philosopher's hands would absentmindedly wander over the boy's shoulders and neck. In spite of this minor distraction, his conversation, delivered in the purring voice of one who has left no passion ungratified, was fascinating.

"It is against every principle of reason that a government that is at the mercy of society's basest elements could ever attain either coherence of purpose or dignity of expression. Even the best of men cannot turn mud into gold simply by squeezing it between his fingers, and in like manner even the most selfless of patriots must find himself hampered and corrupted by allowing himself to become the agent of mob rule. The ideal of rational policy can only be attained when authority is vested in a single individual, and he a philosopher king. Democracy has been a curse upon the Greeks, not least upon the Athenians, who condemned my master, Sokrates, simply because they could not understand the complexity of his thought. My dear Prince, you must try a little honey on those figs. It improves the flavor enormously."

"Yet, Master, is not all government simply an expression of human nature, and should we not therefore be indifferent as to its form?" Aristotle inquired, with just the hint of a malicious smile tugging at the corner of his mouth. "Your own experience with Dion of Syracuse . . ."

Provided one had eyes to see, the look that passed between student and teacher—the flash of irritation, instantly extinguished and covered over with a laugh and a deprecatory wave of the hand—revealed much, and Philip realized, with the slight shock that always accompanies any change in our assessment of the familiar, that Plato, for all his years and vast prestige, was just a little afraid of Aristotle and that Aristotle knew it. And at the same time he was disappointed with himself for being surprised. Plato must have realized that the physician's son from Pella was the most gifted of his disciples and, in a world where intellectual agility counted for everything, why should he not be just a little afraid?

"Ah, yes, that wretched man—such a disappointment!" Plato sighed like an actor in a bad tragedy and consoled himself with a swallow of wine and a glance at his servant boy. "I was speaking merely of what might be. A tyrant may be clever or a fool, virtuous or criminal, a blessing to his subjects or a curse. Anything is possible, even perfection. Democracy, however, is always and of necessity a catastrophe. Athens has become like the people who rule it, and our polity has assumed the character of a porter's wife—grasping, quarrelsome, petty, and contradictory. Our allies and our enemies alike are united in their hatred of us, and for all this we have our democracy to thank."

When lunch was over, Philip persuaded Aristotle to return with him. They would climb the Akropolis together and visit the temple of Athena.

"I have been in Athens for half a year and have never seen it," Aristotle mentioned as they rejoined the road leading back to the city. "I am not quite sure what Plato believes concerning the gods, but displays of piety are not encouraged. Nevertheless, I am given to understand that the building itself is quite beautiful. Also, the statue of the goddess is considered the finest piece of sculpture in the world."

"Excellent. Then I will make sacrifice to my patroness, and you will admire her proportions. It seems likely that aesthetic pleasure and religious awe are both simply aspects of the same movement of the soul toward the divine, so perhaps the goddess will not take offense."

"You are beginning to sound like one of Plato's students."

"Am I? It is probably something about the climate."

"Did you know that Arrhidaios is in the city?"

At the mention of his half brother's name, Philip felt a chill, which he interpreted as mere surprise.

"No," he answered, "I did not. Have you seen him? Is he well?"

"I have not seen him, nor should I advise you to do so. If one wishes to return to Macedon, it is wisest not to compromise oneself by associating with declared traitors."

"Arrhidaios is not a traitor," Philip snapped, astonished at his own sudden flash of anger. "One is not a traitor for seeking refuge from the suspicions of our lord regent. You know as well as I that had he not fled, Ptolemy would have found some way of implicating him in Alexandros's murder."

"I believe I referred to Arrhidaios as a declared traitor. I did not accuse him of anything."

The expression of Aristotle's face suggested that he was amused rather than offended, which was not necessarily preferable. Philip decided that it might be best simply to go on.

"How is he living?" he asked.

"Quite well, I should imagine." Aristotle shrugged his thin shoulders, as if bored to be discussing anything so obvious. "Doubtless he has his patrons—a foreign prince is always an asset."

When Philip looked merely blank, Aristotle smiled and Philip knew at once that he was about to receive a lesson in political sophistication. He did not much relish his friend's tendency to treat him like a raw bumpkin, fresh from the edge of the world, but he supposed he had something of the sort coming. He decided to remain silent and let Aristotle enjoy himself.

"Athens has interests in the north to which Macedon is a potential threat," Aristotle began, in a voice he must have copied from one of his teachers. "She has colonies in Chalcidice and Thrace, and she must always be concerned to preserve her access to the Black Sea. As long as Macedon is weak and in turmoil Athens may do as she likes, and the House of the Argeadai oblige by regularly plotting against and murdering whomever among them happens to be currently occupying the throne. Thus, having Arrhidaios in reserve suits Athens quite well, since it gives her someone with whom she can threaten the Lord Ptolemy—or whoever should happen to succeed him in power. A possible pretender is as good as a small army, and much cheaper to maintain."

He glanced at Philip and smiled again.

"Thus perhaps, at least now, the Lord Ptolemy is not wrong in suspecting Arrhidaios of treason, since, if he has made no overt move against the peace of his homeland, he is at least poised to do so."

Philip felt a giddy sensation in the pit of his stomach. It was a kind of grief, and he knew that it showed. In that moment, and for the first time in his life, Philip discovered that he really hated Aristotle, who was enjoying his distress. The feeling would pass, and with it his anger—this he understood quite well—but for that brief space of time both were quite real.

"A man is not made a traitor by what is forced upon him." He found himself unable to say anything more.

"Then let me ask you a question, Philip—as we have known each other all our lives, I will take the liberty." Aristotle's countenance now showed only a kind of awed pity, as if he realized at last that what he had stirred up with his restless intellectual probing was something akin to tragedy. "If it had been you, forced to flee to escape the plots of your relatives, would you have put yourself at the disposal of Macedon's enemies?"

When Philip did not answer, Aristotle shook his head.

"No, I thought not. You, at least, would have preferred to starve in a ditch."

As they walked in silence, they passed a slave gang—a line of eight or ten emaciated figures trudging lifelessly along the side of the road, a long chain running through the rings of the iron collars they wore around their necks, the end fastened to the back of a wagon loaded with stone. There was a burly man driving the wagon and a guard bringing up the rear of the column, but he hardly seemed to need the whip he carried in his hand. These pathetic creatures had long since forgotten even the possibility of resistance.

"City slaves," Aristotle announced as if answering a question. "One can tell from the way the tops of their ears are notched."

"Then they were probably prisoners of war whose families could not pay the ransom. What a grotesque fate to befall a man whose only crime was to be on the losing side."

"You are too compassionate, Philip—especially for a prince. A slave is nothing more than a tool with life in it."

"What, then, must an exile be? Those men, perhaps, fought for their country. Arrhidaios has not even so much as that to dignify his loss."

19

It was late afternoon before Philip and Aristotle returned from visiting the temple of Athena Parthenos, and Pammenes had not returned to the inn. Instead, he had sent round a note to the effect that Philip should meet him for dinner at the house of one Aristodemos near the Dipylon Gate.

"Do you mind if I accompany you?" Aristotle inquired, with the air of one who knows he will not be refused. "Aristodemos is one of the richest men in Athens, a dabbler in politics and a collector of famous men—his banquets are notorious for their size and anonymity. No one will even notice my presence."

"Then how can I mind?"

They went to the public baths and cleaned off the dust of their excursion. The light was beginning to fail by the time they reached the Dipylon Gate, but they had no trouble locating Aristodemos's house. They had merely to follow the noise.

As Philip and Aristotle entered, a man stumbled past them through the door. When they turned around to look he was doubled over, retching against the wall of the house.

"What a pig!" Aristotle murmured, shaking his head, but Philip merely laughed.

"Don't be so exacting, my friend, for thus you show yourself unaccustomed to the usages of the great. Besides, had this been my father's court in Pella he would not have troubled himself to find his way outside, otherwise his retreat would have been covered by a hail of half-chewed mutton bones."

"I gather, at any rate, that they have started without us."

And so it was. A banquet, no less than a man, struggles through infancy to youth and then, after reaching its full growth, enters the inevitable decline that leads to extinction. It was apparent at once that this particular revel was well advanced into a vigorous maturity. The clattering din of perhaps a hundred different conversations drowned out the musicians, so that the women who had been hired as entertainers seemed to dance to some inner rhythm only they could hear. Even in the great hall, which, had it been empty, might have seemed a large room, the damp heat of so many bodies was overpowering, and the air stank of wine.

The head table was toward the back of the hall, and it took Philip a moment to discover it. Pammenes was there, sitting next to a plump, elderly little dandy whose hair and beard were an unnatural silvery color and elaborately curled. This was presumably their host. Pammenes' attention was all directed, however, toward the man at his right, who was in his middle years and dressed with the simplicity of one who is not interested in being noticed.

"Is that he?"

When Philip nodded, Aristotle smiled with satisfaction. "I thought as much. That is Aristodemos, looking like a pampered old cat. And the one on the other side is Anytos, a member of the Committee of Fifty—a powerful figure, for all that he is only a carpenter. I see we will be obliged to fend for ourselves, since there are no places near the guest of honor. It is just as well. I plan to forget for one night that I am a philosopher and become wildly drunk."

"Will anyone be able to tell the difference?"

Aristotle did not seem to find the jest particularly amusing.

After perhaps an hour Philip began to wish he had stayed behind at the inn and dined on bread and onions. He did not care for the noise, and the man sitting next to him seemed to have made a game out of knocking over his wine cup and scattering its contents all over his neighbors.

If I leave, no one will be offended, he thought. *Aristotle knows the city far better than I do. He does not need me for a guide. And Pammenes is too occupied with business to notice. This banquet is not amusing—I would do better to be asleep in my own bed.*

It was really quite simple. All that was required was to get up from the table and leave—if anyone noticed, they probably imagined he needed to empty his bladder. He dodged around servants carrying pitchers that still dripped from the cellar and shouldered his way through the crowd, which, for some unfathomable reason, clogged the antechamber like leaves in a rain gutter. As he stood on the steps leading up to the house, in the little circle of light that escaped through the door, the first breath of fresh air, simply by virtue of the fact that it was not rank with the odors of wine and humanity, felt as cold as snow. The darkness seemed to beckon him.

"Going home already, Philip? Or do the brothels beckon?"

Philip, prince of Macedon, was not the sort who betrayed surprise, yet with the sound of this voice that appeared to come from nowhere, he froze, his mind racing as he tried to recall . . .

"Arrhidaios? Is that you? Is it really you?"

Something moved among the shadows on the wall of the building opposite—he could not be sure if he saw it or merely sensed it. Then the shadow became the hem of a cloak. Then a man.

It was his half brother, smiling up at him a bit ruefully.

Philip laughed and ran down the stairs to throw his arms around him, kissing him on the face. Soon they were both laughing.

"How did you know where to find me?" he asked, with a mixture of astonishment and pleasure.

"I didn't." Arrhidaios grabbed the beard on Philip's chin in both hands and pulled it playfully. "I didn't even know you were in Athens, but sooner or later everyone comes to the house of Aristodemos. So it was fated . . ."

Another figure emerged from the shadows, a tall, thin youth of perhaps twenty. His hard, rather petulant mouth suggested a certain amused contempt, as though he regarded himself as having risen above the attachments of kinship. He glanced vacantly about for a second or two and then his eyes settled upon Philip, to whom he seemed to take an instant dislike. One could almost have imagined he was jealous.

"Yes." Arrhidaios stepped back. He looked embarrassed. "Philip, this is Demosthenes, whose words linger on the tongue like honey when he speaks in the assembly."

"Then I look forward to hearing him one day," Philip said, offering his hand.

Neither Arrhidaios's compliment nor Philip's hand seemed very welcome. The latter was taken in a limp grasp and then dropped almost at once, as one might after having been surprised to discover himself holding the fingers of a corpse. The former was simply ignored.

"Pleased."

That was all he said, but the one word betrayed everything. For just an instant it appeared to be lodged in his throat, only to come out at last with a kind of puff, giving the impression he meant to propel it some distance. It was apparent that the gods had cursed the great orator with a stammer.

Philip tried to keep his eyes blank and his smile as uncomprehending as any fool's, but a man possessed of a flaw is always quick to detect when it is noticed. The lines around Demosthenes' mouth seemed to harden.

"Are you going inside?" Philip turned to his half brother and tried to make himself forget that they were not alone. "I was just leaving, but . . ."

"No, no, no. I am sure Demosthenes will excuse us—he wishes to meet the great Pammenes, and my presence might be something of an embarrassment."

Arrhidaios laughed nervously, in the manner of one who wishes to be contradicted, but Demosthenes merely frowned and glanced away.

"You must p-please yourself," he said. Without waiting for a reply, he began climbing the stairs up to Aristodemos's front door and was soon lost among the milling crowd in the great man's antechamber.

"Well—it appears we are at liberty to do as we like." Arrhidaios smiled and threw an arm across Philip's shoulders. "Shall we follow your original plan and search out a brothel?"

"My original plan involved nothing of the sort. My original plan was to return to my own bed, which alas is empty."

"But plans can always be changed."

"Yes, I suppose they can."

While it was not precisely a brothel where they ended up, the overall effect was much the same. Arrhidaios knew of a wineshop just at the foot of the Hill of Colonos, which was much frequented by the more elegant young men of the city. There were rooms upstairs for private entertainments, where the wine was served mixed with only three parts of water. The food was excellent, better than that served at Aristodemos's table. There was companionship available, and all inclinations were catered to.

"I had a boy last time I was here," Arrhidaios said as his hand slid over the naked back of the girl who was crouched beside him, pretending to busy herself with the wine as she dragged her nipples back and forth across his chest. "Just for variety—women can grow stale on a man if he doesn't allow himself a change now and then."

"I have never noticed that," Philip answered.

The girl who had been washing Philip's legs was as tawny as a lion and when she spoke, which was not often, it was with an Ionic accent, so she had probably been born in one of the Greek cities along the coast of Asia. Her eyes were as large and as brown as a doe's. Philip liked her eyes best. When she would glance up and smile at him, it made his throat tighten.

Arrhidaios frowned.

"Well, then, of course, you have never been an exile. When one lives among foreigners . . ."

"I live among foreigners." Philip gently placed the sole of his foot against the girl's belly, meaning to push her away, but the touch of her flesh against his toes was such an appealing sensation that he decided against it.

"Yes, but if you go home, it will not be to have your throat cut."

"I don't think I can be sure of that—not as long as the Lord Ptolemy is alive."

"Yes, but for me it would be a certainty." Since fleeing Macedon Arrhidaios had gained weight and already there was a pad of fat beneath his jaw. As he spoke he tucked his chin in against his chest, and his neck seemed to bulge. "You might perish in some palace intrigue, but I would face public execution and my corpse would be crucified over Alexandros's burial mound. By the way, Philip, I had no hand in our brother's murder."

"If I thought you had, you would have been dead hours ago," Philip said, smiling amiably. "Praxis's accomplice is still in Pella—married to my mother."

Philip's doe-eyed girl looked up, as if her attention had been attracted by the sudden silence. When she saw the expressions on the two men's faces, she dropped her gaze.

Then, from one instant to the next, Arrhidaios seemed to lose interest in the discussion.

"I like Athens," he said as he ran his hand admiringly over his girl's back—indeed, he seemed almost to be talking about her. "I have always venerated Athens, but I never conceived what a pleasure it is to live in the most civilized city in the world. There is no pleasure, either of mind or body, that is not available here, and I am under no constraints. I have leisure and, through the favor of my friends, I have money. Indeed, I seem to have all the leisure in the world."

"And what, I wonder, will your friends want of you when at last your leisure comes to an end?"

Arrhidaios raised his eyes and looked at Philip as if he thought him the greatest fool in the world.

"It is possible that one day my friends will succeed in making me king of Macedon," he said, speaking with an evenness that betrayed rather than concealed his anger.

"Our brother Perdikkas is king." The smile on Philip's lips suggested that he had lost the capacity to be shocked by any treachery. "And, should he die without issue, I am to succeed him. Do your friends' plans include both our murders?"

Arrhidaios, in his turn, did not seem offended by the suggestion. He merely shrugged.

"My friends have no idea of murdering anyone. They assume, I would imagine, that Ptolemy will do the work for them."

20

If he lived, Perdikkas, king of the Macedonians, would reach official manhood during the summer of the second year of his reign. No one seemed to take much notice of this approaching fact—least of all the regent, who continued to govern as if he were king in his own right—and Perdikkas felt little inclination to remind him. He was quite sure his stepfather was prepared to have him murdered rather than relinquish power. He never stopped being afraid. His memories of his brother's death were painfully vivid, and some nights he would wake up from a dream, just able to keep himself from screaming as he tried to remember whether it was Alexandros's blood or his own he had seen on the assassin's sword.

Tonight was the worst. He sat on the edge of his bed, trembling all over while cold tears ran down into his beard, looking out into the darkness as if waiting for some enemy to step away from the shadows.

At last he got up and, feeling his way, located the basin and pitcher of water he kept on a table next to his wardrobe chest. He had to be very quiet. The only door led to his mother's room, and tonight the Lord Ptolemy was asleep in her bed. He washed his face with the furtive silence of a man stealing the offerings from a temple altar.

Yet he felt better afterward. He could sit down on his bed again and reconsider the problem that he had gradually become aware was the key to his survival: how he was to kill the regent.

It was not as straightforward a matter as it seemed. The Lord Ptolemy was asleep in the next room, yet Perdikkas knew he could not simply walk in there with a hunting pike and run him through. After all, his mother would be in the same bed, and he could not slaughter the man under his mother's very eyes. The idea itself—the screams and curses, the blood spattered over her naked body—was horrible.

Provided the deed was done out of her sight, Perdikkas told himself, and after she had had a chance to consider the matter, his mother would realize that he had done the right thing, the manly thing, and she would forgive him. Surely she would see that there had been no choice. Surely she could not love this man more than her own child. She would cry and then, after a time, she would see the necessity of it and he would be her son again. Blood, after all, was a stronger tie than desire.

In the darkness of many sleepless nights, Perdikkas had worked it all out for himself. His mother would forgive him. He accepted this as both inevitable and right, and still within his secret heart he doubted. Perhaps, he thought, it was that doubt that stayed his hand.

Yet it was not only his mother he feared. Ptolemy was a tested warrior, the survivor of many battles, and Perdikkas knew himself to be clumsy with weapons. It would not be easy to kill the man openly and it was upon doing it thus that Perdikkas's honor as king depended. No one would blame him if one day he simply drew his sword and spilled the regent's guts out onto the ground. A king may kill anyone he thinks a threat to him, provided he does it as a right, as a thing he is prepared to own before the world. There could be no suggestion of stealth.

Yet to attempt Ptolemy's life that way—as a public act, in front of witnesses—was to take an appalling risk. Perdikkas was not a coward, but neither was he a fool.

It was all a question of opportunity, and the opportunity had not yet presented itself.

Could Ptolemy have any idea of what was in his mind? Night after night, the two men sat beside each other at the banqueting table, sometimes exchanging a look or a word, as casually as if they could see into each other's hearts. Perdikkas found he could not stand these affairs unless he had two or three cups of unmixed wine in his room first. It was like feasting with a scorpion.

Because if the regent ever guessed, Perdikkas knew that his life would not be worth a day's purchase, that his only safety lay in Ptolemy's contempt for him, in the conviction of his harmlessness.

There were days together when Perdikkas forced himself to push all thoughts of violence from his mind—he would be that which the regent imagined him to be, the pliant, trusting fool, no threat to anyone, and then perhaps . . .

But it was no good. The danger was the same, whether he chose to see it or not. If Ptolemy suspected him, merely suspected him, he was as good as laid out upon his funeral pyre.

Once—only once—he hinted at his fears to his mother. They made her smile.

178 ⊠   NICHOLAS GUILD

"You are not in any danger from the Lord Ptolemy," she told him. "You
are his protection."

"From what? From what does the regent need protection?"

"From your brother, you blind fool. He knows that if anything happens to
you, Philip will come back."

"Yes, I can understand that." Perdikkas had nodded, suspecting even then
that he understood nothing. "If I die, the Thebans . . ."

But he was cut off by Eurydike's wild laughter.

"You are an idiot!" she shouted, with sudden ferocity. "Do you imagine
that the Lord Ptolemy is merely afraid that Philip will return at the head of a
foreign army? Let your brother come home alone, with only a kitchen knife
rolled up in his sleeping blanket, and it would be just the same. It is Philip
alone who turns his bowels to ice—he lives in terror of ever setting eyes upon
him again."

It was almost as bad to have his life on sufferance from his little brother as
to live in constant fear of losing it. Sometimes it was worse.

He had to kill Ptolemy. Then he would be free of them both.

A flicker of light from under the door made Perdikkas aware that someone was awake in the next room as well. It was not an unusual enough event
to cause him any alarm. Perhaps the regent's bladder was weakening with age.
It would be pleasant to think that he too was troubled by dreams, but Perdikkas doubted it. Whatever his mother said, he found it difficult to believe that
the Lord Ptolemy was frightened of anything.

The light went out. Perdikkas lay down again, experiencing the dead calm
of despair. He did not fall asleep again until just before dawn.

It was not the regent who had lit a lamp in the middle of the night, but his wife.
The Lord Ptolemy slept on, lying on his side with his face to the wall. He never
noticed when Eurydike slipped noiselessly out of bed.

She hardly seemed to sleep at all anymore. Sleep required some peace of
mind, or at least a certain indifference to fate. Yet, as the circumstances of her
life became less and less tolerable, she found herself correspondingly less able
to ignore them. Her son anxious and moody, contemplating the gods knew
what rashness. Her daughter still trying to conceive a child by the man who
had divorced her and now used her as he might one of the kitchen servants.
And Ptolemy, who drank more wine now than was good for him and was even
more frightened than Perdikkas. They all seemed drawn helplessly into some
vortex from which there was now no possibility of escape.

She held up the lamp to look at her husband, but all she could see was the
back of his head. His hair still a glossy black, although threads of gray were
beginning to show up in his beard.

Merely to look at him gave her a trembling sensation in her breast, as if she were fifteen and in the grip of her first passion. No, it was worse than that. The love she bore this man simply consumed her, as if the gods had chosen him as the instrument of her destruction. Ptolemy was faithless and evil. He would sacrifice anyone on the altar of his ambition. She did not believe, as many did, that he had had any part in the murder of her son—she would not allow herself to believe it, for then existence would be unendurable—but she could not conceal from herself that no scruple would have prevented him. There was no sin of which he was not capable. All this she saw quite clearly, and it made no difference. It was her curse to love him without illusion. And to love him with such blind need that sometimes she felt as if she must break apart, simply shatter like a pot that falls against the stone floor. There were times when she felt she must be going mad.

He stirred in his sleep, muttering something in an urgent, unintelligible voice, and, instinctively, she held up her hand to mask the lamplight. But it was not the light which disturbed him. The Lord Ptolemy suffered from frightful dreams so that sometimes he would wake up covered with sweat, his eyes gleaming with terror. He blamed it on the wine, but it was not the wine. He would never tell her what it was that he dreamed.

He did not need to. She could guess.

Eurydike carried the light out into the antechamber and then sought her daughter's room. She knew Mena would not be asleep.

She was not, although there was no light coming from beneath her door.

"Is that you, Mother?"

"Yes, child." Eurydike raised the lamp that it might illuminate her face, and she smiled. "Have I awakened you?" she asked, quite unnecessarily.

Mena did not trouble to answer. She pushed herself toward the far side of her narrow little bed to make room for her mother to sit down.

The room was very small, so small that the yellow glow of the lamp filled it up to the corners of the ceiling. There was only the bed and a chest and a three-legged stool on which no one ever sat down. Mena dropped her eyes, as if the light troubled her.

"Is he asleep?" she asked.

"Yes. If he awakens, he will reach for the wine jug. He will never even notice that I am not there."

Mena seemed relieved to hear it, although why she should be afraid of her former husband discovering them together was a mystery. Mena had eccentric notions about the propriety of things—as if propriety could be of any concern in this household.

It was strange, but Eurydike had only grown close to her daughter after supplanting her as the Lord Ptolemy's wife. She had never had much patience with children and Mena had been married young, which had had the effect of removing her from sight almost as completely as if she had been sealed up in her funeral urn. Then Ptolemy had set her aside and married her mother.

Eurydike put the lamp on the floor, which had the effect of returning Mena to the shadows. She seemed to prefer it thus.

"I think I am with child," Mena said, in a thrilled murmur. "There was a full moon night before last when he came to my room. I take it as a sign that I will shake off my barrenness."

Eurydike only smiled, having heard something of the sort every few weeks for almost the whole time she had lived under the Lord Ptolemy's roof. It would be a blessing if Mena could become pregnant—it would distract her—but it was not to be.

"You will see. He will love me again if I bear him a son."

"He loves no one," Eurydike answered, reaching down to stroke her daughter's hair. "He does not even love the son he has. He married you out of ambition and then, when I could serve him better, he put me in your place. He loves no one."

"How can you say that? You are his wife."

"Then who should know better? He has treated you wretchedly—surely you cannot be blind to his true nature. He is a wicked man."

"Yet you love him."

"Yes. This is the curse the gods have visited upon me."

When her fingertips brushed Mena's cheek Eurydike felt her daughter's tears.

"You must not weep," she said. "You must put aside your illusions. It would be far better if you learned to hate him. Surely he has earned your hatred. You must never weep for him."

"Yet you weep for him."

In that moment Eurydike felt as if her heart might tear open. She almost wished it would, that she might die at once.

"No, I never weep," she said.

21

Philip woke with a start. He waited for a moment, listening, letting his eyes adjust to the darkness. There was nothing. Every shadow in the tiny room was familiar to him, and the only sound was the quiet stir of Madzos's breathing as she slept beside him.

Perhaps there had been a noise outside. Perhaps he should look and see. Philip climbed out of bed and opened the shutter on the room's only window. The moon had been full just two nights before, so he could see quite clearly. He could make out the individual stones of the city wall. The street, some ten or twelve cubits below him, was empty. There was no sound anywhere. It was the middle of the night, and the decent people of Thebes were all asleep.

Then he heard it again.

The roof of the building across the street was almost level with the window and, perched on the crest, so close that Philip could not understand how he had missed seeing it before, was an owl, staring back at him with gigantic yellow eyes. Its call was what had awakened him.

For a moment the owl stayed quite still, and then it opened its wings and flapped them, as if to call attention to itself before suddenly throwing itself forward and into flight. It wheeled around once and then flew away, heading north.

He did not have to inquire into the meaning of this strange encounter—the goddess's intention was quite clear.

"Are you up?"

Philip turned around and smiled, although he was not sure Madzos could even see him in the darkness. After what had happened, even the smile felt like an act of treachery.

"Yes, I am up."

"What is it?"

Had there been something in his voice? After all this time Madzos could probably read him like a scroll, except that she couldn't read. And a girl raised in a tavern would have an intimate understanding of human weakness and perfidy. There seemed little enough point in lying to her.

"I have to go back," he said, wondering why his words sounded so hollow.

"Back where?"

By now she was sitting up in the bed. In a moment she would light a lamp and he would be able to see the way her long black hair cascaded over her shoulders, half covering her breasts. He had been sleeping with her for nearly two years, yet his longing for her, for the taste of her flesh and the feel of her thighs pressing against his own, had never been stronger.

"Back to Macedon. I have to go home."

She didn't say anything at first. When the lamplight began to throw shadows over her body and he could see her face, she didn't even seem surprised. Yet what could surprise a woman who had been brought to this house at the age of eight and had worked here as a slave until the tavern master married her? A wife at fifteen, a widow at seventeen, and her own mistress for ten years. She was nearly that much older than Philip, yet the difference in experience had nothing to do with time.

"But not tonight," she said, blowing out the lamp, as if realizing that lighting it had been a mistake. "Come back to bed—you can keep me warm until the morning."

And when the morning came Philip went to the house of Pammenes, where he found the great man in his garden, at breakfast.

"You say you must return?" Pammenes asked after listening to Philip's story. He poured the younger man a cup of wine, blended with five parts of water as befitted the hour. "Yet to see an owl in the middle of the night is not so unusual an occurrence that we are compelled to read into it the promptings of the gods."

"One may see the most commonplace thing and know in one's bowels that it is from the gods." Philip grinned, as if to concede the folly of his own words. "I have been summoned, and I have no choice but to obey."

"You Macedonians are a superstitious lot. Yet in your fervor to submit to heaven's call have you calculated how long you are likely to live after you have put yourself once more within the Lord Ptolemy's reach?"

Philip merely shrugged. When Pammenes understood that this was all the answer he was to receive, he nodded.

"I see. Then have you given any thought to how you will proceed?"

"I planned simply to ride out this morning as if I intended to go hunting. You could then report to the regent that I had escaped. You have always been my friend, My Lord, and I had no wish to burden you with a diplomatic problem."

Pammenes made a contemptuous face as he dipped a piece of flatbread into his wine.

"Macedon is not so great a power in the world that Thebes need stand in much awe of the Lord Ptolemy's wrath—I do not wish to insult your patriotism, Philip, but there it is."

His eyes narrowed as he studied Philip's face. Then suddenly he smiled.

"Yet there is nothing to be gained by alerting your stepfather's spies, is there? I assume you plan to travel overland?"

"That would give me the best chance of slipping back into Macedon undetected, yes."

"Yet the journey by horse, particularly at this season, will take you at least twelve days, and a letter carried by ship could be read in Pella after three. There are not so many roads through the mountains that the regent cannot have them all patrolled. I think perhaps an escape is not the best plan."

They were sitting in the shade of a grape arbor, and Pammenes frowned as a linnet perched among the vines. He reached down to pick up a handful of pebbles and threw them with savage force at the bird, who managed to flutter away unharmed.

"My wife used to feed them," he said in a voice that was almost a growl. "And still they come around. When they are disappointed of bread crumbs they peck at the grapes."

It occurred to Philip that he had known the Lord Pammenes for more than two years, and this was the first he had ever heard of any wife. Yet he did not seem destined to learn anything more, for the Boeotarch quickly returned to his original subject.

"There is an envoy leaving for Delphi tomorrow," he said. "His ostensible purpose is to consult the oracle, but his real business is of a more practical nature and need not concern you. You can travel with him for half a day, just until you are well out of sight of the city, and then strike off to the north on your own. I will see to it that the commander of the escort has his orders and will not hinder you. I can provide you with a letter of safe conduct, which will be respected as far as Thessaly, but perhaps it would be better if you did not have it on your person when you cross the border into Macedon."

"I would certainly not show it to the regent," Philip replied, but if he had intended his answer for a joke, it was a failure. Pammenes' frown deepened, as if Philip too had been picking at his grape arbor.

"I am far more concerned that he might find it on your corpse, Prince. Your return will present the Lord Ptolemy with far too direct a challenge to allow him to ignore it, and we both know he is not burdened with many scruples about the spilling of blood. Thus I do not rate your chances of survival very highly."

"It is in the hands of the goddess," Philip said, with a simplicity that made it impossible to imagine he was anything except perfectly serious. "I can only hope that the Lady Athena spares me for some purpose of her own."

"Yes, indeed—piety is all very well." Still frowning, Pammenes surveyed the upper reaches of his grape arbor, giving the impression he expected a cloud of birds to descend upon it. "And if, after tomorrow, ever I hear from you again, Philip, I truly will believe you lead a charmed life."

The ride north was like an escape from prison. Among other things, Philip discovered that he really had been a hostage in Thebes—if not to the Thebans then to his own sense of futility. In Thebes he had felt like the witness to a catastrophe he was helpless to prevent. One brother had been murdered and the other lived at the whim of his murderer. It was intolerable and yet had somehow to be tolerated. Without knowing what he should do, Philip had always carried with him the sense that his enforced idleness was a shameful indulgence of his own weakness and cowardice.

And now the goddess had released him. He knew precisely what was expected of him—that he return to Pella and either kill the Lord Ptolemy or die in the attempt, which was the more probable outcome. But Pella was eight or ten days to the north and in the meantime, riding across the vast, empty grasslands of northern Greece, he enjoyed a delicious sense of freedom, as if he had had but one decision to make in his life and he had made it.

Although he kept to the main road, he would sometimes go all day without meeting another traveler. Winter was giving way to spring, and the rains were beginning in earnest. In the middle of the afternoon, sometimes with no warning, the heavens would open and, for an hour or so, drown the world. There was nothing to be done except to find a bit of shelter, which in that treeless expanse was not always just at hand, and wait. Anyone who had a choice stayed comfortably at home.

Two hours before Philip saw the watchtowers of Pharsalos he was caught in the open by an icy rain that drenched him as thoroughly as if he had thrown himself in a river. Even his sleeping blanket was soaked through. Out of deference to Pammenes, who, without saying so, had implied that he would prefer that his letter of safe conduct be used as sparingly as possible, Philip had avoided the cities, buying food and horse fodder at farmhouses he encountered along the way, but tonight the prospect of a tavern, where he could dine on roasted meat and dry his clothes before the hearth where it was being cooked, where he could sleep in a warm room and a dry bed, was simply more than he could resist.

As it happened, the guards were playing dice as he passed in through the city gates, and did not even glance up. He could have had an invading army at his back and they would never have noticed.

At the first tavern he found he gave his horse to the stableboy and carried his bag and bedroll inside. When he opened the door the sound of laughter and the welcoming, warm, food-scented air seemed to jolt him out of a trance. There was a side of mutton on the fire and, as it turned on the spit, sizzling juice ran down it like sweat. He couldn't remember when he had ever been so hungry.

A short time later, his clothes dry, his belly full, and his head buzzing with wine, Philip sat on a stool in front of the hearth waiting for the ninth hour, when the lamps would be dimmed and the local people would be sent home to their beds. Then the landlord would spread a blanket on the floor for him and he would be allowed to go to sleep. His beard felt warm from the fire and he was enjoying an almost voluptuous sense of exhaustion when he felt a breath of cold air on the back of his neck and, the next instant, heard the door slam shut behind him. He turned to look, not really very interested, and saw that another traveler had arrived.

"Something to eat, landlord—and a jar of that thick Thessalian wine. I have been riding into a raw wind all evening and I need to coat my throat. By the gods, I would not leave a dog outside on such a night."

Philip knew at once that the man was a Thracian, for even by Macedonian standards his accent was barbaric and he wore a heavy woolen cape of a dark green that marked him as a member of one of the coastal tribes. He was tall, as were most of that race, about thirty years old, and possessed of an elaborately curled black beard. The Thracians, when they weren't raiding other people's cattle, were great traders all over the north of Greece.

Where had this one come from? They were only about four days' ride from the border with Macedon. Perhaps the man had journeyed through Pella on his way south. It was with a mixture of dread and anticipation that Philip realized he might be about to hear his first recent news of home in over two years.

"While you wait for the landlord to find his way to the cellar, have a taste of mine, friend," Philip said, dropping into the country dialect that he had first heard at Alcmene's knee. Without rising from his stool, he held up his own cup for the man's inspection. "Thick as syrup and red as blood—you could catch flies with it."

The Thracian took the offered cup and, after saluting Philip with a mischievous smile, drained off the last drop.

"That went down nicely, friend," he said as he lowered himself onto the stool beside Philip's. "I thank you, for these Greeks have no more notion of hospitality than does a cow whose backside is swarming with flies. How long have you been away from home?"

"Two years and more. I've been in Thebes, studying to be a physician, but I'm afraid I haven't made much of a success of it."

Philip grinned like a man making light of his own weakness. He had learned a long time ago that people will believe any evil a man speaks of himself and he wanted to forestall detailed inquiries. He was pleased to observe how forgivingly the Thracian nodded.

"I know how it is—spent more time studying anatomy with the whores than with your teachers, hey? Hah, hah! Well, a fellow is only young once. You wouldn't happen to have a taste more of that axle grease, now would you?"

Half an hour later, when they had shared out the rest of Philip's jar between them, then the Thracian's, and were halfway through another, and Philip had heard all about the intricacies of the hide business—as it turned out, the fellow traded all around the northern lands, from Chalcidice to Acarnania—the conversation at last turned in a promising direction.

"Well, I don't suppose you will be too happy to be home, eh?" The hide merchant shook his head, as if to answer his own question. "I suppose you're from Pella, since everywhere else in Macedon is just a mud hovel. A boring place is Pella."

"Have you been there recently?"

"Recently? Oh, yes. I was in Pella at the beginning of last month. Did a few good strokes of business too. Bought a few hundred horse hides. The Macedonians, I'll say this for 'em, know a thing or two about the management of horses—there wasn't a mark or a blemish on any one of them hides. Still, I was glad to leave."

"And how fares the king?" Philip was conscious of time seeming to stop while he waited for an answer.

"Well enough, for all I know. Why? Is he a great favorite of yours?" The Thracian slapped Philip on the back, laughing with great energy. "Yes, well enough. I saw him once. Rode right past me through the city gates—hunting, I suppose. They say he is very keen on hunting. Fine figure of a man. Admired his horse."

The Thracian took a meditative sip from his wine cup, seeming to relive in memory that one sight of Macedon's king. Or perhaps he was imagining how well the horse's skin would look stretched tight on one of his drying racks.

Yet something was not right. Perdikkas, unless he had improved mightily in two years, was an ungainly rider, always giving the impression that he was in imminent danger of falling off.

"Perhaps then it was not the king you saw," Philip ventured. "Perhaps . . ."

"Oh, yes. It was the king." This followed by several vigorous nods. "I recall someone saying, 'There goes the king.' A man in his fifties riding a black stallion. It was Ptolemy."

Philip felt a shiver of dread through his bowels that was almost painful. Yet a foreigner could always make a mistake . . .

"The king is a young man," Philip said evenly as if it were the most neutral of topics they were discussing. "He is hardly older than myself. When I left home they had just appointed a regent—I think his name was Ptolemy. If there has been a change, I am surprised to have heard nothing of it."

"Well, I heard a man call him 'king.'" The Thracian's tone was belligerent, as if Philip had called him a liar. And then, almost from one breath to the next, he seemed to dismiss his anger. "But perhaps the rogue was mistaken—a regent is as good as a king in most men's eyes. I own I was more interested in this fellow Ptolemy's horse than in him. By the gods, that stallion was a big one! And so fierce he seemed to breathe fire. If Ptolemy wasn't the king, perhaps he should have been, with a horse like that."

That night, as Philip lay in the darkened tavern, with only the embers from the fire to throw a lurid gleam across part of the floor, he tried to calm his wilder fears and to see the thing as it really was. After all, it had been a mere four days since he had left Thebes, and surely if Ptolemy had declared himself king, Pammenes would have received word of it almost as soon as the first ship arrived from Pella. This drunken hide seller, who was at present snoring loudly with his back to the hearth, could offer no intelligence that was not at least a month and a half old. Therefore Perdikkas was still alive and there had been no revolution.

What the Thracian was reporting was simply the climate of opinion. *A regent is as good as a king in most men's eyes.* People had simply grown accustomed to the Lord Ptolemy's assumption of his king's place.

And he had let them, for he had no intention of ever relinquishing it. Doubtless by now no one would be too shocked if Perdikkas were set aside and Ptolemy became king in name as well as in fact.

That is what he plans to do, Philip thought. *And soon.* Perdikkas would be eighteen in another two months, and the regency would then have to come to an end. The only choices remaining to Ptolemy were death or murder, for once Perdikkas broke free he would be certain to order him killed—not to strengthen his rule or even in revenge for Alexandros but out of the vindictiveness born of fear. Perdikkas would crush him merely to prove to himself that he was afraid no longer. And this Ptolemy knew as well as anyone.

The next morning, while the western horizon was still black with night, Philip was dressed and sitting before the cold ashes of the fire, scraping his breakfast out of a pot left over from last night's dinner. The landlord, when he found him there, assumed at once that he was trying to take himself off while everyone was asleep to avoid the reckoning.

"Your money is in that pouch hanging from the roasting spit," Philip said. "Two Athenian drachmas of silver, lest you imagine I intended to rob you."

The landlord, once he had retrieved the pouch and emptied the coins out into his hand, declared that no such suspicion had crossed his mind, but by way of atonement—and because two silver drachmas was enough to pay for a banquet—he offered Philip a cup of wine to clear his throat and made him up a dinner sack with meat and bread and even a small jar of his best Lemnian. For two silver drachmas he would have been content to let Philip lie with his daughter as well.

When the city gates opened at sunrise, Philip's horse was the first one through.

It was a measure of Philip's urgency that on the third night after leaving Pharsalos he slept in the last of the northern Greek colonies, the city of Methone. The next morning, following the coastal road, he met a farmer walking along with his mattock over his shoulder, and when he asked the man the name of the village up ahead, he was answered in the heavy, rather clipped accent of the Macedonian peasantry. He knew then that he was home.

By the early afternoon he was in the city of Aloros. It would have been a simple matter to hire a boat and sail across the gulf to Pella, but he was too well known along the docks of the capital. Someone was sure to recognize him and within an hour, probably, Ptolemy would know that he was back. He had come too far to lose everything for want of a little patience. Thus, although he burned to be home, he decided to keep to his horse and follow the road that curved around the water's edge like a fishhook. He slept on the ground that night, and the next afternoon, when he began to recognize the countryside and knew he was within a few hours of Pella, he left the road and rode inland. He would shelter that night on the plains, where he had hunted and played as a boy, where his mind would be free and he could decide what to do.

It was dark by the time he found a place to stop, and he cooked his dinner in a grove of oak trees close enough to the city where he had been born that he could see the fire against which the guards warmed themselves outside the main gate. It felt strange to be so close and yet not dare to enter—for Pella was the regent's city, and there every loyal subject's hand would be turned against him. By returning home without leave, Philip had made himself an outlaw.

He sat beside his campfire, letting it die out of its own, trying to think of some clever approach that would allow him to get close enough to Ptolemy to kill him before anyone had a chance to intervene. He considered simply riding into the palace courtyard and walking in on the man while he was having his breakfast, but Ptolemy was no fool and no one was allowed to carry arms within the royal precincts. Even if he wasn't arrested, his sword would be taken away from him, and the regent would see to it that he never had another chance. He would probably finish up in a dungeon somewhere—or in a ditch.

No, it had to be in the open. It had to take him unawares so that he would have no recourse but to answer Philip as one man to another, without subterfuge or cunning. And it had to be a public challenge, something he could not dismiss except at the expense of his reputation as a man of courage and honor.

But where? And, more importantly, how? Philip had no solutions. He would have to leave it in the laps of the gods.

It was not until he awoke the next morning—late, it seemed, for the sun was already two hours over the horizon before he opened his eyes—that he recognized the grove. Four years ago, just here, the owl had swept down out of these trees to mark his face with its claws. In a sense, he had come to manhood on this very spot.

"Why have you led me back here, Goddess?" he whispered. "To what end? Show me what you would have of me."

His prayer was answered almost as soon as it had passed his lips, for in the distance, in the direction of Pella, he saw, first as no more than a dark smear on the horizon and then more clearly, a body of horsemen. He saw them first, and then he heard them—the murmur of many voices blended with the barking of dogs, the thin whine of the kennel master's trumpet. It was a hunting party. And, from the scale of it, a royal hunting party.

Philip scrambled to his feet, his heart beating against his ribs like a fox in a trap. Standing in the shade of an oak tree, where he would be concealed, he strained his eyes to make out the forms of the riders as they began to take shape in the distance. The first person he recognized was old Geron, the head groom, and then, on the huge black horse of which the Thracian had spoken, the regent himself, the Lord Ptolemy.

"You are wise, Lady of the Gray Eyes," Philip said as if the goddess were there standing beside him. "Thank you, that you have delivered my enemy into my hands."

And then, almost in the same breath. "Alastor! That son of a whore—he has stolen my horse!"

By the gods, that stallion was a big one! the Thracian had said. *And so fierce he seemed to breathe fire.* Philip couldn't understand why he hadn't recognized the description at once.

"My horse. By the gods, how dare he take my horse."

Good, Philip thought. His anger had grown dull over the years—somehow this put the edge back on it. And he would need anger.

A second later he recognized his brother's face among the riders. So he was not too late.

His horse was tethered just a few paces away, so Philip undid the hobbles and slipped the bridle over its head. Then he took his sword and jumped on the horse's back. The hunters were now no more than a quarter of an hour away.

He rode out of the grove and into the light. He could tell the precise moment in which he was recognized, for the entire hunting party, as if with a single will, reined in their horses and came to a sudden halt. They waited, and a peculiar stillness settled over them, as if they had stepped outside of time—all except the Lord Ptolemy, who was hard pressed to keep the great black stallion from breaking ranks.

They waited while Philip approached and, when he was perhaps no more than seventy-five or eighty paces away, he shouted out his challenge.

"Ptolemy Alorites, I accuse you of treason. I accuse you of complicity in the murder of King Alexandros. I accuse you of plotting to set aside the Lord Perdikkas and to make yourself king in his place."

At first there was no reply, and then abruptly the Lord Ptolemy threw back his head and laughed.

"We have heard such things from the Lord Philip before," he said. "My stepson, everyone will recall, once charged me with plotting his own murder." He turned his head toward Perdikkas, who was just to his right, and laughed again, but if he expected the king to join in his laughter, he was disappointed. Perdikkas turned his eyes away, with a look registering something between fear and embarrassment. Everyone else was silent, waiting.

"What proof do you offer, Philip?" Ptolemy went on, when he saw the faces of the men around him. "You accuse me of terrible crimes, for which I would be expected to answer with my life. What is your proof?"

"The proof lies in your own guilty breast, My Lord. I accuse you before the bright gods, from whom nothing is hidden, and I offer the proof of my own sword. I mean to avenge my family, My Lord, and think you will not dare to refuse me, for I will shout your treason to the heavens as long as there is breath under my ribs. Ptolemy Alorites, I challenge you to single combat."

Philip dismounted and, when his feet were on the ground, drew his sword. He slapped his horse on the rump, sending it cantering out of harm's way.

"Philip!" Perdikkas shouted all at once as if he had just shaken himself free of a trance. "Philip, I forbid this—this has—"

"This has gone too far already to be forbidden," Ptolemy interrupted him, snatching his javelin away from a groom. "Philip, son of Amyntas, you young fool, you have brought this death upon yourself!"

He dug his heels into his horse's flanks so hard that his spurs drew blood, and the black stallion, his eyes wild, screaming like a damned soul, bolted into a run.

For an instant, standing there on the bare ground, Philip's mind seemed to seize up with fear. This man did not intend to fight. He was simply going to run him down, to trample him to death like a frog in the road.

And then fear gave way to anger—the Lord Ptolemy was a coward who had abandoned his honor.

Well, he was not prepared to die under the hooves of his own horse. "Alastor!" he shouted. "Alastor—halt!"

In later years, when those who witnessed it spoke of what happened, they sometimes said that the great black stallion must in that moment have been possessed by some god, for a horse is not a man to treasure his memories over time. Even a dog will know its own master, even should it see him again after the whole span of its life—did not the poet Homer write that Odysseos's dog, old and feeble, licked the hand of the beggar whom all despised, knowing him to be the lord of the house, returned after twenty years? Yet a horse will not. A horse's memory is like a cup made of sand. It will hold nothing. Therefore, men said, it must have been a god who filled the stallion's heart with his own will.

For at the sound of Philip's voice, Alastor fulfilled the prophecy of his name, stopping in the midst of his charge and rearing up and kicking at the empty air. The Lord Ptolemy was thrown to the ground and, as he tried to crawl away, the stallion wheeled about and brought his great hooves down in the center of his back—once, twice, and then a third time, as if he meant to grind the man into paste.

"Stop, Alastor!" Philip came running up, dropping his sword as a thing forgotten and useless. He was full of horror. "Stop."

And, from one instant to the next, the stallion grew calm. He accepted the touch of Philip's hand upon his neck and stood idly by as Philip walked up on his shattered enemy, who had somehow managed to roll over.

Ptolemy made a limp, futile grab at his javelin, which was lying on the ground beside him, but it was too far away.

"I cannot even feel my legs," he said as Philip knelt beside him. "That beast has killed me. He has broken my spine like a rotten twig—your mother always said that he would kill me one day, if you did not."

He tried to smile, but his lips twisted back in a grimace of pain.

"By the gods, is it to end like this?" he went on, his words hardly more than a gasp between clenched teeth. "Finish me off, then—show a little mercy. Where is your sword? Find it and avenge your brother, for that idiot Praxis killed him at my bidding. This you knew. Finish me off, you damned boy. You guessed right, all along. Complete your triumph over me."

A shadow fell across the regent's face. If Philip had but raised his eyes, he would have seen his brother Perdikkas, standing over them with Ptolemy's javelin in his hand.

"That is my honor, My Lord," he snarled.

At the sound Philip glanced up. When he saw what was about to happen he raised his arm as if to fend off a blow and began to say something, but it was too late. With both hands clenched around the shaft of the javelin, Perdikkas drove the point into the Lord Ptolemy's chest, splitting his heart.

22

"I will not forget this, Philip. You have done me a service."

"You shouldn't have killed him."

Philip and his brother, standing over the corpse of the dead regent, would have only a moment alone. Already the other members of the hunting party were dismounting their horses and running toward them.

"Why should I not kill him? He was a traitor—you heard it from his own lips. Or is it simply that you wanted to kill him yourself?"

"Not only that. If he dies at my hands, it is a private quarrel. If he dies at the king's hands, he is a traitor under the law. Now his whole family lies under the sentence of his treason. You can save our mother, but he has a son."

"Philoxenos? Is he a particular friend of yours? For myself, I can bear to be parted from him."

"That is good, for you have condemned him."

No one heard—perhaps not even Perdikkas. As men began to cluster around them, all eyes were on the dead face of the Lord Ptolemy. They had attention for nothing else, as if they found it impossible to believe that such a man could after all have been mortal.

Philip walked away unnoticed. There was one more duty that he owed his brother and he longed to perform it. Perhaps it would erase this ugly scene from his heart.

He found his sword and, among the baggage of the hunting party, a small bronze shield. As he approached the little knot of men who were still staring wordlessly down at the corpse of their slain master, he began to beat the flat of his sword against the shield.

"The king has acted a man's part and rid himself of the traitor Ptolemy!" he cried. "I pledge life and honor to the Lord Perdikkas, king of the Macedonians. Hail, Perdikkas!"

At first they all stared at him as if they thought him mad. And then, one after the other, when they understood what was happening, they drew their swords and beat them against their shields.

"Perdikkas!" they shouted. "Perdikkas—king of the Macedonians!"

In their joy, the dead regent was almost forgotten.

There would be no hunt that day. Instead, it was the body of the Lord Ptolemy that was tied over the back of a packhorse like a prize boar. It was time to go home.

Philip walked up to where Alastor was peacefully eating grass. The great black stallion suffered the touch of his hand with perfect tranquility, and at last, when he lifted his head, Philip slipped the bit from his mouth.

"I promise you will never wear this again," he murmured in the horse's ear as he examined the bit—it was a cruel piece of work, sharp enough to cut the flesh. "Was he so afraid of you, then? And you as gentle as a newborn kitten."

He grabbed Alastor's mane in both hands and jumped lightly up onto his back. At the first touch of Philip's knees, the stallion started forward at a walk—then a trot, then a brief gallop, then a sudden stop. Once more, as in the past, horse and rider seemed merged into a single will.

"I will never surrender you again," Philip said, reaching down to caress the stallion's gleaming neck. Never before that moment had he felt such love, compounded of gratitude and relief, for any living thing. "While we both live, you will be mine and no other's. I swear it."

On the ride home, Perdikkas and Philip, king and prince, rode a little apart from the others.

"In two months I will have reached my majority," Perdikkas said—the thought seemed to expand him with joy. "I will be king in fact then, and not just in name. In two months, ask anything of me and you will have your reward."

Philip turned his head to look at his brother. From the expression of distaste on his face, anyone would have thought he had been offered an insult.

"You are king in fact now, if you will but realize it. You have declared your manhood today. There will not be another regent."

"You think not?"

"No. After what has happened, who would dare?"

This answer seemed to please Perdikkas immensely. With a tight smile, as if trying to suppress his elation, he nodded. "Then name your reward."

Philip did not answer, and for several minutes they rode on in silence.

"I will begin purging Ptolemy's friends at once," Perdikkas went on at last, as if he had forgotten that he owed anyone anything. "I will assemble the council . . ."

"Be careful, brother. There are many good men on the council, men you cannot afford to antagonize. And they are guilty of no crime."

"Is it not a crime to serve a traitor?" Perdikkas asked, just on the verge of becoming seriously angry. But Philip only shook his head.

"If it were, all the Macedonians would be traitors. A few will have to be sent away, to be sure—Lukios for one, since he is fool enough to cause trouble if he stays in Pella—but let there be no executions. The country is weak enough without that."

"You seem to forget that I am king, and not you, Philip."

But Philip, who had never learned to be afraid of his brother, simply turned to him with such a look of disdain that Perdikkas grew ashamed.

"We will send Lukios away," he said, his voice sounding strained and uncomfortable. "His young bride will not like it—can you imagine what it will be like for her, locked up in some mountain fastness with that oaf—but you are right. The man is a dangerous fool."

"Is he married again?" Philip grinned, having decided to accept his brother's unspoken apology. "Who would have him?"

"Our cousin Arsinoe. Is that not a waste to make the gods weep? She is even delivered of a child, although there is some suspicion that it is not Lukios's. Ptolemy arranged the whole affair. He seemed to think it a most exquisite joke."

Perdikkas threw back his head and laughed. He seemed to have forgotten Philip's part in the story, so he did not even notice his brother's struggle to preserve something like composure, nor the uncertain character of his victory.

By now they were close enough to the city walls that one could make out the soldiers of the watch as they patrolled the catwalk along its top. It was necessary to speak once again.

"You see how they observe us?" Philip asked, pointing up at the guard towers. "They wonder why the regent's hunting party is returning so early. Already they know it is I and not Ptolemy who rides beside you. Soon they will notice the burden carried by one of the packhorses, and they will guess it is a corpse under the blanket. In a quarter of an hour it will be all over the city that the Lord Ptolemy is dead. You had best think what you will say to our mother."

"When she knows the truth, she will understand." Perdikkas swallowed hard, as if that truth were bitter for him as well. "He was a bad man—she could not have been so blind to his nature as not to recognize that. When she hears that he murdered Alexandros . . ."

His voice trailed off as he began to anticipate what it would be like to tell her. It was almost possible to pity him.

Philip did not answer at once. He was not bound to his mother by any ties of affection, so he could see the thing more clearly. The nature of Eurydike's passion for the Lord Ptolemy was a mystery to him, no less than to Perdikkas, but at least he knew that he did not understand it.

"Perhaps you should ride ahead and tell her," he said finally.

But Perdikkas only shook his head.

Already a crowd was beginning to gather outside the city gates. The distance was too great to make out their faces, but Philip could see from the huddled way they stood about in little groups that already they knew the regent was dead. There was something tragic in it. The Lord Ptolemy had never inspired much affection, but that made no difference. They mourned not for him but for themselves. What did they know of Perdikkas? Nothing. For the common people, who are wiser sometimes than their rulers, change was always evil.

"I will fall back and ride with the others," Philip said. "You are the king. Pella is your city now, and you must take possession of it."

Perdikkas did not answer, but his face registered a change. It was a mixture of anxiety and triumph, and at last triumph prevailed. No, he did not wish to share this moment with anyone.

Yet the triumph was brief. The king and his companions entered under the main gate, through crowds at once sullen and fearful. No one threw handfuls of mud at the corpse of the late regent and there was no cheering. To avoid antagonizing the Lord Ptolemy, for most of his reign Perdikkas had kept out of the public view. Most people did not even recognize him, and those few who did had no idea what he might be like as a ruler. They saw the future ride by while the past was carried slung over the back of a packhorse. The future was a blank to them. On the whole, they preferred the past.

Similar feelings of apprehension seemed to grip many members of the hunting party, for the greater part of it appeared to melt away between the city gate and the entrance to the courtyard of the royal palace. Perhaps they were afraid they might be targets of vengeance—perhaps they preferred to wait at home for a time and see how Perdikkas reacted to his new power. Or perhaps they smelled deeds of blood when the reckoning for Ptolemy's death would have to be paid and they did not care to be remembered as having witnessed what must come when the king stepped across his threshold. At any rate, by the time the grooms were taking the reins of their horses they were down to a handful.

The Lady Eurydike stood in the center of the courtyard. Her face was white and, for all the tears that streamed down it, immovable as stone.

"Show me his body," she said in a voice that betrayed nothing, that was just loud enough for everyone to hear and carried all the authority of one who had been the wife and mother of kings.

They took Ptolemy's corpse down from the horse and laid it on the ground before her. He was still wrapped in a blanket—she reached down to pick up one corner and pulled it away.

The dead always looked so surprised. Eurydike knelt down beside him and, with a hand that a keen enough observer might have noticed trembling slightly, she closed his eyes. She touched his face and his beard, as she might have a thousand times while he lived. It was a touch that mingled passion with tenderness and was at the same time expressive of the most terrible grief. Her fingers brushed against his chest. They came away coated with blood and as she knelt there, staring at it, a crazed look came into her eyes.

Perdikkas stepped forward and took her by the shoulders. It was the bravest action of his life.

All at once she raised her eyes to her son's face. For a moment they seemed frozen, outside of time, in some reality of their own.

"How did he die?"

"He was a traitor, Mother. He murdered Alexandros—he would have . . ."

"How did he die?" she repeated, measuring out each word so that each carried the same weight. "Who killed him?"

Perdikkas released his hold on her shoulders and stepped away. His courage was at an end. He did not even have enough left to lie.

"I did." His face puckered, as if he would weep. "I had to, Mother. I had . . ."

She sprang up, as one might recoil from a serpent. Her hands came up, her fingers curling into talons. She seemed ready to attack him, to tear his face with her nails, but she did not. The expression on her face was hardly human. She was shaking all over with demented rage.

"I curse you!" she shouted. "I curse the hour I bore you, that I did not strangle you with your birth cord. I curse all the days of your life. May you die as he died, under the eyes of strangers. May your reign end in destruction and may no son follow after you. I curse you, Perdikkas! A mother's curse upon you!"

Eurydike wheeled around and ran back into the palace. She did not even see Philip approaching.

"She is mad!" Perdikkas cried. He put his hand upon Philip's shoulder, possibly because he was afraid his legs would give way beneath him.

"She has been mad for a long time—did you really not realize? The gods know what she will do now. Perhaps it is best if she is not left alone."

"She cursed me. She cursed me to death and ruin." Suddenly wild with terror, the king of the Macedonians clutched at his younger brother the way a child clutches at its nurse. "She must be made to take it back."

But Philip shook his head, appalled to the bottom of his soul.

"She will not take it back. She will never take it back, not if you have her torn into pieces. She knows how to hate, that one."

Gently, with an almost feminine delicacy, Philip disengaged his brother's hands from his arm.

"Someone must see to her," he murmured. "I will go."

It had been over two years since he had been inside the palace. He knew his way, but as one does in a dream, where the familiar is at the same time strange. He passed servants in the corridors who were so surprised to see him that they forgot even to bow.

When he reached the regent's apartments he discovered that the door had been bolted from the inside.

"Mother, let me in. It is Philip, Mother."

There was no answer. A moment later he heard a scream. It did not sound like Eurydike's voice.

"Mother, open the door—now!"

He beat on the rough wooden planks with his fists and then threw his full weight against the door, but it was as solid as a wall.

I will need help, he thought, *before it is too late*. Yet in his bowels he knew that it was already too late.

In the great hall he found Glaukon, who had come looking for him. There was no time even for an embrace.

"Bring two men and that bench," he ordered, the words stumbling over each other in his haste. "And send word to old Nikomachos—we may have need of a physician."

The corridor was narrow and the door was strong. It took them several tries before they succeeded in battering it loose from its hinges. As soon as Philip had climbed over the shattered door and was inside the regent's apartments, he could smell blood.

A servant girl was crouched under a table. She was trembling and sobbing, too frightened even to answer their questions. Her tunic was spattered across the bosom with a thin spray of blood, but she was not hurt. The gods only knew what she had seen.

Philip went into his mother's room alone. He found her there, facedown, lying across the bed. Her head was in a pool of blood. She had cut her own throat.

The knife she had used was lying beside her.

"Your sister is dead too."

Philip turned and saw the physician Nikomachos standing in the doorway. His hands were smeared with blood.

"Mena?"

"Yes, Mena." Nikomachos shook his head as if he could not bring himself to believe it. "I brought her into this world. I . . ."

Philip seemed to feel nothing. He knew that later, when it became real to him, he would know the pain of this moment, but just then he was too shocked even to weep. He picked up the bloody knife that lay beside his mother's body.

"She must have killed Mena and then come in here to kill herself. What could have possessed her?"

The physician said nothing. He had no answers.

"My family seems to live under some curse," Philip went on, astonished at his own words. "And it has not yet worked out its poison."

23

Ptolemy's corpse was taken to the old capital of Aigai, where all the kings of Macedon were buried, and there it was crucified over Alexandros's tomb. His son, Philoxenos, who stood condemned of his father's treason, was brought before the assembly and there put to death, impaled upon the spears of the very men who, less than three years before, had voted to make his father regent.

Perdikkas, as head of the family, lit his sister's funeral pyre with his own hand, and her bones were wrapped in purple and gold cloth and placed in a golden box in the antechamber of her father's tomb. Eurydike, as a suicide, was cremated at night, lest the sight of it offend the eyes of the gods, and her burial urn filled an unmarked grave beyond the city walls.

Everything that was done in those first few days after the Lord Ptolemy's death was sanctioned by law and custom, yet nothing could erase the stain that marked the beginning of Perdikkas's reign. People said he would be an unlucky king, cursed by the last words his mother ever spoke.

And, at first, Perdikkas seemed bent on confirming this impression, for his actions were those of one filled with fear. He surrounded himself with men who had been out of favor under Ptolemy, and who avenged three years of accumulated slights by urging the king to purge all the late regent's close supporters. There were many treason trials before the assembly—so many that the Macedonians under arms grew weary of them and began to balk at convicting men whose only crime seemed to be loyalty to an authority that all had accepted. At last even Perdikkas saw that the trials were unpopular and dangerous, and he put a stop to them.

But the fear did not leave him.

He would even have feared his brother Philip, had that been possible. But Philip's loyalty was of a caste that even Perdikkas could not bring himself to doubt and, besides, Philip seemed to take no interest in power. The deaths of his mother and sister seemed to have unnerved him.

He had been fond of his sister, Mena, although he had rarely seen her after her marriage to Ptolemy. His mother had disliked and shunned him and therefore, perversely, Philip took her death all the harder, for it is an agony of the soul to mourn someone for whom you have never been permitted to have any affection. It was he, her last and unloved son, who dug Eurydike's grave with his own hands, pouring out offerings of wine that her ghost might find what repose it could.

Philip began to believe that Eurydike's curse might have been less her own grief and madness than, in some weird sense, the voice of heaven. It seemed to him that the House of the Argeadai had somehow forfeited the favor of the gods and had been consigned to ruin and extinction. First Alexandros, then Mena, then his mother—all the victims of treachery and madness. Of his real family there was only Perdikkas left, and Perdikkas was now a jealous and apprehensive king, cut off from him, wordlessly estranged. Philip's influence with his brother was sporadic only. Most of the time it was better if he did not speak at all.

But Philip could congratulate himself on one thing—with a word at the right moment he had prevented Lukios from suffering anything worse than banishment to his own estates. At least six of the regent's closest supporters had been condemned—a few anticipated the judgment of the assembly and either fell upon their swords or fled—and Lukios, who had followed at Ptolemy's heels since they were boys, who had even named his youngest son after him, surely Lukios would have been one of their number had not Philip, quite by chance, used his name as an example of those with whom the king should temper his wrath.

For Lukios would not have perished alone. The penalty for treason was the annihilation of one's line—wife, brother, children, down to the babe at its mother's breast. The law made no separation between the guilty and the innocent. And no one, not the king himself, could change the law.

Without intending it, without even knowing that it was about to take place, Philip happened to be part of the crowd that witnessed Lukios's departure from the city. The fallen lord rode through the streets of Pella and into exile, looking at no one, lost in his own private reflections, and behind him came his servants, leaning against their walking staffs as if the journey were at its end rather than its beginning, and, in a wagon covered with a linen canopy, his family. Thus did Philip have his last look at Arsinoe.

She was as beautiful as ever—more beautiful perhaps, for with some women anger has the effect of defining the character of the face. As she trundled past, her eyes searched over the crowd, lighting on one and then another, in the manner of one marking out her enemies for future vengeance.

When she saw Philip—and who can say if she had not been looking for him all along?—her face hardened even more. Then she reached down to pick up her little boy, who was beside her, and held him to her breast. She caressed his hair and kissed him, but her eyes never left Philip's face.

Yes, this is my son, Philip thought. *And she means me to know it. It is the only revenge that is left to her, and it is sufficient.*

Somehow, this seemed the crowning defeat.

So after that, little by little, Philip withdrew into himself. Unless he had business there—and that was rare enough—he hardly went near his brother's court. Although there were apartments in the royal palace set aside for him, he continued to live with old Glaukon, as he had when a boy. He spent his time with common people, soldiers, and artisans. Indeed, he spent so much time at the building sites around Pella that a rumor began circulating that he had apprenticed himself to a stonemason.

The rumor was in error only as to the facts, for it was of precisely such a destiny that Philip, prince of Macedon and heir apparent to the throne, dreamed as ardently as other men dream of wealth or love. He would have given much to be allowed to forget that the blood of kings flowed through his veins, for his birth tied him to the evil destiny that seemed his family's only legitimate inheritance.

To be a stonemason and spend his life thickening the callouses on his hands. Or, even better, to take ship with the merchant sailors who stopped off on their way south from the Black Sea—that would be something, to drift away on the morning breeze and never set eyes on Pella again!

Yet it was not to be, for he was a child not only of the Argeadai but of Macedon. Nothing else remained to him. This he knew, although he tried to deny it to himself. And of this he was reminded when at last he was summoned into the presence of his brother the king.

He found Perdikkas in the room that had been their father's study, a room he had not entered before more than twice in his life, so that it had the strangeness of an unknown continent. Perdikkas was seated at a massive table, and behind him, explaining some detail of a map, stood a chamberlain whom Philip had never seen before. Perdikkas wore a sullen face, but lately this expression had become almost habitual with him so it did not suggest that he labored under any immediate grievance. It was several moments before he seemed to notice Philip's presence, and when he did, his frown deepened.

"Where had you been hiding yourself?" he snapped. "Playing in the mud again with your laborer friends?"

But Philip did not answer nor even look at his brother. Instead, his eyes were fixed on the chamberlain, as if he were trying to decide what the man could be doing there. At last Perdikkas took the hint and waved his hand in dismissal.

"Very well, then, Skopos, you may leave us now. I wish to speak to the Lord Philip alone."

They both waited in silence until the chamberlain had left the room and the door had closed behind him.

"I've hardly seen you the last month," Perdikkas said at last. "You never come to court—people are beginning to comment on it."

"Aren't you going to invite me to sit down? Or am I in disgrace?"

Perdikkas interrupted his brooding long enough to make an impatient gesture toward the room's only other chair, seeming to resent even that.

"I want you to begin attending meetings of the council."

"Why should I? You have other advisors."

"Because you are the heir!"

"Then have you had a premonition of death?"

Philip grinned when he saw how well he had succeeding in nettling his brother. Then he felt a little ashamed.

"You have no need of me, Perdikkas, so I stay away. I will grow old as your heir."

"Nevertheless, your absence from court creates the impression that there is some quarrel between us. We both know how these things go—I do not wish your behavior giving rise to factions."

All Philip could do was laugh, which annoyed Perdikkas even more.

"There is nothing to laugh at," he said with some heat. "Macedon is weak enough that we cannot afford to be divided at the center."

"I was just thinking what a miserable time any partisan of mine would have of it. What would he do? Join me in carrying stones up the wall of the new city granary? A day or two of that and I've no doubt he would remember the duty he owed his king."

Philip shrugged, seeming to dismiss the idea as an absurdity.

"Besides, you did not summon me here to urge me to attend the council. The few times I did come you wouldn't listen to anything I said. I just decided to stop embarrassing you. So perhaps now you'll tell me what you really want."

"What do you know about Elimeia?" Perdikkas, who was evidently glad for an opportunity to stop sparring with his younger brother, pushed the map across the table toward him. Philip hardly did more than glance at it.

"What is there to know?"

"They have a new king and he is in rebellion against me."

Philip smiled as if at some private joke. "Pray don't take it personally, brother—the kings of Elimeia have been in rebellion for over a hundred years."

"Yes, but this one means it. He is sending raiding parties down to the plains and he has to be persuaded to stop. You must persuade him."

"What are you talking about?"

Now it was Perdikkas's turn to smile. It was evident that he had finally achieved his objective of complete surprise.

"I want you to go to Aiane and see what can be done with this bandit who calls himself a king. I need peace along my western borders, and I expect you to get it for me. Bribe him, threaten him, do whatever you think is needful, but persuade him to stop his raids."

"No." Philip shook his head. "Send someone else. Send an ambassador—that is what they are for."

"Derdas would probably send my ambassador back in pieces."

"Then thank you very much indeed!"

"Oh, you will be safe enough." Perdikkas made a dismissive little gesture with his left hand, rather like waving away a fly. "He knows it would mean war if he killed you and, besides, there is some sort of family connection. Can you leave tomorrow?"

Philip was on the point of refusing yet again when he realized that he did not want to refuse. He put little enough faith in Derdas's notions of family feeling, but at least this would be doing something.

For the first time in weeks he felt a spark of interest in life.

"Yes, very well, then—tomorrow morning."

Philip left early enough that the guards at the city gates were the only people to witness his departure. Perdikkas had offered him a military escort, but he had refused, thinking he would make better time alone. Besides, once he reached Aiane, and should Derdas take it into his head to kill him, twenty or thirty soldiers could offer him no protection whatever.

He had allowed himself three days for the journey. "I will endure two nights of this barbarian's hospitality," he'd told Perdikkas. "What cannot be accomplished in that span will never be accomplished. And then I will return. Thus if I am not back in ten days, you will know that I am dead."

"And you shall be avenged," Perdikkas had answered complacently. "But he would never dare—"

"Would he not? I am always astonished at what men will dare."

He made good time on the first day and camped on the western plains, at the foot of the mountains and well out of sight of the sea. After that the terrain grew rougher and his pace slowed. There were fewer cultivated fields and more herds of sheep, but he could have closed his eyes and known that he was entering Upper Macedon—he could hear Alastor's hooves scraping against the stones in the ground.

Along the way he stopped in a few villages to buy food and refill his waterskin. The elders would come to greet him, to hear the news and to indulge themselves in the luxury of a new audience for their complaints. If they asked his name, he would simply tell them, "Philip, son of Amyntas," and they would nod. By itself, a name means nothing, and to these people he was merely a stranger. They told him of the raids along the border.

"The king should do something. We need a garrison here, that the Elimoitai will stay at home."

"Has there been much trouble?"

"My wife's sister married a man from a village two hours' walk from here. He was killed and his house burned down. They may ride fine horses, but these upland nobles are nothing more than thieves."

He glanced at Philip's horse and then looked embarrassed, but Philip merely laughed and turned the conversation to the prospects for a good harvest.

Yet what he had heard of the raids was true. About an hour before sunset Philip passed through a village that had been burned out only four days earlier. Several people had been killed, including three children, and almost all the sheep had been driven off into the mountains. Philip gave them money in the king's name, but he could not promise them safety or even vengeance. He rode away with the sound of the women's lamentations still ringing in his ears.

He made his second camp in the shadow of Mount Bermion, which marked the limit of his brother's kingdom. Tomorrow he would be in the land of the Elimoitai.

Had he been sent here to die? Did Perdikkas expect him to be killed? Such thoughts occur to a man as he stirs the embers of his lonely campfire, far from the safety of home, yet he could not bring himself to credit them. Perdikkas had nothing to fear from him and could not profit from his death. Besides, the country was too weak to sustain a war, even against Derdas of Elimeia, and the army would demand such a war if the heir to the throne were murdered. Yet Perdikkas could risk his brother's life based on a calculation that the king of a petty hill tribe would think like a statesman and not like a bandit chieftain. Alexandros had sent him as a hostage to Bardylis of Illyria, hanging his life on a same slender thread. What was wrong with his family, Philip wondered, that they seemed to love each other so little?

Down on the plains it was summer, but at this altitude one could almost have imagined a hint of snow in the cold wind that blew down from the mountain. Philip had found a bit of shelter below an outcropping of rock and he had his sleeping blanket wrapped around his shoulders, so he was not uncomfortable. He had passed worse nights in the open.

He tried to settle on some plan for approaching the negotiations but at last gave it up and decided to rely on his instincts. The gods alone knew what he would find when he reached Aiane. The gods alone knew what sort of a man he would find in Derdas, who had succeeded his father less than a year before and was little more than a name outside his own kingdom. It was better to have no plan—a plan might only get in the way.

And while he turned the matter over in his mind, it occurred to him that he was happy. He had something to occupy his thoughts that did not automatically fill him with remorse and pain. His gaze was once again turned on the world. He had escaped from himself, which was perhaps as close an approximation of happiness as he could imagine.

The next morning, a few minutes before noon, he saw the first of the Elimiote sentries—a single man on horseback, to the south, at the top of a ridge that stood out against the sky like a knife's edge, perhaps half an hour's ride distant. Horse and rider kept quite still for a long time and then cut away and disappeared over the horizon. He had fulfilled his task. He had made Philip aware of him.

But Philip had felt their eyes on him for some time—one had to be dead not to feel them. This was only the first time one of their number had actually presented himself for inspection. There were others, of course. Philip estimated that there were probably ten or twelve men in the patrol that had been dogging him for the past three hours or so.

These things followed a certain protocol. They hadn't approached him, but they wanted him to know that they were there, if only to assert their king's authority. By now a rider was halfway to Aiane, and they would not act until they had instructions.

Probably they didn't know quite what to make of him. He didn't have a packhorse, so he wasn't a merchant. His horse and gear marked him out as an aristocrat, but diplomats, or even members of the gentry on a family visit, as a rule traveled in far greater state. Perhaps it had crossed their minds that he could be a fugitive, in which case his arrival in Derdas's kingdom might be a blessing or a political embarrassment. They would have been able to form no conclusions, but until he arrived in their capital, the heads of the king's ministers would be kept buzzing with lively speculations.

Good, Philip thought. *Let them simmer.* He wanted to keep all the advantage of surprise on his side.

Since crossing the border he had passed two or three large villages, but he had not stopped in any of them. The women and children ran away at the sight of him, and even the men lowered their eyes as if to render him invisible. Even in the mountains Macedonians were generally welcoming of strangers, but not here. Perhaps they too felt the eyes of the king's sentries and were afraid.

In the early afternoon, as he rode through a narrow valley, there they were, to the right and the left of him, strung out along the trails that girdled the hills to the north and south. He counted eleven in all—with the twelfth man probably this moment giving his report in Aiane. They were close enough now that he could have carried on a shouting conversation with them. Philip would have liked to do that, if only just to rattle their delicate nerves, since by now they were trying to intimidate him, but he kept silent. After all, it wouldn't have been polite.

It was nearly evening by the time he came within sight of Aiane. He looked up and suddenly there it was—a wall and a few towers crowning a low, flattened hill. It was said that some four or five thousand people lived there, but one's first impression was that the capital of the Elimoitai didn't amount to much more than a fortified village.

His escorts, having apparently decided that he had come close enough, now closed on him from both sides. They were driving their horses at a gallop, although there was no need—Philip had reined Alastor in to a halt and was waiting for them. Within a few minutes he found himself surrounded by a tight little circle of armed soldiers.

"Hand over your sword, stranger, and state your business," one of them, presumably their officer, growled in his slightly roughened version of the Macedonian dialect. He was a fierce-looking man—indeed, one might have guessed that he put something of a premium on looking fierce—and he seemed unpleasantly surprised when Philip grinned at him.

"My business is with your king, bumpkin, not with you. And if you compel me to draw my sword, you will probably not live to regret it."

This reply betrayed a few of the other soldiers into a few smothered syllables of laughter, but they quickly recovered themselves when they saw how it angered Philip's interrogator.

"You claim to be some sort of ambassador, then?" he asked, trying to climb down a little without losing face, but Philip was not inclined to let him off so easily.

"I don't claim anything except that you are beginning to become a nuisance. So take a bit of friendly advice and get out of my way."

It was one of those decisions that seemed to make itself. Philip was alone. His claims to authority came down to a letter carrying Perdikkas's seal and his own audacity. There was nothing else. And of these, he judged, audacity was probably the more useful, for if he did not command respect from these rustic bandits, he would not get it.

Besides, for all that this officer doubtless bullied his subordinates, Philip judged that he was no more dangerous than a barking dog. He had probably made it to his present rank by a careful mixture of bluff and servility, but in his bowels he was nothing more than another shrewd coward. Thus he would not be fool enough to kill someone who might be some sort of foreign emissary—Derdas would have him up by his heels before the sun set—nor was he brave enough to risk a quarrel with a man who didn't seem the least afraid of him. Philip was prepared to bet his life that the fellow wouldn't accept his challenge.

In fact, he was betting his life.

"I must refer this to the captain of the watch," the officer said, scowling like he had just awakened with a headache. "He will at least want to know your name."

"Then he can ask it."

The officer colored but said nothing. An instant later he yanked the reins around and rode away at a gallop. Philip touched his heels to Alastor's flanks, urging him to a walk. He did not join, nor even seem to notice, the other men's delighted laughter.

The soldiers dropped in behind him so that he seemed to be leading the patrol back to the city walls.

There was an armed company of perhaps fifty men waiting for him at the gate. Several of them already had their swords drawn, as if they expected to do battle for their lives. An officer stepped forward, but Philip did not stop until his horse's nose was practically touching his breast.

"Now I am asking it," he said. "Your name, My Lord."

Philip threw a leg over Alastor's neck and dropped down to the ground.

"Philip, prince of Macedon," he said lightly. He reached inside his tunic and took out a small scroll. "And this, you can see, bears my king's seal. I have business with Derdas of the Elimoitai, my lord's vassal and servant."

Philip took it as a favorable sign that no one had the temerity to laugh in his face.

24

There was a banquet that night. Philip was informed of this by one of the palace chamberlains, who implied that it was as good a chance as any to fill his belly and that no one would trouble to ask if he had been invited. When he inquired whether the king would be there all he received was a puzzled look, as if the man couldn't understand what difference it would make. In any case, Philip took a bath and put on the one clean tunic he had brought from Pella and went.

No one had waited for him. As soon as he stepped into the hall and looked around him, he understood that his mission was hopeless. There were about a hundred and fifty men present, it was impossible to guess which one of them might be Derdas, and the proceedings had reached that pitch of hilarity that suggested that everyone had been drinking for at least three hours. Several of the revelers were smeared with blood, so apparently they had been out hunting that afternoon and hadn't bothered to change. The servants scurried about like rats, disappearing as quickly as they could to avoid being spattered with wine and food. Judged even by the standards of his father's court, it was an unseemly business.

As he looked about him, Philip noticed that all the men present were about his own age. There were no elders, no leavening of graybeards among all this youth. Derdas, he knew, was just twenty—it would appear that he now surrounded himself with his own friends and that his father's advisors had fallen from favor. For all that he was young himself, Philip recognized that this was bad—bad for his mission and possibly worse for Elimeia, for a man's friends, particularly if they are young, tell him only what he wishes to hear, and a king, to be successful, must develop a stomach for unpalatable truths.

At a table near the door a member of the Elimiote gentry, one of the king's chosen companions, was resting his head in the palm of his left hand while he used a finger of the right to trace pictures in a puddle of spilled wine. He was so absorbed in this undertaking that Philip had to grab him by the collar and shake him to gain his attention.

"Which one of these swine is Derdas?" he asked, smiling benevolently.

The man, to whom it apparently did not occur to take offense, scratched his head and frowned, as if the question puzzled him greatly.

"That one over there," he said at last, pointing to a table nearer the center of the room. "The one with the curly beard is the king."

Philip looked in that direction and saw at once who was indicated. Derdas was a tall, handsome youth with a head and beard full of black, shining curls. His appearance suggested all the qualities of a great king except intelligence, and the rather vacant expression of his eyes might have owed less to any natural deficiency than to an evening's hard drinking. Philip told himself there might be hope after all.

There were three rather elegant youths seated with the king. The one at his right appeared from the way he was gripping the corner of the table to be about to fall under it. Philip decided anyone that drunk would probably be more comfortable on the floor and gave him a little push to help him on his way. He then occupied the man's place, tasted his wine, and, after having decided that the keeper of the king's cellar had been cheating his master, set the cup back down and put his hand on Derdas's shoulder.

"My Lord, you and I have business to discuss."

Derdas could not have appeared more surprised if he had looked back and seen a knife held against his throat. At last, in a voice husky with overuse, he was able to murmur, "What happened to Dipsaleos? He was sitting there just a minute ago. Who are you?"

"I am a messenger, My Lord. And my message is that you should learn to curb your imprudence, for you have offended against the Lord Perdikkas, king of all the Macedonians, and risk his anger."

"If I know what you're talking about, friend, then I'm a turnip." He turned to the man sitting on his left and laughed immoderately. "Did you hear that, Antinous? I'm a turnip!"

This witticism was greeted with universal hilarity—at least among those of the king's companions who were still sober enough to understand what was expected of them. Philip, however, contrived to retain a certain gravity of bearing. Indeed, if anything, it deepened. For he realized now that not only was he dealing with an idiot but no one had bothered to inform this particular idiot of his presence.

"As to whether or not you might be a turnip it is not my province to say. But I would suggest that you make an early night of it, My Lord, for I will wait upon you in the morning."

Derdas sat staring at him, his mouth open, like a man who is not sure whether he has just heard a jest but is inclined to laugh in any case. It was all Philip could do to restrain himself from shoving his fist down the drunken fool's throat, but at last he contented himself with merely rising from the table and stalking out of the hall.

Outside, as he stood in the cloistered walkway that enclosed the four sides of a garden, the night air felt deliciously cool against his face.

"What does the king in Pella want with my brother?"

Philip turned around and saw a young woman, hardly more than a girl, standing behind him. She was very quiet and composed, wearing a white tunic that reached down low enough to cover her feet. She was also startlingly pretty, with black hair all in ringlets and skin as flawless as wax. Except around the eyes, which sparkled with intelligence, the physical resemblance to Derdas was quite striking so that Philip felt no need to inquire of whom she spoke.

"I had expected to have this conversation with the king in Aiane," he said, smiling with pleasure in spite of himself. "And how is it that you know of my mission when he did not?"

"My brother has no wife so I run his house, as I have since our mother died. The chamberlains tell me everything."

"And they did not tell him?"

"He would not listen."

She said this without emphasis, as if presenting a neutral fact. She wanted him to understand, but she did not wish to criticize her brother. It was an interesting balance and offered an insight into the struggle between loyalty and prudence, which probably consumed much of her life.

"Why would he not listen?" Philip asked, less for the answer than for the pleasure of hearing her speak it.

"You came late, and my brother does not like to be troubled with business when he is with his friends."

"So the chamberlains told you, in hopes that you would tell him."

"Yes. And I would have, in the morning. Women are not permitted at the king's banquet. In the morning you will find him—different."

"And will you stand beside his chair, whispering into his ear what he should say?"

Philip smiled with mischief and the king's sister dropped her eyes, which was a great pity since he took such pleasure in looking into them.

"My brother will receive you alone," she replied, making it sound like the answer to a reproach.

Yet she would speak to him in the morning, Philip thought. And perhaps, since she knew his mind, what he heard from her might predispose him to something like reason. Thus it might be useful for her to know more.

Besides, he was enjoying the conversation.

"Then I will speak to him in a way I would not in front of his sister." He allowed his smile to fade into the merest ghost of itself. "I will tell him that he risks the Lord Perdikkas's wrath, for he has raided villages well beyond his own borders, burning and carrying away plunder and leaving many dead."

"The king of Elimeia is not a bandit!" she said with a heat that one suspected was not usual with her.

"Lady, I have seen the charred huts and the graves of the dead—with these eyes have seen them, not two days' ride from this tranquil garden. If your brother is not a bandit, then his soldiers do evil behind his back, knowing it will be he and not they who will be called to account for the innocent blood they have shed. Is he so heedless, Lady? Is he king here or only master of the revels? Which would pain you less, to believe he is a bandit or a fool?"

Once more she dropped her gaze, since there was no possible answer. She had already turned to go when he called her back.

"Lady . . ."

"Yes, My Lord?"

To see her face in that instant was to feel the most tender pity, for she seemed to raise it only to receive another blow.

"Pray, Lady, what is your name?"

"My name?" There was genuine surprise in her voice, as if she could not imagine why he would wish to know it. "My name is Phila, My Lord."

This time, when she disappeared soundlessly into the shadows, he made no effort to detain her, for all that the night seemed rendered darker by her absence.

Phila was mistaken. Late the next morning, when Philip was at last shown into the king's presence, he was not alone.

Derdas was in his stables and, while the grooms prepared for another day of hunting, he and the same three companions who had shared his table at dinner stood about making a breakfast of the bread, goat cheese, and wine that had been set out for them on a small table near the door. He was sober enough now—no man with sufficient wit to find his beard will mount a hunting horse drunk—but his eyes were just as barren of intelligence as they had been the night before. He greeted Philip almost as an old comrade.

"My Lord, come join us. Have they fed you yet?"

"Thank you, but, yes, I have eaten," Philip answered, looking about him with a certain distaste. Normally he would have felt himself insulted to be received by a foreign king in a room that smelled of horse dung and hay, but he had the sense that Derdas simply didn't know any better.

"Then come hunting with us—the boar in the forests a few hours' north of here are as big as plow oxen!"

"And if we don't find any boar," one of the others broke in—last night his name had been Dipsaleos, so presumably it still was—"the king knows a woodcutter's hut up there with five daughters in it. Imagine. Five daughters! Enough for everybody!"

"My Lord, pray spare me a word in private," Philip said after the gleeful laughter had died away a little. "I have made the journey here to treat of matters that should be more important to you than hunting."

"Oh—I trust my friends," the king answered, throwing his arm over one of them. "Speak, My Lord Prince, for you have my undivided attention."

There was a moment of silence, punctuated by one quickly suppressed giggle of Dipsaleos's, a sound that made one think of a donkey braying into a pillow.

"My Lord . . ." Philip took a moment to let his anger mellow into something like contempt. "My Lord, your soldiers have been conducting raids across the border. King Perdikkas has a decent regard for the lives and safety of his people and he requires that you—"

"Requires?" interrupted the man whose shoulder at that moment bore the weight of his sovereign's arm. "Who dares to require anything of Derdas, lord of the Elimoitai? In Pella it may be you are allowed to use such language to a king, but here your words are merely so much . . ."

He was in the midst of a little dismissive wave when Philip caught him by the wrist, squeezing hard enough that the king's friend had to clench his teeth to keep from crying out.

"Dares? Who dares?" Philip released the man with a disdainful push, which made him stumble and fall back onto a pile of horse blankets. "Perdikkas his king dares. You may have heard of him. He is the Perdikkas who is lord of all Macedon and whose grandfather's grandfather set the first Derdas on his throne—that Perdikkas. Or have the Elimoitai somehow forgotten that they are Macedonians?"

It was an ugly moment. Dipsaleos actually had his hand on his sword hilt. There was no knowing how it might have ended had not Derdas, whose puzzled expression suggested that he hadn't the slightest idea what everyone was shouting about, suddenly begun to laugh.

"Serves you right, Antinous!" he shouted as if he had just that instant seen the joke. "My sister warned me we should treat the Lord Philip with respect. Hah, hah, hah!"

And then, as if dismissing the rest of them from existence, he picked up a piece of bread, dipped it in a cup of wine, and ate it, chewing the whole damp wad as thoughtfully as a cow does her cud.

"But he has a point, you know," he said, looking at Philip. "Pella is far away and the Macedonians have many kings—Perdikkas is only one of them. Besides, I have heard nothing of any raids."

Derdas was not sufficiently intelligent to have mastered the art of concealing his thoughts, and Philip had only to look at his face to know he wasn't telling the truth.

"Perhaps the local barons were simply reclaiming stolen property," Antinous said, with a thin smile of malice. "Everyone knows that peasants are always thieving."

"Perhaps that's it." Derdas's face lit up, as if with inspiration. "Perhaps, instead of making accusations against his fellow kings, he should ask a few pointed questions in the villages along his side of the border."

That seemed to resolve every difficulty. It was wonderful. Philip was by now perfectly aware that he was wasting his time—these boors were simply mocking him—but he felt an obligation to try at least once more.

"My Lord, no ruler can either know or control everything that happens in his realm," he began as he tried to cleanse his mind of anger. "King Perdikkas is aware of this and is prepared to overlook the past—provided that he receives an undertaking from you that these raids will cease. Write the king a letter pledging that you will hereafter respect the border and will see to it that your nobles do the same, then everything can be as it was. I leave for Pella in the morning. Let me carry your words with me when I go."

Philip bowed. He would withdraw now, without giving the fool a chance to refuse. Let him think on the matter. Perhaps his sister had some influence— let her have time to use it.

"I shall await your call, My Lord."

Yet the call never came. Food was brought to his room that night and he was told that the king and his companions were celebrating the anniversary of some famous battle and thus the banquet was closed to foreigners. The next morning, he attempted to wait upon Derdas in his private apartments but was told that the king was indisposed and would see no one. By midmorning Philip had had enough. He went to the stable to reclaim his horse and left the city.

This time there were no sentries to watch him. The guard at the main gate did not even salute as he rode past—they knew now why he had come and probably knew that he had failed in his mission, so he was no longer of any interest to them. By the time he was four hours from Aiane he was quite sure that no one was following him.

He stopped for the night in an Elimiote herding settlement near the border, and the villagers too must have sensed that he was not being watched, for his reception was very different from what it had been two days before. The headman invited him to sleep in his own hut and, after Philip had bought a pair of sheep with which to feast the whole village, they celebrated his arrival with beer and honey cakes.

Philip and the headman got a little drunk together. The headman's wife had been dead for five years and his children were all grown, so he was glad of the company. And the beer had made him careless, or perhaps he had just decided that his guest was someone to be trusted. Whatever the reason, it wasn't very long before Philip found the man looking sidewise at him through narrowed, speculative eyes.

"You have been to the great city?" the headman asked. When Philip nodded the headman nodded too, as if the proposition were self-evident. "And did you go there to see the king?"

All at once Philip had the sense that he might be about to hear something of use. The man only needed a little encouragement. So he nodded again.

"Yes." He sighed. "I have been to see the king—for all the good it did me."

"Did you go to ask a favor?" Why else, after all, would a foreigner come all this way?

"I went at the request of the great king in Pella. King Derdas has been raiding villages across the mountains, and I was sent to persuade him to stop. I did not succeed."

"Will there be war, then?"

He asked more out of curiosity than anything else, for wars were not fought by shepherds. Possibly, if a battle were to be fought nearby, the men of this village might walk an hour out of their way to sit on the rocks at a safe distance and watch. They might bring their lunch and eat it while the battle raged. Then, when everything was over, they might rob the corpses of the fallen. Otherwise, war was not something they would feel much concerned them.

"I don't know," Philip answered.

The headman seemed to turn this over in his mind for a while, and then he took another long pull on his beer jug.

"Well, if there is to be war," he began, wiping the foam from his beard with the back of his hand, "I hope you lowlanders fight like you mean it. We need a new king."

"You don't like this one?"

The headman didn't answer for a moment, as if he knew he was on dangerous ground. "The father was good enough, but the son . . ." He shook his head. "Sometimes the nobles raid our villages too. A king should know how to be strong—otherwise everyone who owns a horse and a sword just does what he likes."

During the next two days, while he was on the road back to Pella, Philip was aware that, almost of its own accord, an idea was growing in his mind. Perhaps it was less an idea than a conviction, but he knew that he had reached a great turning point in his life.

He explained it all to Perdikkas before he had been an hour inside the city gates. Without preamble, he simply blurted it out. "You must send an army into Elimeia and topple Derdas."

"Then I take it your diplomatic mission was not a success," Perdikkas replied. He had fallen into the habit of taking a short nap before dinner, and Philip had awakened him. He was not cross, because he had been dreaming about his mother.

"No, it was not a success. The man is a fool who thinks life is a hunting party followed by a feast. His nobles are a leaderless mob and the common people wish him in his grave. We can topple him—it can be done."

"Derdas can field an army of four thousand men. We would need at least six thousand to be sure of success and I cannot spare anything like that number from the northern garrisons without the Thracians and the Illyrians falling upon us like wolves."

"Then raise a new army."

"There is no money. I cannot afford to raise a new army."

"You cannot afford not to. If you do not show your strength and make an example of Derdas, soon all our borders will be under pressure. If that happens, Macedon will crumble into pieces like stale bread."

Perdikkas did not answer at once. For a long time he merely sat on the edge of his bed, glaring at his brother with something like real hatred, which of course meant that he knew Philip was right.

"I cannot afford an army of six thousand men," he said at last, as if that settled the matter.

"You don't need six thousand men to deal with this empty-headed bandit. If you can't manage that number, then give me a thousand."

He said this as his elder brother was just about to rinse his mouth out with a sip of wine, but as Perdikkas listened he stared at the contents of his cup as if it were so much fresh blood. He set it back down on his night table with evident distaste.

"Are you mad?" he asked quietly. "Did a snake bite you up there in the mountains, or did you fall on your head? To send an army of a thousand men into Elimeia would achieve nothing except to precipitate a war with a disaster."

Philip put his hands together and pressed them against his mouth. As he looked at his brother there was almost an expression of pleading in his eyes.

"I have spent most of the last three years in Thebes," he began, speaking as if to himself. "They understand more of war there than anywhere else in the world, and I learned much. Believe me when I tell you, brother, that a small army, properly trained, can defeat a mob of any size. Give me a thousand men, and the summer and winter to train them, and I can break the Elimoitai like a rotten twig."

The two men seemed to watch each other for a moment, as if each were trying to assess the other's motives. Inside the mind of each there lurked the thousand little doubts and apprehensions that had accumulated through their shared childhood. Was Perdikkas too weak to grasp this chance? Was Philip trying to make himself even more glorious in men's eyes? Was it safe to trust him?

At last Perdikkas took the long-delayed sip from his wine cup, bringing his head back, seeming to roll the taste of it over his tongue.

"Very well, then—you shall have a thousand men and your summer and winter to train them. If, at the end of that time, you have performed some miracle with them, you may take them into Elimeia. If not, then they will go north to fortify the garrisons where. And you will go with them."

That was all Philip wanted to hear. When he was almost at the door of his brother's bedroom, Perdikkas asked him a single question.

"Tell me, Philip—when you conquer Derdas, will you take his place and become lord of the Elimoitai?"

"No, brother." Philip forced himself to smile. "When I conquer I will become whatever it is your pleasure to make me, but you will be lord."

25

Perdikkas thought he was mad when Philip announced that he wanted body armor and weapons for seven hundred infantry troops. "Derdas has nearly three thousand horsemen—what are you going to do up there in the mountains with a rabble of foot soldiers?"

"First of all, the mountains are poor terrain for cavalry, so I will have the advantage. Second, by the time I finish, my infantry won't be a rabble but an army. Most of the Theban army is infantry."

"Oh, well, what choice do they have? Greek horses are hardly bigger than dogs."

"Then why are we so afraid to take the field against them?"

Perdikkas stalked off in a huff, but the smiths were put to work forging spears and breastplates. And since the Pella garrison could easily spare three hundred horses for the new army, all Philip had to do was recruit his foot soldiers.

And to find these he turned his eyes to the western mountains, to the lands the Elimoitai were plundering. He wanted men whose courage would be sharpened by the knowledge that they were protecting their own homes.

For a month Philip toured the villages along the narrow strip of lowland through which ran the Haliakmon River, many of which had been ravaged and burned by the Elimiote horsemen. He had powers of impressment—he could simply have rounded up men and marched them off—but he did not use them. He did not need to. There were plenty of shepherds whose herds had been run off and who didn't know how they were going to survive the winter. To these Philip offered a wage paid in Athenian silver drachmas and the chance for revenge.

It was always an event when Prince Philip would show up in some cluster of mud huts with an escort of only two or three horsemen. He would buy sheep and beer with which to feast everyone in the village, many of whom had perhaps not tasted meat in half a year, making them all guests of the king's bounty.

He had the gift of being able to make himself liked, for, although a prince of the royal house and thus hedged about with that awe that the common people felt for the sons of the Argeadai, he never created the impression that he held himself above other men. He would joke with the youths, even the children, and he would take counsel with the elders, rarely uttering a word but listening as a son listens to his father.

Then, in the evening, when men's bellies were full and their hearts cheered, he would stand up beside the remains of the fire, its red and yellow light playing across his face so that he seemed not a man at all but a kind of beacon in the darkness and, starting slowly, almost diffidently, commanding attention by the sheer force of his presence, he would begin to speak in the voice of a neighbor and friend.

"Not half a day's ride to the west," he would say, raising his arm to point toward the last faint rays of the setting sun, "there is a cluster of burned-out houses where no one will ever live again. It was a farming village, where the people were poor, and when the Elimoitai could find no plunder they expressed their annoyance by slaughtering the men and carrying the women and children off into bondage. Now grass grows on the threshing floors and the wind blows over the unburied bones of the dead. Girls who had hoped for husbands will wear out their lives in the households of strangers, old women before they are twenty, for by day their labor crushes the soul and by night they are the bed slaves of their parents' murderers. How they must envy the dead!"

And a murmur of assent would make its way around the fire, for his words seemed like nothing so much as the language of their own hearts, making them see as for the first time that which they felt they had somehow always known. Men said that to listen to Prince Philip was to hear the voices of the Fates whispering in your ear.

"All across these hills, there is weeping tonight. There is lamentation and there is hunger, for the Elimoitai are like a plague of locusts that passes over and leaves the ground naked behind them. They plunder and they destroy, yet who are they? Are they not men like us? Are they not our brothers? Are they not Macedonians? Thus, how have they made us fear them? And why?

"We, the sons of Macedon, seed of the Great God Zeus, are not like other men," he would go on, like a priest reciting an incantation. "The people of the southern lands are ruled by tyrants or councils of fifty or whatever whim stirs the bowels of the greatest number, but we have been faithful to our kings for as far back in time as the memory of man can reach. And over all the petty kings of the Macedonians the gods have set the House of the Argeadai, the descendants of Herakles, to be our rulers. They have been our glory—and, sometimes, our affliction. For a man is not always wise, nor brave, nor just, nor virtuous, simply because he is a king. A bad king leads his people into shame and ruin, inciting them to make war against their brethren, making of their name a curse. Such a man is Derdas, king of the Elimoitai—a little man, vain, wicked, and foolish.

"For has it escaped his notice that there is a king in Pella? And does he imagine that the Lord Perdikkas, his master as well as ours, father to all the Macedonians, will suffer in quiet the murder and rape of his subjects? No! I tell you he will not! He will send fire and sword against the despoilers of his realm. He will drive them into the shadowed lands of death, for Perdikkas the king will see his nation avenged!"

And the village people, who had at last found their voice, would cheer the vision Philip had raised up before their eyes. Wherever he went men begged for the honor of following him into battle so that for every one he chose he had to turn away many more.

"Do not imagine that to be a soldier is easy," he would tell the peasant boys who crowded around him. "The training will be hard and battle will be worse. There is no safety in war. You will know suffering and pain, and some of you will find not victory but death. Yet at the sacrifice of your lives you will have purchased the blessing of peace for those who survive you. Your brothers and sisters will live on the land without fear, and they will bless your memory so that you will be as a father to all the generations to come."

Thus Philip at last led nearly eight hundred men down from the mountains of the west. He established a camp an hour's ride from Pella—there seemed little enough point in tempting these village boys with the pleasures of the city—mixed in about a hundred soldiers from the garrison, and set himself to the task of drilling them into an army.

But an army needs more than drill. It needs to be fed and supplied, and so, on the first morning of his return to Pella, even before he had seen his brother, Philip went to the house where he had been raised to see old Glaukon.

"I need you," he said. "I need someone who will see that my soldiers have fresh meat and boots that do not fall apart after a day in the snow. I need to squeeze the last drop from every drachma. Perdikkas has not been wonderfully generous."

And Glaukon sat silent beside the hearth, which since his wife's death was hardly ever lit, listening with his head bowed. When he looked up there were tears in his eyes.

"Yes, of course," he answered. "Where would I not follow you, My Prince? But I am the chief steward of the king's household and his servant. I need his permission."

Philip nodded, and in that moment he had the look of one whom even a king refuses at his peril. "I will see to it."

Perdikkas did not refuse. Perdikkas, in truth, was becoming a little afraid of his younger brother, for Philip was like one possessed. To watch him drilling his new soldiers was to witness the revelation that comes to a man who has found that which he was born to do.

And if one did not go out to the plains to watch him with his men, one did not see Philip, for he hardly ever left them. He was up with them before dawn. He ate from their campfires, and when they went on their morning march he was with them—he did not ride his horse; he was down in the ranks, wearing out his sandals with the rest of them. In the afternoons he taught them the use of their weapons, swinging a wooden sword in the practice sessions until he could hardly move his arm. And when they had learned enough to begin forming up into the Theban phalanxes that so astonished his officers—how can men fight all jammed up together like that? they would ask—Philip took his place in the front ranks. And when his soldiers began to understand that he meant to be one of them, to try his life in battle along with all the rest, it gave them heart.

His cavalry consisted of two hundred riders, most of whom came from noble families but were, like Philip, younger sons, men who had no great inheritances to look forward to, men for whom war held the prospect of advancement. Philip trained them in the tactics he had learned from Pelopidas, adding refinements of his own that took better advantage of the greater size of Macedonian horses and the skills of their riders. He divided them into companies of forty each and drilled the companies together until their separate wills seemed to fuse into one. When the time came they would have to be able to break up enemy formations without breaking ranks themselves, to offer pursuit without splintering. It was hard for them, for Macedonians had never fought like this before.

And, hardest of all, he taught them that they would have to share pride of place with the infantry, that they were merely one more weapon to be used with the others, and their birth and status earned them nothing. And once, simply to prove to them that he was serious, Philip had a cavalry officer flogged for insulting a foot soldier, and when the man's back was stripped raw, Philip had the man set upon his horse and himself led horse and rider through the camp for every soldier and officer to see. He never had to repeat the punishment, because the incident found no successor.

And sometimes, when the men had been worked almost to the breaking point, Philip would give them a day's rest, have eight or ten oxen roasted for a feast, and then, on the following afternoon, hold games. He himself competed, throwing the javelin and running the longer races—he never entered the horse races, for he said that victory would only prove what everyone already knew, that he was nothing as a rider but that black Alastor was swifter than Pegasos. He only took the laurel once, for a footrace, and on that day the men carried him around the field on their shoulders, for they learned to love him and his triumph had become theirs.

Once, the day after the first of the winter storms, Perdikkas passed by on his way back from a day's hunting. Philip's soldiers only guessed who he was when they saw their commander break ranks, walk over to a party of riders, and help one of them down from his horse.

"They tell me you have performed miracles," the king said as he and his brother watched a mock engagement between a pair of infantry companies drawn up in phalanxes. "They tell me that your men have grown quite agile in this new style of warfare."

"They are not acrobats yet, but at least they don't fall down in the snow." Philip kicked up a plume with his foot—it was nearly a span deep on the ground.

"Where are your boots?" Perdikkas asked, with something like horrified indignation. "You risk frostbite in those sandals."

"As long as one keeps moving, the cold is merely uncomfortable. I wear sandals because they are wearing sandals. When we go into the mountains I will give them boots—I want them to think that, compared to this, the campaign is a debauch."

He laughed, but Perdikkas did not seem to share in the joke.

"Then you really mean to take these green troops in Elimeia?"

"They are not all green. Some of the regular garrison soldiers were with Alexandros in Thessaly. But, yes, I mean to take them into Elimeia. I think I would have a mutiny on my hands if I did not, for they are very keen to fight."

Philip looked at his brother through slightly narrowed eyes. There had been no mention of garrison duty in the north since the day he had received the king's permission to form his new army, but it was in both men's minds.

Perdikkas glanced away.

"Derdas has increased the tempo of his raids along the Haliakmon River," he said finally. "There are those among the council who believe he means to annex the whole valley."

"He already has, brother—after all, he is the one collecting the tribute."

"When can you be ready to leave?"

"After the festival of Xandikos."

"You won't even wait for the spring?"

"No. We can maneuver in the mountains before the rains turn everything to mud. And Derdas will think twice about committing too much of his cavalry while the ground is still icy. When the spring comes I will write, informing you of our progress—I will write from Aiane."

He smiled, but Perdikkas guessed he was in earnest.

The king turned his attention back to the clashing phalanxes, one of which was breaking through the front lines of the other. Had it been a real battle, this would be the climactic moment.

"I suppose now we have no choice," he said.

"No choice at all."

It snowed on the festival of Xandikos, and, as happens sometimes in Macedon, the last snow of the season was the worst. Tree limbs broke off with the weight of ice and the wind piled up drifts, sometimes almost to a horse's belly. And it was a hard snow, stiff and crusted, so that it cut at a man's legs as he tried to walk through it.

The next day Philip led his army out of camp, putting the supply wagons in the vanguard that they might clear a path for his foot soldiers. By nightfall they had gone not even a hundred *stadioi*. The next day there was a thaw, but it was still nearly six days before they reached the base of Mount Bermion.

"We are now in the territory of the Elimoitai," Philip told his men. "The border is still a day's march to the west, but of late Derdas has paid little heed to borders. At any time now we might encounter a large force of his cavalry, so we must put ourselves in such a posture that it does not even cross the enemy's mind to attack us. Therefore tonight, and every night until we sleep in Aiane, we shall erect ourselves a line of defenses."

Under the snow the ground was still frozen, and the soldiers cursed as they dug the trenches and the earthworks. Philip sent out patrols in force. They came back at sunset, white-faced and shaken, for they had found not the enemy but his leavings.

"A village, little more than an hour from here," the captain reported. "We counted over fifty corpses lying in the snow. Old men, women, even children—they seem to have killed everyone. The place stinks of blood."

That night one of the soldiers, a man born in that same village, went mad with grief and threw himself on his sword.

The next day one of the patrols reported contact with the enemy. Philip had given orders to avoid offering battle, but there was a brief skirmish and two men were killed.

"Were any of the Elimoitai killed?"

"One of them dropped from his horse, Prince. If he was dead or wounded, we could not tell."

"I hope he was merely drunk and returns to his king with a bruised backside and tales of how we ran like rabbits. I want Derdas to feel confident. Let his patrols come in close enough to count our numbers."

Nine days after leaving Pella, Philip's soldiers made camp within sight of Aiane. They had seen enemy horsemen watching him, sometimes riding in close enough to shout insults, but there was no more fighting. That afternoon they were left unmolested as they dug their earthworks.

That evening, with only Glaukon for company, Philip took a walk around the perimeter.

"I am frightened," Glaukon said. He sounded so astonished by the fact that Philip had to smile.

"Don't be. Tomorrow is time enough for fear—they will not attack before then. They will not attack at all until we come out."

"How can you be so sure?"

"Because I can think Derdas's thoughts for him. He sees we are a small force and he wants a great victory, in broad day and under the very walls of his city. Thus he is fool enough to let me choose the time and place to offer battle."

"Feel the wind. Has it turned colder, or am I just getting old?" Glaukon pulled his cloak tighter around his shoulders.

Philip, who was not even wearing a cloak, dug his sandaled foot into the earth turned soft and pulpy by the melting snow.

"It has turned colder," he said with evident satisfaction. "Perhaps, if the gods love us, there will be another snowfall before morning—anything to make it harder for Derdas's cavalry."

He laughed aloud. It was a sound that Glaukon found colder even than the wind.

"I have never been in battle," he said. "I have passed my whole life in the king's household, and I have never seen war."

"Neither have I." Philip made a gesture that seemed to take in the whole sweep of the horizon. "Neither have any of us—probably neither has Derdas."

"Yet you are not afraid."

"No."

Was he as surprised as he sounded? Glaukon began to realize how little he knew of this strange man whom he had raised and loved as his own son.

"No, I am not afraid." Philip went on. "Tomorrow, if I discover that I have led you all here to die, perhaps then I will learn to be afraid."

26

The gods did not oblige with a snowfall, but by dawn there was a frost that turned the ground rock hard and, in places, as slick as ice. The sky was full of iron-gray clouds. This high up in the mountains the sun could break through at any moment, or there might be a storm that would last for days. Philip was not disposed to waste his opportunity.

At first light he sent runners through the camp: everyone had exactly half an hour to present themselves in battle dress. Men who knew they might be dead by noon ate a cold breakfast and put a final edge on their swords. They exchanged silent glances. No one wanted to speak of his fear, and there was nothing else to say.

The infantry marshaled beyond their own ramparts, four great phalanxes in depth. The cavalry was nowhere to be seen—it had its orders already.

Just as the sun rose over the walls of Aiane, Philip rode out of camp on his black demon of a stallion. No one was surprised, since the nobility of Macedon had always fought their wars from the back of a horse. As he spoke he crossed back and forth before the two great wings of his army, keeping the reins tight to hold Alastor to a walk.

"The Elimoitai expect to kill you today," he said. "They are many and we are few, and they imagine they will ride over us so that we flatten out under their horses' hooves like wheat in a field. They expect you to break and run because that is what their infantry would do. If they are right, then you will die here on this ice-covered ground. The very blood from your wounds will freeze, and when your corpses thaw out the crows will grow fat on your rotten flesh. That is the fate of the defeated, to lie unburied until their bones are picked clean.

"But you will not break. Your lines will hold, and when you run it will be toward the enemy and not away from him. You will remember everything you

have learned over the past months. You will keep good order, because that is
your only safety. And if the Elimoitai cavalry is foolish enough to charge you,
they will shatter like a beer jar hurled against a stone.

"Let the men to your right and left protect you while you protect them.
Keep your ranks tight, and do not be ashamed to be afraid. A little fear is
good, for it sharpens the mind—a man would have to be a fool not to be afraid
on the morning of his first battle—but drive panic from your hearts, for if you
panic you will surely die.

"And now it is time for me to dismount." He reached down and stroked
the great stallion along his shining neck. "Alastor, as you know, is braver than
any six men and he longs to trample down our enemies, but it is not to be.
When this battle is won, I will ride him through the gates of Aiane to take her
surrender in the name of King Perdikkas, but until then I will fight on the
ground with you. I will command from the inside corner of the left phalanx,
and when I shout an order you will all pick up the cry. We will fight as one
man with one voice and one will and a thousand hearts, and thus shall we
grind Derdas as under a millstone and thus shall our massacred innocents
be avenged!"

As he threw a leg over his horse's neck and dropped to the ground, a great
cheer rose in the throats of Philip's soldiers. They all knew that the place Philip
had chosen for himself, the very hinge of the front line, was where the fighting would be the fiercest. He slapped Alastor on the rump to send his horse
cantering back to the grooms, and men rushed forward to offer him their
spears and shields, even the greaves from their legs. What would they not have
offered him, he who had stepped down from the majesty of his birth to be one
of them, and by that single act had entered their souls?

They had drawn up their ranks perhaps four hundred paces from the city
gate, and still Derdas had not attacked. Philip's soldiers beat their shields
with the butts of their spears, shouting their defiance. They shouted into the
cold wind that blew down from the mountains. It seemed a raw day on which
to die.

The field sloped very gently downward from the walls of Aiane, which
would normally have been an advantage for the Elimoitai, but frost was still
heavy two hours after sunrise and Derdas's horses could have a difficult time
on the hard, slick ground. The momentum of their assault might very well
work against them.

As the challenger, Philip at least had the privilege of choosing the site of
battle. The day before, he had taken Alastor out alone and spent two hours
reading the features of the land. Now he had placed his forces accordingly,
choosing a large patch of stony ground that was good footing for men but

awkward for horses, especially at a run. To the north were patches of trees and low scrubs, which meant that an attack would have to come from either the west or, if Derdas swung his forces around in a flanking maneuver, the south. A small stream, frozen solid now, ran at a slight angle at the upper edge. It was wide enough that the enemy cavalry would not risk crossing it at a gallop, so it would have only fifty or sixty paces to regroup and focus for the charge. And all that time it would be under attack from the Macedonian archers and javelin throwers.

It was not so obvious a trap that Derdas would refuse battle, but it would work against him. Philip was pleased with his choice. He would need the edge it provided against the numerical advantage of the enemy Elimiote cavalry.

Yet it was not the cavalry his soldiers would have first to overcome. As the sun edged up in the sky, the gates opened and the Elimiote infantry began to marshal in front of the city walls.

They were at least fifteen hundred strong, but they were a mob—peasants who had been dragged off their farms, given a shield and a pike and told to fight for their king. They would have little stomach for battle, and Derdas was not such a fool as to count on them for victory. They were a sacrifice. They would die in their hundreds merely to entangle the Macedonian forces and perhaps force them to turn. Then the cavalry would come in to take advantage of the confusion and destroy what was left.

Philip knew that he had to dispose of this first attack quickly, keeping his men under discipline, or everything was lost.

The Elimiote infantry had arrayed itself into three long lines, one behind the other. Not even squares, but merely three lines—they would charge in waves. Philip could hardly believe his luck.

When the first attack came, the Elimoitai gave voice to a great battle cry as they began running down the field. It was a chilling sound, but Philip had told his men to expect it. "They will be out of breath by the time they reach us," he had told them, and they had laughed. Now he could almost feel the Macedonians tensing for that first impact.

The Elimoitai had not even covered a hundred paces when their lines began to break apart. They were not an army now, merely individuals, each one alone with nothing but his weapon and his courage and his terrible longing for life.

Another hundred paces and the first man dropped with a Macedonian arrow through his neck. There were others, many others. Many times when they died they threw their arms out as if to welcome the stroke that killed them.

For the last hundred paces they faced the javelins as well. A javelin seems to cleave a man in half—what an appalling thing to feel that thick shaft of wood suddenly run through you from your breast to your bowels.

The second wave of attack had begun, and these had to face the added horror of running across a battlefield littered with their dead comrades. Yet they came, and they perished in their turn.

The Elimoitai had reached the little frozen stream by then. They had to take care over the slippery ice and then, when they were across and the enemy was only fifty or so paces away, they would glance about them and perhaps for the first time realize how few they had become. To go forward was certain death, if only on the spears of a Macedonian front line that must have looked like a wall, and yet they could not bring themselves to retreat. They seemed not to know what to do, and as they waited, milling about, they were cut down.

What a butcher, Philip thought. *What a butcher the man is to send his subjects out to die like this.* And then once more he became the soldier, the commander with a sliver of ice through his heart, as it occurred to him that the tangle of bodies would further impede Derdas's cavalry.

But it was not only the Elimoitai who were dying, for they too knew how to use their weapons. The man next to Philip was struck in the eye by a javelin—it tore his head open, scattering blood everywhere. Philip kicked the corpse aside, and the next behind in the column stepped forward to take up the dead man's shield and spear. Macedonians were dying everywhere, but their defenses held and when one fell another came up to stand in his place.

And their discipline had its reward. For every one of Philip's soldiers killed, there were as many as eight or ten of the Elimoitai lying dead upon that field of slaughter.

The first two waves of Elimiote infantry had exhausted themselves and the third was just coming within range of the Macedonian archers when Philip decided it was time to end this mortal agony. He raised the tip of his spear high into the air and shouted, "Point!" The cry was taken up by row after row of men until it seemed to roll away from him in waves—it was the signal for the two center phalanxes to advance at a trot while the right and left followed at a slower pace.

The effect was devastating. Where before the Elimoitai had been confronted with a solid wall of shields, from behind which arrows and javelins fell down on them like hailstones, now the wall bowed out at the center and began to advance on them as if to grind them to pieces. To men who had seen their comrades dropping all around them, it was simply too much. They turned and fled, and in their confused and terrified flight they engulfed the final wave of their own infantry. Even those whose advance had hardly reached the perimeters of the battle, when they saw what was happening—when they witnessed the panic of the men who had preceded them—they turned and ran.

Within an hour of its beginning this phase of the battle was over, leaving the Macedonians in possession of the field and with their lines unbroken.

"Let them send their horsemen!" Philip shouted, almost beside himself with exultation. "Let them come if they dare, for they see what awaits them!"

He gave the signal to withdraw back to their original positions and to straighten their lines. They had no more than a few minutes' grace before the Elimiote cavalry began assembling outside the city gates. The final test was at hand.

The massing of the enemy horsemen took nearly an hour—they were easily seven or eight hundred strong, as large a force as Derdas could assemble on short notice—and this time he was beginning to show some tenuous grasp of tactics. He seemed to have divided his cavalry into two uneven groups, the smaller of which was breaking away and deploying itself far out to the south so that the attack could come from two directions at once.

The distance was too great for Philip to identify Derdas among the hordes of riders. It would have been useful to know where he was, for, if he understood the man correctly, the king of the Elimoitai would want to take personal command over whichever of his three groups he felt sure would deliver the decisive blow.

The question answered itself as the mass of the enemy cavalry, which would attack head-on, began to concentrate itself, drawing in at the sides so that the horsemen were disposed in several rows, one behind the other. It looked like the infantry battle all over again.

Philip knew at once what it meant. There would be a wave of cavalry straight on, over the same ground where now lay the corpses of the Elimiote foot soldiers. Perhaps there would be two waves. These would engage the Macedonian forces while the smaller force moved in from the south. Infantry squares were notoriously vulnerable to this sort of side attack, and Derdas hoped to catch the enemy from two directions at once, giving him no opportunity to turn and shield his exposed flank. Then, when the Macedonian lines had been broken and their formations reduced to chaos, Derdas would unleash a final attack to finish them off.

It was a good plan, as far as it went. It did not make the best use of the terrain, which, considering that Derdas had grown to manhood with this patch of ground constantly under his eyes, said much about the mind that had conceived it. But its greatest flaw was that, at least in general terms, Philip had already anticipated it.

The first wave of cavalry started forward at a walk. They were within a hundred and fifty paces before they began their charge. When they were a hundred paces, and already under attack from the Macedonian archers, Philip ordered his two right phalanxes to begin a slow advance. This was what Derdas would expect—indeed, he would be counting on it to draw out the Macedonian flank. It seemed a pity to disappoint him.

When the first of the Elimoitai reached the ice-choked stream that ran across the top of the battlefield they did not break their charge and several horses lost their footing and went down. Those who followed slowed down and, after a moment or two of costly hesitation, began to pick their careful way across. They were easy targets then, and the bodies of men and horses began to pile up on both banks. *The fools*, Philip thought. It seemed they had not even anticipated that the stream would have frozen over.

By now the two forces were no more than forty paces apart, too close for the Elimiote charge to regain its momentum. But the Elimoitai were brave men and they threw themselves at Philip's army with a desperate fury.

The air was rent with the screams of horses disemboweled on the Macedonian pikes, but if many died, many broke through. All along the front of the two forward phalanxes there were great tears where men were trampled to death beneath their own shields. Sometimes horse and rider, having reached the center, would be cut down, and sometimes they would blunder through to safety, scattering the Macedonian infantry as they went.

Some of the Elimiote cavalry veered off to attack the two left-hand phalanxes to the rear. They had greater momentum to make up for their smaller numbers and they inflicted terrible damage.

But Philip's soldiers did not yield to panic. When men fell they were replaced from behind and the ranks closed like the water of a pool into which someone has thrown a pebble.

When the first wave had spent its force, Philip shouted, "Wheel left!" and his two rear phalanxes, like a boat that in midstream must swing round at right angles against the current, began a huge turn, pivoting on the center, to get ready to face the next attack, which was already beginning from the south.

Here the Elimoitai had a better field, straight and clear, and they faced only two of the Macedonian phalanxes. Here, and for the first time, Philip tasted real fear, like a copper coin on his tongue.

There is nowhere to run, he thought as the Elimiote horsemen came down on him—at fifty paces they seemed huge, like a race of giants. *There is no escape from this*. Yet somewhere he found the courage to think, and to issue the crucial order.

"Drop!" he shouted. The one word rippled over the front line as man after man went down on one knee, digging the butt of his pike into the earth behind him so that the point made a long row, about breast high, in front of them.

The javelin throwers now had a clear aim and they punished the Elimoitai cruelly. Men fell from their mounts, spilling backward as if pulled down from behind, and were crushed beneath the weight of their horses as these rolled over the ground, thrashing about with their hooves as they died.

The charge was blunted but by no means stopped. Many of the Elimiote riders would not be stopped, crashing through the Macedonian lines like a stone breaking down a wicker fence. Many held back, waiting for the confusion to give them a better opening. And even some of the fallen horses tumbled against the first row of shields and killed many men while avenging their death agonies.

Philip all at once felt his pike snap in two in his hands as it pierced the breast of a gray dappled warhorse. Its rider fell almost on top of him, and suddenly he found himself fighting for his life, scrambling to avoid the arc of the man's sword. With a timing that was instinctive and unconsidered, he threw himself forward just as the Elimiote had finished his swing, wrestling him to the ground. Before he knew what he was doing, he had the shattered butt of his pike across the man's throat and had crushed his windpipe. The Elimiote's face was a purple, bulging horror by the time he stopped struggling, and there was blood running out of his right ear. Philip did not let up until he was sure the Elimiote was dead, but then, kneeling over the man's chest, he felt a spasm of revulsion and shame so intense he almost vomited.

Not until he stood up again did Philip see that the front of his tunic was soaked in blood—there was a straight, shallow wound from his shoulder to his sternum where the man's sword had nicked him. Somehow that made it better.

This will not kill me, he thought with a sudden flash of joy, and all at once he could not help but laugh. *I will not die of this.*

He found his shield lying in the dust at his feet. Someone handed him a pike and he went back to the front rank. The whole incident had taken no more than a few minutes.

"Straighten the lines!" he shouted, and somehow men who were fighting for their very lives found it in themselves to pick up the cry and to obey. Even in the midst of the Elimoitai's furious attack, the phalanxes firmed up and their ranks closed.

Now it was the Elimiote cavalry that was in turmoil. It could not withdraw to regroup, and after its initial charge each of the two groups that were attacking the Macedonian left and right wings had degenerated into a milling horde. Its attack still dangerous but uncoordinated and unfocused, it would only harass the phalanxes like a swarm of gnats.

The third assault divided itself between the two wings of Philip's infantry, which were almost at right angles from one another. It was another blow, but the phalanxes absorbed it, so that the battle was becoming a bloody stalemate in which the Elimoitai could not shatter the Macedonian ranks and the contest would only be decided, it seemed, when the last man was left standing.

It was then that the Macedonian cavalry attacked.

It had been kept in reserve and out of sight, behind the earthworks of the Macedonian camp, and now, when the Elimoitai had at last committed everything to the battle, it charged. Philip's infantry, when they saw the Macedonian horses tearing over the ground, raised a cheer.

The surprise was total, as if the Elimoitai had forgotten that their enemy were Macedonians and knew how to ride as well as they. Only two hundred strong, they held together and punched a huge hole in the milling crowds of Elimiote horsemen. Suddenly there were dead everywhere, and one could almost smell the panic.

Yet the Elimoitai were fated to suffer another shock, for after their initial charge the Macedonians did not stop. They rode straight on until they had a clear field, then turned, keeping their wedged-shaped formation intact, and charged again.

But even before the second charge, it was over. The Elimiote cavalry had been reduced to a beaten, panic-stricken mob, mere targets for the Macedonian archers and javelin throwers. They simply were not able to offer any organized resistance and thus found themselves confronted with a plain choice—either flee or die. In their hundreds they fled.

It was only then that Philip could make out the figure of Derdas. The beaten king was perhaps fifty paces away, mounted on a beautiful tawny stallion he seemed barely able to control. He was waving his sword over his head and shouting, as if to rally his men, but in the confusion of battle, it was impossible to make out even the sound of his voice.

And it did not matter, for no one was listening. The Elimiote cavalry streamed back toward Aiane, in such numbers that the city gate was clogged with horses. At last Derdas too threw down his sword and ran.

It was then that Philip saw perhaps the last thing he might have suspected—the gates to Aiane beginning to close. The great wooden doors, pushing against that hysterical mass of men and animals, began to swing shut almost in Derdas's face. Someone had given the order to seal the city, leaving the king and what was left of his men to their fate.

How many were left? Four, perhaps five hundred of the Elimoitai were still on their horses. Their refuge was cut off. They knew that unless they sued for peace they would stay only to be annihilated. The sole alternative was flight.

Derdas wheeled about on his great tawny stallion and shouted something—a curse, from the expression on his face. Then he and many others rode north, the only direction left open to them.

"Pursuit!" Philip shouted, and again the cry was taken up by many voices. Two companies of Macedonian cavalry promptly wheeled about and galloped after the king and his companions in flight. Their horses were fresher, but Derdas knew the terrain. Philip wanted him alive, yet the chances were good that he and his soldiers would escape into the mountains to be the problem of another day.

Their departure left the battlefield eerily quiet. Not even the Macedonians could bring themselves to cheer their victory. They waited in silence as, one after another, the Elimoitai dropped their swords in token of surrender.

One of them, a man of perhaps thirty, rode forward, toward the ranks of the Macedonian horsemen. It was obvious that he wished to parley.

Philip handed his pike to the man next to him—time to be a commander again.

"Which of you is leader?" the man shouted. He seemed surprised when the answer came from the ranks of the infantry.

"I am Philip, prince of Macedon," Philip said, hardly raising his voice. "Say what you have to say."

The man rode over to where Philip was standing. It was clear he found the whole business infinitely distasteful.

"What terms will you offer if we throw open the city to you?" he inquired.

Philip favored him with a wolfish smile.

"Better to ask, what terms will I offer if you do not?"

27

"We killed about twenty and captured perhaps a hundred," the cavalry commander reported. He was about Philip's age and his name was Korous. They had known each other all their lives. "But most escaped."

"Did you take Derdas?" It was the only important question.

"No. We had a prisoner identify the slain on the way back, and he was not among them."

He lowered his head just slightly, like a child who expects to be punished for losing a toy. It was obvious he imagined himself to be in disgrace.

Korous was tall, handsome, and blond, and he had always reminded Philip of his eldest brother, Alexandros, as much in temperament as in appearance. It would be a mistake to humiliate such a man.

"At least now I won't have to decide what to do with him," Philip said, grinning as if he had just escaped something himself. "Tell your men they fought well today. They saved us."

And then, out of sheer exhilaration, he started to laugh.

"We have won a famous victory today, Korous—like when we were boys."

They could both laugh now. They were the conquerors, looking down from the absolute pinnacle of their young lives, and Derdas was forgotten.

Half an hour later, in the middle of the afternoon of a day that already seemed to stretch back half a century, Philip, as he had promised, was mounted on Alastor and about to enter the captured city of Aiane. Before him was his army, drawn up in neat ranks, and, sitting on the ground in postures of exhaustion, the thousand or so of the Elimoitai who had bought their lives at the price of surrender. They were all waiting for Philip to speak, for now his was the only voice that mattered.

"This city and all who dwell within her are now under the protection of the Lord Perdikkas, king of all the Macedonians, among whom are numbered the Elimoitai. There will be no looting, nor will there be any reprisals. We are all countrymen again, and we are all brothers. Those who have died today lie together on this battlefield, purged of all enmity—so let it be with us.

"Derdas is gone, having fled when the fighting turned against him. He will not be back. His ancestor was put on his throne by King Alexandros of Macedon, and now a descendant of that king has pulled him down from it. He has forfeited his right to rule and his right to your allegiance, but I say to the men of Elimeia that his fall is not yours. All who take the oath to King Perdikkas, declaring loyalty to him and his heirs, will retain their rank and property. All who do not will number among his enemies. It is for each man to decide alone.

"And to my own soldiers, lest they feel cheated of their rightful plunder, I declare that one third of the treasury of King Derdas will be distributed among them equally, officers and men—we have shared equally in the danger of this enterprise, so let it be the same with the booty. Until that division is made, perhaps the tavern keepers of Aiane will extend us all credit."

There were cheers from the ranks of the Macedonians, for they knew that one-third was the traditional prize of the conquering commander. Even some of the Elimoitai cheered, although perhaps for different reasons. At any rate, it was a long moment before Philip could once more make himself heard.

"Now let us enter this city, which is today once more a Macedonian city, and may this triumph mark a new beginning for victors and defeated alike."

And when the massive doors opened one might have thought that Aiane was welcoming home her own conquering army. People poured out into the streets, out along the great road that led from the city gates. They threw flowers under the hooves of Philip's horse, crowding so close around that Alastor seemed on the verge of panic and it was all Philip could do to keep him from trampling them under. Women wept, holding up their children that they might see, and men cheered. It was as if they had found themselves a new hero.

And why should they not cheer? Philip thought, even as he smiled and waved. *They know the customary fate of vanquished cities. They are grateful to be alive.*

When he rode into the courtyard of the king's palace, whence he had come as a supplicant a mere six months before, there were only servants and a few old secretaries, the drudges of royal administration, there to meet him. The only person of rank he saw was the Lady Phila.

She wore a dark blue tunic, one end of which covered her hair, and her face was drained of expression. She might have been waiting for her executioner.

"I will conduct you to your apartments," she said, her voice showing only a trace of strain. "Since there is no one else to do it."

"And which apartments would those be, Lady?"

"Whichever you wish," came the answer—she appeared surprised that he would see fit to ask—"since this house and all that it contains are now yours."

There was nothing of either bitterness or invitation in her words. She was merely stating a fact. Yet, as she led him inside and they were alone together in the vast reception hall, Philip could not help wondering if she enrolled herself in the list of his new possessions.

"Lady," he said, speaking almost as if to drive the thought from his mind. "Who ordered the gates to be closed on Derdas?"

And when she would not answer, he smiled.

"It was you, was it not?"

"My brother was so confident of victory," she said at last, her anguish visible nowhere but in her eyes. "I knew you would have demanded his surrender as the price of peace, and I knew he would not have accepted. I have no illusions about the sort of man he is. He had lost—that was obvious—and he had made no provision for a siege. Nothing could have prevented you from taking Aiane, now or a month from now, and after what suffering? In the end you would have captured him anyway, and I know what revenge is visited upon cities that refuse to submit to their conquerors."

"And so you . . ."

"And so I betrayed him." Tears, cold as rainwater, ran down her tortured face. "He leaves me his proxy when he is away, and thus people are accustomed to obeying my orders. In this case they were only too eager . . ."

"Of course they were eager—they knew you were saving them."

He looked around him, studying the paintings on the walls, that she might be spared observation while she struggled to retain her composure. His back was almost to her when he spoke.

"Lady, you are both noble and wise—a rare combination. You make me almost glad your brother has escaped with his life."

Aiane accepted her conquest without fuss, and there were no disturbances in the city that night or in the days that followed. Philip had issued a proclamation that hostages taken in raids over the border had only to present themselves to claim their liberty, and over time perhaps two hundred, mostly young women, found their way into the Macedonian camp. The bulk, of course, were from the great estates, most of them some distance from the city, but they too were not hindered from regaining their liberty. No one was disposed to trifle with Philip's word.

But his first priority was not justice but reconciliation. For many days the air was black with the smoke from funeral pyres. The Macedonians had lost not quite a hundred and fifty men, but the Elimoitai had suffered far worse— over a thousand had fallen in those few hours of battle. Philip gave orders that their bones were to be returned to their families without ransom and that those who went unclaimed were to receive honorable burial beside his own soldiers.

These things made their impression on the Elimoitai, who had never been noted for clemency. As the days passed, Derdas's nobles, sometimes in groups, sometimes one by one, presented themselves at his former palace to stand in the presence of his conqueror and to take the oath of allegiance to King Perdikkas, as did the soldiers of the city garrison.

But, since men are sometimes more loyal to the corps of which they are a part than to any commander, Philip made it a rule that the old Elimiote army had to be absorbed into the new army he had created to fight them. This was not difficult with the infantry, since many of them had been impressed into service and now only wanted to return to their fathers' farms, but the cavalry posed special problems. For one thing, there were more of them. Of the Elimoitai who had ridden against Philip's soldiers that day, perhaps five hundred were still alive. It was not enough to put his own officers in command of Elimiote companies, because he did not have enough officers to go round. And Derdas had not been able to mass his whole force in time to face the Macedonians—there were outlying garrisons that did not even hear of the defeat until half a month after it had happened.

But Elimeia was fractured with as many regional hatreds as the whole of Macedon generally—the plainsmen thought that anyone from the mountains of the west had to be a barbaric monster, and men from the other side of the Siatista Pass spoke a tongue so larded with Illyrian that it was hardly intelligible to someone not born among them. The ties of kinship and clan were what mattered. All of them had followed their own nobles into battle and were loyal chiefly to them.

So Philip mixed the survivors together like salt and sand. *Let them learn a new way to make war among new faces*, he thought. *Let them learn to be Macedonians.*

A month after the battle, a group of Elimiote nobles sought a private audience with Philip. He knew what they wanted. He had been expecting them.

"Derdas is gone," they said. "He will not come back—after what has happened, we do not wish him back—and he was the last of his line. We need a new king."

"You have a king," Philip replied. "His name is Perdikkas."

"Perdikkas is in Pella. We know nothing of Perdikkas, and a king is no good if he is always four days' march away. Men want a king they can see."

"What are you proposing?"

"We wish to propose you to the Assembly of the Elimoitai. You have won the right by force of arms, and you are of royal blood. Besides, you are already more powerful than any king, and men will be less ashamed of their defeat if they can pledge their loyalty to you and not to some stranger. We wish to know if you will accept."

"And do the other nobles agree, or do you speak only for yourselves?"

"We are not fools, My Lord Philip. We need a king, or we will begin to cut each other to pieces—so it has always been. Victory makes a man respected, so better you than anyone else."

"I must write to my brother and ask his permission. King or no king, I will remain his subject."

"We understand that."

"Then I will write."

At first, when Perdikkas received his brother's letter, he did not know what to think. "It is largely a question of forms and the tenderness of local pride," Philip had written. "Like anyone else, they would rather be ruled by a king of their own choosing than occupied by foreigners. In any case, I will have to stay here for some time. The reorganization and retraining of the Elimiote forces is a slow business. Perhaps by late summer we can exchange a few companies with, for instance, one of the garrisons on the eastern frontier . . ." Philip seemed to consider the matter purely from a practical standpoint, giving the impression he did not care whether he became king of the Elimoitai. And yet he must care. What was in his mind?

Philip had gone west with an army of a thousand men, mostly infantry, and now it seemed he had picked up, like a copper coin he had found in the street, some three thousand additional cavalry. Further, his reputation as a commander was suddenly enormous—the conquest of Elimeia was on everyone's lips—so that Perdikkas was sick unto death of hearing his brother's praises. And now he wanted to be made a king. Of course he wanted it. How could he not want it?

Perdikkas, who had only recently emerged from the shadow of one brother, now found he had a rival in the other. Philip was creating an army. What would he finally decide to do with it?

"If someone, myself or some other, does not maintain strong control over this region we are inviting disaster. The nobles are jealous and afraid of each other. If we leave them to themselves, how long will it be before some of them begin to seek the protection of outside alliances? Either we control Elimeia firmly, and from the center, or it will slowly slip away from us."

Well, Philip was right about that. The Elimoitai had to have a king, and that king had to be beholden to Macedon.

But not Philip—anyone but Philip.

But if not Philip, who?

A king, it is said, may trust no one. Who could be sent to Aiane who would not begin to fancy himself as an independent power? No one. Absolutely no one.

Except Philip. For, when he reached the bedrock of his feelings about his brother, Perdikkas knew that Philip would never betray him. With Philip as king of the Elimoitai, he was safe on his eastern borders.

And there was something to be said for having Philip in Aiane, far away, embroiled in the squabbles of those mountain savages, rather than in Pella, enjoying his reputation as a conqueror. What honors he would expect! Perdikkas would have to raise him to glory, or the world would judge him ungrateful—and perhaps even suspect him of being jealous. It would be intolerable to have him at home.

Yes, let him be king in his little rock-strewn kingdom—better there than here. Perdikkas decided he would write back at once, giving his permission.

After her brother's flight, Phila had continued to live in his palace and, in the absence of any sign that she should not, carried on the running of the household, just as she had done since her father's time. The Lord Philip used the palace as a headquarters, but he did not live there, preferring to sleep in a tent in the encampment his soldiers had erected outside the city while they built an enlargement to the royal barracks. When it was finished, for all she knew, he might sleep there.

Thus she saw him but rarely, and then only for a moment or two in passing. He might almost have been avoiding her.

Her astonishment was therefore all the greater when one morning she received an invitation—an invitation that, of course, carried the force of an order—to join him at his midday meal in her brother's old council room.

She had not entered that room since before the Lord Philip's arrival, and now she hardly recognized it. In her brother's time it been a bare, melancholy place, for Derdas had had little taste for business and hardly ever used it. Now several of the tables were stacked up against the far wall and of the only two that remained one was covered with papers and maps. The Lord Philip was standing behind it with a small group of officers, both Macedonian and Elimiote, clustered around him. She was ten or twelve paces away and he was speaking in a tone too low to allow her to catch the words, but she could hear the peculiar urgency of his voice and she could see from the faces of the men around him how raptly they listened. For that moment at least, he possessed their souls.

The scene was a kind of emblem, a distilling of all the impressions she had formed of him since the first time he came to try to persuade Derdas to peace. He was serious. He cared nothing for appearances, preferring to see the world as it was and to describe what he saw in blunt, almost brutally truthful words. He was a man other men would follow by instinct.

It was a moment or two before he was even aware of her presence. Then he looked up and, without smiling, said, "My Lords, we will continue with this another time."

A servant brought in a tray of food and laid it on the other table. There was bread and cheese, a bowl of figs, and a small jar of wine. Still standing, the Lord Philip picked up one of the figs and split it open with a knife.

"Be pleased to sit, Lady," he said. He seemed absorbed in the process of scraping the meat out of his fig. "Be good enough to pour us both some wine."

Phila poured the wine into two small cups and set the jar back down on the table. She did not drink, however, nor touch the food. It simply did not occur to her.

"Why have you summoned me, My Lord?"

"Summoned?" He looked at her and at last smiled, as if her use of the word amused him. "Do you know what is to happen in five days' time?"

"There will be an assembly."

"And then?"

"You will be elected king."

He sat down, tore off a corner of bread, and dipped it in his wine. He gave no indication that he had even heard her.

"Will you resent my being king?" he asked. When she did not reply, he leaned a little to the side so that his shoulder touched the wall. For a long time he remained silent, chewing on his piece of bread and studying her face, as if he still expected an answer.

"I will be king not for my own sake but because it is necessary," he said at last. "Derdas, even if he returned and my brother pardoned him, could never rule here again—the nobles will not forgive him for betraying them into a humiliating defeat. You do not like to hear this, but it is still the truth. I will be king because there is no one else."

Phila could not raise her eyes to look at him. She knew herself to be very close to tears, but it was not his words which pained her. She simply could not bear the pressure of his gaze. What did he want of her?

"What do you want?"

The question at least got him to look away. He suddenly became very busy with the bread and cheese, and it occurred to Phila, with something like astonishment, that he was embarrassed.

"I want to be a good king, true to my brother and to the people of this place. I want to rule in peace, to end all division and hostility."

"And what has this to do with me?"

Now he really was embarrassed—enough so that he actually blushed. It gave her a small feeling of triumph to know that, at least for the moment, she had the advantage over him.

"It is the duty of a king to protect his people," he said in what sounded like a rehearsed speech, "both during his own lifetime and after his death. A king needs an heir. I would take you to wife, My Lady."

For a moment she was not sure if she remembered how to breathe. If someone had asked her how she felt, she could not have told them. She did not feel anything really, except a shock of surprise that blotted out everything else.

Was he still speaking? Yes, he was.

"I am sorry, Lady. I have no wish to offend you and I am sure you find the subject distressing, but since you have no male relatives with whom to arrange matters—at least, none who are in a position to act for you—I have no choice but to approach you directly. Yet have no fear that I will compel you to this marriage, Lady. If the idea is distasteful to you, or if you feel you cannot in honor accept, then I will give you one of the royal estates and you can live there as you see fit. It would be for the best, however, if you did accept. You are the last of the old line."

"Is that all you want?" she asked. "Legitimacy?"

"I won my 'legitimacy,' as you choose to call it, with the point of my sword." His fingers closed around the rim of his wine cup and she was not sure he would not crush it to powder, he seemed so angry. "I am to be king by vote of the Elimiote Assembly, and they think I do them a great favor to accept. They are right to think so. But I would put an end to old divisions—for the good of the nation."

"For the good of which nation?" she asked, not even knowing why she felt so wounded. "The Elimoitai or the Macedonians?"

As she sat there, as he watched her through his beautiful blue-gray eyes—eyes as coldly intelligent as a cat's—she felt once more her heart dissolving into tears.

Yet she must not weep. The royal women of Elimeia did not weep before strangers. She would rather die than show the Lord Philip what she felt.

"The Elimoitai are Macedonians." His fingers relaxed around the wine cup and he picked it up but did not raise it to his lips. "We are one people. We must be one people.

"Consider my offer," he said as if they were discussing the price of a horse. "I would like an answer before the assembly meets.

"One thing—if you decide to accept, you must put aside your loyalty to your brother."

"I have betrayed him once already. Is that not sufficient assurance?"

"No." He shook his head. "When a woman marries she leaves one family and joins another. Her husband's enemies become her own. I simply want you to be clear in your own mind what is possible for you."

She rose from the table and, before he could stop her, bowed to him.

"Thank you, My Lord. You shall have my answer before the assembly meets."

When she was alone in her room, when there was no one to see, Phila wept at last. She wept as if her breast would crack. She wept until the tears parched her throat, until there were no more tears left.

And as she lay across her bed, with the door safely bolted, she weighed in her mind what a weak and inconsiderable thing a woman was. Did the Lord Philip want her? For herself did he want her? It was even possible he did, but it would not matter to him if he did not. What he proposed was a dynastic alliance, the sort of marriage she had been raised to expect would be her destiny, yet to hear him propose it was bitter. To be sent away from home, away from one's family, to be the bride of a stranger—this she knew she could have borne with a lighter heart. But to be the wife of Philip of Macedon, and only because he judged it best, *for the good of the nation . . .*

Because she did love him. Perhaps she had loved him since that first moment, in her father's old garden—she was not sure. She only knew that she would have committed any crime he asked of her.

Was that why she had raised the gate against Derdas? She had not thought so at the time, but now she was no longer sure. She would never be sure.

Yes, take me if you want me, she thought. *And I will love you with a woman's abject, ignoble love. Even if you never look at me, if I never see your smile, I will love you until I die.*

28

Five days later, at first light, the Elimoitai met in assembly. A motion was put forward to formally depose King Derdas and it was carried by noisy acclaim. When Philip was hailed as the new king, men gathered around him to beat their swords against their breastplates and shout his name in the traditional display of allegiance. No one had spoken against him because, even if the Macedonian army had not been camped outside the gates of Aiane, there was no other candidate whose election would not have meant civil war. Everyone knew that the life of this lowlander was now all that stood between them and chaos.

When the dog had been cut in half and its blood sprinkled across the road from the amphitheater, Philip led the members of the army, now his subjects, to the temple district, there to purify their weapons and to make sacrifice at the shrine of Zeus. He entered alone, as was the custom, and, as chief priest of the Elimoitai, made sacrifice at the altar fire, offering the thighbone of an ox, wrapped in the animal's own fat. The fire blazed up, which was considered a lucky omen.

Outside, the ceremony over, he found nearly the entire population of the city gathered to hail him. Their cheers rang in his ears, and he raised his spear in the traditional greeting.

Will you be a king, Philip? Great-Grandfather has said I am to be the bride of a great king someday.

Little Audata, clutching her knees, sitting on the rim of a stone cistern, inquiring if he was to be her destiny. Why, suddenly, had that particular memory floated into his consciousness? How long ago it seemed.

"Yes," he whispered to himself, listening to the cheers of people who only a few months before had been his enemies, who now had delivered their fates into his hands. "Yes, I am now a king. But it comes too late for us."

He could not have explained why, at this his moment of triumph, he felt so peculiarly desolate.

Later in the day there was feasting and games. The Elimoitai and Philip's own soldiers competed on equal terms, dividing the prizes between them. Philip, breaking his own rule, competed in the horse race and won.

The next day, very quietly, the Lady Phila's possessions were transported to a royal estate within an hour's journey of the city. As king, Philip now felt obliged to take up residence in the palace, so for propriety's sake she had to leave. She would stay away until she returned as a bride.

They had agreed that the marriage would take place in the month of Peritios, a propitious time. It would be heavy winter by then, but Philip was not sorry for the delay. He wished to be established as ruler in the people's minds before he took a wife from the old ruling house. He did not wish to create the impression that he was trying to strengthen his claim.

As king he now held all of the treasury and royal estates as his personal property. In law, the Lady Phila had nothing. Her very life was at Philip's disposal. Had he wished to, he could have sold her into slavery.

But it would have shamed her to come into marriage thus destitute, so he signed over to her the estate where she was now living, along with thirty thousand Athenian silver drachmas to provide her with a dowry.

They would see each other but infrequently before the betrothal ceremony, only a few days prior to the wedding. It would not be seemly if they were known to be meeting, for all that an hour's ride was hardly the journey of a lifetime.

Yet he had much to keep the Lady Phila from his thoughts. The enlargements on the royal barracks were proceeding at a rapid pace, and Philip, who knew enough firsthand of carpentry and stonemasonry to take a real interest in the work, was on the site every day, often for several hours. The Elimoitai wondered that a king should sometimes carry building stones on his own back or give audience to his ministers while he plastered a wall, but they were not displeased. Men are rarely disappointed to find that their ruler is concerned with everything that affects them, and Philip, it was soon apparent, worked at being a good king.

Glaukon took over the management of the royal household, serving his foster son as he and his fathers before him had served the kings of Macedon for generations. When he was not entertaining his nobles, and there was no occasion to dine in state, Philip would go to the old man's apartments and the two of them would eat their dinner out of a common pot.

Most of Philip's time was given over to the reform of the army. He trained with his men, sparing himself no more than they. The Macedonian soldiers were used to constant drill, but the Elimoitai were not and, at least at first, complained loudly.

"You have tasted defeat once already," he told them, "and near half your number are now in their burial urns. I mean to see that you never dine from that dish again."

The complaints stopped.

There were also financial matters that needed attention. Philip had Derdas's treasurer flogged out of the city, the royal accounts were in such a deplorable state. He introduced a more orderly system of record keeping that he had learned in Thebes and made a practice of checking the accounts himself.

Added to this there were the estates of the Elimoitai to be disposed of. The heirs of men who had fallen in honorable combat beneath the walls of Aiane did not lose their rights—no one would be punished for having done his duty—but the property of those who had fled with Derdas was forfeit, and many among the dead had left no issue. Thus vast holdings in land, cattle, sheep, houses, granaries, and mills had reverted to the crown.

Philip used them to reward those among his own men who had distinguished themselves in the recent battle. Common soldiers received grants of land and livestock so that they could settle in Elimeia and begin a new life. Some he even ennobled. Many took wives from among the local women and settled down comfortably among neighbors who had recently been their enemies in war, becoming themselves Elimoitai. By these means did the new king bind the nation to himself, and to Macedon.

But from time to time, in the midst of these duties, Philip would simply disappear for an afternoon. His ministers and officers would search for him in vain, and even Glaukon professed ignorance.

"Perhaps he has gone hunting," the old man would say, with a slight smile that the nobles of Elimeia found maddening—yet who would dare even to raise his voice to the king's chief steward, who enjoyed his master's perfect confidence?

"That is nonsense. A king does not go hunting alone."

"Even a king does many things alone, and this king more than most. Yet have no fear, for he will return before the gates are closed."

And when he did return, riding his great black stallion but without even the carcass of a wild pig to show for his trouble, if anyone asked him where he had been he would fix them with a stare calculated to ensure they would be careful never to repeat the question.

On these occasions, in fact, Philip was with his intended bride. He knew he should stay away—that simple prudence and a decent respect for custom dictated that he should stay away—yet he was drawn to her, almost against his will.

He was not in love. Love, for Philip, was a curse, a kind of madness that descended upon those whom the gods wished to destroy. His mother had been in love, and that fury had ended many lives. No, he was not in love. He would have said, if anyone had had the temerity to ask him, that he was curious. He wanted to know this woman, to see into her heart, for much might depend upon the temper of her nature. After all, one day she might have a future king suckling at her breast.

Yet what he would not have acknowledged, since he hardly even knew it himself, was that in the Lady Phila's presence he knew at last a little peace. Her gentle voice soothed him, and her smile softened the loneliness that seemed to fill his soul as the air does an empty jar. Philip had grown to manhood knowing himself to be profoundly alone, yet for a few hours, in the presence of this woman, the world seemed a less abandoned place.

Yet he was not in love.

"Next summer I will take you to Pella," he said to her one autumn afternoon. They were strolling through the estate's orchard, and fallen leaves were skimming across the ground in a wind that came from the mountains that looked incredibly distant against the northern horizon but were in fact not even a day's ride away. "I will show you the sea."

"I have never seen it. What is it like?"

"Cold and wet." Philip grinned. He had taken her hand as they walked, and she had not resisted. It was the first time he had ever touched her.

"Will you go to Pella to see your brother?" The question sounded so innocent on her lips that Philip could not help glancing at her to be sure she did not mean something else.

"Yes, to see my brother." He shrugged. He did not want to talk about his brother. He wanted to talk about how the wind caught at strands of her black hair and made them seem to dance. "I suspect he will not be glad to see me, but it will reassure him to find I have left my army at home."

"He does not trust you, then?"

"He is a king. A king trusts no one, members of his own family perhaps least of all."

He saw her face darken a little and wished he had not spoken. Of course she would hear his words as a personal allusion, or at least remember what she had done to her own brother.

"My brother has not had an easy life," he said, trying to draw her mind away. "He had the misfortune of being raised by our mother."

"And you were not?"

"No, I was not. I was put to nurse with the chief steward's wife the night I was born. I have always counted it a blessing, but perhaps it accounts for the fact that people say I have more the look of a stable hand than a king."

She did not smile at the jest.

"I have never heard anyone say such a thing," she answered.

"Then perhaps they do not. Perhaps I only say it to myself. I have never regretted that I am as I am. But it does not make me feel very kingly."

"My brother thought that to be a king was to be above the cares of other men, and it brought him to ruin. I think you are wiser than that."

In a surge of tender gratitude he carried her hand to his lips and kissed her fingers. For a moment they stood like that, her hand folded between both of his, and there were the beginnings of tears in her eyes. He could sense that she was trembling, and he knew that if he reached out to take her, she would surrender herself to him, that in this moment she would deny him nothing. Yet he did not reach out. He wanted her so that his body seemed to ache, but in the end he did nothing. She would go to her bridal bed without self-reproach and, for the moment, it was enough to know he was loved. That knowledge was better than the fulfillment of desire.

The moment passed and they walked on together.

On the third day of the month of Peritios an Elimiote noble named Lachios vacated his house in Aiane in favor of the Lady Phila. Lachios had led the second cavalry charge against the Macedonians, but he had since conceived a great admiration for Philip, who regarded him as a friend and trusted him enough to take him into his confidence. Lachios moved in with his brother-in-law, who was mystified but willing to remain so when told it was the king's will, and the Lady Phila slept that night a mere two minutes' walk from the palace where she had lived most of her life.

The next morning a contingent from the royal household staff, headed by the chief steward himself, arrived to take over the kitchen and to prepare the main reception rooms. That afternoon Philip summoned some hundred of his principle nobles to attend him at the house of Lachios, and when they had arrived and had been offered wine and sesame cakes the king appeared before them, leading a woman by the hand. The woman wore a white tunic and her head was veiled.

"It is my desire to take for wife the Lady Phila, a daughter of the late royal house. Will you accept me, My Lady?"

"I will accept you, My Lord."

"Then I hereby publish our betrothal and make it known to all men."

Except for the fact that the Lady Phila had no male relative to speak for her, all had proceeded according to established custom. Nevertheless, the assembled guests were surprised into a silence that was only broken when someone shouted from the back of the room, "May the gods bless this marriage with many sons!" Lachios stood grinning while everyone else took up his cry.

Thus did the people of Elimeia discover that their king was about to take a consort.

Three evenings later there was a full moon. In her apartments the Lady Phila performed the ceremony of dedicating her childish toys to the goddess

Artemis and then, veiled as before, descended the great staircase to where a much larger company was assembled to witness her marriage to King Philip. Prayers were offered, with the king himself acting as priest, and a lamb, together with a lock of the bride's hair, was sacrificed at the household altar. Then there was a feast, lavish and joyful, but, as the women dined in another room, Phila did not see her new husband again until it was announced that the wedding car was at the door.

Philip was waiting for her at the entrance hall. He smiled, looking a trifle nervous, and held out his hand to her. When the door was opened it was discovered that a snowfall had begun and was already nearly a span deep. This was considered a good omen.

As they stepped into the chariot, which was drawn by a pair of perfect white mares, the guests assembled around it, all of them bearing torches, and began to sing the wedding song. They walked beside the car, still singing, their torches seeming to burn like stars in the cold night air, all the way to the palace, where they were greeted with volleys of confetti that mixed strangely with the falling snow.

A chamberlain brought out a silver platter bearing a single quince, symbol of fertility. Phila took it and, lifting her veil, began to eat. When she was finished the guests raised a loud cheer and Philip reached down to embrace his bride around the thighs. He picked her up and carried her across the threshold.

The guests never stopped singing, not until the wedding pair had been conducted to their bridal chamber, which was garlanded with flowers and scented with oil of hyacinth. The door was closed behind them and they stood together in the vast room. Neither moved or spoke until the laughter of the guests, the very sound of their voices, had died away.

"This was my father's room," she said at last, hardly even knowing why, and, when she saw the expression that for an instant crossed her husband's face, added, "I loved him. I am glad you chose it."

"I settled on this one because it seemed the most beautiful." Philip looked around at the walls as if he had never seen them before. "Perhaps I should have consulted one of the old servants."

"No, you chose well."

It was true. Her reaction might have been different if marriage had brought her not only to a strange man but a strange house as well, but she felt safe in this room. It located things. All the emotions associated with it were familiar. This way, at least, she had only one new experience ahead of her.

It gave her the courage to take Philip's hand, and this, perhaps, encouraged him. After a moment he drew the veil from her face, brushing it aside like a cobweb.

"Everything went well," he said, with a tense little smile—with a slight shock that had as one of its elements a certain feeling of triumph, Phila realized that her new husband was also a little frightened. "Everyone was pleased, I think. I know that I was pleased."

Somehow, although she was not conscious that either of them had moved, they were no longer side by side but stood facing each other. Philip touched the side of her face and then slowly, as if solely for the pleasure of feeling her hair gliding by beneath his palm, brought his hand around to the back of her neck. They were so close now. He might almost have been asking permission. She raised her head to bring it closer to him, letting her eyes half close.

No one had ever kissed her on the lips. The softness of his mouth, the tickling coarseness of his beard—each of these she felt as a separate experience, and each in its turn was submerged in an ardent beating of her heart that was like fear and yet was not. She was not afraid. Whatever might happen now, she would not resist it. She would welcome it.

Her wedding tunic had a wide neck that left her shoulders almost bare. Her old nurse had made it for her—she had begun sewing months ago, as soon as Phila had spoken to her of the king's proposal.

"I will feel almost indecent in this," she had said, but the old woman had merely smiled.

"The veil will cover you, Lady. And for the rest, you will understand well enough in time."

She understood now, as Philip's hands moved down her neck and over her shoulders, pushed the fabric aside so that it slid down her arms until she was naked to the waist.

"You are my lord now," she murmured, putting her arms around his neck, pressing her breasts against the hard muscles of his rib cage. Let him believe what he liked, she meant to ensnare him. "I belong to you, soul and body both. I would not have it other."

She awoke sometime in the early hours of the morning. When she went to the window and opened the shutter, the sky was still black. There was no sound of revelry, so the last wedding guest had gone home, and the servants would not be awake yet for a long time. She went back to bed and crawled in again beside her husband, who slept deeply. He did not even stir. She lay there, listening to his breathing, wishing she dared to touch him.

A few hours ago, on the other side of a chasm bridged by a little sleep, she had been someone else. Who had she been? She could hardly remember. That other self was almost a stranger to her now, and she could only look back to her with a certain amused pity. For now she was the wife of the Lord Philip, prince of Macedon and king of the Elimoitai—Philip, her husband. She must begin to think of him now as simply Philip. In this room, in this bed, that was his only name and title.

And now her womb held his seed.

There had been pain. At first the urgency and power of his lust had been terrifying. But all fear, all pain, all sense of self were quickly overwhelmed.

Was it this way for all women? Had it been this way for her mother? Her mother had died, leaving so much unsaid that it was possible to mourn her loss all over again.

But she could not believe that it could be thus for all women—all women were not married to Philip.

Some men, it was said, shamed the very gods with their mortal splendor, so that they became the darlings of heaven. Surely Philip was one of these. The conqueror of an army that should have crushed him as easily as a hammer crushes a grape, a king before he was twenty—surely he could not be like other men.

And therefore this happiness could not be like the happiness of other women, and therefore it could not long survive.

In the darkness of her wedding night, Phila heard the beating of death's black wings and knew that her hour would be brief.

Yet what was even death, measured against this?

29

"You look tired, My Lord. You should spend less time in bed." This, followed by much laughter. Philip found himself the butt of many such jests during the first few weeks after his marriage. He took them in good part, for he was not one to stand on his dignity and it is the lot of every new husband to provide his friends with occasions to exercise their wit. In this, a king was no different from any other man.

Besides, Philip had decided that he liked his new wife. What had begun as a duty of state was developing into a positive pleasure. When he came home after a day with his troops Phila would rub the stiffness out of his muscles and listen to his descriptions of how the training went. He could talk to her about his plans for the nation because she was not interested in power but in him. It was a great relief simply to be able to speak of these things.

"You may wish to take a concubine," his friend Lachios had told him when Philip had confided his marriage plans to him. "I know nothing of the Lady Phila—I have not spoken five words to her in my life—but these high-born women are not raised to be very comforting. They will bear you sons, but they are too proud and too cold for a man to find much entertainment in their beds. So, when you have done your duty you are free to take a little diversion with some pretty baggage who knows how to spread her legs. I have three or four in my own household who would do nicely. When you are ready, let me know and I will make you a present of whichever pleases you best."

It was an offer kindly meant and, as they had both been a little drunk at the time, Philip had thanked him profusely and called him a good fellow, clapping him on the back until he almost knocked the wind out of him. Yet now, after just a few days of marriage, he did not see himself visiting Lachios's slave girls to make a selection.

The Lady Phila was neither proud nor cold. She welcomed him into her bed with what almost amounted to gratitude and, while she seemed to know absolutely nothing about the commerce between men and women, she was eager to learn and even more eager to please. Madzos, who had been fond of saying that a tavern girl in Thebes ends by understanding more of the senses than all the whores in Corinth, would have laughed to know that some of her vast knowledge in these matters was now being hungrily received by the sixteen-year-old consort of a barbarian king.

This passion was different from any other he had known in his life. With Arsinoe, during their one night together, he had been consumed almost as much by fear as by desire—fear of that unknown, dreaded, yet enticing thing, the body of one's beloved. Perhaps, had they had the chance to know each other a little, it might have been different, but as it was their brief coming to-gether had remained in Philip's memory as an experience of almost inhuman intensity, a moment incapable of being repeated. A moment he was not even sure he would wish repeated.

With every woman he had known since, the whores of Thebes and Athens, even Madzos, there had been only lust, which was perhaps the most business-like of all the appetites that afflict mankind. It was like getting drunk, except that one enjoyed it with a certain cold detachment. Madzos, for all that they had slept together so long a time, did not even weep when he had to leave her. And for himself he had never spent a moment in longing for her. It was simply over, and the flesh has no memory.

But with Phila it went beyond mere flesh, and yet, strangely, it was as re-laxed and unalloyed a satisfaction as the eating of a good dinner. It was like having a purse full of money to spend on nothing but one's own amusement. And there was something too of the gentle, unself-conscious happiness one feels in the company of small children, a sense of the world's original good-ness and innocence. It was the pleasure of giving pleasure. It was an escape from the tyranny of the self.

"Is it different for a man?" she asked him once.

"The poets say that when Tiresias, who for a time inhabited a woman's body, was asked by Zeus and Hera which of the sexes had the greater pleasure in love, he declared in favor of women. I myself am not in a position to con-firm his judgment, but I suspect that it is not far wrong."

And Phila blushed when she heard this. Even in the dim, flickering light from the single oil lamp that rested beside their bed, he could see that her cheeks were flushed—it was not much different from when she was in the throes of her passion. Philip discovered that the sight aroused him, and he buried his face between her breasts.

"I think it is sharper for a man," she said at last, stroking his hair while he kissed the tips of her nipples. "It seems almost like pain."

"Sometimes it is."

. . .

But it was not his marriage that filled Philip's life. His marriage, happy as it made him, was merely a resting place, a refuge at the end of the day, a means of escaping. What occupied his mind, and took pride of place in his heart, was the task of kingship. This, he was beginning to understand, was the reason he had been born.

And the task demanded his full attention, for a change of rulers always draws the eye of ambition. And when a king has been deposed or killed, neighboring powers, like the wolves that follow a herd of deer, waiting to pull down the weak and the stragglers, look for the signs of chaos and disunity. They hope to exploit a weakness, to gain some advantage or merely to plunder. So it was when the Fates pulled Ptolemy down—many besides Derdas saw a chance to raid across the border into Macedon. So it was when Philip pulled Derdas down.

By spring Philip was receiving letters from his brother Perdikkas that the Eordoi, whose kingdom was just north of Elimeia, had entered into some sort of treaty with King Menelaos of Lynkos, which put them at liberty to threaten the cities of the western plains. Edessa was already under more or less constant attack.

"Apparently they are not impressed by the example of the Elimoitai," Perdikkas complained. "I cannot afford to reinforce the western garrisons."

"You cannot afford not to," Philip wrote back. "Raise an army and show King Aias and our beloved uncle that you still have your teeth."

"I raised an army," Perdikkas replied tartly. "You have it."

Which posed Philip an interesting problem—he was his brother's subject and his new army, made up of Macedonians and Elimoitai, needed blooding. But he was also the king of Elimeia, and his subjects would not relish the idea of fighting a war simply to accommodate the king in Pella. He required a pretext.

Fortunately, Aias was happy to oblige.

On the fifth day in the month of Daisios, when the snow had begun to disappear from the ground, Eordian infantry ambushed a squadron of Elimiote soldiers conducting a peaceful border patrol. They caught them in a gorge and rained down arrows from the heights until the patrol commander was forced to surrender. Then they massacred the survivors. They even cut the throats of the horses.

Aias offered a lame apology, claiming that the patrol had strayed into his territory, but it was merely a test to see how much the new king of the Elimoitai was prepared to swallow. By the time he received it, Philip and a force of fifteen hundred infantry and four hundred horse were already on the march north.

Philip was at war; he had no interest in conducting raids. The villages through which he passed were required to provision his men and horses, but they were not otherwise molested. He was across the border for only eight days and fought two engagements.

The first of these was little more than a skirmish. It lasted not even an hour, by the end of which two hundred and seventy men, most of them the enemy, were left dead on the field. Two days later Aias had assembled over three thousand men and the battle lasted all morning and half the afternoon, but long before then it was clear that the king of the Eordoi simply did not know how to deal with this new kind of warfare. He squandered wave after wave of cavalry trying to crack the Elimiote infantry formations, and in the end he had to call a truce and inquire if King Philip would be willing to settle for terms. Philip counted up the casualties—one hundred and twelve dead and seventy-two wounded among his own men against nearly a thousand of the enemy, almost all of them either dead or dying—and demanded a hundred thousand silver drachmas in tribute, thirty-six villages, a repudiation of the treaty with Lynkos, an end to the attacks against Edessa, and Aias's two eldest sons as hostages. Aias had no choice but to accept.

When Philip returned to Aiane, he wrote to his brother, "By your leave, I will bring my bride to Pella this summer to be received by you. I will also bring King Aias's eldest son and heir, who is a well-mannered boy but very frightened. I have promised I will not let you chop off his head and eat it. We will have no further trouble with the father."

Perdikkas, who had already received the Lynkestian ambassador and therefore knew what had happened, was apparently not amused. In his reply he made hardly any reference to the victory, but he demanded the return of the two hundred horse that had made up Philip's original force of cavalry.

By the time this exchange of letters took place, both of Aias's sons, who were nine and twelve years old, had adjusted to captivity so well that indeed they hoped it would never end.

The elder of the two boys, Deucalion, was just old enough to look about him and be struck by the differences between Aiane and home, between King Philip and his own father. Some of these became apparent to him during the course of his first night in the Elimiote capital, when he was distinguished from his brother Ctesios by being allowed to attend a banquet of the king's companions.

"Brothers, let me make known to you our honored guest," King Philip roared, climbing onto a table to make the announcement and half dragging the still terrified boy up after him. "This fine lad here is Prince Deucalion, son and heir to Aias, king of the Eordoi. Let us welcome and befriend him, for he has the makings of a Macedonian. What say you—is he not old enough to eat with the men?"

This suggestion was greeted with cheers and followed by an extraordinary initiation ceremony in which the king and his nobles took turns carrying the boy around the banqueting hall on their shoulders. When it was over, and he had been welcomed into the company of the companions, Deucalion was so flushed with happiness and pride that he would have laid down his life for King Philip.

Such a thing could never have happened at home. For while King Philip seemed to trust his nobles sufficiently that they dared to speak their minds in his presence and to treat him as a man among other men, a first among equals but still an equal, in his father's court the king was accorded almost godlike honors by men who were constantly intriguing against him.

Deucalion knew that one day he would succeed his father as king, but as king of what? Aias was little more than a tribal leader, endlessly threatened by his nobles, each with his own retainers, loyal only to him, and his own ambitions. Any one of these might be scheming to supplant their king. It was not even certain that Aias would survive the crisis of his defeat at the hands of the Elimoitai, that he would even be in a position to pass on the crown to his son. Once he realized that he would not be mistreated by his captors, Deucalion was very well pleased to be out of Eordia, where, if his father fell from power, he and his little brother Ctesios were certain to be murdered.

How different was the atmosphere of the Elimiote court, where all authority seemed to flow from a single source, where every man, noble, and common soldier alike was the king's man, his loyal servant. This was not power that, like a snake grasped too far back from the head, turned to wound the hand that held it. This was power that operated for the safety of all.

And how different a man was King Philip.

Deucalion could not have said how long he had been aware that his father was widely hated. Such an understanding is like a mosaic that is created in one's mind piece by piece until gradually, in a process too slow and indirect for one to be genuinely aware of it, a general outline of the truth emerges. He simply knew that everyone, from the nobles to the slaves who swept the stones of the palace courtyard, looked upon the Lord Aias with a mixture of hatred and fear. If he had thought about it at all, it had struck him that being hated and feared was a perfectly normal consequence of being a king. How could it be otherwise when men will obey nothing except the power that otherwise threatens to destroy them? Such power cannot help but make a man cruel, since he must be cruel if he is to keep it. "Everyone is envious," his father had once told Deucalion. "Everyone wishes he were in my place—you will learn this well enough when you are king."

Yet King Philip said that cruelty was an admission of weakness, that men are cruel only when they are afraid. "If you must frighten a man into obedience, he will betray you when he has the chance. And sooner or later he will have the chance. Loyalty is not made by breaking bones."

He did not even like to whip his soldiers. When Deucalion asked him why, he seemed not to understand the question. "Why should I whip them? They do their best. Each man knows his survival in battle depends on the courage and skill of the men next to him. That is enough."

And it was true. Philip's soldiers—that was what they called themselves, "Philip's soldiers"—were ashamed to be thought slack. It was actually considered an honor to fight in the front ranks. "That is where our king fights," they would say.

Our king. So they called him, this foreigner, this lowland Macedonian—*our king*. No soldier was so humble that King Philip did not seem to know his name and the names of his children. Men twice his age seemed to love him with a son's love for his father. He was their pride, for they felt his pride in them.

For Deucalion and his little brother, King Philip moved quickly from dreaded enemy and captor to friend to something almost akin to a god. They simply worshiped him, as if one of the great heroes of fable had come back to life to teach them the right way to bind up their sandal straps. Every morning they breakfasted with the king, and afterward he might take them along with him to drill with his invincible army. He had even engaged a tutor from Athens to teach them to read from *The Iliad*, because he said that a warrior and a ruler of men should know how not to be a savage.

Philip was like an elder brother to them, even a second father, and they never suspected that his kindness was a matter of deliberate policy, to create in them a sense of loyalty to him personally and to the idea of a united Macedonian state of which Eordia would one day be no more than a province.

In Pella, however, Perdikkas, king of all the Macedonians, had no thought for that greater state his brother was busy inventing in the mind of an adolescent prince. He was thinking about the Athenians.

Athens was fighting a war with the Chalcidian League and had captured two port cities on the Thermaic Gulf, Pydna and Methone. These had been Greek trading colonies for as long as anyone could remember and had never posed any threat, even though they both were within a day's march of the old capital of Aigai. Yet the situation was different with an Athenian fleet at anchor in their harbors. Now they wanted an "alliance," which meant sending cavalry to help then in their operations against Amphipolis. It was blackmail—what would be Macedon's reward, even if Athens triumphed?—but Perdikkas knew he had very little choice.

But the Chalcidian League was allied with the Thracians, and sooner or later Thebes would come in on their side, which meant war between Athens and Thebes. Ordinarily Perdikkas favored Thebes, since her ambitions did not bring her so close to home. He was even supplying timber for the fleet that Epaminondas intended to launch in the spring. Now that would have to be forgotten. He did not want Athens developing a strong base in the Upper Gulf, but he simply could not afford to antagonize her as long as she threatened him so directly.

So Athens would have Macedonian cavalry with which to frighten the Chalcidians, and Epaminondas would have to look elsewhere for his timber. Such was the price of peace.

"At least, if affairs go against the Athenians, My Lord can always break this alliance with an untroubled conscience. Sooner or later, Athens always betrays her friends."

Perdikkas raised his attention from the letter of the Athenian admiral Timotheos, which was spread out on the table before him. When their eyes met, Euphraeos smiled, as he always did, giving the impression that something had upset his stomach. Indeed, the little Athenian was a martyr to his digestion.

Euphraeos had been a student of Plato and it was as a tutor in philosophy and government that he had originally come into the king's service. The Lord Ptolemy had thought to keep his stepson thus amused, but Perdikkas had never taken to a life of study. It was only after the regent's death that the middle-aged sophist began to make an impression on the young king, who discovered in him a wealth of understanding about matters somewhat below the ideal. Since then he had risen in his master's service until he was virtually a minister of state.

And he hated Athens. For reasons that he seemed to prefer to leave somewhat vague, he could never return to the city of his birth. Perdikkas made no inquiries—he did not care. If Euphraeos was a rogue, at least he was a clever one and the king's devoted servant. That was enough.

"If Timotheos stumbles in Chalcidice and the Theban fleet is ready any time this summer, then everything will have changed," he went on, suggesting the mutability of events with a shrug of his thin shoulders. "Then you can have your pick of alliances."

"Particularly if our cavalry acquits itself well against the Chalcidians."

Euphraeos nodded approval.

"Particularly then, My Lord."

Perdikkas's eyes wandered over the table and came to rest on a scroll covered with his brother's large, inelegant writing.

"Philip is coming within the month," he said as if to himself. "He wishes me to receive his new wife."

"There is no harm in that, My Lord."

"Perhaps I should give him command of the forces I am loaning Timotheos. Perhaps this time he will get himself killed."

"Or win another impressive victory." Euphraeos shook his head slowly—he understood to a hair's breadth the king's ambivalence toward his brother. "It is never wise to raise a subject too high in the general esteem. The effect of too much praise on a young head can be the gravest danger to the state."

"The Lord Philip is entirely loyal to me," Perdikkas answered, with something of reproof in his voice. After all that had happened, it seemed unworthy to entertain even a doubt.

"Now he is loyal—yes. It is simply well to see that he remains so. Perhaps you could let him nominate a commander."

Perdikkas gave his servant a hard look, but in the end he nodded assent. "There is no harm in that," he said.

"No, My Lord. No harm."

"And perhaps at least part of the force could be found among his own soldiers."

"Perhaps a large part, My Lord. The ease with which he overwhelmed the Eordians would suggest that his army will not suffer from having a few company of cavalry trimmed away."

And thus it was that, even before Philip had brought his bride to Pella, nearly half of his cavalry, under the command of Lachios, had already passed through the city on its way to support the Athenians at the siege of Amphipolis.

"I won't insist that you take the command," Philip told him as the two of them shared a wine jar during a rest from drill. They were sitting with their backs against the wheel of a supply wagon and their horses, some four or five paces away, were being wiped down by a groom. It was the first really hot day since the beginning of spring. "You are my first choice, but Chalcidice is far away and I will understand if you refuse."

"Refuse? Why should I refuse? I wouldn't miss it for a kingdom." Lachios grinned and then finished off the wine, handing the empty jar back to Philip. "I just wish you were coming. I don't like the idea of fighting under a foreign general."

"I'm a plainsman."

"Yes, but I have decided to forgive you for it. And at least you're not an Athenian. This Timotheos, from what I hear, is not even a real soldier."

"He is a politician."

"A what?"

"He wishes to enlarge his influence in Athens, so he wishes to make a fine showing in this campaign. You are right not to trust him. That is why I want you to go."

Lachios shook his head and then wiped his eyes, as if he had just been startled awake. "You've lost me," he said.

"I don't want him letting our men be butchered to spare his own. I want you to see to it that the Athenians don't fight to the last Macedonian."

"May a subject ask his king a question?"

"Ask it."

"Why is your brother sticking his finger into this particular tar pot?"

Philip stood up, looked up at the sun, and frowned, and then tossed the empty wine jar to the ground, where it rolled a bit and then stopped. The rest period was over and it was time to go back to work.

"I don't think he has any choice."

Late in summer, Philip took his bride and young Deucalion and an honor guard of some fifty men and turned his eyes east to Pella. He was not in a hurry and Phila seemed to tire easily, so they were six days on the journey, stopping at Aigai for one day in between to rest and make sacrifice at the burial mounds of Philip's father and eldest brother. On the fourth day they came within sight of the sea.

"Tomorrow we will take ship for Pella," Philip said, grasping his wife by the hand. "Come—we will walk in the surf, and then you will know I have not lied to you."

"About the sea being cold and wet?"

"Yes."

For half an hour they strolled over the pebble-strewn beach south of Aloros, as careless as two children. They watched the seagulls dropping mussels onto the rocks to crack open the shells.

"Tonight we'll have a turbot for dinner," he said. "We'll make them find us one the size of a cart wheel."

Phila reached down to wet her hand in the waves. "The water really is salty," she said, licking her fingers.

This made Philip laugh, and so he kissed her lest she grow offended.

The next day they sailed across the gulf and then upriver to Pella. King Perdikkas and a large company were there to greet them at the dock.

"Great news! Wonderful news!" he shouted, throwing his arms around Philip and kissing him. "The Athenians have been forced to surrender at Amphipolis."

30

Philip heard the story from Lachios, who had just brought his men back all the way from the Strymon River.

"Anyone with eyes could see how it was going to end," he said as soon as he was alone with his king. They sat together at the kitchen table in Glaukon's old house, the one place in Pella they could be sure no one would be listening. Lachios was not a man who frightened easily, but his eyes wore the haunted expression of one who has looked upon an appalling disaster. "The Athenians were not equipped to mount a long siege, and even with their fleet they could not cut off the city's supply lines. Timotheos must have known from the beginning that he had no chance of success."

"He is a creature of the Athenian Assembly, which possesses too many minds to think clearly and too many eyes to see at all. He must do what he can with what he has."

"Well, you will observe that he did not tarry long enough to see the outcome, but took himself off and let someone else surrender to the Thracians. Your brother had returned to Pella well before that, leaving me in command. I stayed until Timotheos left and then I withdrew my men."

"You did the right thing," Philip said in the tone of one observing an impersonal truth. "We are not under such obligations to the Athenians that we need feel obliged to sacrifice our soldiers just to save face. What did Perdikkas say about it when you returned?"

"Nothing." Lachios shrugged his shoulders, his face registering the most profound bewilderment. "In the fifteen days since my return I have not been admitted into the king's presence. I have no idea whether he intends to congratulate me for my prudence or have me executed for desertion."

"Did he issue a specific command that you should stay?"

"No."

"Then you were simply following your own best judgment, which is what is expected of a field commander. No doubt he has been waiting to see how events worked themselves out. He seems mightily pleased at Athens's surrender, so you are probably safe enough. At any rate, he will not move against you if I make an issue of it with him, and if it comes to anything, I will."

"Thank you, Philip."

Philip made a gesture indicating that he was ashamed to be thanked for such a trifle, his eyes searching over the room. Alcmene's stool was still beside the hearth. As a child he had played on this floor, and at this table Glaukon had taught him how to do his sums. Now Alcmene was dead and Glaukon was in Aiane, keeping the accounts for the royal household. The hearth was covered with dust, and the kitchen smelled of disuse. It depressed him horribly.

"How long was my brother at Amphipolis?" Philip asked, keeping his face blank.

"A month, or perhaps a little longer. He was already there when I arrived."

"What was your impression of him?"

Lachios studied his master's face for a long moment before he answered. Kings, he knew, were unpredictable creatures where their family pride was concerned. With Derdas, one had hardly dared to tell him anything he did not want to hear. But Philip was not Derdas. With Philip, he decided, the greatest danger lay in telling him anything except the truth.

"No one can call him a coward," he said at last. "He is brave enough. I will give him that. He would make a good company commander. But he lacks the imagination it takes to make a general. He works out a plan, using the tactics we all learned as boys, and then, if perchance it doesn't work, he takes offense. He expects the battle to conform to what he has in his head, rather than the other way round. I would not be pleased to trust my life with him again."

Simply by looking at him, no one could have guessed how Philip took this assessment. His expression was impenetrable. Finally he reached across the table and put his hand of Lachios's arm.

"I thank you," he said. "You have spoken as a friend. Now let us leave this place and find somewhere with a fire and a little wine. I feel as if I have been sealed up in my burial urn."

When, after three days, Philip went to the king's private apartments, early in the morning that he might at last have some chance of seeing his brother alone, Perdikkas was very little disposed to discuss the recent campaign. He had other news.

"If you stay out the month, you will be here to see me married," he said, with the smile of a man who is conscious of delivering unwelcome intelligence. But if he expected his heir apparent to betray even a hint of disappointment, he was disappointed himself, for Philip's response was to embrace him.

"I congratulate you, brother," Philip said, almost laughing. "A good woman can make a man very happy. Believe me—I speak from experience. Who is she, then? Do I know her?"

Perdikkas, when he saw that his brother really was pleased, decided, for reasons he could not have explained, to be pleased himself. The smile transformed itself into something almost approaching a grin.

"You know the family certainly. She is the daughter of Agapenor, the one who has such large estates up near the border with Lynkos. I think it does no harm to give him a family reason to remember that I am his king and not Uncle Menelaos. Besides, she comes with a large dowry."

"But does she please you in herself? Is she pretty?"

"The betrothal ceremony will be in ten days' time, and I will find out then." Perdikkas shrugged as if at the unavoidable decrees of the Fates. "She is judged to be a beauty. I am sure she will do well enough."

Now Philip really did laugh. "You will not be so indifferent ten days hence—may she make your bed as hot for you as a roasting pan and may you father ten sons by her before you are thirty!"

Perdikkas withdrew from his brother's embrace and sat down at the table, where the remains of his breakfast had yet to be cleaned away by a servant. He looked about him as if his presence in this room, which had once been Alexandros's study, were the singular achievement of his life, yet he did not seem pleased. He had been afraid of his elder brother, who had taken a certain pleasure in mocking him for lacking his own grace and brilliance, and it always seemed to Perdikkas somehow a mark of disrespect that Philip was not likewise afraid of him. There were moments, such as this one, when he could not entirely convince himself that Philip was not also mocking him.

"You should not be so quick to take offense," Philip said quietly, for he had at last penetrated the enigma. "Would you wish me to behave like your subject, even in private?"

"You *are* my subject." Perdikkas tried to appear coldly angry, but he could not sustain it. "You *are* my subject," he repeated.

"I am also your brother, Perdikkas—and murder, treachery, and madness have taken a heavy toll on this family. All that remains are you and me. If I cannot jest with you about your marriage, then you have no one with whom you can be anything except a king. We are all either of us has left."

Instead of answering, Perdikkas stared at the wall behind Philip's head. He seemed absent, giving the impression that he had forgotten he was not alone, or that some stream of memory carried him resistless in its current. It is a way some men have of not facing their own embarrassment.

"Your cavalry fought well at Amphipolis," he said at last, as if the conversation had never been about anything else. "I may keep them garrisoned in Pella for a time."

Philip's eyes narrowed dangerously. "What is in your mind?"

"Only that we have perhaps been fighting the wrong enemy."

The king of the Macedonians picked up his wine cup and, after glancing inside to satisfy himself that it was empty, set it back down on the table. He did not refill the cup from the jar that rested beside it. He seemed to forget it entirely, as if it had answered its purpose.

"Athens should be kept out of the north," he said, once more carefully looking at nothing. "She should satisfy her greed selling pottery to the Asians. The Chalcidians know that I was forced into that alliance, and now they are sending emissaries. Perhaps this is the moment to change sides."

"And do what?"

"And push the Athenians out of Pydna and Methone."

He smiled as he said it, as if the thought and the deed were almost the same thing.

"First of all, the Athenians will not be pushed out of the north," Philip answered hotly. "At least, not by us. Think of it, brother—we are too weak and threatened from too many different directions to pick a quarrel with Athens over Pydna and Methone."

"The garrisons they have left there are small, and they have just suffered a defeat. Their assembly will not be so eager to vote money for reinforcements, not after the way our cavalry fought at Amphipolis. Besides, we would have both Thebes and the Chalcidian League for allies."

"Both the Thebans and the Chalcidians will be delighted to see us attack the Athenian garrisons. If Athens responds—and she will, since she will have no choice—neither of them will lift a hand to help us."

"I think you are afraid." Perdikkas stood up, assuming a posture that would have been challenging if the two men had not been three or four paces apart.

"Of this? Yes! If you start a war with Athens, you will be committing a piece of folly that will be remembered for a thousand years. Shall that be your memorial, brother? Are you so eager to be the last king of Macedon?"

"I think you are afraid," Perdikkas repeated, precisely as if Philip had not spoken. "You have made a great name for yourself by crushing a few hill tribes, and you cannot bear the thought of seeing your glory eclipsed—*not even by your elder brother and king!*"

Philip glanced at the door, wondering whether anyone had heard the shouting and would come bursting in to see if the king was being murdered. Perhaps it was well that neither of them was armed, for Perdikkas was quite red in the face and the veins in his neck stood out like cords.

"So it is about glory, is it?" Philip asked, provokingly calm. "You would be a great conqueror? Then don't go to war with Athens. If you like, I will undertake to stay home in bed next time there is a border incident with Eordia. Just don't go to war with Athens. If I truly saw myself as your rival, I would encourage you to do this thing, for in your place I would never do it."

"Leave my presence, Philip."

For a long time after Philip had gone away, Perdikkas sat at the table in his room, drinking what was left of the wine that had been brought him with breakfast. The wine was mixed with water at two parts to five, but Perdikkas was normally abstemious in his habits so even thus weakened it blurred the edges of things nicely. If it had not been for the wine, he thought, he might have choked on his own anger.

Why did his younger brother have this effect on him? He did not really believe that Philip begrudged him a share of triumph. Jealousy was simply not part of his nature, and he had never been anything except the most loyal of friends. In their childhood Philip had always defended him, even against Alexandros. Perhaps that was the reason. It was galling to be under the protection of one's little brother.

Yet he could not in justice blame Philip for that. Somehow he would have to make this disagreeable squabble up with him. Besides, he would need Philip's support if anything went wrong with this Athenian venture.

Not that anything would go wrong. What with the Athenians still smarting from their defeat at Amphipolis, Euphraeos thought this an excellent opportunity to drive them out of the gulf—and Euphraeos was a far shrewder judge of these matters than Philip. Philip was a good soldier, but he was no statesman.

It is always more difficult to patch up a quarrel than to make one. Perdikkas thought it might be enough to signal the end of his wrath with some public compliment, but when he found out that Philip was actually making preparations to depart for Elimeia he at last had to humble himself to the extent of going to his brother and admitting that he had simply lost his temper. It was well that Philip was not one to nurse a grievance, admitting that he too had probably spoken intemperately and dismissing the whole business as a stupid misunderstanding, because Perdikkas had gone as far as he felt his dignity as king would permit him.

In any case, when the day came Philip was still in Pella to attend his brother's betrothal ceremony.

The bride was indeed a beauty. Her name was Arete and she had honey-colored hair, delicate features, and skin of such clarity that one could almost see through it. She was about fifteen and seemed a quiet girl, completely overwhelmed by her sudden elevation. Philip noticed that she hardly dared raise her eyes to her intended husband's face.

"I think, to use my brother's phrase, she will do well enough," Philip told his wife that night as he lay on their bed, watching her braid up her hair. She sat in front of a bronze mirror, her naked back to him, and he thought, as he did almost every night, that Phila had very fine arms. "I hope, when she ceases to be afraid of him, she will be clever enough not to let him know it. Perdikkas will be better pleased by a show of the most dreadful awe."

"Are you very disappointed in him, then?"

Philip did not move, but his wife, had she turned around, might have noticed that her fine arms no longer held his gaze. His attention was turned inward as he considered if he had said too much.

He did not like to criticize Perdikkas, but that, it seemed, was what he had done. Yes, he decided, he was disappointed, although it would not do to say so.

"I spoke a few words to her tonight," she went on, when she realized that the only answer she would receive was silence. "She seems pleasant and sweet—perhaps she will make your brother happy."

"Not as happy as you have made me."

She glanced over her shoulder and saw that he was smiling, which at least meant that he was not offended.

"But the chief happiness Perdikkas expects from a wife is a son. He will breathe easier, I think, when he has another heir than me."

After a few minutes, Phila blew out the oil lamp and crawled into bed beside her husband. She ran the palm of her hand over his chest and down where she could feel the ropelike muscles along his rib cage. His whole body, she thought, was like living stone.

"Will you breathe easier when you have an heir?" she asked.

"Perhaps my subjects will."

It took a moment before the implications of the question made their impression, but when they did it was as if he had been struck a blow. He simply stared at her, his mind unable even to form a sentence.

"I am with child," she said at last, out of simple mercy. "I had suspected even before we left Aiane, but now I am sure. Are you pleased?"

She pressed herself closer to him as, apparently, he tried to decide.

"I . . . I . . . I don't know—yes, of course I am pleased. Are you really sure?"

With great care, Philip placed his hand on her naked belly.

"You won't find any change yet, and, yes, I am sure." She brought his hand up to her breast. "The baby is months away yet, and in the meantime I won't break."

.   .   .

Within a month of its beginning, Perdikkas's campaign to liberate the cities of Pydna and Methone came to grief. The snow from the last winter storm was still fresh on the ground when he marched his army down the road that ran along the western coast of the Thermaic Gulf, and by the beginning of spring he was sitting in a tent, across a table from the Athenian general Kallisthenes, discussing the conditions on which the king of Macedon would be allowed to sue for peace.

He had not even the consolation of a glorious and dramatic failure, for there had been only two engagements, during both of which the only strategic choices open to the Macedonians were a hasty withdrawal or total annihilation. The Athenians had reinforced their garrisons at breathtaking speed, with the result that Perdikkas's rather pitiful offensive was simply overwhelmed.

Kallisthenes, when they met to parley, seemed rather amused by the whole business. Like someone slapping a small child's hand for stealing apples, he offered remarkably easy terms. He demanded an indemnity of one hundred thousand silver drachmas, ransom for all Macedonian soldiers held as prisoners, and a restoration of the alliance. Considering that there was really no force worth mentioning between his soldiers and Pella, it was a surprising display of generosity. In person he was very considerate of the young king's feelings, almost consoling—his triumph had been that complete.

"War is a hard teacher, but eventually a commander learns to know the limits of the possible," he said, offering his former antagonist a cup of wine. "As a young man I made some horrific mistakes, just as bad as this, but fortunately I was still a subordinate officer. It is a cruel thing to have the full responsibility thrust on one so early."

It was a punishment more bitter than death to have to listen to such things and know they were not the worst that could be said. The worst would come when the prisoners were returned.

When Philip learned that several of his Elimiote horsemen had been captured, he wrote inquiring about the amount of ransom demanded for them and sent it as soon as he received his brother's reply. The silver was brought under military escort and Perdikkas had it within half a month of his surrender to Kallisthenes.

His own treasury was nearly empty and he would be hard pressed to meet the rest of the Athenian demands. He toyed with the idea of using Philip's silver to ransom his own soldiers and leaving the Elimoitai to wear out their lives as quarry slaves, but in the end he simply didn't dare. He knew Philip would never forgive him such a piece of treachery and he needed his brother's loyalty more than ever now. It rankled almost as much as defeat itself, but he simply could not dispense with Philip.

And so Perdikkas was condemned to suffer the return from captivity of the Elimiote cavalry, and among them was their commander, Lachios.

It was a miracle the man was even alive—a miracle yet, from Perdikkas's point of view, very far from a blessing. A javelin had gone straight through his thigh and killed the horse he was riding. The only thing that saved him from bleeding to death was the fact that the Macedonian defeat had been so swift that he was captured and put under the care of Athenian physicians almost as soon as he hit the ground. Twenty-five days later, he had to be carried back across the truce line on a litter.

When Lachios arrived in Pella he was offered the use of apartments in the royal palace, but instead he moved into a vacant house near the harbor, where he was attended by his own servants. A slave woman who had been his concubine for years cooked his meals, going to the public market every morning to purchase fresh vegetables and meat. He would have nothing from the king's kitchen. No physician was allowed to dress his wounds except old Nikomachos, and he only because Lachios had once heard Philip speak of him as a man to be trusted. Whether this behavior was motivated by fear of assassination or by a simple disinclination to accept anything from Perdikkas's hand was not easy to say.

The king visited him once, and only once, a few days after his arrival in the city. Lachios was still in a weakened condition, but during that visit his shouting could be heard all over the house.

"And when you write to King Philip," he bellowed after Perdikkas as the latter tried to take his leave, "you may assure him that I will be back in Elimeia as soon as I can sit a horse! And you may further tell him that it is my intention to remain there as long as his blundering fool of a brother is king of Macedon!"

Perdikkas's reply, if any, is not recorded.

31

In Elimeia the winter was slow to release its grip. The ground remained frozen even late into the month of Xandikos, and as Phila neared her travail the clouds above Aiane were dark and laden with snow.

It had been a difficult pregnancy. She had begun to bleed almost as soon as they returned from Pella, and the bleeding had never really stopped. On the advice of her physician, a clever little Cypriot with a pointed beard who enjoyed a great reputation in treating women's complaints, Philip took her to a royal hunting lodge closer to the mountains, but the solitude seemed only to depress her. When she began to fancy that the child was dead in her womb, he brought her home again. It made no difference to her health, but at least she was quieter in her mind.

At the beginning of the seventh month, the Cypriot said he did not like the color of the blood she was passing and ordered her to keep to her bed.

"Protect your child and yourself," he said. "Do not allow yourself to become excited, for there is nothing to fear." Privately he told Philip that if she began to show little rosy patches in her face, he despaired of her living to reach full term.

One morning at the beginning of her last month, Philip noticed what looked like a little spider's web of broken veins on her left cheek. He said nothing to her, but later that day he went to the shrine of Hera, goddess of childbearing, and made offerings of a wheat cake and some cuttings from his beard.

Perhaps the goddess was pleased, since Phila lived out that final month.

Yet she must have sensed the loss of some inner harmony, for she knew she was in danger. "I can accept death if our son lives," she said suddenly one evening, while Philip was trying to distract her with a letter he had received from Aristotle in Athens.

"You will not die, and the child will not die." He smiled and took her hand. "And the child may be a daughter."

"The child will be a son. I can feel him kicking at night—I know he will be a boy."

She said no more after that and he continued to read to her from the letter, but he could tell from the expression on her face that she was not really listening.

She hardly slept at night and when she did she was tormented by frightful dreams. The physician said there was nothing sinister about a woman's having nightmares when her womb was heavy, but it frightened Philip a little that his wife never wanted to tell him what she dreamed. Sometimes she woke him with her screaming, and he would hold her in his arms until she was calm again, but if he asked what had frightened her, she was always silent.

At first he thought it was just another dream when one night he was awakened by a sound like wailing and the pressure of her hand on his face.

"It is only the wind you hear," he said, still half-asleep, and he turned to offer her the comfort of his embrace.

"Get the physician. My pains are beginning."

He was wide awake now. With a single quick movement he was on his knees beside her, his hand resting on her swollen belly. He was suddenly more afraid than he had ever been in his life, even in battle.

"Are you sure?"

"Yes, I'm sure. Get him."

In the next instant Philip was running down a palace corridor, struggling to cover his nakedness with a tunic while he tried to remember where he was going. For the last several nights, he had given orders that a servant was to be stationed outside his door, but when the moment came the fellow was asleep on his stool and, in any case, Philip did not even notice him or remember his existence.

The physician had been given a room close to the king's own apartments. Philip kicked at the bottom of the door and shouted as if to raise the whole palace.

"Machaon! Wake up in there! We need you now. Wake up!"

The door opened and there stood the little Cypriot fully dressed and looking as if he had been awake for hours.

"I thought it would be tonight," he said calmly. "The wind, you see. Don't ask me why, but—"

"I won't—just come!"

For the next half hour Philip waited in the antechamber to his bedroom, pacing up and down the tiny room, listening for the smallest sound and cursing the wind. When the physician came outside to speak to him, he took the man by the shoulders as if to shake him.

"It is only the beginning, My Lord," Machaon said, not even glancing at the hands clutching him—proof that one can become hardened to anything. "We have still a long wait ahead of us. I have told her to sleep, but I doubt she will. I am telling you the same. Find a bed somewhere and use it. Your child may not be born for many hours and, with respect, Lord, here you will only be in the way."

This was excellent advice. Philip knew that it was excellent advice, so he went into his study, where he kept a sleeping roll, and spread it over a couch. He lay there for perhaps half an hour, as rigid as a building block, unable to close his eyes. He wondered if Machaon had ever fathered any children.

It was actually a relief when there was a tapping at the door and old Glaukon put his head through.

"I heard her travail has begun," he said, his eyes glittering like pieces of glass. In that moment Philip remembered that Glaukon and Alcmene had lost their only child at birth. He wondered if that memory was what he saw shining in the old man's eyes. "I thought . . ."

"Come. Stay with me." Philip held out his hand. "I am full of fear tonight."

The two of them sat together on the couch, not exchanging a word, for over two hours. It was a comfort to them both.

"Perhaps you ought to go see how it is coming," Glaukon said at last.

"Perhaps I ought."

Philip rose and went to the door of his bedroom. He stood there listening for several minutes, not daring to knock, before it opened and a woman servant carrying a basin of bloodstained water almost ran into him. She shut the door behind her and went scurrying away, but not before Philip had a glimpse of his wife's face, shiny with sweat and the color of candle wax.

A moment later the physician came out to speak to him. The sleeves of his tunic were rolled up to the armpits and he looked grim.

"The labor is sluggish," he said, lifting his chin as if he meant to stab Philip in the chest with the point of his beard. "Her travail is hard, harder than I would have expected so early on, but the baby does not move. And she is losing a great deal of blood. I am not hopeful about the outcome."

"Is there nothing that can be done?"

"Nothing, Lord. A physician can only ease the course of the inevitable, but in the end it rests with the gods."

"I am only in the next room. Call me if anything . . ."

"Yes, Lord—if there is any change."

Philip returned to his study and conveyed the cheerless news to Glaukon.

"What happened to Alcmene's child?" he asked, putting his hand on the old man's knee. "Does it pain you to speak of it?"

"No more than to think of it," Glaukon answered, shaking his head, "and how can I not think of it tonight? Everything went well, but the child was born with his birth cord wrapped around his neck. It choked out his life."

"Did Alcmene suffer greatly?"

"Only in her mind—only until you came to us. I think had it not been for you she might have followed our son to the funeral pyre."

"You fill my heart with cheer," Philip said.

"It is better to be prepared against the worst. I never thought of death, so the shock was all the greater. If all goes well, someday you will remember this conversation and smile."

For five hours they waited, listening now and then through the open door of his study to the slap, slap, slap of sandaled feet passing back and forth through the antechamber to the royal bedroom. Philip tried to judge the progress of events by the sound of the servant women's footfalls, whether or not their speed conveyed a sense of urgency, but he knew this was folly.

It was his sense of helplessness that most oppressed him, the feeling of having surrendered his life to the play of chance. He was by nature active and had always seen himself as the chief agent of his own destiny, yet now he had to accept the fact of his own insignificance. Phila and her child would live or die, and it would have nothing to do with him. He could not help them.

At last he heard the measured tread of a man. The study door opened a little wider and Philip saw the physician gesturing to him. He had only to look at the man's expression to know all.

"The child is dead," he murmured. "I think he died some hours ago, but there is no way to be sure."

"It was a son, then?"

"Yes." And then, for the first time, a look of real anguish crossed the little Cypriot's face. "I am sorry, My Lord. All that the healing arts can do was done, but it was not enough."

"Does my wife know?"

With a deliberate slowness, Machaon shook his head. "It is for you to tell her, if you think it right. Her bleeding has been fearful, Lord, and it has not abated. She cannot last more than another hour or two."

"She is dying?"

"Yes. She is dying. And there is no hope of recovery. If you wish to speak to her, you had best go now."

It was only with the most extraordinary exercise of will that Philip was able to walk the few steps into the next room, where his wife lay on their blood-spattered bed, her beautiful face ravaged and white as paste. Her eyes were closed, making her look as though she might be dead already—it would almost have been a relief if she were.

He knelt beside her, forcing himself into an icy, passionless calm, thinking all the time that if he failed her now, it would be a sin for which he could never atone. At last he took her hand and, a moment later, she opened her eyes.

"We have a son," he said quietly, as if afraid of startling her. At the words he felt the slightest pressure from her hand folded inside his own.

"Let me see him."

But Philip shook his head. "He is with the wet nurse. After you have rested awhile they shall bring him back to you."

"But he lives? You have seen him?"

"Of course he lives," Philip answered, giving the impression he thought the question a little absurd. "From the way he howls he will make a fine king."

"Then it is worth dying for."

She closed her eyes again with a resigned weariness, really giving the impression that now she could peacefully consign herself to death.

"You will not die." Philip could feel his own burning, unspent tears, but his voice remained calm. "You have been through an ordeal, but it is over and now you will . . ."

All at once he realized she could not hear him. He stayed there beside her while she slept, until it became the sleep from which there is no awakening.

Philip never saw the corpse of his son. He did not wish to see it, and at last the tiny body, which had never known life, was wrapped in linen and placed beside his mother's, and both were consumed together by the purifying fire.

While it was considered unseemly for a king to grieve over the loss of a wife, a son was another matter and Philip might safely have allowed himself the luxury of mourning. Yet he seemed to feel nothing—nothing except a sullen disappointment, in himself and in the workings of the Fates. He had failed to provide his subjects with an heir. He had failed to protect Phila. He felt almost as if he had murdered her. His only consolation was that she had died without ever learning that her life had been sacrificed to no purpose.

To his friends he seemed no more than perhaps a trifle more serious, his smile a trifle less ready. They never guessed at the long periods of abstraction that afflicted him when he was alone, when time would seem to stop for him and he would lose all sense of present reality as his mind darkened until it could reflect nothing except the memory of those last few minutes with his wife.

Did she know that their child was dead? Was she a flickering shadow down in Hades, forever bewailing her loss? The idea tormented him. Perhaps, he sometimes thought. Perhaps he should have told her. Yet she had suffered so much, and how much more could mere flesh endure? He had been right to let her die in peace—if only she could remain in peace.

He missed her. Sometimes at night he missed her horribly so that he found himself straining to catch the sound of her voice in the darkness. Yet he blamed himself that he did not miss her more, that his heart did not crack from it, that it was not more than he could bear, that he did not wish his breath to stop. In this too he felt he wronged her, because she had loved him so much. She had died to please him. Was she not worth the tribute of a little pain? He could live, overcoming grief, while she faded more and more into the inaccessible past. This too seemed an injustice, almost an affront.

"You need to marry again," Glaukon told him about three months after Phila's death. The two of them sat over dinner in the old man's suite of rooms near the servants' quarters. Neither of them had spoken for several minutes. "I know you miss her more than you show, but you cannot turn your back on your grief as if it didn't exist. You need a new wife."

Philip smiled, thinking that Glaukon was perhaps the only man alive who would dare to speak to him thus—and certainly the only one to whom he would listen.

"You did not marry again," he said.

"I am a subject, while you are a king. You must have an heir. Besides, I was older."

"Will a new wife make me forget the old one?"

"No."

"I am glad, for otherwise I would never take another wife." He shook his head, as if he had just decided something. "I will marry again when I can love again. That will not be soon."

"Did you love her, then?"

"Yes."

Yes—he had loved her. That was the discovery he had made after losing her. That was the weight burdening his soul.

32

Perdikkas, king of all the Macedonians, had abandoned any hope of driving the Athenians out of Pydna and Methone. In defiance of the peace treaty he had signed with Kallisthenes, he continued to send troops to fight for the Chalcidian League, but even Athens's final defeat at Amphipolis, where she was obliged to burn her fleet, did nothing to change Macedon's essential weakness. No one was going to help her drive Athens from the gulf, and Macedon could not do it alone.

Even Euphraeos seemed to have lost interest in the struggle, for more and more he was directing the king's attention to other dangers—the Illyrians had formed an alliance with Menelaos of Lynkos and were once more threatening the northern borders.

"Perhaps I should send Philip to frighten them," Perdikkas told him, acknowledging in jest the fact that for well over two years now the west had been perfectly quiet. Euphraeos smiled his peculiarly unpleasant smile.

"No one, it appears, cares to challenge the king of Elimeia," he replied, knowing how little his master relished hearing Philip praised. "Men are careful not to tread on a coiled adder."

"Leave me, Euphraeos."

Not a flicker of surprise showed itself in the philosopher's expression as he received his dismissal. He bowed himself out of the king's presence, knowing he had made his point.

Because Perdikkas had understood perfectly. He was not even angry as he sat behind the big table in what had been his elder brother's study, his fingers toying with the hilt of a broken sword his father had kept as a souvenir of some long-forgotten battle. The emotion he experienced was closer to gloom than to rage.

For Perdikkas had come very gradually to understand that as king of the

Macedonians he was marked out for failure. He did not understand why this should be. It was not for want of ability, since his gifts were in no way inferior to those of either of his predecessors. He was not a fool and he was not a coward, yet his reign had been a succession of disasters.

Had he lived, would Alexandros have had to face all this? Or would the blind favor of the gods, which had only deserted him in the last moment of his life, have somehow smoothed his way? It would be comforting to think not, but it was also difficult to imagine Alexandros sitting in a tent being lectured by an Athenian general on the virtues of learning from his mistakes.

And their father, who had reigned for so long, had he not suffered reverses in his youth? Had the Illyrians not once even driven him from his throne? Yet the times had been different, and Amyntas had been elected king after a long period of chaos and internal strife. It had been his achievement to die leaving the succession undisputed and the nation weakened but at peace. No, their father did not provide a reassuring parallel.

Philip did not even enter into his calculations, because his younger brother, after all, was nothing more than a lout whom Fortune had raised and would surely cast down again. Philip, in the end, counted for nothing.

So what was left, except the feeling that events had slipped out of his control, that he and Macedon were moving toward a ruin that he was helpless to prevent or even to predict? The Athenians had established garrisons almost at his doorstep, the Thracians and the Chalcidian League had formed an alliance that threatened his eastern borders, and now there was this business with the Illyrians. It was like living in a room where the walls were collapsing inward.

Over the years Bardylis of Illyria had subjugated his neighbors until his vast mountain empire was clutching at all the Greek-speaking kingdoms to the east like a hand trying to rob a basket of apples. Now, secured in the north by his alliance with Lynkos, the old bandit had invaded Molossis, and Arybbas, king of that country, was able to do little more than to harass the enemy while his subjects were systematically plundered. Arybbas was not a friend, but his displacement was a threat to her southern border that Macedon could not possibly ignore. The question was what to do about it.

The easiest and perhaps the wisest course would be to follow his own joking suggestion and send Philip. Philip had experience of mountain warfare and knew the Illyrians at first hand. Besides, whatever other limitations he might be burdened with, Philip was a good soldier.

Yet there was much to argue against it.

For one thing, Bardylis was no petty rebel chieftain and Philip would require an army of possibly three thousand men. And if he triumphed, he might become more dangerous than the Illyrians. King of Elimeia, with an army that size and with his already considerable prestige enhanced by yet another victory, Philip would not long be a subject but an equal. There would be nothing, utterly nothing, restraining him except such personal loyalty as he might feel he owed his brother and sovereign. Yes, Philip was loyal—now. But a king, if he is to be a king, must be in a position to demand loyalty, not beg it as a favor.

In any case, Philip was not a magician. If Bardylis could be brought down, other men besides Philip could do it. Perdikkas was reasonably sure he could do it himself.

And if he could not—if the gods really meant to destroy him—a military campaign against the Illyrians was as good a way as any other to meet his fate.

At twenty-three the king of the Macedonians sometimes felt like an old man, used up and finished. He was weary of being king; in certain moods he was weary of life. He was weary of the sense of uncertainty that enveloped him. He felt an almost overpowering desire to push things to some grand crisis, after which all doubts would be settled. Perhaps that was the great attraction of war, the source of its fatal glamour, the fact that it transformed everything.

Perdikkas decided he would do no more work that day. Tomorrow he would begin the preparations for a thrust north—if Bardylis was in the south, looting villages, then it made good sense to attack him where he was weakest— but today he would do nothing more. He went to visit his wife and son.

His marriage was at least one thing in life that had not disappointed him, if only because he had entered it with limited expectations. Perdikkas had always thought the pleasures of physical conjunction overrated—the poets praised it, but they also praised drunkenness and horse racing—and it was not to his wife that a sensible man turned for companionship. Arete was virtuous, quiet, submissive, and fecund, which was all that Perdikkas required of her. A year and a half after their marriage she had presented her husband with a son, and six months later both she and little Amyntas were thriving. Philip had lost both wife and child and showed no inclination to tempt his luck again, so in this at least Perdikkas had enjoyed an advantage.

The boy pleased him. Amyntas was a fat, sturdy child with the stumps of two teeth sticking through his gums, and he crawled along over the fur rugs of his nursery at a reckless speed. It was a pleasure to spend an hour with him, supporting his compact little body while he tried to stand, listening to his mother describe his latest triumphs. Perdikkas knew that it was not quite dignified to take such an interest in one's infant children, but existence held few enough pleasures that he felt entitled to look in every three or four days. It gratified him that the boy always seemed to know his father, greeting him with a huge smile.

But even this pleasure was tempered with uneasiness, for Perdikkas had not forgotten how his own mother had cursed him, almost with her dying breath. *May you die as he died, under the eyes of strangers. May your reign end in destruction and may no son follow after you.* And so the king of Macedon was at some pains that no harm should befall his heir. Prince Amyntas had his own physician, and his food came not from the main kitchen but was prepared for him specially under his mother's eyes. Even the nursery maids had been warned that they would be flogged if the boy so much as skinned his knee. Amyntas would follow his father to the throne—Perdikkas had every intention of making certain that he did. Eurydike had not spoken with the voice of heaven, and she could not bring down her son and all his house with a word. Eurydike had been dead for over three years, and in all that time her curse had achieved nothing.

Besides, there would be other princes. Arete was young and strong, and there would be many more fat baby boys. Why shouldn't the rightful succession stretch down through time and into eternity?

"You will be Amyntas the Fourth," Perdikkas would sometimes whisper to the child who sat in his lap, playing with the rings on his father's fingers. "You will rule after me, and Philip will grow old and die as my servant and yours."

Philip also had received intelligence of Molossis's plight. He had established friendly relations with his neighbor Pitheas, king of the Tymphaioi, and he was in receipt of letters describing how refugees were daily pouring over the western mountains to escape the savagery of the Illyrians. At this time of year the high places were already filling up with snow, and the Molossians could expect little enough in Tymphaia, but it seemed they preferred to risk freezing and then starving to whatever fate they anticipated under the Illyrians. The stories they brought with them into exile made one's blood run cold.

The great prize, of course, was the Zygos Pass—whoever controlled it commanded access to all the kingdoms of southern Macedon. Arybbas was still harassing the enemy on their descent into Molossis, but his was essentially a holding action against inevitable defeat and Philip was not prepared to trust to them for his own protection. He quickly came to an arrangement with Pitheas, who after all was in the more immediate danger, and installed a garrison of five hundred men at the summit of the pass. Bardylis could kick against the stopper as much as he liked, but the jar was sealed.

Next Philip wrote to his brother suggesting an alliance with the Molossians, which Arybbas was in no position to refuse, and an immediate attack from around the far side of Mount Pindos while the main Macedonian army marched north to frighten the Lynkestians into neutrality and to cut the Illyrians off from their home bases.

The letter was sent by dispatch rider, who was told to wait for a reply. When he returned he informed Philip, "I was not admitted into the king's presence. On the third day after I arrived a minister told me that King Perdikkas would send no reply. He said you were to await the king's commands." The rider was a boy of about sixteen, and from the embarrassed way he delivered his report one might have gathered that he found it strange that anyone should presume to tell the king of Elimeia—his king—to await commands.

"What was the minister's name?"

"Euphraeos."

Philip understood well enough. There would be no campaign. Nevertheless, he sent a second rider with another letter and the same instructions. This time the rider did not return for twenty days, but at least he brought a reply in Perdikkas's own hand.

"Do not presume, little brother, to lecture me on the arts of war," Perdikkas wrote. "I will deal with Bardylis in my own way and in my own time, and until then I am content that you keep him at bay in the south. In any case, it is too late in the season for campaigning."

Lachios happened to be with him when he received the letter. They had been out hunting and were still in the stables, watching the grooms rub down their horses. It was almost sundown and the smell of hay and horse sweat was very pleasant. When Philip was done reading he handed it to Lachios without comment.

"Whenever I think about your brother commanding an army, all my scars begin to ache," Lachios said, carefully rolling the letter back up before returning it to Philip. "I do not relish the idea of crossing the mountains at this time of year, but does Perdikkas imagine the Illyrians will be any easier to defeat after fattening for the winter in Molossis?"

"I have the most dreadful feeling about this." Philip took the letter and crumpled it into a wad. Then he opened his fingers and looked at it as if at something he suspected might make him sick if he ate it. "I see the pit trap straight in his path, but as loud as I shout I cannot make him look down at how the ground gives way beneath his feet."

"No one ever had to set a trap for the king of the Macedonians. He arranges his own disasters. Believe me, if he wishes to destroy himself, there is nothing anyone can do about it, least of all you."

Lachios threw his arm across Philip's shoulders in a gesture that was almost pitying.

"My own suggestion is that we get very drunk tonight."

"I think that is an excellent idea."

33

The melting snow made a misery of life. Nothing stayed dry, and on some mornings one awoke to find that the water that had seeped into one's boots all day yesterday had now congealed into a sheet of ice. Here and there one saw a few cases of frostbite, but the misery was out of all proportion to the danger of a few blackened toes. And now the food was showing signs of rot. Conditions were so bad that the soldiers had stopped grumbling. A sullen silence had fallen over Perdikkas's army, but he knew without being told that they blamed him for their suffering.

He had thought to make a lightning dash north while the ground was still hard, following the route Philip had outlined in his letters, and to sweep down on the Illyrians in their winter quarters. And the plan might have worked if it hadn't been betrayed by an early thaw that turned the roads to slush. Now, in the lake valleys west of the Pisoderi Pass, the very faces of the stones were covered with running water that trickled down from the surrounding mountains. The army's advance had slowed almost to nothing as they labored with every step to pull themselves free from the clinging mud. If at the end their labors were crowned with victory and the whole of old Bardylis's empire were yielded up to them for the taking, it would be but a poor compensation for all they had been obliged to endure.

And this morning, just before dawn, it had started to rain.

Perdikkas was awakened by the sound it made beating against the walls of his leather tent. The drops were the size of grapes and exploded with a loud pop the instant they hit something. He looked outside and saw how the cooking fires hissed and smoked under the downpour—it seemed unlikely that the soldiers' dispositions would be improved by a cold, rain-drenched breakfast.

They were camped by the side of a huge lake that did not even appear on any of the maps. One could stand on its shore and look across almost to the horizon, with only the mountains as a faint, misty presence on the far side. Now, with the gray rain pelting its surface, it appeared to boil and steam like a cauldron. It was a ghastly landscape, fit only for the purging of men's sins.

An officer came running up—less eager, one suspected, to receive commands than to have a moment in out of the wet—and saluted the king from beneath the safety of his tent flap.

"Give them half an hour and then issue the order to prepare to march," Perdikkas told him. "If this is going to keep up all day, we might as well be soaked through moving as standing still."

As the man hurried away, Perdikkas watched with disgust as the heavy, steel-colored clouds moved across the sky. This was merely a shower—in another hour it might be a torrent. He was not looking forward to a day on horseback, with the rain dripping inside his breastplate so that the woolen tunic underneath became a sodden, itching horror. It was impossible to keep dry in such weather. One might as well not even bother with a cloak, which, in any case, soon got so heavy with water that it felt as if it were made of lead.

Today his men would struggle through a sea of mud, and by nightfall, when they sat down on the wet ground for a dismal, cold supper, they would count themselves lucky if they had covered as much distance as would do for a two-hour walk in fine weather. Be he a cook's helper or a king, every soldier's life was a wretched business.

By noon the rain was coming down so hard that at fifty paces the sound of a man's voice was drowned by it. Perdikkas had to keep wiping the water out of his eyebrows in order to see, but it made hardly any difference, since the entire Illyrian army could have been closer to him than he was to his standard-bearer without running the risk of his noticing them. The rain simply enveloped one, shrinking the appreciable down almost to nothing.

A rider, whom Perdikkas recognized as a man named Elpenor, master of the watch, an officer old enough to have fought under King Amyntas and who had stood high in favor with Alexandros, came up beside him, splashing mud so wildly that Perdikkas's own horse shied away.

"Beg to report, Lord. The scouts are beginning to report an enemy presence farther up the valley, possibly an advance patrol."

"Has anyone actually seen an Illyrian?"

"No, Lord, but they have found fresh horse droppings not an hour from here, and they say they sense something . . ."

"Sense something?" The king of all the Macedonians permitted himself a brief, mirthless laugh. "Anyone can ride a horse, and the Illyrians have no reason to believe a hostile army is within ten days' ride of here—would you be out looking for a phantom enemy in this weather? This rain plays tricks on a man. The scouts are probably starting at shadows."

Elpenor frowned and clutched at his reins as if struggling to keep his horse under control.

"Lord, these are good men—experienced men. When they say they believe the enemy may be nearby, I think one is obliged to take their reports seriously."

Perdikkas sighed wearily. "Very well, then. What would you suggest?"

"I would suggest, Lord, that we begin sending out reconnaissance in force. If the Illyrians know we are here, and catch us strung out on the road, it will go very badly for us."

"You have my leave to double the patrols. Let them spread their nets as wide as they like."

But at the end of two more days, during which it never stopped raining, the scouts could not report any contact with the enemy.

"I told you it was all shadows," Perdikkas said, favoring Elpenor with a nod at a council of senior officers held in the king's tent. It was crowded and the smell of damp wool and unwashed bodies was oppressive, but at least they didn't have to shout to make themselves heard over the constant clattering of the rain.

But Elpenor shook his head, looking very grave.

"Lord, these mountains are full of little hidden valleys that could hold an army of ten thousand men. This is the Illyrians' home ground, not ours—they will know how to keep themselves concealed."

"Yet they would be sending out patrols of their own, looking for us as hard as we are looking for them," replied Toxaechmes, a young officer, handsome and agreeable, who had served with Perdikkas at Amphipolis and stood high in his master's favor. "Large numbers of horsemen cannot range across the countryside without leaving a trace."

Elpenor managed a tight smile, as if at the interruption of a child. "When the ground is as wet as it is now it will not hold a hoofprint for more than an hour.

"My point, Lord," he went on, turning to Perdikkas, "is that we simply do not know if the Illyrians are tracking us. It is perfectly possible they may be and it seems obvious to me, therefore, we must act on the assumption that they are. Otherwise we risk disaster."

Perdikkas raised his eyes.

"I think the rain is abating," he remarked as if there were no other topic of discussion. For a moment they all listened in silence as it drummed against the roof of the tent. "Yes, I am quite sure it is not so heavy as it was even a quarter of an hour ago. Perhaps now we will be in for a few days of fine weather."

"Then we should make the most of the opportunity," Toxaechmes said, seeming very pleased with this happy thought. Several others nodded their approval. "In ten days, with a little luck, we can be over the mountains and into northern Molossis."

"This is not the time to be thinking of a quick dash over the mountains," Elpenor snapped angrily. "The men are exhausted, unfit for either battle or a forced march across bad terrain. We should find ourselves some good defensive position so that we can dig in and look about us a little."

It was not a popular speech, and particularly not with he to whom it was principally directed. Perdikkas showed his displeasure in the expression of disdainful surprise that crossed his face—he looked almost as if Elpenor's rebuke had been directed at him.

"The men," he began, with telling emphasis, "will be all the better for getting away from these infernal, swampy lakes. After what we have endured here, the mountains will seem like a stroll through an apple orchard. I see no reason to sit here in the mud waiting to be attacked by an enemy who is probably asleep in a nice dry barrack somewhere in Molossis, without a thought that there could be a Macedonian any closer than the garrison at Edessa."

He looked around at the other officers present, who looked first at him and then at the smiling, bland face of Toxaechmes, which expressed his complete agreement with every syllable the king had uttered, and then one after the other they muttered their assent.

As the meeting was breaking up, Perdikkas gave a discreet signal to Toxaechmes that he should remain behind. For a long time the two men sat in silence, sharing a jar of wine that somehow had taken on the taste of rainwater.

"I want you to take over command of reconnaissance from Elpenor," the king said at last. "Perhaps I should have rotated him to other duties before this, since it is a post bound after a time to tell on any man. He is beginning to see Illyrians in his dreams, I should fancy, and I would not be surprised if his excessive apprehensiveness is communicating itself to the men under him. You may wish to replace some of them."

"It shall be as you see fit, Lord."

And the rain did abate. For three days the clouds overhead were the color of tarnished iron, as if pregnant with some great storm, but they did not make good on their threat. The ground dried a little, and everyone felt better for a few hot meals. The scouts, now under Toxaechmes' command, reported no sign of the enemy.

Perdikkas found that his disposition was improving with the weather. He was beginning once more to feel quite positive about this campaign, the way he had felt when he and Euphraeos had been planning it back in Pella. In a few more days they would be in the mountains, and once on the other side they would fall on the Illyrians like a bolt of lightning out of a summer sky. It would work—they would achieve complete surprise.

And he had been right to leave Philip out of his calculations. He did not need Philip. After all, Arybbas was still in southern Molossis and still in command of perhaps as many as fifteen hundred men, not sufficient to allow him to engage the enemy but enough to harry them. Once the Macedonians had achieved a few victories, however, Arybbas was certain to rally his forces and attack the Illyrians from the rear. He would do quite as well as Philip.

And how Philip would grieve over the success of this campaign—for Perdikkas had quite convinced himself that his brother's principal motive in proposing a two-pronged attack had been fear of losing his share of the glory. Philip was no doubt quite vain of his reputation as a commander, but, where the Elimoitai and the Eordoi were little more than hill tribes, the Illyrians were, after all, the Illyrians. A victory over them would put all of Philip's exploits quite properly in the shade.

So it was with a good deal of pleasure that the king of the Macedonians considered his future as he led his army across this vast and inhospitable landscape, densely pockmarked with lakes and swamps. Perhaps at last his fortunes were beginning to change.

The third day put the lakes behind them. The mountains were no more than two days away and did not look very formidable. Perdikkas sent out an advance party to look for a convenient pass. He would keep his soldiers on the march as long as the ground remained level and then give them a rest until the scouts returned.

On the morning of the fourth day the rains started in again, at first no more than a light drizzle but persistent. By evening it was a steady downpour, as enclosing as a dense fog. On the fifth day a horse returned to camp without its rider.

"Someone has had an accident," Toxaechmes declared.

"Nevertheless, put out a few extra patrols and see if they can make contact with the advance party. It will do no harm to see what happened."

Perdikkas did not anticipate any real danger. And at the very least he would hear something of how the terrain through the mountains looked.

He did not order any earthworks dug for that night's campsite. Special fortifications seemed unnecessary and, in any case, the men were exhausted.

The attack came just before dawn.

When the alarm trumpets woke him up, Perdikkas wasn't sure he hadn't been dreaming. The first thing he was aware of was that he could no longer hear the rain on the walls of his tent.

No, it wasn't a dream. He could hear the trumpets now, and the sounds of shouting. Just then the tent flap was thrust aside, almost as if someone had hit it at a run, and an officer came inside.

"Lord, the Illyrians are massing!" he shouted excitedly.

Perdikkas picked up his sword. His breastplate and greaves were lying beside his bed, but he never even glanced at them. There was no time.

Outside, in that last, darkest hour before the dawn that now might never come, the king had no difficulty knowing from which direction the threat was aimed—he had only to follow the shouting. At the northwest edge of the defensive perimeter, surrounded by a knot of soldiers, he found one of the watch riders lying on a blanket, his hand clutched to his left side as blood oozed thickly between his fingers. One of the camp physicians was crouched behind him, cradling his head and shoulders in his arms. The man was obviously dying.

"We ran into their advance columns not a quarter of an hour from here," the man said as Perdikkas knelt beside him. "It was an accident on both sides, Lord—we just collided with them at the edge of a stand of trees. I got a javelin in the belly, but I managed to break away and ride back. Did any of the others make it?"

Perdikkas raised his eyes to look at the faces of the men standing about, but one by one they shook their heads.

"How many were there?" he asked.

The man let his head roll back, as if the question overwhelmed him. "No way to tell, Lord, not in that darkness. It seemed like a large force, though—it wasn't a patrol. As soon as they knew we had seen them they went for us. I think they didn't want anyone getting away to report back."

"Well, you have done that," Perdikkas said, putting his hand on the man's shoulder. "It may be that you have saved us all."

But even as he regained his feet, he knew that no one would be saved. Elpenor had been right—the main Illyrian force was massing out there in the night, preparing to attack. His men were exhausted, in no condition to fight, there were no defenses prepared, and the enemy would probably be upon them within a quarter of an hour. Perdikkas needed no one to show him how utterly he had blundered.

The Illyrians were notorious for their cruelty to prisoners. He had led an army of four thousand men into the mountains to be butchered by savages. It would be the inevitable conclusion of all his great hopes and plans, of a piece with his whole career. Everything he began ended badly. His failure, both as soldier and as king, was now revealed to him as absolute.

May you die under the eyes of strangers. May your reign end in destruction.

It was all coming to pass—he could see that now. His mother's curse had come full circle, to encompass the end both of his life and his ambitions.

If this, then, was to be his extinction, Perdikkas was determined that at least he would not be found wanting in the courage to face it. At least it was in his power to spare himself the final indignity of a coward's death.

"Order the men to defensive stations!" he shouted, his voice, perhaps for the first time, carrying the authority of assured command. "Light all the fires—burn the wagons if need be. Let us prepare a proper welcome for our visitors."

34

It was some time before the outside world heard that King Perdikkas, together with four thousand of his soldiers, had been massacred by the Illyrians. There had been few survivors, and the handful who had escaped were many days finding their way through hostile territory and then back to Edessa to tell their story.

When the garrison commander there realized the scope of the disaster, he immediately sent a dispatch rider to Aiane—not to Pella, not to the capital, where the king's heir was still an infant and there was no one to take command and control the inevitable panic, but to Aiane. In this crisis, he reasoned, there was but one man left to whom the Macedonians would give their allegiance, whose age and bloodline qualified to rule. Pella could wait. It was all up to Philip now.

"I would not be he for worlds," the commander confided to his secretary. "The nation is a lamb compassed round by wolves. Whichever way she turns, one must fall upon her back and when they all join in for the kill she will be torn to bloody tatters. I would not be king of Macedon at this hour."

The king of Elimeia was having dinner with his officers when he received the news. The chamberlain came in to tell him there was a courier from Edessa waiting. Philip rose from the table and left without a word. He received the courier in his study, alone.

He knew the instant he saw the man's face that the news was bad. The courier saluted and handed him a scroll bearing the garrison commander's seal.

"Do you know what this contains?" Philip asked him.

"Yes, Lord."

"Then say nothing of it to anyone. You are doubtless tired and hungry—my chamberlain will see to you."

He waited until he was alone before he broke the seal.

It is to Philip's credit that his first emotion was simple grief. His brother Perdikkas was dead. Four thousand of the king's soldiers were dead with him. Philip did not think what this might mean for himself, not at first. He simply held his head in his hands and wept.

Then, after a time, he remembered who he was and sent for Lachios and Korous, his two most trusted lieutenants.

"The king my brother, along with his entire army, has been slain by the Illyrians."

Lachios and Korous, who had fought on opposite sides when Philip seized the throne of Elimeia, now exchanged a glance as they sat across the council table from the master they both loved. They both had a very clear conception of what this news meant.

"I must go to Pella. Korous, since you are entitled to a place in the assembly, I wish you to organize an escort and accompany me. Lachios will be in command here, with full powers, until I return—I may not return for a long time."

"Take an army with you and make yourself king," Lachios said and then looked to Korous, who nodded his approval.

"Lachios is right, Philip. The assembly will elect you if you show them you do not mean to be refused. In this emergency they will have no choice."

At first the lord of Elimeia was silent. His face was set and grim and he simply stared into space, as if contemplating a future only he could see.

"I will not use force to displace my brother's child," he said at last. "Only the assembly may choose a king of Macedon, and the son of Perdikkas is closest in line of succession. How could I possibly command the loyalty of men whom I had threatened into electing me king? What you are proposing is an invitation to civil war. Make up a guard of fifty men, and I will take that to Pella."

"Then there must be a regency." Korous shook his head, very slowly, as if he could not believe such folly. "You are the only possible candidate, but all regencies suffer from the same weakness—as the boy king grows up, men begin to think of the future. Your power will founder on court jealousies."

Philip uttered a short, mirthless laugh.

"Korous, if five years from now there is still a Macedon to be jealous over, then I will gladly yield. Until then, I think I will have little enough to fear from a babe who is still cutting his first teeth."

He stood up—slowly, as if he were accustoming himself to some great weight.

"When we leave for Pella, we will take the boy Deucalion with us. It will remind his father that he has something to lose if he thinks of switching his allegiance from us to the Illyrians. Lachios, double the guard at the Zygos Pass. Let us at least keep this door closed on the enemy.

"And send an envoy to Bardylis to inquire on what terms he will give us back the king's body for burial—after all, Perdikkas was his great-grandson."

He smiled wanly, as if conscious that he had made a poor jest.

"More than that, there is nothing more to say. Be good enough to leave me now."

When he was alone again, he closed his eyes and tried to clear his mind. It was simply too much to deal with in a mass. He felt like a harp the strings of which have all been plucked together, as if the discord of his own thoughts and feelings had blended into a meaningless hum.

He knew he could not afford to think of his brother, whose corpse, unless Bardylis had had the decency to burn it, was even now feasting the crows. He could not allow himself the luxury of mourning. There could be no great oaths of revenge, for the gods alone knew what sort of arrangement he might have to come to with the Illyrians. He must think of Perdikkas's death solely as it affected the safety of the nation—there could be no room for private feelings.

He must confine himself to the situation. Perdikkas was gone, together with an army of four thousand men, about half the total strength of the army. Thus there was almost nothing standing between the Illyrians and the north-western provinces. Relations with Athens were bad, and the Paionians and Thracians were, as always, hostile and threatening. It was perfectly possible that these four would simply divide the nation among themselves, leaving Macedon a truncated dependency of whichever among her conquerors could put their pretender on the throne.

And all of this it was his task to prevent. He alone stood between Macedon and chaos. There was simply no one else. Philip did not even consider the possibility of failure, for even to approach the thought made him giddy with fear.

In the morning, before departing for Pella, he would go to the temple of Athena and make sacrifice to the Lady of the Gray Eyes. Soon he would need her.

But for now he went to Glaukon's rooms near the servants' quarters, where he knew the old man would be studying the household accounts, his usual relaxation before going to bed. Philip brought a jar of wine with him.

He did not trouble to knock at the door, for a man needs no invitation to enter his father's house. Glaukon did not seem surprised to see him—why should he have been surprised? He merely raised his eyes from his writing table and, when he noticed the wine, he smiled.

"We are on our travels again," Philip said, breaking the jar's seal with his thumb. "Can you be prepared to leave for Pella in the morning?"

Glaukon took down a pair of cups and put them on the table. "What has happened?" he asked as he watched Philip pour the wine.

"Perdikkas is dead. His Illyrian adventure has ended in a great slaughter."

For a long time the king's steward made no answer. He merely stared at his wine cup as though it were filled with blood. At last he took it and raised it to his lips.

"Then your great moment has come at last."

"Do you mock me?" Philip asked, approaching as near to anger as he had ever come with the man who had raised him. "I do not think I have been guilty of ambition."

"I was not speaking of your purposes, but of the gods'." Glaukon, who was not in the habit of reproving kings, spoke almost as sternly as Philip had. "Every man has his own peculiar destiny, his own place in the great design that we are not privileged to understand and yet cannot doubt rules our lives. Mine has been to be steward to four kings and to raise you into manhood— an obscure destiny it might be said, yet I think, on the whole, a greater one than many kings can boast."

He paused for a moment, lifting the cup to his lips for a taste, as if to be sure the wine merchant had not cheated him. Philip said nothing, content to wait, for he knew the old man was not to be hurried but would make all things clear in his own time—it had been no different when Glaukon had explained to him, as a child of eight or nine, the various grades and qualities of olive oil and how one arrived at a price for them.

"Without disrespect, My Lord, most kings are paltry beings, their greatness an illusion, for they are no different from other men. It makes no difference if their reigns are long or short; they strut about for a time and then they are dust. They are but pebbles dropped into the pool of mortality— the water closes over them and very quickly the ripples die away. As soon as they are shut up in their burial urns it is as if they never lived, and no one but the chroniclers even remembers their names. So it was with your father, the Lord Amyntas. So it was with your brother Alexandros. And so now too with Perdikkas. I do not believe that this is the fate the heavens have marked out for you."

"Then you are saying I will never be king of Macedon?"

"I am saying it makes little difference whether you are or not." Glaukon shook his head, as if Philip were still the small boy he once taught to tally the accounts and he had made a mistake with his sums. "That is why you were wrong to imagine I accused you of ambition. Ambition is for little men. I speak of a glory that far transcends any title to a kingdom. I speak of the greatness that only the gods may bestow upon a man as their free gift—or perhaps as their curse, since it follows not his purposes but their own. This I know you have carried in you all your life. I have known it since that first night I carried you home in my arms, when Herakles burned so brightly in the black sky. And now, I think, it is about to take possession of you."

. . .

By the time Philip had taken horse and was on his way home the news of Perdikkas's death had spread across the broad plains of Macedon like a grass fire driven by the wind. Every shepherd boy knew what it meant—the nation was hedged in by enemies, half the army was dead in some wilderness beyond the mountains, and the heir of the throne was not even old enough to walk. A time of trial was coming, during which the king's disaster would make itself felt in the remotest village and the humblest peasant cottage.

This knowledge was written on the faces of the men and women who stood by the roadside to pay their silent homage to the last of Amyntas's sons as he rode toward Pella. They did not speak. They simply followed him with their eyes as he passed. He had only to glance at these people to know that they looked to him to protect the homeland and to keep foreign invaders from their doors. Such was the ancient duty of the Argeadai, who had given Macedon her kings since the days of the heroes, a duty which now fell to Philip.

And at Aigai, an hour's ride from the gates of the old capital, the road was choked by foot soldiers and cavalry from the city garrison.

"What do they mean by this?" Korous exclaimed, reining in his horse as he lifted his hand to bring the escort to a halt. "Have they raised a mutiny?"

Philip merely laughed. "At least I have the consolation of knowing they cannot be in mutiny against me, for I have no authority over them." He touched his heels to Alastor's flanks, urging the great stallion forward. "Come. Let us see what they want."

As Philip approached, the garrison commander rode forward to meet him. He was a man of about forty with a red face and a slightly bulbous nose that somehow made him look angry. Once he had been a rising young officer in the royal garrison at Pella. Philip could remember from his childhood being very frightened of him.

"Epikles, why the reception?" he asked now, not frightened in the least—he noticed, as a matter of no great importance, that the man appeared to start a little at being recognized. "Do you mean to stop us, or is this intended as a display of hospitality?"

"Neither, Lord Philip. We wish to accompany you to Pella." Epikles waited for a moment, as if expecting some reaction, and then continued. "You are the last of the royal line, Prince, and no one must be allowed to deny you your brother's crown. The soldiers have voted among themselves, and we are yours to a man."

"You are in error, for I am not the last of the line. Perdikkas left a son."

"A sucking babe cannot be a king," Epikles replied with some heat. "The soldiers will choose you. We mean to see to it."

For a long moment Philip regarded the garrison commander with what looked like disinterested curiosity—he might have been studying a problem in geometry. Then he put his right hand behind his neck and shrugged, as though despairing of the solution.

"If you and your men wish to travel with me, you are welcome," he said at last. "I cannot stop you and I would not if I could, for every Macedonian under arms has a right to his place in the assembly that will choose our next king. But do not imagine I will subvert the ancient laws. You will not make me the leader of a coup."

After a second's deliberation, Epikles nodded vigorously. "Fair enough, Lord. We will leave it to the assembly."

That night Philip slept in the garrison, having refused the apartment that had been prepared for him in the old royal palace, unoccupied for over fifty years. The next morning, while he was still at breakfast, he was informed that a delegation had arrived from Beroia and desired an audience. They too pledged themselves to his cause and asked to accompany him to Pella, and they too were accepted on the same terms. In the same hour he received messages from the garrison commanders at Meiza and Aloros.

"I assume you know what all this means," Korous said to him as they at last mounted their horses in the garrison courtyard. "They mean to make you king, whether you will or no. They have no choice and neither have you, not if the nation is to survive. You had best give some thought to what you mean to do with the child."

Philip felt something like a sliver of ice going through his vitals, for he knew precisely what Korous had in his mind.

"Yes," he said, looking about him as if he were counting the soldiers in his escort, "I know what it all means."

Three days later, when at last he arrived in Pella, the crowds that came out to meet him were large and, on the whole, silent. He might have been an invader entering a conquered city, for they watched his arrival with what seemed a mingling of curiosity and fear.

Yes, of course they are frightened, he thought. It was not unreasonable. Over the last several years he had lived very little in Pella, and Perdikkas's ambivalence toward him had doubtless communicated itself to the citizens of his capital. They did not know what to expect from this stranger.

This was not unfair, since he hardly knew what to expect from himself.

He left his escort at the garrison and rode into the courtyard of the royal palace alone. Most of those who were gathered there to meet him were old servants who remembered Philip from his boyhood, but among them were Euphraeos and the Lady Arete.

The sight of his brother's widow, whom he had not seen since her wedding day, made Philip's throat contract painfully. He embraced her and wept, but apparently even the comfort of a shared grief was to be denied to him, for Arete held her arms to her breast, as unyielding as stone.

"The gods know it is hard," he said, his voice still full of tears. "Our family seems to gather sorrow to it like a mother clutching at her children, but we might at least have been spared this."

She did not answer at first but merely stared at him, as if gauging an actor's performance in a tragedy.

"You will not cheat my son of his birthright," she said finally. "My son is king now."

She shook off his embrace and, as Philip tried to find some word of explanation, she began walking, almost running, back toward the palace.

"You will not set my son aside!"

The words were like a curse and vibrated in the air for several seconds after she had disappeared inside.

"She is afraid of you," Euphraeos stated with his usual bland authority. He had stepped forward and made an elaborately courtly bow to Philip. "She believes you are the most dangerous of the many enemies that surround her and her child—she would prefer Bardylis to you."

"And who put such ideas into her head?"

The philosopher managed one of his grim, dyspeptic smiles.

"Her husband, I should imagine."

"And who put them into his?"

Euphraeos was silent for a moment, as if he had not heard the question— or did not like to think what it might mean. Presently his gaze drifted away from Philip and he appeared to survey the stonework in the courtyard walls.

"She is a danger," he said and smiled again. "She and the child will always be a focus of opposition to your rule. In the present crisis, I do not suppose you can afford that."

"What would you suggest?"

"That you have them both killed."

The remark was quite casual, as if the point were so obvious he was a trifle embarrassed at having to mention it.

"I could be of use to you."

"In killing them? I do not need you for that, Athenian—the means are always at hand.

"In other ways. I could be of service."

"As you were of use to my brother? You have done enough mischief."

Euphraeos's eyes returned to Philip's countenance with a kind of snap. He appeared shocked. This, it would seem, was the last response he had expected.

"The assembly will meet in two or three days," Philip continued, his voice hard and calm. "You would do well to be on a ship by then. I would not be too particular about its destination, because after the Macedonians have made their will known, if I find you in the city, I will have your head mounted on the point of a spear."

When the assembly met, Philip took his place on the tier of seats reserved for the Argeadai—nothing could have represented more starkly the choice facing the Macedonians, for he sat quite alone. He did not speak to anyone and he took no part in the debate.

The amphitheater was almost completely full, for nearly every garrison in the realm had sent as large a delegation as they could. The winter sun shone on the breastplates so that one could hardly bear to look at them.

First came prayers and sacrifice—the bone and fat from a bull's hindquarters burned on an altar in the center of the well—and finally the commander of the Pella garrison stood up. Dardanos was a man past sixty and so stout that his lieutenant had to help him to his feet, yet he had been a famous soldier in old King Amyntas's day. By ancient custom it was his right to speak first.

He raised his hand to command silence.

"We have but two alternatives," he began. "We can declare the child Amyntas, son of the Lord Perdikkas, to be king and appoint his uncle the Lord Philip regent during his minority, or we can set Amyntas aside and declare the Lord Philip king in his place. These two are the last of the royal line whom death or treason has not disqualified.

"In normal times the line of succession flows from father to son, but if the natural heir is judged incompetent by reason of defect, or if the present danger demands it, the assembly has the right to let its choice fall to another.

"So the question becomes not who will rule, for the substance of power must now surely fall to the Lord Philip, but who will be king. We must look to the times for our answer, and there is no one here who does not know as well as I the crisis to which King Perdikkas's death has brought us. As well we know that if the Lord Philip is to lead us out of it—if such a thing is even possible—he will need all the authority that it is in the power of this assembly to place in his hands. Thus let us decide, can we afford the luxury of a child king, or do we need a man and a proven soldier upon the throne of Macedon?"

After that there was little doubt how the vote would go. Dardanos resumed his seat amid a murmur of approval. The next man on his feet, the garrison commander from Aigai, formally moved that Philip, son of Amyntas, be named king of Macedon.

No one spoke after that—no one could have made himself heard. The entire assembly rose as one man and filed down into the well of the amphitheater that they might stand before the new king and display their loyalty by shouting his name and beating the flats of their swords against their breastplates. The sound made the very air shake.

Philip stood up. He was surrounded by a wall of drawn swords and he reached out to touch the points of those closest to him, thus affirming his acceptance. He did not speak—his new subjects wanted no words and, in any case, no one would have heard—but waited for a path to be cleared for him to the entrance. He would now perform his first duty as king and lead his army to the temple of Herakles for the purification of their weapons.

It is odd the tricks that memory can sometimes play on a man. As he stood before the entrance to the amphitheater, as the gathered citizens of Pella cheered him, he seemed not to hear them. He seemed, to himself, to be part of another vast, adoring crowd, looking up from his place by the side of the road, watching with his brothers Perdikkas and Arrhidaios as Alexandros was hailed as king. They were all alive again in his mind, untainted by treachery and death. What a hero Alexandros had looked at that moment!

"My Lord Philip!"

The sound of a woman's voice, like the wild cry of an animal, full of mortal terror, brought him back to himself. He hardly knew who she was as she rushed forward, a bundle in her arms. She prostrated herself before him, reaching out a hand to touch his foot in supplication.

Then she lifted her head to look at him—it was Arete. She was cradling her child in her arms. The crowd fell into a numb silence.

"My Lord Philip, I beseech you to spare the life of your brother's son," she sobbed. "I make my submission to you. I beg you for his life."

All about him Philip could hear the shuffling of feet and the whisper of swords drawn from their scabbards. The officers surrounding him, many of whom could not see what was happening, did not know what to expect—was this perhaps the prelude to an assassination attempt?—and they were little inclined to mercy, for too much depended on the life of this one man.

"Put away your weapons," he said, his voice at once firm and calm, as if he were directing a servant to clear a table. "There is nothing to be alarmed about."

"I beg you for his life," Arete repeated, the word trailing off into a sob. Her outstretched hand still touched the top of his foot.

"Best to kill them both," someone murmured behind him. Philip could not recognize the voice—he did not wish to. "We are at war with half the earth, and a displaced heir breeds treason. Best to kill them now."

"And must I make war on heaven as well?" he answered, without turning around. "I will not stain the beginning of my rule with the shedding of innocent blood."

He knelt and took his brother's widow by the shoulders, lifting her up.

"You are safe and he is safe."

He took the child from her and held him in his arms.

"This boy is the son of my brother Perdikkas," he announced. "I will stand in a father's place for him and, while I have no son of my own, he is my sole heir. He lives under my protection. Let any man who would rob him of his life remember that, for his enemies will be my enemies."

He returned the child to his mother, who knelt and would have kissed his foot if Philip had not forced her to rise.

"Enough, Lady—you were a king's wife. Do not humble yourself more."

They stood there a moment together and it was apparent that the citizens of Pella approved, for they cheered all the louder now. But it was not to them he listened.

You see? They have made their choice, he heard himself say, in the voice of the child he had been. And he saw the face of his half brother, Arrhidaios, smiling a little wanly.

Yes—they have made their choice.

35

The month of Artemisios covered the grasslands near the Thracian border with blue flowers. Philip and his party had ridden down from Heraklea Sintika and were camped on the southern shore of Lake Kerkinitis. They were only a hundred men and the enemy was no more than an hour's ride away, but those were the terms King Berisades had insisted upon.

"I think he means to cut your throat, march in, and install your cousin Pausanias on the throne," Korous muttered as he stirred the fire with the point of his sword.

"You will ruin its temper doing that," Philip said.

Korous took his sword out of the embers and laid it on the long grass, still wet with that morning's dew. It hissed like an adder.

"Nevertheless, he means to kill you."

"And would Pausanias really make such a bad king?"

Philip smiled and scratched his beard. He had slept very well, as he always did in the open, and he was feeling mischievous. But the jest was lost on Korous.

"They say he has grown immensely fat in exile," Korous answered glumly. "And he always was a cowardly, vindictive little worm. Do you remember, when we were children, how he caught us feeding apples to his horse and turned us over to stable master to be whipped?"

"We probably fed that horse twenty apples—we deserved whipping."

"He will make an excellent king from the Thracians' point of view."

"Then I will try to remember not to allow Berisades to cut my throat."

"What are you going to say to him?"

"To Pausanias? Why? Do you have a message for him?"

"Try to be serious, Philip. This business frightens me and you are playing on my nerves. What are you going to say to Berisades?"

Philip tilted his head a little to one side, giving the impression he was think-ing the matter over for the very first time. The truth was that he had thought of little else during this first month of his kingship.

"I will not tell him anything he does not already know," he said finally. "The great point will be to remind him that I know it too."

The arrangements had been carefully worked out. In almost his first act as king, Philip had dispatched emissaries to Thrace and Paionia, but it had taken the better part of a month to erect a framework for this meeting with King Berisades. King Agis of Paionia, his ministers made it known, was too advanced in age and too feeble to leave his capital, but anyone could have seen that this was diplomatic bluff—Agis was a crafty old bandit who would wait to see what Berisades could wring from the young king of Macedon and then ask for more. This gave the first meeting all the greater importance.

Philip had made the first concession by agreeing to come into Thracian territory, but he had asked in return that the encounter should take place outside the city of Eion, in the narrow wedge of land the Thracians occu-pied on the west bank of the Strymon River. This meant that at least he would not have to retreat back over water should Berisades set him a trap, but it represented a very narrow advantage because Eion itself was heavily fortified.

The site of the meeting was a great expanse of flatland bounded on the east by the river and on the south by the sea, which was visible only as a faint gray haze upon the skyline. West and north the waving, flower-dusted grass seemed to stretch on forever, making it one of the poorest places on earth for an ambush.

In three columns of five the main party of the Macedonians rode toward the river, which was far over the eastern horizon. Two patrols of ten each were on the northern and southern perimeter—no one was disposed to take any-thing on trust. When they saw a line of horsemen in the distance they came to a halt and formed themselves into a long row to give the Thracians an op-portunity to number their exact strength. Then the center of the row, twenty-five men in all with Philip in the midst, rode forward toward a precisely equal party of Thracians, which was advancing on them.

When the two groups were separated by perhaps two hundred paces they both came to a halt. Philip took his sword from its scabbard, waved it over his head, and then let it drop to the ground. Then a figure in the center of the Thracian line, presumably Berisades himself, drew his sword, flourished it, and let it fall. This was the signal for both men to advance toward the center of the empty plain, leaving their escorts behind.

As soon as they were about ten paces apart they both stopped, as if this too had been agreed in advance. For a moment the only sound was the whisper of the wind through the tall grass.

"You are younger than I anticipated," Berisades announced as if he expected his auditor to be as surprised as himself. He leaned forward across his horse's neck for a better view, and as he did so he grinned, showing a couple of broken stumps of teeth. "You are hardly more than a boy. The Macedonians might as well have chosen Perdikkas's little brat."

It was not an accusation anyone would have leveled at the king of the Thracians, whose throat was puckered in little folds and who already had the cynical, bored eyes one sometimes saw in the faces of men who had lived long enough to grow weary even of their sins. He was in fact about thirty-two years old, having reigned for eight years, since the death of his father, whose murder many believed him to have compassed.

"It was a close thing, but in the end they decided they needed someone who at least had all his teeth."

The new king of Macedon smiled, honing the point of the insult, and waited until Berisades' eyes darkened with recognition. The Thracian had a reputation for reckless violence that made him widely feared, even by his allies, but Philip judged that if he allowed himself to be bullied once by this man, who had the appearance of one who had never not yielded to an impulse, there would be no end to it.

At last Berisades threw back his head and laughed.

"I was told you have a sharp tongue. Be careful lest you cut your throat with it." He was still laughing, but his eyes narrowed in warning. "You are not in a position to make many enemies."

"I am not here to make enemies," Philip answered him, but in a tone that suggested that another, more or less, might not prove unbearable. "I have no shortage of enemies. I am here to persuade you to let me deal with them—one at a time, and in my own way."

"And why am I here?" He posed it as a real question. "I have only to raise my arm and Philip of Macedon can begin numbering out his life in minutes rather than years. What is there to prevent me?"

"The fact that you have already worked out for yourself that I am more dangerous to you dead than alive."

Berisades smiled, acknowledging, as far as he was able, that he had been surprised. He urged his horse forward a few paces, as if, in that vast emptiness of which the two of them were the center, he wished a more confidential word.

"Go on," he said. "I will listen a little longer to this impertinence."

"Is it impertinence for two kings to recognize between themselves their various points of weakness? We each have ambassadors to tell our lies for us, which leaves you and I the luxury of frankness."

Philip did not smile as he said this, and his blue-gray eyes held Berisades in their gaze with an intensity that was almost cruel. He waited until the other man was forced to glance away.

"My kingdom is threatened with dissolution," he went on. "The Illyrians are poised to take over the west, and the Athenians will try to seize control of the Thermaic Gulf as soon as it occurs to them they have the chance. In the north the Paionians will pick up what crumbs they can."

"And I too am not without my ambitions," Berisades broke in, looking at the king of the Macedonians exactly as if he wished to eat him, horse and all.

But he did not believe it. He was only exacting his revenge on Philip for not being able to frighten him, so Philip did not take it personally. Instead, he went on as if he had not heard the interruption.

"I think the Athenians will strike first. The Illyrians have not followed up their victory over my brother, so I believe they will wait—the gods know why, since it is not what I would have done in their place. But the stronger the Athenians grow in the Gulf, the more they will press upon the Chalcidians, until the league is forced to go over to them, and when that happens they will seal up all Thrace's approaches to the sea."

"I can stop them," Berisades murmured, half to himself. Philip noticed that he was glancing nervously about, as if afraid the waving grass about his horse's hooves might be hostile infantry. "With my help the league can continue to resist."

Now it was Philip's turn to laugh.

"The league will not look to you," he said with something akin to scorn. "What is Thrace but a thinly peopled waste on the edge of the world? You cannot field the army that Athens could buy with a month's harbor dues. Do you understand now? If I fall, how long before it is your turn? My survival is your survival—we need each other."

For a moment Berisades looked at him with real fear. It was not Athens he feared, or the collapse of his alliance with the Chalcidian League—it was Philip himself, who, for all his youth, gazed out at the world with such cold, knowing eyes. Philip made him feel his vulnerability, feel it as he might a cold wind, and his own fear was made all the more terrible by his growing suspicion that this boy might not be afraid of anything.

"What is it you want from me?" he asked finally, a little surprised by the sound of his own words. It almost seemed as if he were the supplicant.

"Time." Philip reached down and ran the palm of his hand over Alastor's black neck. He did not even look at the Thracian king. "Time to rebuild my army. Time to look about me and get ready for war against the Illyrians. I am prepared to pay for peace with Thrace, but I would warn you against driving too hard a bargain. If I perish, in a year's time there will be an Illyrian king on the throne in Pella and I don't imagine you will care for Bardylis as a neighbor—after all, what will there be to stop him from riding east until he has conquered all the lands between here and the Bosporus? And then the old bandit will be the Persian king's problem, because you and I will both be dead."

Once, when he was a very small boy, Berisades had been caught in some minor offense—at this distance of time, he could not even remember what it was—and his father had ordered him flogged like a slave and locked naked in an iron oven in the kitchens. His father had told him that he would decide later whether to start a fire under the oven, but that for the time being he was to stay there, in the dark, huddled in a space so tiny he had to keep his head between his knees. He had been left alone like that for three hours, and all the time the only thing he could think of was the fact that his father was precisely the sort of man who would be capable of ordering his only son roasted like a joint of mutton. He had never forgotten the experience. Even into manhood it still haunted his dreams, putting him back in that black hole, waiting for the walls to heat up. It had taught him to hate his father, in whose death he had rejoiced, and it had taught him the terror of utter helplessness.

And that was why he hated the king of Macedon, who was once more slamming the iron doors in his face. One day, he promised himself, he would have his revenge, just as he had had his revenge against his father, but that day was not yet. For the present he knew, and he had known then, that his only chance lay in acquiescence.

"And what am I to do about the Lord Pausanias?" he asked. "Do you propose it as part of our arrangement that he be killed?"

For a moment Philip seemed lost in some private abstraction so that he hardly seemed conscious of where he was. And then he turned his eyes on the king of the Thracians and smiled the coldest smile Berisades had ever seen.

"Yes," he said. "It is part of the arrangement."

Philip's conversation with the king of the Thracians lasted hardly more than an hour. When he returned to his own escort it was impossible to tell from his face whether there was to be peace or war. When Korous asked him he only shook his head.

"What did you offer him?"

"A chance to survive," Philip answered, "along with one hundred and fifty gold talents."

"One hundred and fifty?" Korous shook his head incredulously. "How can you possibly pay such a sum?"

"It is a trifle—the king of the Paionians, when he hears, will doubtless ask for two hundred."

"What will you do?"

"What will I do?" For a moment he seemed absorbed in the task of adjusting his horse's bridle, then he managed a sidewise glance at Korous and grinned. "I will cultivate all the arts of a king. I will lie, cheat, and grasp at every pretext for delay. I have pledged myself to fifteen talents within the month and the rest over ten years, but I haven't the slightest intention of keeping that pledge—I think even Berisades understands as much."

"A year from now he will expect to be paid again."

"I may be dead by then, but if I am not, we will see if he has the temerity to press his claim, or if I have the strength to refuse."

Philip said no more, and Korous did not press him, for he had learned to respect the closely guarded silences with which his royal master surrounded himself. What Philip wished him to know he would hear from his own lips—for the rest, the king's mind was open to no man's inspection.

They camped on the same spot as the night before, on a bluff close to Lake Kerkinitis. The evening was very still and they could hear the water lapping against the shore. Philip talked about horse racing, which was a sure sign his mind was elsewhere.

"I should have liked to ride Alastor in the Pithian Games, but he is too old now—he still has his stamina, but I am afraid he might tear a muscle running against two-year-olds. After all, he might lose and then I would have offended against his dignity. The first year I owned him, though, he was a match for any horse from here to the Peloponnese."

After a time he gave up even the pretext of conversation and lapsed into a moody stillness.

The next morning Korous woke up about half an hour before dawn and found his king already building a fire.

"Didn't you sleep?" he asked.

"I have an itch to get away from here," Philip answered, smiling as if he found something ridiculous in the fact. "I have the feeling that something unpleasant is lying in wait for us here."

"Are you expecting Berisades to ambush us?"

"No." Philip shook his head. "No, if he intended anything like that we would already be dead. Not that, but something . . ."

During the ride back to Heraklea Sintika he seemed to forget about it. He jested with the soldiers in his escort and listened with evident amusement to an obscene song about a donkey and a boatman's daughter. He was his own self again, the Philip Korous had known all his life.

And then, about an hour short of noon, Alastor seemed to grow nervous, whinnying and shaking his head. Philip reined him in and held up his arm, not so much to force a halt as to command silence.

"What is it?" Korous asked.

"I don't know—is . . ."

Philip turned his great stallion to face the direction from which they had come. He put a hand on the black neck and leaned forward.

"You sense something, don't you?" he murmured, almost in the horse's ear. "Do you know yet what it might be?"

But there was nothing. Philip stared back at an empty skyline.

And then, at last, there was something, no more than a tiny speck in the distance, like a grain of sand rolling soundlessly toward them.

"It is a man on horseback." Korous watched with the keen attention of a hunting dog, his eyes screwed almost shut. "One man, no more. He is riding fast."

"Then we will stop and let him catch up with us—if only out of compassion for his mount."

The wait was harder on Philip's men than on him, for they naturally feared the worst. A few of them slid down from their horses and knelt on the ground to retension the strings on their bows.

"One man does not make war against a hundred," Philip said. "Whatever he wants, he means us no harm. Let no one do anything foolish."

Long before they could hear the beat of the horse's hooves, they saw that the man was wearing Thracian dress. The wind was blowing toward them, and by the time he was close enough to hail they could taste his dust on the wind.

When he was about seventy-five or eighty paces distant he pulled his horse to an abrupt stop. For a moment he surveyed the line of men ranged against him, as if to be sure of not making a mistake, then he pulled something from a leather bag tied to his waist—something about the size and shape of a melon—and threw it contemptuously to the ground. In the next second he wheeled about and galloped back the way he had come.

Philip waited several minutes, long enough for him to get well away.

"Let us see what Berisades has gone to so much trouble about," he said at last.

It was a man's head, badly battered yet still recognizable. The lips were torn and hideously swollen, and one eye was missing. The condition of the bruises suggested that most but not all had been inflicted before death.

The last time Philip had seen it, it had rested on the shoulders of his cousin Pausanias.

He dismounted, took off his cloak, and wrapped the head in it.

"I want this purified and buried. A gold coin in the mouth—the whole ritual." His face, when he looked up, was like a stone mask.

"Why?" Korous asked, accepting the bundle. "Why did they do this to him?"

"They killed him because that was part of what I bought with my hundred and fifty gold talents. The gods know why they chose to do it so savagely.

A warning perhaps—or to avenge themselves for having been obliged to betray him. Does a man like Berisades need a reason?"

Philip shook his head, as if abandoning some treasured illusion.

"Yet I am no better than he, for this blood is more on my hands than on his. We are just the same. We are what a man becomes when others will make of him a king."

36

As he approached his ninetieth year Bardylis, king of the Dardanians, was forced to concede that he was in the deep twilight of his life. It had been a long time coming, but now, as he felt his strength ebbing almost from day to day, he could sense the approach of his last hour the way one can feel a hint of winter in the wind. His own guess was that he would be dead within two years.

And, as a consequence, he had no choice but to turn over more and more of the burden of power to his grandson Pleuratos. This was a greater grief to him even than the approach of death, for he disliked and feared Pleuratos. Not for his own sake, since he had lived too long to treasure any fear for himself. His fears were centered on the future he would not survive to see.

No man relishes the prospect of his life's work going down to destruction, and Bardylis knew, with almost the clarity of memory, as if he had watched it happen and could recall at his leisure the stages of the catastrophe, that his grandson would never be able to hold together the empire he had so painstakingly accumulated. Even now, while he was still alive, he had to witness Pleuratos blundering into this useless war with Macedon.

"I don't know why you're so anxious about it," Pleuratos had said in his usual tone of injury. "We have extended and solidified our control over the whole border region—Lynkos is virtually a province. We have destroyed the Macedonian army and their king is dead. I had expected to hear myself congratulated for the completeness of my victory."

"They have another king now, or hadn't you heard?"

"Philip?" Pleuratos indulged himself in a contemptuous shrug. "He is no more than an impetuous boy. I have taken his measure."

"Or so you thought once before, when you tried to have him murdered."

It was an old grievance between them. Bardylis knew all about the pact his grandson had made with Ptolemy and, the breach of hospitality aside, he had never been able to forgive the flagrant stupidity of the whole enterprise. It was the sort of crass ploy that gambled everything in hopes of winning a trifle. He could date from that incident, from the morning he had put Philip on a horse and told him to run for his life, the hardening of his doubts into a conviction. Pleuratos was not fit to be anything more than a tribal headman. He lacked any sense of his own weaknesses as measured against the strengths of others. He had no understanding of diplomacy, which was no more than the art of turning weakness into the appearance of strength—he seemed to have no understanding of anything except perhaps war. His reign would have the character of an extended raiding party. If there had been anyone else—if even one other of his sons or grandsons were still alive—Bardylis would long since have arranged to have the idiot's throat cut. He would have done it himself, cheerfully.

And to think how easily Philip, instead of this oaf, might have been his successor.

"It remains a fact that their army has been destroyed," Pleuratos answered after a long, sullen silence. "A king is not much of a king if he has no army."

"Philip will have an army soon enough. But that isn't the point."

"Then what is the point?"

"The point is that we don't want Macedon, because we haven't the strength to hold it—I learned that lesson while you were still playing with wooden swords, when I drove Amyntas out of Pella. He came back—I couldn't keep him out. I found I could not hold so much territory, which remained aggressively hostile, without being overextended. It is better to have Macedon as it is now, weak and pliant, than to end by becoming so weakened ourselves that soon we will not be able to hold on to anything."

"You seem to forget that I won!" Pleuratos almost shouted. "Perdikkas, along with most of his army, is dead!"

"I think you will discover one day that Philip is a very different bowl of porridge."

"Is that why you insisted that his brother's body be returned to him? Is it possible you are afraid of him?"

"No, I am not afraid of him." Bardylis shook his head at the impossibility of making himself understood. "But you should be."

But it was not for reasons of policy alone that the king of the Dardanians forbade his grandson to pursue war against Macedon. His real motives were not those of a practical ruler, nor were they of a character that he would have dared reveal to Pleuratos.

The truth was that the approach of death had freed Bardylis from one kind of ambition only to enslave him to another. He had spent a lifetime acquiring a vast empire, and the fact of the empire itself was what mattered to him—only that. He had begun by wishing to see his own nation a great people, rulers over their neighbors, masters of vast wealth and power. After all, was he not their king? Was not his final loyalty to them? Once, perhaps, but no longer. Now he looked upon this tribe of brutal savages with something approaching contempt. He no longer even thought of himself as a Dardanian. The Dardanians were merely one more among his instruments, another possession like his horse.

What mattered was that his own blood should continue to hold sway over the territories he had forced into submission to his will. With time—and it might be the work of generations—these territories would be enlarged until one day his descendants ruled all the lands between the Adriatic and the Black Sea. But he had outlived all his sons, and Pleuratos was an idiot. In the one thing upon which he had set his heart he was baffled, rendering empty the long series of triumphs that had filled his life.

Yet there was Philip, who was also of his race. In Philip Bardylis saw himself as a young man. Philip, had he not been a Macedonian, had he not suffered the crushing disadvantage of being born into the royal house of that fractious and excessively civilized kingdom, might have become . . . Well, he might have become almost anything.

It was a great pity. In a year or two, probably, Philip would be murdered or would perish in battle, after which there must inevitably follow a long, murky struggle for the succession while what was left of the House of the Argeadai poured its royal blood into the ground. If he chanced still to be alive by then, Bardylis thought he might with luck be able to procure the election of a candidate favorable to himself, but it would hardly make any difference. The king of Macedon was always destined to be a nonentity, simply by virtue of the fact that he was king of Macedon. The title carried with it the twin curses of obscurity and defeat.

Philip had been such a promising boy—it was all very much to be regretted.

The king of the Dardanians had an almost daily reminder of precisely how much in his great-granddaughter Audata who, at eighteen, should long since have been married off to one king or another. She remained in her father's house because Bardylis, in his old age, had discovered that he loved this bewitching girl far more than any of the multitude of children who could claim to be his descendants. He loved her enough, in fact, that he had once foolishly made her a promise that he would never force upon her a husband not to her taste—a promise that had turned out to have been a serious mistake, for little Audata, the glance of whose catlike eyes had captivated more than a few of the world's great men, had steadfastly turned away every suitor who had found his way to Bardylis's court. So many, in fact, that it had become something of a diplomatic embarrassment. When he had taxed her with it, asking her why she persisted in being so unreasonably fastidious, she had revealed her secret heart to him—had confided to him the thing that, perhaps, he had least wished to hear.

"Do you remember, when I was a child?" she had asked him as if obliging him to reach far back into the distant past. "Do you remember that you told me once I would be the wife of a great king?"

"Yes. I recall it perfectly," Bardylis answered, smiling at the memory—for her so remote, yet for him so recent. "There are many such in the world, and you have refused full half of them. What, for instance, is amiss with Lyppeios of Paionia? He is a presentable boy and the eldest son of an old and sickly father. Only wait a year or two for Agis to die. Or is Paionia not good enough to satisfy your ambition?"

"A handsome nonentity who happens to rule over a vast and wealthy dominion is not a great king."

She pronounced this sentence with such quiet assurance that the king of the Dardanians, who considered himself great by any standard, was much taken aback. When had she formed such settled opinions? It would be worth something to know, yet one could hardly ask. Bardylis could only marvel and wish that fool Pleuratos had half his daughter's insight.

"It is clear you set a high standard for greatness," he said at last. "I wonder if any man living can meet it."

"Only two have met it."

She turned a little away from him, as if embarrassed, and favored him with a sidelong glimpse of one of her shy, subtle, feline smiles. She was playing on his vanity and his affection for her—this he knew perfectly well, and knew that she knew he knew. It made no difference, for the smile had its desired effect.

"You are the first, Great-Grandfather, and in all the world you have but one peer."

"And I gather that Lyppeios of Paionia is not he."

"No. This man is of your seed. He came here once as a prisoner. I have never forgotten him."

Bardylis, king of the Dardanians, felt a sinking in his heart such as a man might experience on the brink of combat when he sees that his enemy's strength is overwhelming, for how far had Philip of Macedon ever been from his own thoughts?

"He was hardly more than a boy then," he said, noticing only after he had spoken that he not thought it necessary to pronounce the name. This somehow profoundly humiliating discovery prompted him to take his revenge. "It would appear he has forgotten you, since he has already taken and buried one wife."

When he saw the change in her face, Bardylis instantly regretted his own cruelty—Audata always had that advantage over him, that she could make him feel whatever she felt.

"Besides, I love you too much to give you to him," he went on quickly. "He will probably be dead before the winter. You are too young to be a widow and, besides, no king of Macedon will ever be great."

"He is great already," she answered, with unsettling seriousness. "It is a quality in himself. He would have it if he were the master of your stables."

"Well, it is unlikely he will ever have much chance to show it."

Poor child, she seemed destined to misery, for what could be more hopeless than the love that attached itself to a doomed man? Surely she was destined to shed many tears.

Yet perhaps not right away. Bardylis could still derive some pleasure from thwarting the lunatic ambitions of his grandson, so the day when the new king of Macedon was to be crushed had not yet come.

Come it must, though. And then, when her dream was shattered and she was forced to submit herself to the commonplace glory of someone like Lyppeios of Paionia, little Audata would taste the full bitterness of her grief. It was enough to make an old man glad at last to part with life.

37

Arrhidaios had never really adjusted to life in exile. Athens was an entertaining and comfortable city, and certain friends with trading interests in the north had provided him with a pension suitable to his rank and his potential usefulness, but he had never felt at ease there. It was not that he was homesick. It was not Macedon or his circle of friends and family there he missed. It was something else he had abandoned that night after the death of Alexandros, when he had fled the purge he knew the Lord Ptolemy was about to unleash against anyone among the House of the Argeadai who might have constituted a threat to his power. It was rather the sense of being taken seriously. In Athens he simply was not important enough that it would cross anyone's mind to have him murdered.

Thus his reaction, when he received Philip's letter, was complex.

It was delivered with disagreeable informality by Aristotle, who had just come back from visiting his father in Pella. The two young men had known each other from childhood, but in Athens they hardly ever met. Aristotle, doubtless, was only displaying a very natural caution, understandable enough when one remembered that Arrhidaios had been attainted before the assembly as a traitor, yet it was not an omission that was likely to go unresented—Arrhidaios, like all exiles, had developed a long memory for slights. Thus, when Aristotle called one morning at the house Arrhidaios rented not far from the Stoa of Zeus, and a servant showed him into the small walled garden where the master was having breakfast, his reception was not particularly cordial.

"How many years has it been?" Arrhidaios inquired without preamble. When Aristotle failed to reply, he smiled thinly.

"Six, or perhaps even seven," he went on, answering his own question. "I think, therefore, I am entitled to be surprised."

"You are no more surprised than I." Without waiting to be asked, Aristotle sat down on a marble bench next to the tiny fountain that occupied the center of the garden. "You of course are offended that I have avoided you all these years, but under the circumstances that is rather childish of you—Pella is not Athens, but I prefer to be at liberty to return to it now and again. I am not in a position to ignore the prejudices of the mighty."

"Then why are you here now?"

"Because the mighty have sent me."

Arrhidaios was sufficiently startled that, without thinking, he filled a cup of wine and handed it to Aristotle.

"And how does Philip enjoy being a king?" Arrhidaios inquired when he had regained his composure.

Aristotle, after tasting the wine, made a face and set the cup down.

"I don't have the impression he thinks of it in such personal terms," he said, somehow managing to make the reply sound like a rebuke. "He is very active, but he was always that. I would say he is much the same."

"Yet a man would have to be made of wood if he did not find some pleasure in such eminence."

"I think he would trade all his 'eminence' for half a month's rationing of his army. You know him. He was never proud. One hardly notices that he is a king."

When Arrhidaios began to smile with something like contempt, Aristotle merely added, "Yet I think he has more real authority than did even his father. Does that surprise you? Men may still call him 'Philip,' but they obey him in the same way they breathe—without considering why."

"And what does he want of me?"

"I have no idea." Aristotle seemed to look at nothing as he spoke. "He is a king, remember? On this matter I am not in his confidence."

He reached into a fold of his tunic and brought out a small scroll, which he offered to Arrhidaios, who stared at it a long moment before accepting it. The scroll was closed with a daub of wax impressed with the seal of Macedon. When Arrhidaios broke it open he could see that the parchment was covered with a loose, flowing script that was unmistakably Philip's.

"I will leave you now," Aristotle murmured, somehow contriving to sound as if he had just made the decisive point and was savoring his triumph. "Doubtless you are anxious for privacy."

Yet Arrhidaios had been alone for some time before it occurred to him to read this letter from the king of the Macedonians—for perhaps a quarter of an hour he simply held it in his hand and looked at it, as if the mere fact of its existence were sufficiently astonishing to prevent him from inquiring further. There was even a sense in which he almost dreaded to know what it said.

At last, however, he unrolled the parchment.

"My beloved friend and brother," Philip began—a promising start, Arrhidaios thought; at least it did not begin like a writ on condemnation—"I wish you to hear from me what I hope you would have understood without being told, that you are at liberty to return to Pella without fear. You will of course have to present yourself before the assembly, since it is not within even a king's authority to set aside the indictment that stands against you, but everyone knows that you had no hand in Alexandros's death and I have only to say, 'This man was falsely accused and enjoys my full confidence in his innocence,' and the matter will be dropped forever. Have no fear on that point, since your trial will be no more than a form, but the forms of the law must be respected. Once that is done, your property will be returned and you will be free to resume the life to which your rank entitles you. I would make what amends are in my power for the injustice you have suffered."

Arrhidaios put down the scroll for a moment, glad there was no one present to witness the tears that were welling up in his eyes as he seemed to feel, and as if for the first time, the weight of his eight long years of exile burdening his soul. *To resume the life to which your rank entitles you.*

He could hardly imagine what that life might be like. He had been little more than a child when his brother Archelaos had roused him from his bed in the small hours of the morning with the astonishing news that they had to flee for their lives. *Lord Ptolemy has already spoken of us as rejoicing in the king's death. It is but a short step now to an accusation of treason and murder, and to be accused from that quarter is to be condemned.*

Poor Archelaos, who had died of a fever in Corinth during that first wretched year of exile. Who would make amends to him? Arrhidaios found all at once that his heart writhed with anger against the whole House of the Argeadai, against the living and the dead, who had so despoiled his life.

His eyes fell on the last few lines of Philip's letter.

"Come home, my brother, for I have need of you. The wolves are circling and I will be easier in my mind for having those about me whom I can trust."

Trust. What a sentiment—what a sickening jest! In a family that writhed with conspiracies like vipers in a sack, who but Philip could ever have been naive enough to use that word to a kinsman? Among the sons and grandsons of Macedon's kings, the trusting ones were all dead.

Yet it did not enter Arrhidaios's mind to doubt the genuineness of Philip's offer. The only question was how best to make use of it.

Arrhidaios's mother, Gygaia, had been Amyntas's first wife, but for many years she had proved barren and the old king had married a Lynkestian princess who bore him a son, Alexandros, followed by a daughter. Then Gygaia, her lord's favorite but long since despaired of, had unexpectedly borne three sons in four years. Had Alexandros not outlived their father, Archelaos would

have been king in his place and the line of succession would have run to Arrhidaios, since, although Menelaos, the eldest of the three, had died before
reaching manhood, Archelaos had been a year older than Perdikkas, just as
Arrhidaios himself was two months older than Philip. Thus had chance been
the arbiter of all their destinies, so that Philip was now king and Arrhidaios
was an exile, suffered at last to return to his homeland as a useful and harmless instrument, when there was not a hair's breadth of difference between
their claims by birth.

It had not mattered when they were children, neither able to imagine any
life for themselves except that of subject, minor princes fit to fight in the
king's wars and, perhaps, sit at council with the other nobles. Then they had
loved each other, never giving a thought to the obscure quarrel that divided
their elders. But the Fates had intervened and swept away almost all of the whole
of the House of the Argeadai, leaving them to their unequal destinies. Now it
did matter.

Now, it seemed to Arrhidaios, the world was no longer quite big enough
to hold both him and Philip. It appeared a cramped place, where they must
constantly be disagreeably rubbing shoulders, making the presence of each a
grievance to the other. Perhaps Philip felt this as well as he, but a king will
always have the means to make himself comfortable. Philip, probably, hardly
even noticed.

Arrhidaios did not believe his brother to be guilty of condescension—he
was not small-minded enough to injure him with that accusation, not even
in his private heart—but that the offer proceeded from a genuine affection
and was meant to redress an injury that Philip took almost as his own somehow made it worse. It galled Arrhidaios thus to have his birthright returned
to him as a favor, to see himself offered up as an example to posterity of
Philip's generosity and sense of justice. What claim, superior to his own, did
Philip have to be the dispenser of magnanimity? Who was Philip that he
enjoyed the power to pardon or condemn while Arrhidaios, a king's son as
he was, in no way his inferior—was not Arrhidaios the elder, and had not his
mother been the great-granddaughter of Alexandros the First, called the
"Philhellene," when Philip's mother was a mountain barbarian, hardly better than a savage?—was made to feel so utterly at his mercy? It was simply
intolerable.

Such was his frame of mind when, in the afternoon of that same day, he
received another visitor, this time his friend Demosthenes.

Philip was not the only one who had prospered since the three of them had
met on the steps of Aristodemos's house all those years ago. Demosthenes had
flourished in the law courts, accumulating a considerable personal fortune
and, more importantly, at least to him, had come to be thought of as one of

the prime movers of the Athenian state. He had never lost his air of dissatis-faction, however, and as he sat on a bench in Arrhidaios's reception room he looked, for all the gold thread in the border of his tunic, as if life had some-how cruelly disappointed him.

"I am informed you are to be congratulated," Arrhidaios said to him when it looked as if his visitor would never speak, so busy he seemed in counting over his grievances. "Everyone is talking about your prosecution of Andro-tion. I hear your speeches quoted everywhere."

"The man is a fool," Demosthenes answered as if the statement were simul-taneously an incontestable fact and the flaw that robbed his victory of its sweetness. "He imagines, after all these years, that we should still follow a policy of hostility toward the Persians—can you credit such a thing? One day I will succeed in driving him from public life."

"One wonders what you will do then." When the great statesman raised an eyebrow, perhaps as much an expression of astonished inquiry he was capable of, Arrhidaios smiled and went on. "It is simply that your life seems fueled by your hatreds, my friend. What will become of you when you have vanquished all your enemies?"

Demosthenes acknowledged the justice of the observation with a faint smile of his own.

"Then I will take Athens's enemies as mine and vanquish them—as a na-tion we seem to have enough to last me."

"Well, it is possible you may soon have one less."

But if Arrhidaios had expected the pleasure of surprising his guest twice he appeared to have been disappointed, for Demosthenes' features underwent not the slightest alteration. For a moment Arrhidaios couldn't even be sure if he had heard him.

"I take it, then, that you have received some word from your brother the king of Macedon."

Demosthenes' voice expressed a certain resigned boredom, as if the world had grown so predictable that he could hardly bear to live in it, but of course someone had told him of Philip's letter. Arrhidaios was not stupid enough not to have guessed long ago that his servants were paid to inform on him—it simply hadn't occurred to him that they were paid by Demosthenes.

"Did he invite you to return home? What did he promise you? Whatever it was, you would be a fool to accept it."

"You are rather too fond of calling everyone a fool today," Arrhidaios re-plied, not really offended—not even by the fact that his friend had appar-ently placed a spy in his household. "Yet I am curious. Why would I be a fool to accept it?"

"Because at the moment Macedon has too many enemies ranged against her, and no powerful friend to keep them at bay. It is obvious to anyone who takes the trouble to look that Philip's reign will not last out another year. And if you go home, you will most assuredly share his fate. Provided, of course, that he does not have you killed the first hour you are inside his borders."

"And why would he have me killed?"

At first the only answer was a cruel little laugh.

"My dear Arrhidaios, I should have thought that point would not need to be explained to a member of your family." Demosthenes shook his head and seemed about to break into another fit of laughter, but suddenly he became quite sober. "What king can bear the presence of a rival, and how can your brother, in his precarious position, afford to leave you alive when your claim to the throne is as good as his? No, no, my friend—if you go home you are as good as dead."

For the first time since he had received Philip's letter, Arrhidaios felt a stab of fear in his bowels. Yet it could not be true . . .

"I have known Philip all my life," he said, his face a grim mask. "He loves me. And, besides, he is not treacherous. It is simply not in his character to betray me."

"You remember him from when you were boys together. He is not a boy now. He is a king. And kingship changes a man—it makes him see things differently, which is why Athens has long since put aside her kings. You cannot trust your life to the impressions of childhood. Besides, he has already had your cousin Pausanias put to death."

Yes—Arrhidaios had heard the story. But certainly that was different. That was . . .

"Pausanias had committed treason. Already in Alexandros's time, Pausanias had declared himself the rightful king and had called upon the people to revolt. And besides—"

"And besides, Pausanias was not Philip's dear brother and friend," interrupted Demosthenes, his expression one of contemptuous pity. "Yet the kings of Macedon are not famous for honoring the ties of affection. And remember that Philip sits uneasily upon his throne—he is unlikely to be so precise in his understanding of what constitutes treason."

A servant came into the room with a tray bearing a pitcher of wine and two cups. Guest and host sat across from each other in silence as the slave girl set the tray on the table between them and padded away soundlessly on bare feet. The interruption lasted no longer than half a minute, but, like a break in a storm, it was long enough for Arrhidaios to look about him and survey the wreckage of his life.

He did not know if he trusted Demosthenes or not, but trust, in this instance, was not a precondition for belief and he believed it was possible that Demosthenes, for reasons of his own, might be speaking the truth. In any case, he could see that he had been naive to imagine he could simply return to Macedon and resume his old life.

He did not know if he believed Philip capable of so calculated a treachery as to invite him home and then have him murdered. He did not think so. Yet he recognized that it was in his interest to believe it—he wanted to believe it. He wanted an excuse to avoid submitting himself to the will and fortunes of his brother. He found he had no desire to be Philip's loyal subject, so perhaps after all Philip had really forfeited any claim on his loyalty. It was almost a relief to suppose that his brother might have put a dagger in some assassin's hand.

Sometimes it takes no more than half a minute for the pattern of one's whole life to reveal itself.

"So what would you have me do?" he asked when once more the two men were alone—Demosthenes, he noticed, was watching him from the other side of the table the way a fox watches a chicken. "If I stay in Athens, if I do not accept this invitation, then certainly Philip will number me among his enemies."

"That he almost certainly does already." Demosthenes smiled as if at some private triumph. "But I am not recommending that you stay in Athens. I think you should return to Macedon."

At first Arrhidaios could only stare blankly at his guest, as if he had been posed an insoluble riddle, and then, quite suddenly, he grasped the full significance of the suggestion.

"I wonder, my friend Demosthenes," he said at last, "if you might be able to stay for dinner."

Although still officially a student, Aristotle had ceased attending lectures. He kept his rooms at the academy and made abundant use of its library, pursuing his own inquiries in biology and politics, but there was hardly anyone there under whom he felt it would profit him to study. And this was not simply the vanity of a self-consciously brilliant youth. Plato was old now and took little part in discussions, and the intellectual tendencies among the younger men who were destined to succeed him were not much to Aristotle's taste. Speusippos, for instance, whom everyone thought likely to fill the master's place one day, was so in love with geometry that he imagined all philosophical questions could be reduced to mathematics. Art, law, medicine, the management of governments, the nature of society—to men like Speusippos these things were little more than vulgar shadows. No, when Plato was in his burial urn it would be time to go.

But in the meantime there was the library, perhaps the finest in Greece, and Athens itself was an education to anyone who took the trouble to look about him. During a single evening Aristotle might learn more in the houses of the mighty, houses that were always open to bright young men from the academy, than he would in a month of pondering over dusty old scrolls. He did not mind the dusty old scrolls—in fact, he rather liked them—but knowledge of a practical character had its uses too. For one thing, it gave him something to put into his letters to Philip, who, since becoming king, had paid him a regular stipend to be his eyes and ears among his enemies in that city.

There was nothing secret about the arrangement. Everyone knew that he had grown up with the lord of the Macedonians, and Aristotle was just as willing to be bribed for information about Philip as he was to take Philip's silver for spying on the Athenians. He would never have sold out his friend, but the rulers of Athens were generally fools who imagined they had learned something of significance if they heard that Philip, whose very name none of them had ever heard even half a year since, could quote Homer, was an excellent horseman, and cared nothing for the sexual attentions of little boys. Simply by virtue of the fact that he could describe the new king of Macedon, Aristotle had become a popular guest at the tables where political discussions were fashionable.

Beyond this, one gathered that the great men of the city, opposed as they probably were to monarchy as an instrument of government, took a certain pleasure in the thought that their names might appear in a letter that would be scanned by the eyes of a king. No doubt it raised their sense of their own importance to know they had been mentioned as one of those belonging to such-and-such a party advocating such-and-such a policy. And, besides, it was always remotely possible that this young and unknown king might outlast the first year of his reign. It was not unthinkable that his influence might one day count for something in the obscure power struggles of the northern barbarians—one or two of the more farsighted among Athens's democratic rulers had even offered Aristotle gifts of no negligible value if he could make their views known in Pella.

But Demosthenes was not among them, and no doubt he would have been happy to decline the honor of being reported as both a frequent visitor in the house of Arrhidaios and an advocate of a more active and hostile policy against the weakness of the Macedonian state. After all, Philip was likely to see some connection between the two.

"There is much talk of some sort of expedition," Aristotle wrote to him. "I do not know if it will lead to anything—there is always talk of expeditions, but the Athenians do not spend their money willingly—yet I believe you must assume that Arrhidaios is lost to you. It has been a week since I delivered your letter and I have heard nothing from him. If he had any thought of returning home, surely he would have given me some message for you. Not wishing to force him into declaring himself, I have not visited him again, but there is nothing to suggest he contemplates a journey. He still accepts invitations, and he has not notified the owner of his house that he intends to vacate. If Demosthenes' plots ever come to anything, I think you will find your brother ranged against you."

Aristotle sealed the letter with a blob of hot wax and put it in a drawer. There was a ship leaving for Methone in the morning, and one of the crew members was a Macedonian who could be trusted. In a week Philip would know that he was betrayed.

38

Philip was at dinner when he received word that an envoy had arrived from Lynkos and craved an audience at the king's earliest convenience. He kept the ambassador waiting for half a month. There was no hurry. Waiting, after all, was every ambassador's true profession, and relations with his uncle Menelaos, who had signed a treaty of alliance with the Illyrians, could hardly be worse. Besides, Philip had already guessed what the man would have to say to him.

Menelaos had probably learned by now that, dangerous as the Illyrians were as enemies, they were even more dangerous as friends. He was reported to be under pressure from his allies and wanted to reach an accord to keep Bardylis out. Very well. Menelaos was a treacherous fool, but Lynkos was part of Macedon and Philip was loath to see her overrun. The problem was that he had no means of preventing it.

All the more reason to keep the ambassador waiting.

In the meantime he sent dispatch riders to all the garrison commanders along the northwestern frontier, ordering them to send spies into Lynkos to discover if men were being conscripted out of the villages. It was harvest time, and in two months the mountain passes would begin to fill up with snow—if Menelaos was putting the country on a war footing it meant that he expected to be at war with the Illyrians before the end of summer.

And in the meantime he received Aristotle's letter. It seemed he might be at war himself in a short time and, in any case, Arrhidaios was not coming home.

He showed the letter to Glaukon, whose reaction was not what he expected.

"Which did you feel first," the old man asked, "grief or anger?"

"Grief—then fear. I dread a war with Athens."

"But your heart did not harden against Arrhidaios?"

"No."

"And you would have welcomed him back?"

"Yes. He is my brother and my friend."

"That only proves you have not yet learned to see life through the eyes of a king, for whom those nearest to him in blood are to be trusted least. I only hope your faith in family affection is not your undoing."

This made Philip laugh. It was not a pleasant sound.

"I am unlikely to make the same mistake again," he said. "There is no one left."

Glaukon shook his head, as if he found the jest to be in questionable taste.

"You should marry again, Lord. You should breed up sons in whom you can invest your love."

"Because it is my duty as a king?"

"It is not the king's suffering I pity, Lord Philip, but yours."

"If Arrhidaios brings an Athenian army against me, and if I live, I will be the means of his death."

"I know this. I know."

After he had spoken with Glaukon, Philip burned Aristotle's letter. He did not mention it to any of his lieutenants. He never spoke Arrhidaios's name. He merely told them that they must watch for any signs that the Athenians were strengthening their forces in Pydna and Methone.

On the fifteenth day after his arrival, the ambassador from King Menelaos was shown into Philip's study.

His name was Klitos. Philip remembered him from his one visit to Lynkos, and he seemed an odd choice if Menelaos had sent his envoy to beg for aid, for he was a large, loud, overbearing sort of man, in his middle years and openly rather contemptuous of anyone he might consider as being in any sense his inferior, be it in rank or wealth or even experience of life. Perhaps, it occurred to Philip, his uncle imagined he could be bullied into an alliance.

"I have been in Pella for some time already," Klitos began, hardly even troubling with the customary pleasantries. "I am not accustomed to be kept waiting."

"It is the usual fate of petitioners."

Philip smiled pleasantly—he might have been discussing some third person about whom they were both naturally indifferent.

"I am even a little surprised that my uncle would have sent a person such as yourself," he went on, after giving the insult a moment to penetrate. "But perhaps he felt that, after all, it is the message that is important and not the messenger."

It was a sort of test. If Klitos was not accustomed to waiting, he was also not accustomed to the necessity of controlling his temper, and Philip was

more than a little curious to see just how much rudeness the man was prepared to suffer. It would serve as an indication of how afraid he was of returning home having failed in his mission, which in turn might say something
about the real situation in Lynkos.

Klitos's face darkened as the muscles in his jaws worked, but he said nothing. He even tried to act as if he hadn't heard. Clearly, Menelaos was in serious trouble.

"It was a great disappointment to my brother Perdikkas when the Lord
Menelaos chose to form an alliance with the Illyrians." Philip walked over to
his desk and sat down, without inviting Klitos to take the chair opposite. "It
was an insult to the loyalty he owes to the royal house of Macedon and, worse
than that, it was a mistake."

Significantly, Klitos left both assertions unchallenged. He merely looked
uncomfortable, as if the delinquencies of which Philip spoke were all his own,
and he was at last being called to account to them.

"I assume that my uncle has entrusted you with some message for me."

To hear these words was obviously a relief, for the king of Lynkos's ambassador instantly straightened his shoulders, as if an immense weight had
been lifted from them. Now, at last, he could trust himself to speak.

"The Lord Menelaos remembers with pleasure how the Lord Philip,
wounded and in flight, came to the Kingdom of Lynkos as to a place of safety,"
Klitos began, reciting a piece he had obviously been at some trouble to commit
to memory. "He was beset with enemies then, and the ruler of the Lynkestians
gave refuge to his sister's child. Now, once again, when Macedon is torn and
harried like a fawn set upon by savage dogs, Lord Menelaos would extend to
you his protection not as one king offers alliance to another but as an uncle
takes a father's place for his orphaned nephew . . ."

There was more, all in the same vein. Philip listened with perfect composure, not even allowing himself to smile. It was impossible to know if Menelaos actually believed this awful nonsense, or if he thought Philip might, or if
he was merely trying to salvage his dignity.

The thrust of it was, of course, that Menelaos was prepared to renounce
his treaty with the Illyrians and to enter into an offensive alliance with Philip.
They would attack Bardylis and drive him out of Upper Macedon. The plan
would gain Philip nothing, since even if they succeeded, Menelaos would still
be an independent ruler, now virtually a coequal with the king in Pella, and
Macedon would be left defenseless in the south and east. But all of this Philip
was expected to overlook in the name of family sentiment.

At last Klitos finished speaking. He lifted his head a little, as if he expected
an immediate and positive answer.

"It is a serious matter," Philip said, looking grave—he wished to appear as
if he were fighting back the temptation to embrace the man in gratitude. "In

matters of war and peace I must consult with my council. You would oblige me with your patience."

Klitos made a courteous bow, which Philip returned, and the interview was brought to a conclusion.

The next day Philip left Pella on a tour of the western garrisons. He wrote the Lynkestian ambassador a letter, to be delivered after he had already left the city, stating he would have an answer for Menelaos when he returned, which would not be for nearly a month.

"In another month there will not be enough of the fine weather left to organize a campaign," Lachios observed. The morning sky was still a pearly gray as an honor guard of fifty men rode out through the western gate. He and Korous, who were both a little taller than their king, exchanged a glance across Philip's back.

"Precisely." Philip smiled to himself. "It saves me the embarrassment of a blank refusal."

All three of them had read the reports indicating preparations for war in Lynkos.

"You will leave Menelaos to his fate, then?"

Philip nodded. At first it was the only answer he made.

"I have no choice," he said at last. "Except, perhaps, to go down with him."

"Which is not something he would do for you," Korous announced, with an almost ferocious satisfaction.

"Nor should he." With a frown and a shake of his head, Philip seemed to be dismissing a doubt, or perhaps only a temptation. "A nation is not the property of its king, to be squandered at his pleasure. Should men be required to fight and die at the whim of personal squabbles and loyalties? Would any sensible man give his allegiance to a king who asked this of him? The king who consults his private feelings over the good of his people is not fit to live, let alone to rule."

"Yet this is what most kings do," Lachios answered. "This is what they have always done. It is even what is expected of them."

Philip laughed and goaded his horse into a trot, forcing the other two to catch up with him.

"Perhaps that is why the world is such a quarrelsome place," he said.

And in the apartments he occupied in his grandfather's palace it was very much a private quarrel that occupied the attention of Pleuratos, who in his own mind had already succeeded as king of the Illyrians. He hated Old Bardylis, whom he never thought of except as "Old Bardylis," as if his great age conferred the only title he was fit to bear—as if thus Pleuratos could dismiss the ties of blood between them. He hated him for standing in the way, for counseling patience, for demanding attention to his will, for denying him the name as well as the absolute and unchallengeable sway of the king. He hated his grandfather for not having the decency at last simply to die.

And so Pleuratos had decided to destroy him even while he lived. Little by little, he would take away the power that meant so much to the old man, that was almost the last pleasure he was capable of enjoying, almost his last tie to life. If Pleuratos could not rule through the sheer authority of his unquestioned word, then he would rule by stealth. Yet in the end he would rule, and that would be his revenge.

And the instrument he had chosen was one Xuthos, a commander of indifferent abilities whom Bardylis had sent to head a garrison near the approaches to the Pisoderi Pass, where he would be safely out of the way. Xuthos was a man of prominent family and he felt the humiliation keenly. Pleuratos had led him to believe that great things awaited him in the next reign.

"You will create an incident," Pleuratos wrote to him. "You will pick some small and unimportant village just inside our borders with Lynkos, and you will send fifteen or twenty of your most trusted men to raid it. Burn the houses and put the inhabitants to the sword, even the children and the women— perhaps especially the women. Allow your soldiers to amuse themselves, as I wish this deed, for which the Lynkestians will be blamed, to inflame men's hearts. When this is done, wait patiently for your reward and know that I will not fail you."

But, once again, Pleuratos's timing was faulty.

"He has delayed too long," Philip said when he heard of the raid—it never crossed his mind that Menelaos could be guilty of such a piece of folly; that it was a provocation was obvious. "The weather will hold off perhaps long enough for Pleuratos to establish a force this side of the pass, but even the Illyrians cannot conquer a country that is up to their horses' withers in snow. Menelaos will be able to hold out at least until the spring thaw."

But the invasion of Lynkos, which now was inevitable, gave added significance to another piece of news that arrived almost in the same dispatch bag. Aias, king of the Eordoi, was said to be dying.

Philip waited until dark before he commanded that Deucalion be brought to him. When the young man appeared in his tent, he handed him the report and waited in silence while he read it.

"I have not seen my father in nearly five years," Deucalion said as if slightly awed by the discovery.

"You must see him now." Philip sat behind the little table he used as a desk when in the field, playing nervously with a writing stylus, remembering the night Amyntas had died. "You must be there when . . . He may wish to speak to you. And then you will be king in his place."

This contingency had apparently not occurred to the lad, and his face darkened.

"Tomorrow you will take horse with an honor guard of twenty men," Philip continued as if he had seen nothing. "They will take you as far as the border, where you will be met by whatever escort your father's ministers think to send. I dispatched a rider this afternoon, and part of the message he carries is that the king of Macedon recognizes Deucalion, son of Aias, as the rightful heir to his father's throne—he and no other. I think they will take the hint and your claim will not be challenged. But wait until you have received the oaths of loyalty before you write to me. Then you can make whatever arrangements you think best for your brother's journey."

"You will let Ctesios return with me?"

Philip shook his head, as if he did not understand the intent of Deucalion's astonished question. "Not *with* you—*after* you. The first hours of a new reign are always dangerous, but my possession of your brother will afford you some protection. After all, if some rival kills you, I will still have the rightful heir. It is time enough for Ctesios to come home when you are firmly in control.

"Yet that is not what you and I must discuss tonight. Macedon will soon be at war with the Illyrians—indeed, we are already at war, for the Illyrians are this moment preparing to invade Lynkos. I would know which side the Eordoi will take."

For a moment Deucalion looked as if he had been struck in the face.

"If you will release my brother, then you must know that I am loyal to you," he said, almost fiercely. "We both are. You have been like a father to us."

Philip remained impenetrably grave. "When you are a king you will learn that there are greater claims on you than friendship. The Eordoi sometimes forget that they are Macedonians."

"Yet you have made me remember that we are one people." The heir to Aias's throne took a step forward, his eyes wet with unspent tears. "At your bare word I would . . . Say what oath you require of me and I will take it."

"I need no oath." At last Philip allowed himself to smile. "I simply needed to know your heart."

"What would you have of me?" Deucalion asked, looking almost relieved.

"Nothing." Philip rose from behind his table and came to put his arm across the younger man's shoulder. "We will speak more another time. For now, go back to your tent. Avoid the company of others—your father is dying, and this may well be your last chance to be alone with your grief."

. . .

Deucalion had proved himself a good soldier and he was popular with Philip's men. Therefore, the next morning, when the king embraced him and wished him a safe journey, the army of Macedon sent him on his way with a cheer.

"Our young friend wears a grim face," Lachios observed, watching the honor guard as it rode off toward the western horizon.

"This surprises you?" Philip raised a hand and waved, although Deucalion was probably too far away to see. "He will soon bury his father and become king over the Eordoi. He is not much to be envied."

Lachios uttered a short syllable of laughter. "It is not what awaits him that oppresses his soul but what he leaves behind. Philip, do you not know that boy would rather command a wing of your cavalry than be king of Persia?"

"Good. Then perhaps he will keep his nobles from allying themselves with the Illyrians when Bardylis overruns Lynkos."

"Is that all you ask of him?"

"If I asked more, I might end by getting his throat cut. When the king is hardly more than a boy, his nobles think they need obey only when it suits them. And it might not suit them to throw in their lot with us rather than the Illyrians, particularly since just now we must seem to them the weaker side. Yet they might be persuaded to sit and wait until the outcome has grown more obvious. Never fear, though—Deucalion will bring the Eordoi over to us when the moment is right."

Philip turned his gaze to Lachios and showed him a tight smile, a smile that somehow managed to suggest the perfect confidence of one who cannot afford to be wrong.

"I have letters to attend to," he said, perhaps just a trifle too carelessly. "Should anyone need me, I will be in my tent."

Yet when he had closed the tent flap behind him, a sign to the guard that he did not wish to be disturbed, his writing box remained closed. Philip sat on the edge of his bed, struggling to control the impulse to weep.

In the years since his wife's death he had submerged himself in work, hardly allowing himself the luxury of a private impulse. Glaukon said that he had not yet learned to see life through the eyes of a king, yet he had tried. He had cultivated an icy dispassion, willing the man to disappear inside the ruler, hoping somehow that it would be easier to be king of Macedon than simply Philip, who felt himself adrift in the world.

Yet the departure of Deucalion affected him strangely. Suddenly it was as if he were still kneeling beside Phila's bed, whispering lies to her about the stillborn child she had thought it worth her life to bring into the world. He could almost feel her cold fingers closed around his hand. Wife and son had been laid together on the same funeral pyre, their bodies consigned to the purifying flame.

Deucalion remembered her too. From that day to this, they had never spoken her name, yet they both remembered. It was a bond between them.

And now the bond was broken and Philip knew that he was utterly alone. *Better to get used to it,* he thought. *What king is not alone?*

It was almost midday when he was distracted by voices outside his tent. "Well, he will want to be disturbed for this!" he heard Korous shouting.

Philip stepped out into the sunlight, which was surprisingly harsh.

"What is it?"

"A rider . . ." Korous made a wild gesture with his arm as if it indicate someone right beside him. There was no one near. "From the south, Philip. The Athenians have landed in force at Methone."

39

There had been a rainstorm on the gulf the night before, and the decks of the Athenian triremes were still streaming with water. Arrhidaios had been dreadfully seasick the whole voyage, and the dense, moisture-laden air did not make him feel any better. He stood on the prow of the commander's vessel, watching the shoreline swing up and down like a bit of cloth fluttering in the wind, his mind clouded with a dull, hopeless resentment.

Macedon, he thought. *Occupied by the Athenians, but Macedon nonetheless.* He wondered a little why the sight of home failed to move him. He found, on the contrary, that his native land stirred nothing in him but a faint distaste that was indistinguishable from the nausea that had risen in his throat like the smell of decaying flesh. *Macedon.*

His purely physical suffering, however, only partially accounted for his bad temper. The fact was he had come to understand his real helplessness. Demosthenes and his party might be prepared to help him become king, but they had no intention of recognizing him as anything except their instrument. They had their own dark purposes, and he was along merely to provide a plausible excuse for this fairly typical specimen of naked Athenian aggression. He had not even been consulted about the route of march.

Well, they would learn their mistake soon enough. Once he was established in Pella—once Philip was dead and the assembly had made its submission— then Arrhidaios planned to teach the Athenians the folly of having underestimated him. He would make the north so hot for them they would never come back.

But in the meantime all he wanted was to scramble onto dry, motionless land and to never again be obliged to feel his guts being heaved up into his mouth. Macedon, at least, would be good for that.

"By the day after tomorrow you will be hearing yourself proclaimed king in Aigai."

Arrhidaios started at the nearness of the sound and turned around to see Mantios, nominally his lieutenant but in fact the expedition's commander, standing almost beside him.

"I wish I could be there to see it," Mantios continued, smiling in a way that hinted at an almost pitying contempt.

"But surely you will be there."

Arrhidaios, fighting back a sudden surge of panic, raised his hand as if in a gesture of supplication and then slowly withdrew it.

"Alas, no." The Athenian shook his head, still smiling. "It was judged unwise—after all, you do not wish to appear to your subjects as the client of a foreign state. We will remain in Methone."

"I cannot be expected to seize Aigai alone," Arrhidaios replied with some heat. Strangely, it was at that precise moment he noticed that his seasickness had left him.

"Indeed not, nor will you be. The mercenary force will accompany you, along with your own Macedonians. A few Athenians will be of the company, but you must understand that, for your own sake, we cannot make up a noticeable presence."

Mantios paused for a moment, during which he appeared to be studying the coastline as if he expected to find something there.

"And of course," he went on, "should it come to that, I and my ships and my companies of soldiers will be in Methone, hardly even a day away. Yet it will not come to that."

"You are so sure?"

"Your brother Philip is conscripting men to rebuild the army that perished with King Perdikkas—there is bound of be discontent. Besides, Aigai is the ancient capital and the old aristocracy feels the loss of prestige. They will rally to you."

"And of course they will know that I am supported by Athens."

"Of course."

"And what of this army that Philip is rebuilding? If you do not believe he will fight, you do not know him."

Mantios dismissed the threat with a shrug.

"Farm boys are not turned into soldiers overnight," he said with an evenness of tone that betrayed his contempt for the rustic Macedonians. "They are little more than a rabble, I suspect. And you have a core of hardened troops."

"Mercenaries."

The Athenian shot him an annoyed glance, and then he smiled, as if reminding himself of the folly of losing his temper.

"By the time Philip even knows you have landed, you will control Aigai and most of the southern plain. The Macedonians have no taste for civil war just now. They will abandon him when they realize your strength. Believe me—he will think himself lucky to escape with his life."

Yet there flashed through Arrhidaios's mind a memory of his brother when they were only boys together, playing at war, fighting with barrel staves in the palace stable. How old had they been? Seven or eight, no more. Arrhidaios had set an ambush, waiting patiently behind an empty oil jar, silent as a mouse as he thought how he would surprise Philip when he climbed down the only ladder from the hayloft. Yet Philip had spotted him through the cracks of the hayloft floor and had jumped—a boy of nine had risked a drop of perhaps fifteen cubits—and had landed directly behind him. Arrhidaios could still remember the surprise when he felt the sting of Philip's barrel stave against his back. "You haven't the gift of cunning," Philip had said, laughing. "But I have."

The Athenians had at least provided Arrhidaios with a beautiful horse, a white stallion. It was not as large as the Macedonian horses, but it was impressive enough—a horse a king might ride. With his army he was somewhat less pleased.

The core was six companies of Corinthian and Theban mercenaries under the command of one Timoleon, a brutal, cynical man whose notion of conversation was to show off his scars and to explain how he had acquired each one. Demosthenes had hired him, offering twice the usual rate, to be paid out of the Macedonian treasury when they had seized Pella, and Demosthenes vouched for his abilities in the field. But mercenaries fight for pay and only a fool, Arrhidaios was quick to remind himself, believes in their loyalty to anything else.

Another hundred or so men were Macedonian volunteers—exiles, like himself. And like Arrhidaios, they knew that they could expect no mercy in defeat. In that sense, at least, they were dependable, but on the whole they inspired even less confidence than Timoleon and his hirelings.

Some of them were common criminals, murderers, and thieves, but most were simple malcontents: younger sons, aristocratic and portionless, who had quarreled with their families; rebels by temperament, men who would have quarreled with any regime; ordinary adventurers, out for plunder and perhaps some unspecific revenge. One or two actually seemed half-mad.

And the quarrels were endless—they were like women. For not quite a month Arrhidaios had been almost constantly in company with these men, and in that time three of them had been killed. One had been stabbed by a jealous lover, another was beaten to death with a stool in a gambling dispute, and the third, only the morning before they left Athens, was found sitting against the barrack wall, strangled with a bowstring that had been pulled so tight around his neck that when it was removed it was found to be crusted with dried blood. Arrhidaios suspected that the murderer's identity was widely known—doubtless he was with them this very hour—but for reasons as obscure as his end the dead man had not been popular and no one seemed interested in rendering him justice.

And when they were not fighting among themselves they were bragging of all they would do, the time they would have and the scores they would settle, when it was their foot on someone and everyone's neck back home. *Back home*—a phrase that seemed to have no meaning for them except as the scene of some malicious and apparently endless debauch. Each of them expected to be enriched and ennobled by a grateful king, their old comrade in arms, such that there would not have been land and wealth enough in ten Macedons to satisfy them. Oh, a rare flock of courtiers they would make! Arrhidaios had privately decided that, should it come to a battle, he would put his honored countrymen in the front ranks and let Philip wear himself out killing them. As for the survivors, as soon as he felt himself to be sitting firmly on his throne, he would find some pretext for having them all condemned to death. Doubtless, after a month or two of witnessing how they conducted themselves, the nation would be grateful to him for putting down that mob of brigands. It might become the foundation of that real popularity that a king needed if he was to survive.

Philip, the Athenians assured him, was already widely hated.

Arrhidaios felt his stomach contract painfully and realized, for the twentieth time since midday hour, that it had been a great mistake to miss breakfast this morning. He had felt himself too excited to eat—after all, by the end of the day he would probably be lodged in the old royal palace, the real seat of the nation, king of Macedon in fact if not yet in name—but he should have forced himself at least to eat a few spoonfuls of porridge. Now, mounted on this beautiful horse, at the head of an army and perhaps no more than an hour or so away from the effortless triumph that would be his occupation of Aigai, he was beginning to experience a certain giddiness. That was all it was, the protest of an empty belly. He must be careful not to confuse it with fear.

So to distract himself he thought about the road. It was the same road that had taken him into exile—it was on this road that he had first learned what it was to be alone.

He and Archelaos had traveled together at first, taking horse two hours before dawn and traveling fast in case the Lord Ptolemy had sent search parties after them. They had been exhausted by the time they reached Aigai.

"We must part here," Archelaos had said, whispering to him in the darkness of the room where they had slept that night in a tavern by the western gate. "They are looking for the two of us, so in the morning I will ride west and you south. We can meet again in Athens."

Arrhidaios would never forget how afraid he had felt, how the sound of his brother's voice, as disembodied as if he were already a restless shade, had filled him with dread.

So the next morning he had set out alone, on this road. And they had never met in Athens because Archelaos had died in Corinth—Arrhidaios didn't even know where he was buried.

A rider, from one of their forward patrols, was coming toward them over the crest of the hill they were approaching. He was traveling fast and Timoleon, who had taken his position in the column just behind the future king, cantered a little ahead to meet him.

When he rode back his face was set and expressionless.

"The gates at Aigai are closed," he said when he had drawn his horse up to Arrhidaios's so that the two men's knees were almost touching. "It would seem they have had warning of our approach."

It meant nothing, Arrhidaios told himself. The garrison commander, informed that an army of some three or four hundred men was on its way up the coast road, would very naturally withdraw inside his walls. After all, it might be anyone.

"Possibly they have spies in Methone," Timoleon went on. "I have not noticed any scouts. In fact, it is a little surprising that we have met hardly a soul along the road."

"They would close the gates even if they knew who it was. They will want to be in a position to make us bargain for their support."

"Doubtless that is the explanation."

Yet somehow Timoleon did not look as if he quite believed it.

When they reached the crest of the hill they could see where the road turned inland and, perhaps an hour distant, they could see Aigai, looking as shut up as a merchant's money chest.

"We will know soon enough," Timoleon said.

It was the middle of the afternoon before they were in hailing distance of the walls, and still no emissary had come out to meet them. But it was not until they were close enough to make out the faces of the men standing on the rampart that Arrhidaios began to feel hope dying in his breast.

I know him, he whispered in his soul, looking up at a man standing with his arms crossed. He was in the middle of life, red-faced and fierce looking, and he wore a soldier's cloak. He was the garrison commander. *I know him— he was in the royal guard at Pella when I was a child.*

"Epikles!" he shouted. "Epikles! Do you not know me?"

For a moment there was only silence.

"I know you," came the reply at last. "You are Prince Arrhidaios. You slipped away like a thief and now you have returned leading an army. What do you want?"

"Come down, Epikles, for some things are better explained in private. I guarantee your safety."

"My soldiers guarantee my safety, Prince. I will ask you but once more—what do you want?"

"There is nothing for it but to answer, Lord," Timoleon murmured, his mouth almost touching Arrhidaios's ear. "If you were ever eloquent in your life, this is the moment."

Yes, this was the moment. And Arrhidaios felt his heart emptying like a cracked jug.

"I would bring you freedom, Epikles!" he shouted, conscious of a certain hollowness in his voice. "I would guarantee every decent man's liberty. I would rid you of—"

"Of what, Prince? Of what would you rid us with a rabble of foreign mercenaries at your back? Or of whom?"

It could have been excitement, it could have been anger, but the old soldier's face seemed to darken from moment to moment, as if he were holding his breath.

"Speak, Prince—from whom would you save us?"

"I would save you from tyranny, I would—"

"Oh, then it is from Philip that you would save us—that is it. You would do us the kindness to rule over us in his place."

Epikles looked around at the officers who surrounded him, as if taking a silent count.

"Then you needn't trouble yourself, Prince. We have taken his measure and we have taken yours, and we prefer the king we have."

From the wall was a little ripple of appreciative laughter at this—Arrhidaios could even hear a faint echo of it behind him. In that moment he knew that Demosthenes had tricked him, that he would never be king of Macedon, that he would never be anything, ever again. His humiliation boiled in him like molten iron.

"You will deliver the city and its garrison over to me, Epikles, or I will take it!" he shouted. "I will hang you from the main gate. I will leave you for the dogs to eat!"

"It will not be my carcass upon whom the dogs will feast, Prince, for if I am any judge, Philip is already on the march."

Epikles drew his sword and threw it so that it flew glittering through the air until it fell in the dust, close enough to Arrhidaios to make his horse start.

"I do you this final courtesy, Prince, for I was a soldier in your father's service before you were born and I honor the House of the Argeadai. Take my sword and retire to some private place to fall upon it. I offer you a quiet death, with still a shred of dignity to it. The king your brother is unlikely to show you so much mercy."

Arrhidaios, full of fury, was about to scream back his defiance when Timoleon reached across to grab him by the cloak, almost yanking him off his horse.

"You imbecile, be still," he hissed between clenched teeth. "The city cannot be taken, not even by four thousand men, not in a day or two. Can't you see the game is lost?"

As quickly as it had come, Arrhidaios's rage left him, to be replaced by a terrible, quaking fear. This man, who only an hour ago had referred to him as a king, now reviled him. *Imbecile*—Timoleon could use that word to him. Then truly he was utterly deserted.

"My brother will not have a large force." He heard the tremor in his own voice. It was a miracle he was able to speak at all. "We can defeat him . . ."

"Defeat him yourself, for I have heard it said that your brother is no sucking lamb. Do you imagine we will risk all for your sake? I am taking my men back to Methone—you can come if you like, or you can conquer King Philip by yourself."

Thus, without a blow struck, Arrhidaios's campaign to make himself lord of Macedon came to its end. What would become of him? Perhaps one of the Macedonians would think to sneak into his tent tonight and cut his throat. Perhaps his head would be presented to Philip as a peace offering. Or perhaps—and this was the worst—he would live out his life, would grow to old age, forgotten except as a kind of jest.

Someone caught the bridle of his horse and led him away. He had to listen to common soldiers cursing him, jeering at him for a fool and worse. They would not be paid now, and they blamed him. His mind was numb. He had become as nothing.

He did not know how long he continued thus before he was roused by the shouts of alarm all around him. He had only to turn his head to see the reason. To the north, across the flat countryside, he could see the dust raised by a long column of horsemen.

"Well, you shall have your wish after all," Timoleon growled. "We can't outrun him, so we shall have to make a fight of it."

He leaned forward a little over his horse's neck, shading his eyes to get a better look.

"Say a prayer, Prince, for your brother the king will be upon us within the hour."

40

"The Athenians have decided to gamble that by taking the first bite they will be able to tear off the biggest piece," Philip had said when the news reached him that several companies of men had been landed at Methone. "They will march toward Aigai."

His officers exchanged glances.

"They must know they cannot succeed until they have engaged and defeated you," Korous very sensibly pointed out. "If I were the Athenian commander, I would strike straight north with my forces intact and threaten Pella—that would be most likely to draw you into a fight."

"That is what I would do too, but Arrhidaios will need to have himself proclaimed king and Aigai is the old capital. His first thought will be to seize it."

"Your brother is in this?"

"Oh, yes," Philip answered, nodding slowly. "The Athenians are great respecters of appearances and they will wish to present themselves as liberators. They will expect the garrison to be impressed by a show of strength and throw their support to Arrhidaios—after all, it is not so unreasonable."

"Then we must intercept them before they reach Aigai. We are in the field already and it is less than a day's march. We can be there waiting for them. I will give the order to break camp."

But Philip put a restraining hand on his shoulder as Lachios rose to go.

"We will not leave before tomorrow morning. I want the Athenians to see for themselves that I command the loyalty of my subjects. And if I do not, then perhaps I deserve to be overthrown."

He smiled in an odd way, as if making his brother's treason his own, and with a gesture of his hand indicated that he wished to be alone.

In the evening, as they sat around a dying cooking fire, the king's officers watched the thin line of yellowish light that showed through his tent flat. Philip had not come out for supper.

"They are half brothers, then?" Lachios inquired after a long silence, as if the precise relationship would somehow explain everything.

"Yes. Arrhidaios was the child of the old king's first wife."

"And were they close as boys?"

"Close enough that he feels it as he does." Korous held a wine cup between thumb and first finger, as if hoping to catch something in it. Finally he set it down next to his foot. "It has been a bad day for him—first Deucalion leaving, and now this. Although I suppose no one is surprised by it except Philip."

"Is this brother any kind of a soldier?"

"Who can say?"

"We should have marched on Aigai at once," Lachios pronounced glumly. "It was a mistake to wait."

"Perhaps he needs to prove something to himself, even if it is only the loyalty of a single garrison."

"Will they hold, then? Even with the Athenians in Methone?"

"Epikles is not a man to care for all the Athenians who ever lived."

"Yes, but his officers might take a more pragmatic view. You lowlanders have not always been so steadfast to your kings."

Lachios grinned, just to show that he was jesting, but Korous appeared to consider the question very seriously.

"I cannot believe it," he said finally. "I think the garrison would mutiny and cut their officers' throats if they abandoned this king. It is just a thing one senses about him, that he is somehow different—that he is like no other man, that there is some element of him that is uniquely his own. His soldiers feel it. They trust their lives to it. I feel it, and I have known him since we were children."

"Then perhaps he is wise to wait."

"Yes, perhaps he is."

With a single impulse they turned their eyes back to the sliver of light that came from the king's tent.

"I wonder how he bears it," Lachios said, almost to himself.

When Arrhidaios's foreign army was within sight, Philip rode to the crest of a low bluff for a better view of its dispositions. His own infantry numbered less than a thousand men, but he had an advantage of cavalry, even if they only numbered forty or fifty. It might be enough.

"Draw up our cavalry in two wings, with most of the weight on the right side," he ordered. "Give them about a hundred and fifty paces before you advance to meet their infantry. If I am any judge, their lines will have begun to disintegrate by then—hit them from two sides at once. They must never have a chance to regroup."

His commanders, now including Epikles and his ranking officers, formed a circle around him while he used the bronze tip of an arrow to draw his plans in the dust. No one else spoke. No one thought to raise an objection, for one does not question a fact and Philip had the gift of bringing an extraordinary vividness to his analyses. It was as if he had already waged this battle in his imagination so that the actual fighting would be an anticlimax, the enemy doomed in advance like the protagonist in some tragic drama.

"Break through their infantry lines here, between the left wing and the center. Our infantry will pour into the hole, and I think that will finish them. These men are mercenaries and their campaign has come to nothing, so now they will have no object except to stay alive. It is my will that the Aigai garrison shall have the honor of leading the offensive—they have earned it."

Two hours later, just at sunset, it was over, and Arrhidaios's defeat had been overwhelming. What had been the field of battle now belonged to the dead and the dying, and almost the only sound came from pack animals too badly wounded to rise from the ground. They screamed like women in childbirth.

The mercenaries were vanquished and fully half of them, including their commander, were dead. Most of the remainder had been taken prisoner—they stood around in disconsolate little clumps, the heart so gone from them that they hardly even needed guarding. The Macedonians who had come with Arrhidaios, knowing what surrender would mean, were also dead.

Yet perhaps it was not quite over. A tiny force, still in possession of their weapons, had sought refuge and the illusion of freedom on the crest of a hill, away from the main battle. Their position was hopeless. They could only wait and marvel that somehow they had not been overrun. It was as if, in the course of the fighting that had flowed around them, they had been forgotten.

But they had not been forgotten. Philip merely stayed his hand, ordering that six companies be deployed to make any attempt at escape impossible. The light was fading, so they built huge bonfires around the base of the hill.

As he listened to his commanders reporting their losses and the identities of all notable prisoners Philip sat on the tongue of an overturned wagon while a physician from Aigai cleaned out a wound on his arm with the bronze tip of an arrow that had been heated to a dull red. The physician was nervous to find himself attending a king and perhaps for that reason the procedure was taking a long time, which did nothing to improve his patient's disposition.

"Epikles is dead," he was told. "It was almost an accident—a wounded horse rolled over and kicked him in the head while he was dispatching its

rider. Fewer than thirty men from the Aigai garrison were killed, and he had
to be one of them."

Philip might not have been paying attention. In his mind he heard the
voice of a red-faced old soldier telling him, *We are yours to a man.*

"Have you found my brother?" he asked at last. It was impossible to tell
whether he anticipated the answer or dreaded it.

"He has not been captured. If he is among the slain, we will probably not
know before tomorrow. It is quite certain he has not escaped—no one has
escaped."

"Send men out with torches to inspect the battlefield. I want to know if
Arrhidaios is still alive."

Philip did not say what he would do if he was. Perhaps he did not know
himself.

It was two hours before midnight when a badly frightened Athenian with
a careful little margin of beard around his jaw, who looked as if he had never
been a soldier, was shown into the king's presence.

"He is from the hill," his guard said. "He came down bearing emblems of
truce, asking to be brought to you."

"Is my brother alive?" Philip asked him, even as the man was making his
bow. "Tell me that first, and then I will let you bargain for your life."

"The pretender is in our keeping, My Lord King, as well as some ten or
fifteen of the Macedonian rebels who followed him. The rest are mercenaries,
along with a few Athenians like myself—peaceful men who came only to
observe and who took no role in the fighting."

He actually managed a cringing smile, as if he expected Philip to be grateful that he had taken no role in the fighting.

"Then here are my terms," Philip answered, his voice cold and without expression. "My brother Arrhidaios will be delivered to me unharmed. The rest
of you will surrender yourselves by dawn, without preconditions, or face
another trial by arms in which you must expect no quarter."

"But surely, Lord, there will be mercy for the noncombatants. Surely, My
Lord . . ."

The words died away as the Athenian's eyes searched the conqueror's face
for some clue to his fate.

"You have until dawn." Philip made a gesture to the guard that he might
escort his prisoner away. "I would suggest you make haste back to your friends,
as you will have hardly any time left to decide."

Philip had little sleep that night, and that little was restless and tormenting.
He awakened with a start, unable to remember his dream, which had left no
trace in his consciousness except an unfocused panic that drained away only

very slowly. When he lit a lamp he discovered there was blood on his fingers—
he had torn open the wound on his arm.

The physician was called for, and he stitched the wound closed with a sail-
maker's curved needle and a hair from the tail of the king's horse. This time
Philip was almost grateful for the pain. He found it cleared his mind.

When dawn came he discovered the remains of Arrhidaios's force had surrendered and were waiting for him at the bottom of the hill that had been
their last refuge. Some ten or twelve of the Macedonians had drawn lots to cut
each other's throats rather than face the punishment for treason, but Arrhidaios himself was alive. His hands had been lashed behind his back, doubtless
to keep him from also taking his own life.

The mercenaries, who perhaps expected it less, were too proud to beg for
mercy, but the Athenians fell on their faces the moment they beheld the face
of their conqueror.

"Get up," Philip said with a distaste he could not, did not wish to hide.
"This is unseemly. Get up. Get your noses out of the dirt."

Reluctantly, as if loath to abandon the tactical advantage of their abase-
ment, the prisoners first pushed themselves up with their arms and, when they
saw that even a kneeling posture was forbidden them, finally regained their
feet. After an exchange of glances, one of them stepped forward. He was the
same man to whom Philip had spoken the night before.

"Please be so clement as to accept the ransom our families and the assembly will offer for our release," he said, risking an occasional glance up from
the ground, as if the gaze of Macedon's king would burn him to ashes if he
dared to meet it. "We are all men of substance, and our—"

"You will be provided with horses and escorted back to Methone," Philip
interrupted him. "I will accept no ransom for your lives, and you may tell your
assembly that Philip of Macedon desires only peace with Athens and will look
with favor upon her ambassadors if they come to him with an offer of friendship. This conflict was of your making, not of mine, and I will do nothing to
carry it forward."

He lapsed into silence, his eyes hard and unforgiving as he surveyed the
last remnants of the army that had been hurled against him.

"As for the rest," he said at last, "they will hear my sentence soon enough."

He turned on his heel and walked away, his principal officers trailing
after him.

"Do you have any concept of what you have thrown away?" Lachios demanded as soon as he caught up with him, his voice a suppressed cry of rage.
"Your treasury is empty, and you let them ride out of here as if they had been
your guests for dinner? Those men would easily have been worth a hundred
talents of gold!"

"And right now peace with Athens is worth a good deal more than that,"

Philip answered without looking around. "Those smooth-handed politicians will be home before the moon has had time to wane, and they will remember but two things: the generosity of their captors and their own fear. The latter they will never speak of, for nothing shames a man like the recollection of how he groveled for his life, so what do you think they will report to their fellow citizens? The assembly is a mob, Lachios, and mobs are greatly impressed by generous gestures."

"Yes, perhaps—but the leaders who arranged this little expedition, who are not a mob but as coldhearted as any king who ever lived, they will read your generous gesture as a sign of weakness."

"And they will be right. We are weak. We are so weak that we gain nothing by attempting to hide the fact. Let us settle for what we can get. Believe me, it will be some time before our enemies in Athens will be voted the money to try again."

Philip put his hand on his friend's shoulder, and the two of them slowed to a stop.

"It is done, Lachios," he said, almost as if he were consoling a child. "Now do me the kindness to have my brother brought to me. I would see him now."

When he was brought to Philip's tent, Arrhidaios already had the look of a condemned man. His tunic was smeared with mud and his eyes appeared sunken, as if he had not slept for two or three days. He seemed past fear. The first thing Philip did when they were alone was draw his sword and cut his brother's bonds.

"How long has it been since you have eaten?" he asked, but Arrhidaios only stood there, rubbing his wrists where the lashes had rubbed them raw.

"Would you like some food?"

"Some wine perhaps," Arrhidaios answered at last with a vague shrug. "Am I permitted to sit down?"

Philip made a gesture toward the bed that occupied one corner and Arrhidaios did not so much sit down as collapse on top of it. He took the cup of wine that was offered him, drank it off in what seemed one swallow, and then held it out to be refilled.

"Have you brought me here to offer me pardon, brother?"

Philip shook his head. "If I could spare you, I would, but I cannot. You knew that already."

"Yes, I knew it. Thank you at least for having the decency not to trifle with me. Then what is it you do want—to gloat?"

"Can you believe that of me?"

Arrhidaios allowed himself a short, joyless laugh.

"Under the circumstances, I could believe it of any man. When will the assembly meet to condemn me?"

"I take no pleasure in this, brother. I only want to know why."

"I asked first," Arrhidaios snapped. And then, as if with a deliberate effort to control himself, "When am I to die?"

"Your trial will be in Pella. Two or three days, I should think. Why did you make war against me?"

"Isn't it obvious?"

"Not to me."

For just a moment, until he remembered himself, Arrhidaios wore the expression of a man who has known the sudden grief of witnessing the death of some sustaining illusion. It was the thing of an instant, just something that flickered briefly across his face, but it was enough to make Philip understand.

"You thought I would betray you," he said, an edge of cold disgust in his voice. "You thought I had invited you home in order to have you murdered."

When Arrhidaios did not respond, Philip shook his head.

"There is no one here except us two," he continued. "At this extremity I have no reason to lie—I swear to you, I had no such intention."

"If you have no reason to lie, you also have no reason to tell the truth."

Arrhidaios showed his brother a tight half smile, as if affirming the unbridgeable gap between them. No, they would have nothing together this side of death, not even a common understanding.

"Yet there is one thing you might tell me," Philip said, accepting the fact of this final estrangement. "And that is the names of the men in Athens who led you to this folly."

"Why would you want to know?" Arrhidaios answered, obviously surprised.

"That someday I might avenge you."

41

The triumph over Arrhidaios and his mercenaries was a new beginning for the Macedonian army. Trifling as it might have been in purely military terms, it canceled out Perdikkas's defeat at the hands of the Illyrians. The day before Aigai, almost no one imagined that the nation could stave off collapse. The day after, there was hardly a man under arms who was not positive of their ultimate triumph. They felt themselves ready for any test.

The difference, they believed, was Philip. He was invincible. He could see into the minds of his enemies. The men who had fought with him in Elimeia and in the campaign against Aias told fabulous stories about him. The position he defended was impregnable. The position he attacked was doomed. Even the Elimoitai horsemen who had fought against him beneath the walls of Aiane bragged shamelessly of his genius and courage—it seemed that to have been defeated by Philip of Macedon conferred almost as much distinction as victory.

But for the object of all this praise the days following the rout of the Athenian expedition were full of a bitter darkness, for it was Philip who had to stand before the Macedonian Assembly and accuse his own brother of treason. It was Philip who had to watch that same brother perish under a rain of spears as soon as the verdict had been pronounced. It was Philip who had to preside over the crucifixion of the guilty man's corpse, that the crows might make a feast of him and his soul wander this earth forever, unable to cross over into the realm of the dead. These were duties that law and custom imposed upon the king, duties that he could not shirk. These things, he felt sure, would poison his life forever.

The House of the Argeadai has been cursed, he thought. *Only witness how the gods pick us off, one after the other.*

It was actually a relief to hear that Agis, the old king of Paionia, was dying, since war left no place for black reflections.

"We will march north as soon as we can marshal sufficient strength," Philip ordered. "It is only Agis's weakening health that has thus far inclined the Paionians to accept our tribute money. As soon as his son Lyppeios is on the throne they will attack us. Our only real chance is to strike first."

It was on the day before he had appointed to leave Pella to join his army, which was assembling at Tyrissa, that he received the ambassadors from Athens. They quickly agreed to a treaty accepting the occupation of Methone, provided it was the northern extremity of Athenian expansion.

"Let them have their garrisons," Philip said after they had gone. "I cannot drive them out now, and their greed makes it certain they will sooner or later give us an excuse to repudiate this treaty. At least for the moment Athens and Macedon are great friends, and that, let us hope, will be long enough."

There were four thousand soldiers waiting for their king at Tyrissa. They were the first fruits of a reign that had witnessed the sacrifice of both treasure and national pride, of whatever the lord of Macedon could barter away that would purchase a few more months in which to prepare this force. They were men who had spent nearly a year being drilled in the formations and tactics that had carried the day at Aigai. They had seen the miracle for which they had prayed. They had been made to believe in themselves.

"You are late," Korous announced, even before Philip had dismounted from his horse. "The dispatch rider arrived this morning—Agis died six days ago. Where have you been?"

Philip looked around the camp with narrowed eyes. The wind already carried sharp little flakes of snow that stung a man's face. They had perhaps another month before winter would put an end to the campaigning season. In Lynkos the Illyrian advance had already bogged down under nearly a cubit of snow. Korous was right to be anxious.

"Playing in the dirt with some visitors from the south," he answered. "I had hoped the old bandit would hang on a little longer—what do you suppose he expects in the netherworld that he hastens so to abandon his life?"

But Korous either did not hear the jest or did not appreciate it.

"Lyppeios will have finished his seven days of mourning tomorrow." He too looked as if he had felt the snow's burning lash and had read its meaning. "He will be upon us then. He can field perhaps as many as seven thousand men. Have you thought about that, Philip?"

"The thicker the wheat grows on the ground, the more the scythe takes at a stroke." The king of Macedon smiled bleakly. "Besides, what choice do we have?"

"None, but a man can't help worrying."

At dinner that night Philip received a more complete account of events in Paionia.

"It seemed Aias's decline was quite sudden. The heir was out of the country and only returned after his father had lapsed into a coma. It is taken as a bad omen that he missed the old king's blessing."

"Aias has been reported dying for the last five years at least," Philip said, shrugging his shoulders as he chewed a piece of flatbread. "It had attained almost the status of a tradition, but I think Lyppeios may be forgiven for not hanging about at court. Where was he?"

"In Illyria, it is reported—courting. He has been there several times in the last few years. No doubt he dreams of an alliance."

"What he dreams of, people say, is old Bardylis's granddaughter. They say she has him bewitched."

"She is his great-granddaughter." There was an edge in Philip's voice that caused Lachios and Korous to exchange a glance. "Her name is Audata."

"You know something of this girl?"

"I met her when I was Bardylis's hostage. She was only a child then."

Something in his face made Lachios decide to change the subject.

"Well, Lyppeios is home now—and king, with or without his father's blessing. If he is eager for an alliance with the Illyrians, he will want to make a show of strength at the very beginning of his reign."

"That serves our purpose," Philip responded, nodding grimly. "I don't want this campaign to degenerate into a series of raids. I want to meet the Paionians straight on. Nothing will serve but that we humble them before the whole world."

He lapsed into silence, staring at the fire as if he had forgotten his companions' existence. One could not even guess what he was thinking.

Eight days later, on a windswept plateau where even late into the morning the ground was still hard with frost, the two armies came within sight of one another. It was almost as if they met by appointment—there had been skirmishes between their advance parties for almost three days while Philip and his antagonist engaged in a cautious, dancelike series of probings, each trying to assess the other while they searched for some advantage in the terrain of what was soon to become their battlefield.

Now at last they faced each other, across perhaps five hundred paces of almost featureless earth rendered strangely lifeless by the cold.

"Notice how he has concentrated his cavalry on the left," Philip observed to his commanders. "The ground there is uneven enough that I would not care to lead a charge across it. I think he made his plans too far in advance and does not now have the presence of mind to change them."

"He must have something like five hundred horsemen," Korous observed with a grudging respect.

"When you make your attack, go straight for the center. I don't care if he has five thousand horsemen—if we can separate them from his infantry, we can cut them to pieces at our leisure. I will be with our infantry, on the inside pivot of the right wing."

"Are you mad, Philip? When the Paionian cavalry reach our lines . . ."

"Yes, I know. They will go straight for the inside pivot of the right wing. But we will have the advantage of terrain."

"If you are killed in this battle, Macedon is finished."

Philip's laughter had in it something of the quality of relief. "If we lose today, it will not matter if I am killed. If I am to command, I must be at the crux of the battle."

"In war, a king should take better care of his life."

"In war, a king's first duty is to win, Lachios."

He then dismissed the subject with a twist of his body as he made a sharp gesture toward a point in the Paionian infantry lines.

"Hit them there," he said. "Crack the spine and watch the legs fold."

Half an hour later Philip was in the front rank of his infantry, watching the approach of the enemy cavalry.

A charge is useless unless it can be executed at a full gallop, and at that pace the formations of Paionian horsemen were spreading out over the broken, stony ground like a flock of birds in a rainstorm. By the time they reached the Macedonian lines they would have lost all focus and their attack would have little more force than a child pushing against a stone wall. Whether they realized it or not, they were riding into a massacre.

When the Paionians were a hundred paces away, Philip crouched to the ground and angled his spear forward. All three front lines followed his lead, giving the archers behind them a clear field. There was a throb of bowstrings and the first flight of arrows, so thick that for an instant one could see its shadow on the ground, whistled over their heads. One . . . two . . . three . . . Philip discovered himself counting as he watched the arrows rise and then begin to curve down toward the earth. Four . . . five . . . six . . . He was almost to ten before the first of the Paionian cavalrymen fell from his mount. The man had not even hit the ground before perhaps one in seven of the enemy horses were riderless.

The second flight of arrows seemed to have an even more devastating effect.

"They are hill savages," Philip whispered to himself. "They have never known battle against disciplined infantry." Somehow the thought came to him as a kind of grief.

After the fifth flight of arrows, when the enemy's lead horses were no more than forty paces away, Philip stood up, balanced his spear in his hand and hurled it. Then his line melted into the line behind them. There was time for all three rows of javelin throwers to have a turn, then Philip was back in the front line with his long pike and his shield, ready for the shock of the Paionian assault.

"Fight now to stay alive!" he shouted to his soldiers. "Hold your ranks together, for we have already beaten them!"

One can say what one likes, it is still a terrifying experience to have a horde of cavalry galloping straight for one. It takes courage to stand one's ground and face that charge. But Philip had fought beside these men before and knew that they would not break if he did not. He felt their wills behind him like a wall so that even the threat of death lost its terror.

The first Paionian horseman to reach their lines came straight for the inside corner, as if he knew whom he would find there. He tried to squeeze through the line of pikes, but Philip's point caught him just under the ribs, tearing him from his mount, breaking the pike's shaft with his fall, and spilling his guts out over the ground as if someone had emptied them from a basket. While he died, another made it through, close enough that Philip could hear the whistle of his sword slashing at the man next to him, who lurched over without a sound, his skull split open. Philip had to wipe the blood from his eyes. But the horse stumbled, going down on its knees, and before it had a chance to scramble back up five or six pairs of hands reached up to pull its rider from its back—the man was dead before he had a chance to scream. That was how it went.

And in a quarter of an hour it was over. The first attack had spent itself, and there would not be another. Macedonian cavalry cut through the ranks of the Paionians, most of whom had seen how the battle was going and had already fled. One had only to stand and watch as the battle ground down into a series of pointless skirmishes.

"Bring me my horse," Philip said at last.

He rode about the field, receiving the reports of his commanders, trying to assess his victory. In his mind he was already considering how best to exploit it.

"Lyppeios has fled," someone told him. "We have reports from several prisoners that he left the field as soon as our infantry broke through his lines. Our pursuit cavalry is not far behind him, but he got away. He has lost half his army, either dead or captured."

"He might have saved more of them had he stayed. And the rest will not be eager to fight for him again."

Philip shook his head in disgust. He thought what it would be like for Lyppeios when he had to face the men he had deserted. It would be better to lie here, a stinking corpse, honorably dead.

Nevertheless, it would be necessary to reach an understanding with the man.

"Are there any nobles among the prisoners—or did they all run away?"

"Perhaps a few," Korous answered when he could make himself heard above the laughter. "We haven't had time to sift through them."

"Find one."

He was Lyppeios's cousin but seemed to have a bit more spine, since he had neither surrendered nor run away. He had been knocked unconscious by a fall from his horse and had almost killed the soldier who, thinking he was dead, had tried to strip him of his body armor. It had taken another crack on the head to subdue him. But the bravest men are not necessarily the cleverest and this one, upon being brought into his conqueror's presence, apparently assumed that he was going to be put to death as part of the king of Macedon's victory celebration—the Paionians were notorious for their harshness to prisoners—and was quite intemperate in the abuse he heaped on Philip, who merely smiled politely, the way one does in the presence of an unruly child, and offered him a cup of wine.

"You are the Lord Dekios?" he asked, merely as a token of respect. "And you are the second son of the Lady Aletheia, the king's father's sister?"

Dekios, who was perhaps twenty, darkly handsome with a neck like a bull, sat staring at his interrogator as if trying to remember where he had seen him before.

"You are unarmed," he said at last. "I could kill you with a blow—what is to prevent me?"

"Nothing, except that you might not succeed. I am not quite as harmless as I look. Besides, my guards would come rushing in at the first sound and kill you, and then you will not be able to go home and speak to your cousin for me. But you have not tasted your wine."

The second son of the Lady Aletheia looked at the cup on the table in front of him, considering it and, perhaps, the interesting possibility that he might after all survive the evening, and then picked it up, weighed it for a moment in his hand, and took a swallow.

"What would you have me tell the king?" he asked suspiciously, as if the matter were one in which he had some choice.

"Merely that he and his soldiers are of no use to me dead," Philip replied with unsettling calm. "I have no ambitions in Paionia, but I have no intention of leaving it until I am sure it will never threaten me again. An arrangement, on suitable terms, would therefore be useful."

For some reason this suggestion seemed to anger the Lord Dekios.

"Lyppeios still has an army at least as large as your own," he said hotly, setting the wine cup back down with sufficient force to spill half its contents onto the table. "He has merely to regroup and he will attack you again."

"You think so?" Philip raised his eyebrows speculatively. "I think he is beaten. I think he knows he is beaten. Half his army is dead or captured—if he cannot conquer with seven thousand men, how can he with three?"

"We were merely unlucky today."

"You were more than unlucky."

"You expect me to advocate surrender?"

"I don't expect you to advocate anything. Merely inform your king that Philip of Macedon is willing to discuss terms."

"And if he refuses?"

Philip allowed himself the slightest of smiles, as if the suggestion amused him but he would have considered it ill-bred to laugh.

"He will not refuse."

In the morning the Lord Dekios was given a good horse and told that he would have half a day's start before the main body of the Macedonian force began its advance on Lyppeios's capital, some three days' march to the north. A man on horseback can cover that distance much faster than an army on the march, so the king of the Paionians would have perhaps as much as two days to decide between peace and annihilation.

And Philip did not hurry. He allowed his soldiers a leisurely pace, sent out plenty of advance patrols, made very sure of himself. He did not want another battle, for all that he had no doubt concerning its outcome. Battles were expensive, and in his private thoughts he had already moved beyond this long autumn and the Paionians. The spring thaw would bring war with the Illyrians, and he must be ready for that.

So it was a relief when, the day after his scouts had reported seeing the low granite walls of what, in this wilderness, must pass for a city, an emissary came riding into his camp with an olive branch tied to his spear, in token of truce.

It was arranged that the two kings would meet alone on a stretch of open ground that was within sight of their two armies. Lyppeios was rather sulky and at first would not look his conqueror in the face.

"I will accept suitable hostages and such tribute as will compensate my men for their sufferings," Philip told him. "Beyond that, I will offer you a military alliance, which I suspect will be of service to us both."

Philip knew he had been right when he saw how the light changed in Lyppeios's eyes—having lost his first battle, the man was now afraid of his own nobles. His power and probably his life were at risk, and if he wanted to keep them, he would need at least the tacit support of the Macedonian king.

Very well, then, but he would have to pay for it.

"You cannot, however, be both my friend and the Illyrians'," Philip went on blandly. "You will have to choose."

From the expression of pain that crossed his face it was really possible to believe that King Lyppeios might be in love with old Bardylis's great-granddaughter, for he had the look of one who had been asked to sacrifice his dearest wish.

"Why did you attack us?" he asked, speaking for the first time and in a tone of injured innocence. The question, however, was merely an evasion, an excuse for putting off the inevitable. "You had sent tribute money to my father—why were you afraid of him and not of me?"

"I was more afraid of you."

Lyppeios's eyes narrowed slightly, as if he imagined himself insulted. He was doubtless under terrible strain, so his temper was unpredictable.

"Your father was too old and enfeebled to take much interest in war," Philip continued, as if he had noticed nothing. "But I knew you would move against me as soon as you were king."

"How could you know that?"

"Because it is what I would have done."

This answer seemed to ease the tension between them, and Lyppeios was at last able to raise his eyes.

"I was already marshaling my forces when word came that you had crossed the border," he said, almost as if it were a boast. Perhaps it even was.

"I know that. Otherwise you could not have fielded so large an army."

"They did me little enough good."

"War has changed," Philip said, with the polite shrug of someone making a general observation. "Numbers count for less—this is something I learned as a hostage in Thebes."

For a moment the two kings faced each other in silence, and suddenly Philip felt very old and tired. He was only twenty-three, and Lyppeios could not have been more than a year or two his junior, but the gulf between them seemed unbridgeable. It was not age that separated them, nor even experience, but Lyppeios seemed such a boy. There was a kind of innocence about him. Philip did not think he himself had ever been young in that particular way.

But the moment passed and Lyppeios reined in his horse so that the animal took perhaps half a step back.

"I accept your terms," he said, "since I have little choice. An envoy with full powers will come to your camp tomorrow to work out the details."

Philip watched him ride away, and suddenly he discovered that he almost envied the king of the Paionians. *You have taken a knock*, he thought, *but tomorrow you will still be alive, and a year from now you will hardly remember. Such a defeat would have destroyed me.*

42

Philip and his army crossed into Macedon in the midst of a blinding snow-storm. It was only by the merest chance that the Lynkestian scout did not ride straight past them.

"King Menelaos is but a few hours behind me," the man said. "His escort numbers fewer than twenty men, and he craves a word with you, My Lord."

"Yes, very well, but not here," Philip answered, gesturing at the snow that swirled around them like smoke. "There is a town not a morning's ride to the south, where my soldiers will be able to sleep out of the snow. I will wait for my uncle there."

"I hope we will be able to find it," the scout said, shaking his head. He looked rather scandalized when Philip laughed.

"Menelaos will know the way," he said. "In my father's day he once raided the place."

And so it was that, seven hours later, in the dining hall of a house owned by a local noble of doubtful loyalty—the man did not know to whom he should bow lower, his own king or the king of Lynkos—Philip and his uncle sat in front of the fire drinking wine mixed with only two parts of water, trying to pretend that they met as kinsmen rather than as sovereigns, trailing behind them a long history of rivalry and mistrust.

"I wept when I heard what had happened to your mother," Menelaos said after a long, brooding silence. "I wept, but I was not surprised. Even as a child she was willful and passionate. When she was seven years old our father gave her a ferret as a pet, and she seemed fond of it. Then one day she threw it into the kennel and stood there watching as the dogs tore it to pieces. She was whipped for that, but she would not cry. She would not explain why she had done such a thing and she would not cry. I think she was always a little mad.

And now her shade wanders the earth, banished forever from the realms of the dead."

"That at least it does not. Before her corpse was burned I slipped a gold coin into her mouth that she might pay the ferryman for her voyage across the River Styx. I buried her myself and left offerings in her grave."

Menelaos raised his eyebrows in astonishment. "You committed an impurity. Yet perhaps it was one which the gods could forgive—a son's act of pity can never offend too deeply. I am glad you told me."

Philip did not relish the subject of his mother and he made a slight, peremptory gesture with his hand to indicate that he wished to speak of these things no more.

"My mother has been dead for nearly seven years, and you are under siege by the Illyrians," he said with perhaps more edge in his voice than he intended. "I do not think you rode all this way in a snowstorm merely for the pleasure of unburdening your grief. What do you want, Uncle?"

For a moment the king of Lynkos seemed to be debating with himself if he should take offense, but if that was the case, he decided he would be better served by a display of faint amusement. Accordingly, he smiled.

"Everyone, it appears, is impatient with me." He picked up his wine cup and appeared to study the pattern under the glaze. Then he set it down again as if he had forgotten its existence. "The Illyrians think I have reigned too long and wish to chase me from my throne—either that or kill me sitting on it, whichever is more convenient—and my nephew thinks I waste his valuable time with insincere family chat."

He smiled again, the whole time studying Philip's face for some hint of a reaction, whether of embarrassment or something else it was impossible to say. At last he gave up the search as fruitless and his smile slowly vanished.

"You show great promise as a king, Philip. You have learned very quickly to be hard."

"I will ask again, Uncle—what do you want? And what are you prepared to surrender to get it?"

But Menelaos, who had balanced his enemies against each other for long enough to have developed a certain faith in his own agility, was not to be rushed into anything against his will.

"You have developed into something of a military wizard, Philip," he said, shaking his head in what seemed like astonished admiration. "You inherited a broken, demoralized army and a country hedged about by enemies, and now, not even a year later, you have won two major battles and are reckoned dangerous enough that the Athenians have signed a treaty of peace with you. I must concede you my respect—frankly, I had expected that by now you would already be dead."

"Are you disappointed?"

"No. I have not grown so lost to all human feeling that I would rejoice in the death of my sister's son."

"And, besides, now you need me."

"And, besides, now I need you."

Menelaos took a deep breath and let it out in a long, weary sigh. It was as if the accumulated strain of many anxious months had at last caught up with him.

"Do you know Pleuratos?" he asked.

"Yes. I met him while I was Bardylis's hostage."

"Yes, of course—you would have. I had forgotten." Menelaos absentmindedly touched the faint purplish birthmark that was visible on the right side of his face to about a finger's breadth above the beard, and for the first time Philip noticed how much gray had become mixed in with his kinsman's curly brown hair. "Well, for all that the old king lives, Pleuratos seems to be the one in authority. I could always deal with Bardylis, but his grandson is a different matter."

"I gathered as much from the fact that his soldiers now occupy about a quarter of your territory."

Philip smiled mirthlessly, and Menelaos looked as if he felt the thrust.

"They are bogged down in the snow," he said. "We are safe enough through the winter, but the spring will be another matter. Unless Pleuratos can be persuaded to withdraw, by the beginning of summer he will be in possession of Pisoderi and I will be dead or in exile. On the whole I would prefer death."

"Do you think there is any chance he will withdraw?"

Menelaos shook his head. "Why should he? If he can take Lynkos from me, I have nothing left with which to bribe him."

Plainly the king of the Lynkestians was not enjoying this conversation. He paused for a moment and swallowed deeply from his wine cup, as if nerving himself to go on.

"When the snows melt Pleuratos intends to finish me off quickly and then he will march south. Lynkos will be merely a preliminary skirmish, in itself a prize hardly worth the taking, but Lynkos is the gateway to Lower Macedon. It is you he yearns to destroy, not me. Thus by summer you will find yourself at war with the Illyrians—it is something that you cannot avoid. I am not even sure you wish to avoid it."

He looked into his nephew's blue-gray eyes—eyes so much like his dead sister's, the child of his father's second wife—perhaps searching them for some confirming sign, but he found none. Perhaps all he found there was the awareness that Philip's heart, like his mother's, hid its secrets well.

"And when you and Pleuratos meet," he continued, "there will be a great battle, perhaps the greatest battle since Troy. And in this inevitability I find my one hope of survival—that it takes place before and not after I am myself vanquished. It is a slender hope, for I think it probable that you will be defeated, but it is my last hope. Pleuratos offers only death, or that which, for a king, is worse than death. What do you offer, Philip?"

Philip glanced away for a moment, and then returned his gaze to Menelaos with an intensity that was almost painful.

"Support, Uncle. Such support as I would feel myself obliged to offer a kinsman—and a subject."

Menelaos gave a little cough of astonishment, as if he could not believe that defeat could come so quickly, so little heralded, so like a trap that lies unconcealed and yet strangely invisible. Philip, it was clear, would not bargain. He would only announce the terms on which he would accept surrender—terms that did not admit of a refusal.

For four generations the House of the Bakchiadai had reigned as masters of Lynkos and of their own destiny, ignoring the Argeadai's ancient claims of lordship. They had made war and peace as absolute sovereigns, treating with the kings of Lower Macedon as equals. But now, it seemed, all of that was to end, and at a word from the boy Menelaos had once caught poaching his boar.

"Very well," he said, with a slight shrug. "It would seem, Philip, that I have tethered my fate to yours."

The next morning, before Menelaos began his return journey to Lynkos, he took formal leave of Philip and acknowledged him as his sovereign master and king of all the Macedonians, obliging the members of his escort to do the same. Then he turned and rode away, back to the ice-choked mountains that, at least while the cold weather held, were his only security.

"Do you think he will honor his pledge?" Korous asked as he and Philip watched the Lynkestians disappear into the swirling snow.

"I think that even at this moment he is wondering how he can betray us to the Illyrians," Philip answered without turning round. "But I think he knows that Pleuratos will break any promise he makes."

"Then we are sure of him."

"No. He knows we will fight the Illyrians during the next campaigning season, but he may hope to remain neutral and then deal with a victor who is too exhausted to pose a threat to him. That is why, when the spring comes, we will move north before Pleuratos can begin to move south. When my uncle sees us at his doorstep, and understands we give him no third choice between being our ally or our enemy, even he will realize that he has seen the last of his opportunities for treachery. We will be sure of him then."

"Will we be ready to face the Illyrians by spring?"

Philip glanced over his shoulder and smiled thinly. "Have we a choice?"

. . .

From the walls of her great-grandfather's citadel, Audata watched the cavalry exercises in the long, sloping valley below. Men and horses appeared as nothing more than black smudges against the snow, which in places was deep enough that the horses sometimes had to jump to push their way through.

Winter had only just settled in, and Audata had not yet grown hardened to the cold. She wore a sheepskin cloak with the fleece on the inside, but the spot where she was standing was high and exposed and there was a damp, steady wind.

The cavalry exercises made no sense to her. She could detect neither pattern nor intention, only a series of frantic, random movements. All she understood of them was that their ultimate purpose was to destroy the only man she had ever loved.

"Is it only the wind that brings these tears to your eyes?"

The nearness of his voice startled her—that was all. She turned around to find Bardylis, king of the Illyrians, standing within arm's reach.

"You should not climb so many stairs, Great-Grandfather," she said to him. "There must be—"

"There are forty-seven. Yet sometimes one must do what one oughtn't, if only to prove that one is still alive." He smiled so that his ancient, seamed face appeared to crack open in a hundred places, and looked out over the plain, where men who had sworn loyalty to him unto death were throwing up great plumes of snow as they rode back and forth. "Have you developed an interest in military matters?"

"No."

"Really not? Well, then, perhaps there is someone among my nobles to whom you have taken a fancy."

She glanced at him with a baffled expression and then, suddenly, appeared to understand and dropped her catlike eyes.

"Only once before have I known you to come up here to watch the soldiers disporting themselves," he went on with that amusement the old sometimes feel in tormenting the young, "and that was when young Philip was among us. Are you thinking of him now?"

"I think of him constantly," she answered, with a matter-of-fact sincerity that made Bardylis regret his intrusion, because it reminded him that her heart was one of the few things in his world he did not command.

"Your father is levying soldiers in every corner of the realm. By spring he will have raised a force sufficient to allow him to field ten thousand men against Philip. And the strange thing is that he does not even suspect how you feel toward this king of Macedon whom he yearns so to destroy."

"Would it make any difference?"

"No." The old king shook his head. "No, for the wound to his vanity is deeper than that. If he knew, he would hate Philip all the more, but everything nourishes such hatred as your father's. And the summer grass will already be tall over one of their graves—I am glad for your peace of mind that it will not be within your power to choose which."

"Do you believe Philip will be crushed, Great-Grandfather?"

"Does it matter what I believe, child?" He smiled joylessly, knowing that she understood his thoughts. "But perhaps what Philip believes is of somewhat greater importance."

43

All through that winter Philip's nights were plagued by a dream. He was a boy again, summoned to his father's deathbed. He would enter the room and find the House of the Argeadai all there, even Arrhidaios, his body torn by spear wounds, who this time had somehow contrived to arrive ahead of him.

"Here is Philip, late as usual," his mother would say, the front of her tunic drenched in the blood that trickled from the slash across her throat, and the others, all except Pausanias, who held his battered head between his hands, would nod in disapproving agreement.

"Save your tears for the funeral," Alexandros would announce sternly. He was naked and shining with oil, with the wounds from Praxis's sword showing below his rib cage, and standing beside him was Perdikkas, dressed in mud-spattered armor, the gash from an Illyrian sword stroke running across his face. Perdikkas always turned his eyes away when he saw Philip and, in a voice too low to be intelligible, said something to Ptolemy, who would smile with bloodstained lips.

Nothing is ever surprising in a dream, so Philip never felt any astonishment at the discovery that all the assembled members of his family were dead. After all, most of them had been dead for years, and the dream, which was not a memory but a dream, existed not in the true past but in that past that is also the present. Therefore Philip the boy in the dream accepted all this as natural, and Philip the dreamer, the helpless spectator, witnessed it with horror.

Only the old king was alive. His eyes would come to rest on Philip and he would make a small, feeble gesture, beckoning him closer. Amyntas's lips would move soundlessly, forming the words, "The king's burden . . ."

And then Philip would wake up. In that first moment, when he realized it was merely the dream again, he would experience an odd mixture of surprise and disappointment. The ghastly faces of the dead were gone, but Amyntas's last words remained unspoken. *I will never know what he meant to tell me*, Philip would think. *I will never know.*

And sometimes, while the winter sun shone brightly as the king of Macedon drilled with his soldiers for the battle with the Illyrians that would decide all their fates, he would be seized with a terrible feeling of regret, as if his life were blighted and all his labor destined to come to nothing because asleep or awake he had never heard the sentence Amyntas, his father, had left unfinished.

I will never know.

At such times he felt utterly abandoned, cut off from gods and men. These were his thoughts, this the yawning pit of despair that opened before him as events carried him toward the great crisis of his life.

"We must have ten thousand soldiers before the spring thaw," he told his officers, who exchanged worried glances, as if they imagined his mind to be cracking under the strain.

"Ten thousand, no less," he went on, almost daring them to refuse. "Pleuratos will have at least that many, and we cannot afford a victory that leaves us so weak we might as well have been defeated. If we fight this battle on equal terms, we have some chance of keeping our losses tolerably low."

"How can you hope to raise such a force?" Lachios asked him, giving form to the question that was in everyone's mind. "It has hardly been a year since King Perdikkas lost an army of four thousand prime troops. The recruiting officers are stripping the villages naked—we will be lucky if by spring we have eight or nine thousand men under arms in the whole country. We cannot leave the garrisons empty, Philip."

"I will have ten thousand men if I have to march north with every soldier in Macedon at my back."

"If you lose, the nation will be defenseless."

"If I lose, there will be no nation to defend."

It was not a proposition with which anyone could argue, so the training camps soon grew bloated with conscripts, farm boys, most of whom had never held either sword or shield in their lives. These Philip and his officers drilled until their knees were ready to fold beneath them, until they knew their weapons better than the faces of their wives and mothers, until they forgot they had ever been anything except soldiers.

During the first week they would nurse the bruises on their shins where they bumped against the rims of their shields, and they would complain endlessly about the drill.

"Carry your shields higher," the veterans would tell them. "You will find that less vexatious than an Illyrian spear through your guts."

"How can anyone do battle all jammed up like this, with the next man's elbow almost in his face? My mother's uncle won enough booty fighting for old King Amyntas to buy forty head of sheep—in his day all a soldier needed was courage."

"Do you want to be a dead hero? This king keeps his men alive, and he wins. You take my advice and practice your drill. I have served under the Lord Philip since Aiane and, believe me, he knows what he is doing. That is him there."

"That is the king?"

It was something they acquired along with a knowledge of the proper way to manage a pike staff and how to pad their greaves to keep them from chafing, this conviction that their king, who walked among them in an old brown cloak and was not too proud to drink soldiers' beer, was the darling of Ares, the war god's favorite son. He was never weary, never afraid, and never wrong. It was deemed a stroke of luck to stand near him in battle, for the line in which the Lord Philip fought could not be broken. He was at once perfectly familiar and the object of the most dreadful awe, and the confidence he inspired in his men was absolute. The green recruits learned it from the veterans of past campaigns, who told stories of the battles they had fought and the victories they had won, hardly conscious of the myth they were creating. Their king had become the wall sheltering them against a time of disasters.

And if Philip believed in the myth, no one could say, for his doubts and his dreams he kept locked away in the privacy of his soul. It was his nature to have many friends but no confidants. His father had spoken of the king's burden with his dying breath, and what, after all, was the king's burden if not this?

It was also in his nature that when he received a letter from the new king of the Eordoi he carried it around with him for half the day before at last looking at it.

"It is from Deucalion," he told Korous as they sat on the ground, resting their backs against the wheel of a supply wagon while they waited for dinner.

"What does it say?"

Philip scanned halfway down the scroll and then put it back in his pocket. "It says he is alive and safe and will be with us in the spring."

"How does he like being a king?"

"He doesn't mention it."

It was not until that night, alone in his tent with no company except the flickering light of an oil lamp, that he looked again at Deucalion's letter.

"My throne seems secure," the king of the Eordoi wrote. "I owe this as much to your uncle Menelaos as to you, since my nobles seem to have profited from his experience with Pleuratos and realize that if they hope to avoid being overrun by the Illyrians, they need a king who commands universal support—I enjoy the luxury of being the only available candidate.

"And behind me, of course, they see you. We are perhaps a barbarous people, but we hear a little of what happens in the larger world and reports of your victories have found their way to us and have freshened memories of my father's defeat at the hands of a certain king of the Elimoitai. News that the Athenians and Paionians have suffered a similar fate has done much to soothe my nobles' wounded vanity. Their attitude toward you is one of fear mingled with a certain pride, for, if you are not an Eordoi, the Eordoi are at least Macedonians and thus your triumphs become in some sense ours.

"So for the moment I feel myself safe from challenge, and I am making it understood that the Eordoi have a stake in the outcome of the great conflict that is coming, that we must choose sides while there is still time, that it is simply not in our power to remain neutral spectators. This is less difficult than you might imagine, for my nobles are at least not fools and have a great yearning to be on the winning side. Beyond this, they have before them the example of King Menelaos and know that the Illyrians are no less dangerous as allies than as enemies. I have not been an open partisan of Macedon, for it is better if my nobles draw the right conclusion for themselves and this is thus a decision that seems to make itself. Yet I have no doubt of the outcome.

"Thus, when the spring comes, I will be able to offer you perhaps a thousand infantry and eighty to a hundred cavalry. I am training them in the tactics I learned from you, so perhaps they will not utterly disgrace us.

"Be of good cheer, Philip, king of all the Macedonians, and know that your enemies are mine. Your friend and faithful servant . . ."

And as king of all the Macedonians Philip was pleased. His careful cultivation of the boy who had been his hostage was being repaid handsomely. It was on a more human level that he read Deucalion's pledges of allegiance as almost a reproach.

Deucalion's assessment was largely correct. The Eordoi could not help but be drawn in on one side or another, and they had more to hope for from Macedon than from the Illyrians. Philip knew, however, that his young protege's estimates were based more on the impulses of personal loyalty than on the cold-eyed appraisal of a situation that should mark the calculations of a king. Deucalion had chosen Philip as his personal hero—after all, Philip had gone to some trouble to ensure that choice—and a hero, by definition, is always victorious. Therefore, the Macedonians would triumph over the Illyrians. How could it be otherwise?

Yet what if he lost? Philip was not a callow boy to be blinded by a reputation, even his own—perhaps most especially his own. He put his own chances at no better than even. His own defeat was even a probability, and what then? What if, like Perdikkas, he was simply overwhelmed and destroyed? Philip knew that if he perished, his allies would perish with him and then he would have betrayed this boy, whom he loved almost as a younger brother.

Thus he was aware that, at least in one sense, he was betraying a trust. That such betrayals were a king's business in life, that it was his duty to make whatever use he could of whatever instruments were within his grasp, was not a consolation. He was privately appalled at his own ruthlessness.

Well, then, he thought as he blew out the tiny flame of his oil lamp and lay down for what he knew in advance would be a night of tortured sleep, *I suppose then I have no choice but to win.*

By the middle of Panemos, that month when the snow was still deep but was beginning to take on a certain cheesy softness that is the earliest hint of warmer weather, Philip moved his base camp to within a few hours' ride of the border with Lynkos to be ready to march north with the first thaw. The camp was made large to accommodate eight or nine thousand men, but the soldiers from outlying garrisons were still making their slow way to the assembly point, so there was only a small force with Philip when the patrols reported back that a group of fifty riders was on its way down the mountain trails.

"They were no more than two hours from the plains when we spotted them, but their horses will be nearly spent after such a journey. They are probably three or four hours behind us."

"Could you identify them?"

"No, Lord, but from that direction they must be coming from Pisoderi."

"Then they are probably emissaries sent by King Menelaos. Dispatch an honor guard to receive them."

But Philip's conjecture was not quite borne out, for King Menelaos was himself a member of the party—along with four or five men in the dress of Illyrian nobles. They arrived half an hour after dark and were all exhausted, having been forced to sleep in the snow for two nights together. They were given a hot meal and a tent with a brazier in it, so the Illyrians in the party were not in a mood to take offense that the king of Macedon did not receive them that first night. They had probably all been asleep for an hour when Philip had a private audience with his uncle.

"Who are your friends?"

The two men walked together along the camp's defensive perimeter, where they could be sure no one would overhear them. There was a slow but icy wind. Even inside the fleece-lined cloak, Menelaos looked profoundly miserable.

"They arrived six days ago, under token of truce," he said as if even to admit this much was a humiliating concession. "I presume they carry some sort of offer for a peaceful settlement."

"You mean you don't know?"

The king of the Lynkestians shook his head. "They made it plain their embassy was to you, not to me—all they wanted was safe passage through such territory that I still control. I thought it best to come along, however, since it is my fate they have come to discuss."

He stopped for a moment to fumble with a pair of gloves and for just an instant, before he noticed the appraising expression in his nephew's eyes, allowed the full measure of his despair to show in his face.

"I suppose I shouldn't have brought them here," he went on. "Everything they see will be reported back to Pleuratos, but I—"

"There is no harm done." Philip, perhaps to save his uncle's feelings, seemed preoccupied with tracing the outline of the earthwork's crest against the gray-black night sky. "I will have them on their way again by the morning after tomorrow, if only to give them the impression that I am concealing something, but the intelligence they carry home with them will be misleading—it will be at least five days before we even begin to approach full strength. What is your guess as to their mission?"

Menelaos's answer was a long time in coming. The two kings had resumed their walk, and the silence between them seemed to have become permanent.

"I have given up being clever," he said at last. "When they tell you, and if you elect to take me into your confidence, then I will know. It makes little difference anyway, since Pleuratos is not a man to be trusted."

He seemed astonished when Philip began to laugh.

"We are none of us men to be trusted, Uncle. Nevertheless, I would value your impression of these hill bandits."

"They think they have won already. While they were in Pisoderi they swaggered around my court like they had come to pick out their share of the spoils."

"Will you join me tomorrow when I receive them? You understand the situation in the north better than I."

Menelaos nodded, visibly pleased but valiantly struggling to conceal the fact, and they headed back toward the center of the camp.

The next morning, when Pleuratos's envoys were shown into Philip's tent, the king of Lynkos was present, standing beside his nephew, appearing as if that fact alone constituted a complete revenge.

The Illyrians looked embarrassed, which corresponded to Philip's intention—it seemed unwise to begin negotiations, however remote their prospects of success, by accepting so marked a snub to his ally and close kinsman. The envoys' mortification manifested itself in an impenetrable arrogance of manner; they kept glancing at King Menelaos as if they could not understand how he had arrived ahead of them.

For the rest, they had the appearance of prosperous savages, parading their wealth in massive gold earrings and the silver bands they wore on their bare upper arms. One of them, a squat, solidly built man in the middle of life, with a long, ragged scar on his forehead, Philip remembered from his time as Bardylis's captive.

"What brings you all this way, Xophos?" he asked the man, whose expression went from surprise to pleasure to something akin to disappointment at having been recognized—ten years ago he had been Bardylis's man, so perhaps his loyalty to the heir apparent was still suspect and it did not suit him to be received on such familiar terms by Pleuratos's old enemy. "I might have thought this season of the year would find you at home, fighting mock battles in the snow with the other children."

Xophos laughed in spite of himself and then, perhaps thinking that he had nothing more to lose, allowed himself a wide grin.

"My Lord Philip always loved to go over to the attack," he said in heavily accented Greek, "but, as I hear you have discovered for yourself, real war is much more amusing."

"Well, it appears then we will all have a jolly summer. And now, My Lord, let us know what message you have brought, for there is nothing to be gained from prolonging this visit."

After a little shrug, as if at the impatience of a rude boy, the Illyrian turned back to his colleagues. They exchanged a few whispered words in their own language, and then Xophos, who perhaps by default had become their spokesman, cleared his throat—the formal preface, one gathered, to the business that had brought them.

"My Lord Bardylis, great king of the Dardanians and of many other races, is not without mercy toward his beloved great-grandson and is prepared to make an offer of peace—"

"And what is the price of the king's mercy?" Philip interrupted, his eyes narrowing in a display of suspicion. "The Bardylis I remember would have sold his whole family to push the borders of his empire forward another two hundred paces. Exactly what is the going rate in great-grandsons?"

Menelaos, standing just outside his field of vision, uttered a short syllable of laughter, but Philip never so much as smiled.

"What price, Xophos? What does the old thief want in return?"

"Price, My Lord?" Xophos, along with his fellow subjects of the great king, contrived to look appalled at this shocking lack of filial piety. It was not a particularly convincing display. "He asks no tribute, nor any extension of territory. He is content that things remain as they are . . ."

"Oh—is that it?" Philip shook his head. "As long as my great-grandfather is allowed to keep what he has stolen, he is content for the present to steal no more—I am filled with admiration for his generosity."

"It is a good offer, and kindly meant. My Lord Philip would be well advised to accept."

And then, after glancing at Menelaos, whom apparently he had not forgiven his unseemly levity, Xophos, with another of his eloquent shrugs, dismissed him from existence.

"Besides," he went on, "why should you wish to go to war when not a dirt clod of your own lands has been threatened?"

"Has it not? You surprise me," answered Philip, looking not in the least surprised. "I might remind you that I am king of Macedon."

The Illyrians merely looked blank, giving the impression that they were dimly aware of something having eluded them.

"Yes, but Lynkos . . ."

"Lynkos, My Lord Xophos, is part of Macedon. It has always been part of Macedon. The Lynkestians are Macedonians—my subjects, for, like my fathers before me, I am king of all the Macedonians. They look to me for protection and redress of their grievances, and it is to them and to the immortal gods that I have given my oath as king. You may tell Bardylis that it is not in my power to concede to any other king so much of the sacred soil of Macedon as will fit comfortably inside a horse trough."

"Is this your answer, then, My Lord?" Xophos wore an expression of settled gravity, as he might in the presence of some distasteful folly.

"There is one more thing." Philip picked up his sword, which happened to be lying across the writing table at his right hand, and held it out as if offering the blade for their admiration. "On the day of my election I washed this weapon at the shrine of Herakles—an ancient rite of Macedonian kings."

Slowly he raised the point, until it was not more than a finger's width from Xophos's throat.

"When the snows melt I will wash it again, this time in Illyrian blood."

For a moment no one moved. It was even possible that Xophos thought that his death was upon him. Then Philip lowered his sword and smiled.

"My Lords, this interview is at an end."

When the Illyrians were gone, Philip carefully replaced the sword on his writing table and collapsed into a chair.

"I was afraid you might have accepted," Menelaos said at last, perhaps only for the comfort of hearing his own voice.

"What would have been the point? If Bardylis sent this embassy, I am sure he did not expect me to accept. He is a clever old scoundrel and doubtless has achieved his real objective—now his ambassadors have had their look and can go home."

"And now there will be war for certain."

For a moment Philip appeared not to have heard, and then, very slowly, he nodded.

"Yes. Now there will be war."

·　·　·

Two days before the Macedonian army, now numbering eight thousand strong, was to break camp for the march north, one of the watch soldiers came at first light to Philip's tent to tell him that his great black stallion Alastor was dead.

"He simply collapsed." The man stood wringing his hands, seemingly afraid to look Philip straight in the face, as if afraid he would be thought to blame. Everyone knew that the king put a great value on this particular horse. "It happened not a quarter of an hour ago. His knees suddenly buckled and he was down."

"I would like to see."

Alastor was lying on the ground, his eyes open and his head at a peculiar angle. The tether rope was still around his neck.

"Their hearts burst, I think," Geron said. The king's chief groom, who had put Philip on his first horse when the boy was no more than two, shook his head. "It is a thing one sees from time to time with some stallions. It is as if their own strength destroys them."

"Perhaps. No, doubtless you are right."

Yet it was somehow terrible that Alastor should have died thus—some horses, like some men, should never die until they are killed. Even Geron felt it.

"Burn his body," Philip said, looking away, as if the sight of the dead animal hurt his eyes. "Have a funeral pyre erected, and I will make sacrifice for the repose of his great soul. I will not have the crows making a meal of him."

Geron looked troubled—to him it seemed almost an impiety, but he said nothing. The king's will was not to be ignored.

"See to it." Philip turned on his heel and walked away.

He kept to his tent all that morning, until the chief groom came to tell him that all was in readiness. Men said that as he held the torch to the logs of the funeral pyre he looked as stricken as if he had lost his dearest friend.

"I wonder what it means," Lachios muttered to Korous as they strolled away together afterward. "The king's horse drops dead just before we are to go on campaign—it is an omen, whether for good or ill I cannot guess."

"That was the horse that killed the Lord Ptolemy," Korous announced, seemingly having just remembered the fact.

"I had heard that story. Well, he will kill no more of the king's enemies."

"Yes, it is the end of something. Or the beginning."

44

As soon as the spring thaw was under way, Pleuratos began moving the main body of his army up to northern Lynkos, which his soldiers had held all through the winter. This was not because he felt any sense of urgency about the situation there—the Lynkestians were defeated and demoralized, trembling on the verge of collapse, and the Macedonians, for all Philip's wild threats, were not a serious opponent. No, Pleuratos's real motive for inflicting on his men a long march over muddy terrain was simply to escape from his grandfather, who was making his life a misery.

Old Bardylis had not been encouraged by the report of his envoys, who had estimated the Macedonian force at no more than a few thousand strong.

"Xophos said the camp looked as if it had been laid out for perhaps as many as six or seven thousand men," he kept saying. "Menelaos probably still commands a thousand or so, plus cavalry. Suppose you find yourself facing an enemy army of eight thousand. What then?"

"I will have ten thousand, along with five hundred cavalry. I am not a boy anymore, Grandfather. I fought my first battle before young Philip was even born. Are you suggesting that without a crushing advantage I must despair of victory?"

When the old man remained silent, Pleuratos shook his head in disgust.

"Besides, the camp was probably a bluff."

This made Bardylis laugh. "You mean he built it all on the off chance that we would send someone to look at it? You think he has nothing better to do with his time?"

"Then perhaps he built it to keep his men occupied during the winter."

"You really are a dolt, Pleuratos. I really think your mother must have been playing my son false, because otherwise I am at a loss to explain how you came to be such a fool."

These conversations only made Pleuratos hate his grandfather more, if such a thing was possible, so that the mere sound of the old king's voice grated on him like a carpenter's file.

So he was more than happy to trade the conveniences of the court for the rigors of campaigning. He did not object to the mud or the almost daily rain-storms that left one soaked and freezing and without hope of finding even a dry piece of firewood. Each day's march, he felt, carried him one day closer to the decisive victory and would silence his grandfather forever. The last time, Bardylis had spoken as if the defeat had been his instead of Perdikkas's, whose corpse he had brought home slung over the back of a horse, but the coming battle with Philip would have an outcome admitting of no equivocation. In a few months, when Lynkos was reduced to an Illyrian province and there was not a Macedonian left in arms from the mountains to the sea, then the old man would be left with nothing to say. It would be almost as good as if he were dead—perhaps, in some ways, it would be even better.

And by the time they reached the first Illyrian encampments on Lynkes-tian soil the rain had stopped. The ground was still a sea of mud, but the snow had disappeared. A few days of sunshine and the mud would dry.

"Philip has been in Pisoderi for half a month. It is rumored he has close to eight thousand men with him."

He received the news even before he had dismounted his horse. The garrison commander, who owed his position to Pleuratos's favor, looked as if he expected to be whipped as the bearer of evil tidings.

"I did not think there were eight thousand Macedonians left." The heir to King Bardylis's empire laughed, but a certain narrowing of his eyes betrayed his real state of mind. "How many horse does he command?"

"There is no way of knowing."

"You mean to tell me you haven't thought to send out a few patrols in force to take a look?"

"The Macedonians have sealed off all the approaches to the south. It will take more men than I command to break through."

Pleuratos decided that, yes, he probably would have the man whipped. He climbed down from his horse and, without another word, went into the hast-ily constructed wooden building that housed the garrison command. That night, he took a jar of wine to bed with him and sat up drinking alone until almost dawn. The next morning, no one had the courage to wake him, so he slept until just before noon.

He awoke with a frightful headache, but his temper was improved. It no longer seemed to matter that Philip's army was almost equal in strength to his own. Philip was a boy whose experience of war was almost nothing—a few cheap victories did not make a great commander. Pleuratos was quite confi-dent he could crush him.

"His soldiers for the most part are green," he told his officers. "After all, the best units of the Macedonian army fell with Perdikkas."

When, with the greatest possible tact, it was pointed out that this green army had beaten a much larger force of Paionians, Pleuratos had his answer. "Lyppeios is notoriously an idiot who could not lead a successful attack on a brothel. My daughter has several times refused to marry him, in spite of the fact that he is handsome as a god—that should tell you something about his powers of conquest. I think there is nothing useful we can learn from the example of Lyppeios."

He glared around the table at his officers, seeming to dare anyone to dispute his judgment, and when he was satisfied that the silence would remain unbroken he nodded.

"Since young Philip is so eager for a fight, we will give it to him. We will allow our men ten days in which to rest, and then we will march south. I will take my oath on it—in half a month's time the road to Pella will be clogged with dead Macedonians."

Deucalion had kept his promise and arrived at the assembly point outside Pisoderi with an army of nearly eleven hundred men, including a hundred cavalry. Attending their lord was almost of the entire nobility of the Eordoi, many of whom had fought against Philip but now greeted their former adversaries with the enthusiasm of old comrades in arms.

Three days later Deucalion joined Philip's leading commanders as they accompanied the king on a tour of the northwest perimeter, just an hour's walk beyond which the army of the Illyrians was crouched like a cat waiting beside a mouse's burrow. Now and then they would even come within sight of enemy patrols, which would always stop for a moment, probably to take a count, and then canter away, as if they had orders not to engage the Macedonians.

"They are waiting," Philip said. "They do not want to provoke us into taking the offensive. They prefer not to surrender the initiative. I am content that it should be so, provided only that the battlefield remains of our choosing. Let them imagine they decide when to fight if we can say where."

His officers exchanged glances but said nothing—Philip was merely thinking out loud. They were accustomed to their master's curious ways and knew he would explain his intentions when he thought the time was right.

Two hours later, as they were passing through a broad meadow that seemed to pour out of a notch between two hills like water out of a broken pot, Philip suddenly dug his heels into his horse's flanks and broke into a gallop, leaving his astonished companions scrambling to catch up. After covering a distance of perhaps three hundred paces he wheeled about, coming to an abrupt stop— Deucalion could see that he was laughing, although the sound of it was drowned in the pounding of horse's hooves—and then just as suddenly gal-loped off at an angle. He seemed to be daring them to catch him.

The game, if indeed that was what it was, lasted for perhaps half an hour. Mounted men raced across the wide expanse of grassland, switching direc-tions at random as if to no purpose save that of wearing out their horses.

And then, as unexpectedly as it had begun, it ended. All at once Philip swung a leg over his horse and dropped to his feet. When his officers reached him he was contentedly sitting on the ground, chewing on a blade of grass.

"The battle will be here," he said, making a gesture with his hand that swung around, taking in the whole meadow, right up to the break between the rocky hills. "Unless the Illyrians mean to take a walking tour of Lynkos there aren't more than two or three points at which they will dare move south in such force—we must be very sure he comes through that pass. This is where we will be waiting for him."

Deucalion was about to say something, but a glance from Lachios checked him. Lachios was perhaps closer to the king than any of them and knew his master's mind and temper, when to speak, and when to let the flow of ideas run unchecked.

"We will fortify the other positions," Philip went on, taking the waterskin someone handed him and washing the dust out of his throat. "This one too, but the gap is so wide here and the hills so low that Pleuratos will see that it is impossible to defend. He will be looking for an ambush, of course—we will engage his scouting parties in a few sharp little skirmishes just as they come in, and that will set his mind at rest. Pleuratos is at bottom a stupid man and probably a coward. I should hate to see him seized at the last moment by an attack of idiot caution."

"What advantage do you think this site gives us?" Korous asked. It was merely that, a question. It was the same question that was in all their minds. All of them expected Philip to have an answer and all were surprised when he shook his head.

"None—we will not be setting a trap, if that was what you were thinking. We will give the Illyrians what they want but probably do not expect, the chance for an equal fight. The ground is flat and one has only to look at the thickness of the grass to tell that it is not too rocky Have we not just been dem-onstrating its fitness for cavalry operations? I am sure it will suit us both very well—Pleuratos would probably have picked this spot himself. No, the point is not what we gain by forcing the battle here. The point is what we do not lose."

Deucalion had always prided himself that he knew Philip, that he under-stood him with the intimacy of a close and trusted friend, almost of a brother. For years he had lived with this man as a virtual member of his family, had listened to him playfully teasing his wife over breakfast, and beheld at close range the agony of his grief when his wife died. Who could know him better?

Yet now there was a look on the king's face that Deucalion had never known before, the look of one haunted by a vision, and he knew that he was in the presence not of Philip the man or even Philip the ruler but of some third being who was a stranger to him. He knew that in that moment Philip was not among them but in the midst of the battle that would soon be fought on this empty stretch of grassland, which he saw in his mind as if it were happening now, before his very eyes. The child of his imagination had become real for him.

There were such men, it was said, born with a special gift for war, as if Ares had touched them with his own divine genius. If this was blended with a natural cruelty so that they were blinded to all but war's glory, such men were greatly blessed, but Philip was not cruel. Nothing was hidden from him and therefore he was spared nothing. If he saw victory, he also saw suffering and death. If he saw war's glory, he also saw its senseless horror. Deucalion could not find it in his heart to envy him.

The king of Macedon smiled, as if breaking the charm by an act of his will. It was a smile to turn one's blood to ice water.

"This site will allow both sides perfect freedom of maneuver," he went on. "Our cavalry formations will hold together as they would not over broken ground and our infantry will be able to use their superior discipline to full effect. We need every advantage we can gain because it will not be enough merely to defeat Pleuratos. He can withdraw and fight again another day, but we cannot—we are stretched too thin for that. If we only defeat Pleuratos, then he will come back another time and defeat us, for we will be too weakened to withstand him. Thus we must utterly destroy him or we ourselves are lost. We will never have another chance like this."

Pleuratos was growing impatient. The sun had shone brightly every day he had been in Lynkos, and his men were rested and fit. He had sent spies into the Macedonian territory, but none of them ever returned—some had even been found with their throats cut inside the Illyrian lines—and thus he had no notion of Philip's strength or dispositions. Every day he waited, he felt himself more a prey to unreasonable fears. He knew he had to engage the enemy soon or his own anxiety would betray him into some mistake. Six days after arriving in Lynkos he issued orders that his great army would march south at dawn.

He had decided to make his breakthrough at a wide gap between two hills, the weakest point in the enemy line. His advance parties informed him that the position was fortified but not heavily, and less than an hour of easy fighting proved enough to secure his soldiers from ambush. The defenders, when faced with so massive an attack, simply melted away.

But the moment he was through to the broad meadow that opened up on the other side, Pleuratos grasped why the Macedonians had withdrawn with such indecent haste—it was almost as if Philip had invited him in.

Yet it was not a trap. After that first panicky instant of recognition, when he saw that he had merely followed a lure, Pleuratos had only to look about him to realize that this could not possibly be a trap. A thousand paces across the meadow he could just make out a few Macedonian horsemen, but his scouts reported that the enemy presence was not yet large enough to pose a threat, and the terrain itself did not especially favor either side. Philip had merely chosen this as the site of their engagement, and Pleuratos had to admit that he had nothing to complain of.

It took well over three hours to move the entire Illyrian force through the pass and onto the field of battle, and while he waited Pleuratos listened to the reports of his scouts. Philip was marshaling his army. The Macedonians numbered ten thousand infantry and perhaps as many as six hundred horse. That boy was obviously prepared to make a fight of it.

For the first time, Pleuratos felt the darkening shadow of doubt. It was not so much that the enemy matched him in numbers since, after all, the bulk their forces had to be completely untested and therefore almost useless. More than anything it was the dawning recognition that Philip genuinely wanted to do battle. Philip had accepted the challenge, had assembled a huge army, had even picked the field. The initiative was his.

He isn't afraid, Pleuratos thought. *He welcomes this.*

It was almost as if he could hear old Bardylis's mocking, scornful laughter.

45

"The Illyrians are forming their infantry up into a defensive square."

Lachios, in command of the cavalry's left wing, dismounted his horse and crouched beside his king, who was sitting on an overturned water bucket, mending a sandal. Philip was frowning with concentration as he trimmed the end of a leather strap—at first he seemed not to have heard.

"How extraordinary," he said at last, as if to himself. "They like to go on the attack, so Pleuratos must be frightened. Only one square?"

"Only one."

"How are they positioning their cavalry?"

"The bulk are clustered on the right."

"In what numbers?"

"By rough count, about five hundred in both wings."

Philip put his cobbler's knife back into a little wooden toolbox and slipped the sandal onto his foot. Then for the first time he turned his full attention to Lachios.

"They will be good for only one charge, but that will be ferocious. All we have to do is give them a target and they will attack—they will not be able to help themselves. We will absorb that first charge as best we can and then you and Korous hit them as they try to regroup."

Lachios nodded. He had heard all this before, but he did not resent being reminded, because it was something that Philip always did. One grew accustomed to it. In fact, it was almost reassuring.

"And then we will go for the opening," he answered as if continuing his master's sentence.

Philip nodded in his turn.

"Yes. The infantry will crack them on the right corner—since they are so intent on guarding it, that must be where they feel their weakness—and then the cavalry will do the rest."

"You are not to be dissuaded, then?"

"No. The key will be the infantry assault, and that is where I must be."

"A king should take better care of his life, particularly if he has no successor. If you are killed, it will be worse than if we lost."

The king of Macedon laughed.

"We have had this conversation before," he said. "Admit it, Lachios—you simply think it is undignified to go into battle without a horse between one's knees."

Lachios smiled and gave a little shrug. "There is something to what you say. I am offended by the idea of you rubbing shoulders with peasant boys. It is not the way a gentleman should fight."

"It is the way the Thebans fight."

"Who claims the Thebans are gentlemen?"

They could both laugh now.

And then for a moment neither man spoke. A soldier on the eve of combat learns to deal with his fear as best he can, knowing that courage will come when it is needed, yet it is good at such times not to be alone.

"How many times have we been through this, Philip?"

"You mean fighting on the same side?"

They laughed again, and the burden lightened for a moment.

"I know what you mean, though. There always seems to be just one more battle we have to fight, and then we will be safe. So we fight the battle, and then there is one more. Sometimes I think it will not end until the gods grow sick of our folly and destroy the race of men utterly."

Lachios shaded his eyes with his hand and looked up at the sun. "It is already an hour past noon."

"There will be plenty of time—never fear. We had a full moon last night, so we can keep on fighting well past dark. I wonder if it has yet dawned on Pleuratos what will happen if today goes against him."

Lachios gave his head a mystified shake.

"I did not like to speak of it before," Philip went on. "It seemed bad luck. But I did not choose this spot simply because the ground is even and good for cavalry. Did you see how long it took the Illyrians to make their way through the pass?"

"Then you *have* set a trap." Lachios smiled with wolfish rapacity. "We can retreat in good order, but if the Illyrians try to flee, they will block up their only escape like apples trying to pass through the neck of a wine jar. The slaughter will be terrible."

"Yes, it will be terrible. I have not forgotten that these are the men who massacred my brother and four thousand of his soldiers. I propose to make certain that none of them will ever kill another Macedonian again."

. . .

As Philip had predicted, the battle began with a massed charge by the Illyrian cavalry. For Lachios that was the hardest moment, to watch them galloping across the battlefield, many of them straight at the outside corner of the third infantry square, where the king was waiting for them in the front line. It did not seem possible that men on foot could possibly survive, let alone repel such an attack.

Yet the squares held. Perhaps a hundred of the Illyrian horsemen never lived to get within twenty paces of striking a blow—the open space between the two armies was strewn with fallen men and horses—but many more than that reached the Macedonian formations to spread panic and death. The front line was a tangle of fighting as some of the Illyrians, oblivious to the long pikes, even jumped their horses over the wall of shields to land crashing down on the tightly packed columns of men who had nowhere to run. It was an appalling thing to watch.

Yet the squares held. Common soldiers said that the king's presence turned a line of soldiers into an iron wall, and that day it seemed no more than the literal truth. The Illyrians, who at least were not cowards, struck out with their swords and slashed at the men whose greedy hands reached up to pull them down. Thus they killed and died, and at last those who were left alive found they had to fight their way free. And behind them the front ranks of Philip's infantry simply refilled and closed.

Then suddenly, above the noise of battle, there arose from the Macedonian lines the sound of swords being beaten against shields, a rhythmic pulse that seemed to make the very air shake. That was the signal Lachios had been waiting for.

"The king lives and triumphs!" he shouted, holding his sword above his head. "Strike now for Philip and for Macedon!"

The Illyrian cavalry, when it saw that now it was under attack, made one last confused effort to regroup, but it only managed to concentrate its numbers enough to make itself even easier prey. Hit from two sides at once, it would fall back from one blow only to meet another. The slaughter was terrible. Lachios himself killed four of the enemy in the first charge, one at such close range that the man's blood spattered his face.

Once they had broken through, the Macedonian horsemen wheeled about, reversing their formation, just as they had done in countless drills, and turned to attack a second time, but the Illyrians, those who were not already in full retreat, were so spread out that they were no longer capable of any coherent defense.

"Leave them to the bowmen!" Lachios shouted.

He took a quick look about him and estimated his losses at perhaps twenty.

They had destroyed the Illyrian cavalry as a fighting force and were now in unquestioned possession of the no-man's-land between the two opposing armies. A cheap success and certainly the last to be won with so little Macedonian blood spilled. Now the battle belonged once more to Philip and his foot soldiers—might the gods show them a little mercy.

With a wave of his hand he signaled his horsemen to follow him as he rode off the field. Even before the cavalry was out of the way the two squares that made up the left wing of the Macedonian infantry began a slow inward turn, their first move toward engaging the main enemy force.

"It is beautiful in its own way." Korous had ridden up beside him on a small patch of high ground that allowed a view of the battleground. "Philip is perhaps the only commander in history to turn war into a work of art."

For just a fraction of a second Lachios was angry. He even began to say something, but then was struck by the perfect justice of the observation. It was beautiful—better than four thousand soldiers weighted down with body armor and great unwieldy pikes, wheeling around with the precision and economy of a door swinging on its hinges.

"Now—see? He begins his advance."

He begins . . . Yes, all those men moved to but a single will. They had become Philip's creations.

Lachios screwed his eyes almost shut trying to pick out his lord from among the moving block of men, but he could not. Behind their shields, their faces half-covered by their helmets, any one of them could have been Philip. Had the king disappeared in the midst of his army, or was it the other way about?

Moving now at a trot yet somehow managing to keep their lines perfectly even, the two squares of the left wing began to close with a corner of the Illyrian infantry—it was like watching the slow, irreversible collision of worlds. Three hundred paces, now two hundred and fifty, now two hundred . . .

But long before the two great masses of men crashed together, flights of arrows skipped back and forth between them so that the advancing Macedonians left a trail of corpses in their wake. At a hundred paces the Illyrians let fly their first volley of javelins, almost all of which fell short. At seventy paces the Macedonians stopped for just an instant and answered back in kind, only to renew their advance even before the first of their javelins had found its mark.

At thirty paces the front ranks of both armies dropped their spears into place so that their lines seemed to bristle. This was war in cold blood, Lachios thought—what an appalling business simply to walk into those rows of spears, offering one's belly to be torn open.

Not that the Macedonians walked. The last twenty paces were covered at a dead run, so that the two armies smashed into each other with an impact that could be heard even at a distance of seven hundred paces. It seemed to make the very earth shudder.

And then war became war again. The elegant dance was over, instantly replaced by the familiar chaos of battle as men struggled and fought and were trampled under by friend and enemy alike. The harsh clang of metal against metal blended with hoarse, frightened shouting and the screams of the dying as the two armies pushed against each other like half-mad bulls.

It seemed endless. One had the sense that time had simply stopped, that it had been replaced by an interminable cycle of killing—confused, lethal, and endless, a millstone grinding men indiscriminately to death.

"What a way to die," Lachios said, half under his breath. "What a brutish crush in which to surrender one's life . . ."

"He has done it!"

Korous leaned forward over his horse's neck, pointing frantically with his sword. He seemed beside himself with rapture.

"Look! The Illyrians have lengthened their line to meet the attack, and now it is starting to buckle. Philip has done it!"

Lachios strained to see, to find some pattern in the fighting, and at last he understood. The Macedonians were beginning to push their way through as the corner of the enemy square collapsed, and the Illyrians were weakening along all their lines as they tried to fend off the assault.

And as if in response to some invisible signal, the right wing of the Macedonian infantry began moving on the Illyrian center. Within a quarter of an hour of Philip's first advance the Illyrians found themselves attacked from two directions at once.

For a time they seemed to hold and then, quite suddenly, their lines started to sag and then to break. More quickly than would have seemed possible, the fighting began to change character. What up to then had been a battle was becoming a massacre. The great square, comprising perhaps as many as ten thousand men, was simply falling to pieces.

"Now it is our turn again," Korous announced, with an almost ferocious exultation. "Philip and his peasant boys shouldn't be allowed all the glory."

He slapped his horse on the rump with the flat of his sword and bolted back to his own men. Even as the hoofbeats of Korous's horse were fading away, Lachios's cavalry wing had begun forming up for the attack.

"You know the drill!" he shouted to them.

"Yes, we should," someone called back. "We have been through it often enough."

Lachios permitted himself a moment to join in the general laughter and then held up his arm for silence.

"Still, one last time. Charge straight through at an angle, then regroup and hit them again face on. When they are completely scattered, form up into pursuit squads and hunt down anything that is left moving. All right?"

His answer was a cheer and then someone took up the battle cry, "For Philip and for Macedon!" Soon they were all hurtling across the empty grassland toward the battle.

It happened when Lachios was perhaps forty paces from the Illyrian spear carrier he had marked out as his first target. He was driving his horse hard, his sword already raised when, in the last instant of his life, he must have seen something out of the corner of his eye and reflexively turned his head. The arrow pierced his left eye. Without ever feeling the blow that killed him, he slipped from his horse's back. He was dead before he hit the ground.

Pleuratos led the first cavalry charge himself. He even recognized Philip, carrying a shield and spear in the front rank of the Macedonian infantry, and tried to kill him before being driven off—what sort of king, he asked himself, commands his army on foot, fighting beside common soldiers?

The charge, of course, was a disaster. It failed to split the enemy defenses and the Illyrians were badly mauled by the Macedonians, who somehow attacked with more force than Pleuratos had expected. Perhaps their horses were bigger.

Yet he did not relinquish hope of victory until he saw how Philip's infantry broke open his battle square like a fox cracking the shell of an egg with its teeth. Then, as the panic among his own men grew and spread, and the battlefield quickly changed into a killing ground, he knew that everything was lost.

He managed to rally some thirty of his horsemen, hoping for a last charge at the attacking infantry, but the enemy cavalry, attacking from two directions at once, soon made this impossible. The Macedonian cavalry, in one furious assault, shattered his army, turning it into little more than an armed mob with no thought except to save their lives and no plan except flight. Suddenly Pleuratos and his few remaining followers found themselves in serious danger of being overrun by their own troops.

"We must get away from here!" one of them hissed at him. "We must escape before this crowd of cowardly riffraff so clog the pass that a man on horseback will have no chance!"

"Better to die here—better to fall in battle under the eyes of our enemies, lest they think we are all women . . ."

But no one was listening. Pleuratos looked about him and discovered he was alone. It was the most awful moment of his life.

There is no life for me now, he thought. *Not after this. It really is better to die here.*

He drew his sword and tried to urge his horse into a trot—he would show young Philip what he was made of; when they found his corpse, at least all the wounds would be in the front—but the mobs of his fleeing soldiers, swarming around him now, made any progress impossible.

And then, and with real horror, Pleuratos realized that hands were reaching out to him, that some of them thought to drag him from his horse that they might use it for their own escape. This was the only death that awaited him—to be pulled apart by a terrified rabble.

All at once he could think of nothing except getting away from those hands. He lashed out with his sword and struck off someone's thumb. He had time to be astonished at how the man hardly seemed to notice, and then he reined in his horse and wheeled about to flee the way he had come.

The Illyrians were in terrified flight and the only possible escape was back through the pass, which was strewn with boulders everywhere except down its center, a space hardly wide enough for five to walk through it abreast. Now that narrow passage was almost choked off and foot soldiers were clambering up the broken hillsides to escape the bands of Macedonian cavalrymen who were riding back and forth across the mouth of the pass killing anyone who came in their way. The corpses of the slain were almost as much an obstacle as the rocks.

And over these—and over the bodies of living men, already trampled half to death by those luckier or more ruthless—Pleuratos urged his horse, which had been seized by the general panic and hardly needed urging. He flailed away with his sword, as if to cut a path for himself, cursing like a demon, half-mad with a mixture of fear and rage. The gods alone knew how many of his own soldiers he maimed or killed.

It took him what seemed an eternity to make his way through, a distance of no more than a few hundred paces, and as soon as he could see the ground spreading out in front of him his heart swelled with a strange exultation. He was free. There was no one ahead of him, and doubtless his pursuers were as hindered by the mobs of fleeing Illyrians as he had been himself. He made no attempt to curb his horse as it broke into mad, headlong gallop.

But a man's luck, once it has deserted him, never comes back. The pass was not even half an hour behind him when his horse stumbled and threw him and, perhaps seeing its own chance of freedom, lingered hardly an instant before disappearing at a limping, ungainly run. The filthy animal was already out of sight by the time Pleuratos was able to roll over and sit up.

This was the end.

He was still there, the tears running shamelessly down his face, when, just before sundown, a patrol of Macedonian cavalry found him.

46

Nothing travels faster than bad news. Within ten days of Pleuratos's defeat one of the few survivors from the Illyrian cavalry who had managed to elude the Macedonians was on his knees before King Bardylis. Subsequent accounts only confirmed the scope of the disaster. An army exceeding ten thousand men had been utterly destroyed. Perhaps as many as seven thousand were dead and the rest were scattered. If Philip took it into his head to move west, there was no force left to oppose him. The Illyrian empire was at his mercy.

An emissary was dispatched to inquire whether the Macedonians might be willing to come to terms—any terms offered would probably amount to abject surrender, but there was no alternative—and to discover, if possible, the fate of Bardylis's grandson. The emissary returned after a month and made his report.

"The king received me personally," he said with just a hint of pride. Apparently he had not expected such a courtesy.

"Which king? Menelaos?"

"No, King Philip himself."

"Then he is still in Lynkos?"

"Yes. Menelaos was present, but he never spoke. Philip is clearly the master. The next morning I was shown the battlefield, which is now a huge gravesite, for the Illyrians who died fighting have been given decent burial. I was told that of those who surrendered or were taken captive ten were selected by lot to have their throats cut as sacrifices over the grave of some close friend of the king's who was killed in the battle and the rest were released to find their way home."

Bardylis looked grave but offered no comment. Such displays of humanity he normally interpreted as signs of weakness. In this case, however, he was not so sure.

"And my grandson?"

"The Lord Pleuratos is alive and a prisoner."

"You saw him?"

"Yes, ah . . ."

"Out with it."

"He is kept chained in the cage beside the royal kennels," the envoy replied with obvious reluctance.

"Chained?"

"Yes, he is manacled, and there is an iron collar . . ." He made a vague embarrassed gesture toward his neck, as if he could not bring himself to speak of the matter. "He is fed the kitchen scraps."

"What ransom is Philip asking?"

"He would not say." The envoy raised his eyebrows, dissociating himself from the matter. "He was perfectly polite, but he said he was not prepared to discuss his conditions for peace with anyone except My Lord King."

"He wants me to come to Lynkos?"

"Yes. He said he would be greatly pleased to welcome King Bardylis as his guest in Pisoderi."

The Illyrian nobles were unanimous in rejecting any such proposal. It was a trap. If the king ventured into Macedonian territory, he would certainly be killed as a prelude to a war of conquest against the entire empire. Bardylis had little patience with them.

"If Philip wants my kingdom, there is nothing to stop him from marching in and taking it," he pointed out. "His possession of my ancient person would not give him the slightest advantage—he doesn't need an advantage. Besides, I am invited as a guest. King Philip is cunning, but he is not treacherous."

And Bardylis had his own reasons for feeling hopeful, reasons he did not see fit to confide to his nobles.

"It is a long journey at my age," he told them. "Yet I will undertake this duty for the sake of my people."

He sent a dispatch rider ahead to let Philip know that his invitation had been accepted and then set off himself with an escort of a hundred men. He was an old man and he would take his time. Bardylis only hoped Pleuratos survived until he reached Macedonian territory, for he was looking forward to the spectacle of his grandson's humiliation.

Twenty-three days later he found the king of all the Macedonians waiting for him before the gates of Pisoderi.

"You must be tired," Philip said. "You will wish to rest."

"I wish to talk first. I would hear your terms for a treaty of peace."

Philip shrugged, as if he had not considered the matter before and was not sure it was important. "A return of all tribute money received during the reigns of my two brothers."

"Done. Now, what of my grandson?"

At first Philip seemed to ignore the question. He rode in silence beside the king of the Illyrians as they passed beneath the city gates. When they were in the palace courtyard he dropped quickly to the ground and himself helped Bardylis down from his horse.

"Do you wish to see him?" he asked at last. Before the old man had a chance to answer, Philip raised his hand in a gesture of summons and a pair of grooms appeared out of a stable doorway, holding up Pleuratos between them.

A murmur of suppressed astonishment rippled through the Illyrian escort as their king's heir apparent stumbled into the light. His hair and beard were a filthy tangle and he looked pale, flabby, and dispirited—hardly surprising with a man who had spent more than two months sitting on his haunches in a cage. He looked about him with bewilderment, giving no sign that he recognized anyone. Even Bardylis could not entirely quell a pang of compassion.

"Why have you done this?" he snapped. "He is a prince of the royal blood. He is—"

"You can ask me why?" Philip seemed to note the old man's anger with perfect indifference. "How many women are widows this day because of his folly? How many children have lost their fathers? There will be famine among your own people this winter because the men who should be gathering in the summer's harvest are sleeping in the earth. I do not speak of the Macedonian dead, for I know you will be heedless of them, but I lost many good soldiers and one dear friend in this war that was forced upon me and I grieve for them all. Yet you ask me why I suffer him to live thus. Inquire rather why I suffer him to live on any terms."

It was not until late that night, when Bardylis was sitting up alone in a strange bed in this citadel of his enemies that he at last realized Philip's intention. If Pleuratos had fallen in battle, it would have been a different thing, but now, while he was a prisoner, to kill him would constitute an insult the Illyrians could not overlook. Whatever else Philip wanted, he did not want to create that sense of grievance, so Pleuratos would not be killed and Philip would certainly return him when his price was met. Yet he meant to destroy Pleuratos, and he had done precisely that. The members of Bardylis's escort who had seen him chained like a beast would not forget the sight, and when they returned home everyone would know the full measure of Pleuratos's humiliation. The Illyrians were a proud people and they would never accept his shame as their own. Thus they would never accept him as their king. Philip had as good as killed him.

Clever boy, the old king thought, half tempted to laugh. *Clever, clever boy.* In its way, it was almost beautiful.

Yet Bardylis knew his own honor was at stake, so his grandson could not be allowed to remain a hostage. Pleuratos might be good for nothing now, but it was still necessary to buy him back.

The next morning the kings of Illyria and Macedon took a walk together around the fortifications of Pisoderi.

"It is just like the old days, when the situation was reversed and you were my hostage," Bardylis said, supporting his bad leg by resting a hand on Philip's shoulder. "Except now I have to reach a little higher—you have grown."

"It has been eleven years, Great-Grandfather."

"And now, instead of protecting you against Pleuratos, I must protect him from you."

"It is not from me that he needs protection."

Bardylis nodded, acknowledging the truth of the observation.

"No, not anymore, for the damage is done. You have broken him so that he can never be made whole again."

"I have done what was necessary to protect my people," Philip answered, perhaps a little more stiffly than he had intended.

"Don't imagine that I blame you." The old man moved his hand in a gesture of protest. "I would have done the same in your place. Yet understand, while we are haggling over the terms of his release, that Pleuratos has become a liability to me now. I will redeem him from captivity only to satisfy the demands of honor and, as you know, no true Dardanian values his honor at too excessive a price. I would advise you to be moderate in your demands."

He looked up at his great-grandson and smiled, but they both understood that the jest had been in earnest.

"Then you had best hear right away what I will accept as his ransom."

When Philip told him, the king of the Illyrians threw back his head and roared with laughter.

Then five days later, when Bardylis felt fully rested, the Illyrians began their journey home. Pleuratos was among them—his chains had been struck off that morning and he was given a horse. He rode beside his grandfather, and for two days he did not speak a word.

On the third day, when they were at last back in their own domain, he broke his silence.

"What did you pay him?" he asked, his voice strained and rusty sounding. Then he cleared his throat and spat on the ground.

"What he asked," Bardylis answered calmly.

"And what was that?"

"Your daughter."

"Audata?"

"Have you another? Yes, of course Audata."

"She has refused every suitor who has sought her hand. She will not consent."

"She will be delighted."

They rode on in silence for a long time.

"That boy will imagine himself as having a claim upon the throne," Pleuratos said at last.

"I doubt if such was his motive, but if it is so, I would welcome it." The old king favored his grandson with a smile full of mischief. "I have need of a successor."

Yet no one who saw King Philip at his betrothal ceremony could have imagined that he had contracted this marriage for reasons of state.

It was nearly winter before the Lady Audata arrived in her future husband's capital. She had traveled as far as the border with Lynkos attended by a large company of her great-grandfather's retainers, not only to do her honor but to safeguard the fifty talents of gold that accompanied her—there was a certain polite diplomatic confusion as to whether this constituted the lady's dowry or was the first repayment of tribute under the terms of the new treaty of peace, or might perhaps do service for both. Once she had crossed into Macedonia, however, she was under the king's protection and Philip himself made up one of her escort.

It would not have been considered seemly for the young couple to meet face-to-face outside the presence of the bride's family, but as he rode beside her covered chair as they followed the road south it was sometimes possible for them to exchange a few words through the curtain that shaded her from the observation of the world. That seemed to be enough. Philip was too obviously pleased with his choice of a wife to even notice the amusement of his friends.

Once they had arrived in Pella, Philip abandoned his own apartments to the Lady Audata and went to Glaukon's house to use the bed he had slept in as a child. Every dawn the old steward made breakfast for himself and his king, and then Philip, too restless to attend to anything else, usually went hunting. He was not so much irritable as distracted, but the effect was much the same. Everyone was glad that the betrothal period was to be short.

It was Glaukon who saw the king's bride every day, and at night Philip would question him closely about how she looked and what she said and whether she seemed happy. In the mornings he performed a similar service for the Lady Audata. It quickly became apparent to him that these two young people were very much in love, a fact that pleased but at first also mystified him. How had such a thing happened when they were almost unknown to one another? The lady, who was not even twenty, had been still a child when Philip was a hostage among the Illyrians. Certainly in all those years Philip had never mentioned her, and yet the strange intimacy between them seemed a thing of long standing. It was a riddle.

But then many things about Philip were a riddle.

Glaukon happened to be standing behind them during the betrothal ceremony, and he noticed how, while Philip pronounced the ritual formula announcing his intention to take this woman in lawful marriage, their hands sought each other, the fingers sliding together as if from established habit.

They will be happy, the old man thought. *And perhaps at last my boy will find a little peace.*

On the night of their wedding everyone said there would be snow by morning, but the skies were still clear by the time the wedding car took the king and his new wife through the streets of the royal quarter. Glaukon had arranged the feast for the king's guests and stood on the palace steps waiting to welcome his master when he arrived and to tell him that nothing had been left undone. It was a brief moment of quiet in a long and hectic day that was far from over.

In the night sky he could see the constellation of the Toiling Man shining in the west, and he remembered another night when he had left these precincts carrying a newborn child home for his grieving wife to nurse. Who could have expected . . . ?

And yet, in a way, he had always expected it. The gods did not make promises idly.

In the distance he heard the sound of many voices—it was the wedding song. Philip, king of Macedon, was coming home.